"One of our brightest crime fiction stars."
—Adrian McKinty, *New York Times* bestselling author of *The Chain*

"If you haven't read Candice Fox yet, you're missing out! I can't wait to read what this talented writer does next!" —Chevy Stevens

"A bright new star of crime fiction."
—James Patterson

"Definitely a writer to watch." —Harlan Coben

"Sign me up as a big-time Fox fan!" —Lee Child

"If you are not currently reading Candice Fox, you need to remedy that right now." —*Bookreporter*

CANDICE FOX

FIRE WITH FIRE

Tor Publishing Group
New York

FIRE WITH FIRE

A Forge Book
Published by Tom Doherty Associates/Tor Publishing Group
120 Broadway
New York, NY 10271

www.tor-forge.com

Forge® is a registered trademark of Macmillan Publishing Group, LLC.

ISBN 978-1-250-87597-6

Our books may be purchased in bulk for promotional, educational, or business use. Please contact your local bookseller or the Macmillan Corporate and Premium Sales Department at 1-800-221-7945, extension 5442, or by email at MacmillanSpecialMarkets@macmillan.com.

First Edition: May 2023
First Mass Market Edition: April 2024

Printed in the United States of America

0 9 8 7 6 5 4 3 2 1

For the *Troppo* team

FIRE WITH FIRE

FOUR DAYS AGO

Something in the water grabbed her calf. Her brain screamed the word.

Shark.

Mina's body collapsed inward from her elongated freestyle. She twisted and kicked out, the cliffs above and the dusty, gold-lit horizon off Abalone Bay smashing together in her wide-eyed panic swirl. A yelp escaped her throat, making way for sea-foam to be sucked back in. It was a man who'd grabbed her. Not the dreaded white pointer, haunter of her early-morning, high-kneed dash into the dark waves. She was coughing as she tore his hands off her, kicked him in the stomach, the alarms in her brain still sounding even as some other corner of her mind slumped with relief.

"Oh my god! Oh my god!" she gasped. "What the—"

His tattooed, bloodless arm reached for her, and he blew out seawater with the word, "Help!"

He went under again. Mina kicked into high gear: out of survival mode and into rescue mode. She reached blindly into the depths, grabbed a handful of long hair. A wave lifted them both, sea gods thrusting them together, and she caught him under the armpits, clambered around behind him.

"I can't." He shuddered. "I can't keep going."

"I've got you," she said.

She didn't. He was impossibly heavy, not kicking, his head lolling against her shoulder. Now that he'd reached her, he'd given up. She went under, struggled upward, twisted back and forth looking for assistance. When she'd entered the waves only an hour earlier, the horizon smeared red above the slate-gray sea, there had been people everywhere. Fishermen standing like black-coated cormorants on the rocks around Portuguese Point. Joggers pounding the distant trails and a small gathering of regulars at the edge of the tidal pool in the cove. Now it seemed as if an uninhabited coast spread before her, the steep hillsides beyond the beach apocalyptically motionless. Mina had no choice. She hugged the man around his chest, turned, and kicked.

She hauled and kicked, hauled and kicked, floating frequently, his naked backside against the hips of her wet suit. She kept telling him that she had him, though time and again when she straightened and kicked down, hoping to feel sand beneath her feet, there was only ice-cold emptiness. East Beach, her destination, grew no closer. Her terror ratcheted higher and higher as she noticed the wounds on the drowning man. A chunk torn from his chest. Bruises and gashes on his arms. Mina waved and waved. No help came. She scanned the swell, every tip a flicking, ink-black fin.

When her feet hit sand, she cried out in triumph.

The man seemed to tap into some reserve of strength as they hit the rumbling breakers, planting his feet, stumbling, hanging a hairy arm around her shoulders. She helped him hobble a few steps before two surfers materialized just in time to stop him from collapsing on top of her.

On the sand, his ribcage expanded and contracted

as he fought for breath, making the sprawling blue tattoos rise and fall. She knelt by him, shaking with exertion, her eyes wandering over skulls, eagles, guitars. The surfers were oblivious to the inked landscape, one brushing strands of lank brown hair from the man's battered face and beard, the other heaping a pile of towels and gear at Mina's side. She held a towel against the chest wound while the first surfer spread another towel over the man's naked waist.

"Hey, buddy? Buddy? You all right? Stay with us, bro!"

"Was it a shark?" The second surfer touched Mina's arm. He was older than the other surfer, his bare shoulders peppered caramel.

"No . . . Uh, no," she said. "I don't know. I don't think so."

"So what the hell happened?"

"I don't know."

"Where are his clothes?"

"I don't know! I don't know!"

The drowning man grabbed Mina's forearm, the same death grip he'd used in the sea.

"Phone," he said.

"An ambulance is coming, bro. Just hang on," the younger surfer said. Mina followed his gaze to a pair of joggers who were watching from the trail, one with a phone clamped to her ear, her eyes wide as she recited details, pointing as though the operator could see. Nearby, a flock of seagulls stood watching, wings folded, disapproving.

Mina looked back at the bearded man. His eyes were bloodshot and fixed on her.

"Phone. Now. Please."

Her bag was in her car. But the older surfer produced a phone, put it in Mina's hand, and shrugged. Mina realized a ring of observers had formed around them. A flash of anger. Where had all these people been while she was out there in the waves, struggling?

The raw exhaustion dragging at her limbs made her feel as if she'd been fighting the current for hours. But maybe not.

Mina handed the phone to the bearded man. With difficulty, he rolled onto his side, one badly trembling hand gripping the phone as the other struggled to dial.

Mina, the surfers, the gawkers, the gulls, they all watched as the man from the sea lay in the sand and defied unconsciousness, waiting for the call to connect. The morning was so still, so quiet, that Mina heard the woman's voice on the other end of the line.

"Hello?"

"Hellfire, hellfire, hellfire," the bearded man said. Once the words were out, he let his head fall back. He was taken so fast, Mina couldn't tell if he was asleep or dead. She pulled the phone from his limp fingers and held it to her ear.

"Hoss?" the voice on the phone said. "Jesus, Charlie! A-a-are you sure?"

TWO DAYS AGO

The sewing needle penetrated the thick, starchy fabric of Lamb's coal-black uniform shirt too fast, spearing the soft flesh of her index finger. She yelped, sucked the digit, looked around the locker room to see if anyone had heard. She was alone. It was her nerves that had driven everyone away, she guessed. Nerves were contagious, and this was a job in which trembly hands, a sickly pallor, and a jolting step weren't useful.

She hunched in her underwear on the worn wooden bench between the stacks of lockers, replaying the past few humiliating moments in her mind. Arriving at the Van Nuys police station and presenting herself at the spit-screened front counter, as she'd been told to do, rather than swiping through the staff doors at the back. Being shown to the locker room to change, her nostrils flaring like a spooked horse at the unfamiliar sights and smells of the ground-floor bullpen. Tripping and stumbling on an electrical cord taped to the carpet, right in front of two plainclothes detectives.

She had noticed the button on her breast pocket hanging loose from a curling black thread as she changed out of her civilian clothes. *Christ. Why now?* All weekend, she'd darted back and forth to her bedroom closet, staring at the uniform, reverently touching its spotless sleeves, without noticing the loose button. The sewing kit had been at the bottom of a backpack bulging and sagging with precautionary items. Hydralyte tablets, aspirin, Band-Aids, tampons, snacks, a spare set of civvies, three types of hair ties, in case the one she'd used wasn't regulation. *Why the fuck didn't the handbook say anything about hair ties?* Lamb finished sewing the button back into place with numb fingers and pulled on the shirt, smoothed it out firmly.

She caught a glimpse of herself in the mirror inside her locker before she closed it. There was still no color in her face. She went to the paper towel dispenser, ripped off a handful, reached into her shirt, and dried her pits for the tenth time that day. Then she walked to the door and put a hand on the knob.

She closed her eyes and whispered to herself.

"You deserve to be here."

Lynette Lamb, P1 officer in the Los Angeles Police Department, drew a deep breath and let it out slow. Then she pushed the door open and walked into her very first day on the job.

In the hall outside the locker room, she was the new kid in the schoolyard; frozen, vulnerable. When she reached the bullpen, the officer who'd led her to the locker room was standing at the coffee station, one hand on the counter, the other pinching the bridge of her nose. The *fuck my life* pose. The colleague she was listening to touched her elbow in a consolatory manner and walked away.

Lamb straightened and jutted her chin. She understood. This woman, whoever she was, had probably just been told that Lamb was her baby to sit for the day. Lamb appreciated the disappointment. Rookies were annoying. But Lamb was a fast learner, had excellent retention and an eye for detail. Her grades from the academy proved that. It was black and white, on paper: *she deserved to be here.* Lamb forced a smile and went to the officer, standing at attention.

"Ready when you are"—Lamb looked at the older officer's ID badge—"Officer Milstone."

Milstone wouldn't meet Lamb's eyes.

"Come with me, Lamb," she said instead, and walked away.

Lamb followed eagerly, nodding and smiling at officers who were watching from their cubicles, some on the phone, some peering around their computer screens. Milstone and Lamb took a corridor to a stairwell and climbed in silence to the upper floor. Offices, a row of interrogation rooms, a waiting area. Milstone stopped outside a frosted-glass door with a nameplate that read *Lieutenant Gordon Harrow.*

Of course, Lamb thought. *Meet the boss first.* She gave silent thanks to the universe that the terror in her heart was slowly transforming into excitement. Her cheeks felt hot. She'd studied up on Gordon Harrow in the weeks since she'd been informed of her assignment to Van Nuys. She knew his history, major cases, marital status, love of surfing and golf. Lamb was eager to hear a speech about the valley, how the team operated. *Around here, we work hard and we play hard.*

Lamb was ready to do both.

Milstone rapped once on the door.

"Yeah," a voice said.

Milstone held open the door. Lamb waited for her to go in first. She didn't. When Lamb didn't move, Milstone swept the air, annoyed. *Get in there!* Lamb scooted inside. Behind the battered metal desk stacked with papers sat a tired-looking version of the Gordon Harrow that Lamb had been staring at on her computer screen for a fortnight. He seemed strangely incomplete without the peaked police-issue cap he wore to press conferences. He ran a hand over the brushy cut that crowned his small head and offered Lamb a surprisingly limp handshake.

"Sir, good morning," Lamb started. "It's really nice to meet—"

"Sit down."

She sat.

He consulted the computer screen to his left, appeared to be reading. Lamb felt the wave of excitement that hit her at the door cresting, pausing, plunging.

Harrow turned away from the computer and folded his hands.

"Lynette," Harrow began.

That's when she knew.

Lynette. Not *Officer Lamb*.

This was bad.

"I have to ask you some important questions," Harrow said. "And, look, I want you to understand: how you answer these questions isn't going to affect the outcome for you here today. That's already all sewn up. It's out of my hands. I'm just the messenger."

"Okay," she said.

Lamb waited for a punch line. There wasn't one. Beyond the frosted glass of the door, people were walking by, talking, laughing, answering phones. She listened, hoped to hear the telltale whispers and snickers of her future cop buddies that would reveal this to be some harmless initiation prank on the new rookie. None came. The world out there was carrying on without her. The wave was crashing down. Down and down and down, impossibly heavy, impossibly fast.

Harrow's gray eyes were fixed on hers. "A week ago, on the evening of the eleventh of October, you went out in the city. You were celebrating your graduation from the academy. You were in the company of some of your friends. Fellow cadets. Is that correct?"

Lamb tried to nod, but her neck and head were locked in place.

"Yes," she said.

"You went to a few bars in the West Hollywood area?"

"Uh. Y-yes. Yes."

"And in the early hours of the morning, around 2:00 a.m. on the twelfth of October, you split off from the group," Harrow said. "You booked an Uber. You traveled home with a man who told you his name was Brad. You and Brad went to your apartment in Koreatown. Correct?"

Lamb couldn't speak. Her tongue was dry, adhered to the roof of her mouth. *It's just a prank,* she told herself. *A hilarious prank!* Cops were about to come bursting in and slap her on the shoulder, ruffle her hair. There'd be a welcome party in the break room. Cake. Harrow waited for her to emit some kind of response, letting the silence drag on and on. When he decided she was incapable, he gave the sigh of a farmer tasked with shooting a sheep that's wedged in the combine harvester.

"Let me just put this all out there." Harrow made a sweeping gesture over the surface of the desk. "The guy you took home that night was a very, very bad man. It's not clear to us whether he targeted you specifically or if he was just trying to get any one of the girls in your group to take him home. But he knew for a fact that you and your friends were all recently graduated probationary officers."

"What—" Lamb's words hitched in her throat. "What is this all about?"

"That guy, Brad Alan Binchley? He's a patched member of an outlaw motorcycle gang called the Death Machines," Harrow said. "You heard of them?"

"N-no," Lamb stammered. "Y-yes. Uh, I've maybe seen a news article—"

"Yeah, well, they're bad." Harrow cracked his knuckles. "And they're clever. Brad flirted with you and you took him home, and while you were asleep, I assume, at approximately four o'clock in the morning, he accessed a computer located at your residence."

"He *what*?" Lamb yelped.

Her mind raced. She remembered Brad's body. His cigarette breath. His laugh. She'd been strangely thrilled to find her apartment empty the next morning, the flipped-up toilet seat the only evidence that he'd ever been there. *Naughty, naughty, Lynette!* She'd smiled to herself. This wasn't her. Nights out in the city, meaningless hookups, her dream job, payment plan paperwork for a brand-new car on the coffee table. This was the new Lamb. The grown-up Lamb.

Harrow continued, shattering Lamb's memories and bringing her tumbling back to the present. "Brad Binchley used your secure LAPD log-in to access your staff email account."

"That's not possible," Lamb said. "It's just not possible. My password isn't written down anywhere. It's not—"

"There are ways to get around that." Harrow flicked his hand. "Keystroke trackers, whatever. Binchley's a hacker. They're modernizing, the gangs. Bringing in people like him. They have to."

Lamb swallowed.

"Binchley sent an email to a detective named Christopher Keon over at the Civic Center," Harrow said. "Keon opened it. It was internal mail, so he trusted it. The email contained a virus. Brad Binchley and his gang were able to access top-secret police documents through that virus."

"I don't know about any of this." Lamb held her face in both hands, and peered through her fingers at Harrow. "I don't know about *any of this*!"

Harrow plowed on. "Among other compromising details, the gang learned about an undercover officer police had planted in their gang approximately five years ago."

Lamb doubled over, pressed her face into her knees. The wave was crushing her, rolling her, smashing her into the sand.

"They took that officer out to sea on a boat and tortured him," Harrow said.

At this, Lamb reached forward, grabbed the waste-paper basket sitting on the floor at the corner of the desk, and retched into it. Nothing came up, but the retching wouldn't stop. Dimly, she was aware of Harrow lifting a phone on his desk and asking someone to bring her a glass of water. When the retching finally eased, Lamb realized the crotch and armpits of her uniform were drenched in sweat.

Officer Milstone was there with the water and then gone again, wordlessly, leaving the glass on the edge of Harrow's desk. Lamb didn't trust herself to pick it up. She just stared at it, trying to breathe.

"Is he dead?" she managed eventually.

"No. Oh, no, he's not. Sorry. I should have said that." Harrow gave a short, awful laugh that he reconsidered and choked off. "He escaped, swam for shore. Prevailing currents and his efforts ended up bringing him in to a beach near Palos Verdes. He'll be okay."

Lamb nodded, holding her stomach with one hand and gripping the edge of the desk with the other. Harrow sat back in his chair with the groan of a man relieved at having performed his coup de grace and wanting to begin the process of forgetting it.

"I'm going to have to ask you to go back downstairs now," he told Lamb, "and take off that uniform."

CHAPTER 1

Two seconds after Dr. Gary Bendigo pulled into his parking space outside the Hertzberg-Davis Forensic Science Center and turned off the car's engine, a bird shat on the windshield. He looked at the thin white splatter, heard the unmistakable woodwind cooing of mourning doves in the trees above, and instead of recognizing it as the omen it was, he bitterly counted back the hours since he'd washed the now-soiled vehicle. It was nine.

He sighed. Half the reason he'd washed the car in the first place was because, only a week earlier, he'd been blindsided in this very location. Arriving at his parking space outside the lab, McDonald's cappuccino in the cup holder, tie undone, hanging around his neck. A young male reporter with waxed eyebrows and a painted-on suit had ambushed him about the backlog, cameraman hovering behind him. Bendigo had watched footage of the stunt on *Dateline*. He'd noticed, alongside the nation, that the neighbor's kid had traced *WASH ME!* in the dust on his back window.

None of it looked good.

Dr. Gary Bendigo: can't find the time to tie his tie.

Or make his own coffee.

Or wash his car.

Or get through more than five hundred untested rape kits for the Los Angeles Police Department.

He'd hoped he could easily change America's perception about one of those things. The birds thought otherwise.

There were no suited reporters in the parking lot today. And, strangely, there had been no security guard manning the open boom gate, though Bendigo had seen an officer on duty the past three Sundays when he had pulled into work. Another omen he ignored. Beyond the fences, State University Drive was quiet and the freeway was dark. For three weeks, seven days a week, Bendigo had been clocking in before the morning mist in Los Angeles's University Hills district had cleared and clocking out to walk the lonely stretch to his car under the glare of orange sodium lamps. He was growing accustomed to spotting the occasional racoon or possum, other nighttime creatures braving the open plains of concrete.

He swiped his entry through one of the large glass doors and walked across the airy foyer, glancing out of habit at the big Cal State crest over the reception desk, a happy yellow sun wedged beneath insignias for the sheriff's and police departments. The door to the wing of the building that housed the Trace Evidence Unit gave him trouble, as usual, requiring him to swipe his access card three times before the little red light went green and an approving bleep sounded. He flipped on lights as he walked down the hall, his shoes squeaking on the linoleum. Fluorescent tubes blinked on over sprawling, sterile evidence-collection rooms.

He flipped more lights, illuminating a computer lab, a file room, and then a plaque on the wall advised that he had passed into the forensic biology and DNA section of the building. Bendigo went right to the break room and turned on the coffee machine, scanned the noticeboard above the sugar, sweetener, and tea canisters for anything new. Since yesterday, here had

appeared a sign-up sheet for a staff Christmas barbecue, divided by unit. Three people had already put their
names in the "Salads/Sides" column. Bendigo looked at
his watch and sighed again. It was mid-October. Only
scientists planned a salad three months in advance.

Mug in hand, he was still thinking about the distant-
future salad neurotics when he turned into lab 21 and
stopped at the sight of people standing there in the
dimness. It took a moment for him to put it all together, for his mind to begin screaming. Because what
he was seeing wasn't unusual, in a sense. There were
plenty of guns in the lab. Guns moved in and out of
Bendigo's section by the dozen every week. But the
particular gun he was looking at now, held by a man
wearing a denim jacket, wasn't tagged.

And it was pointed directly at Bendigo's face.

That was unusual.

A woman was holding another untagged gun, this
one pointed at a security guard who was curled on the
floor with his arms bound behind his back.

It wasn't the guns, or the blood, or the zip-tied
wrists that terrorized Bendigo. It was their assembly.
Their unique composition. Bendigo felt his stomach
plunge. The man in the jacket, whom Bendigo didn't
recognize, moved the pistol's aim from Bendigo's face
for an instant to gesture to his coffee mug.

"Good idea," the guy said. "We'll need some more
of that."

They told him to get on his knees. Bendigo just stood
there like an idiot, the coffee mug still clutched in his
fist, wondering how the hell a person does that. How
they stop being, say, a regular guy in his midsixties
who's just arrived at work, en route to the inevitable
slog through his email inbox, and become—what? A
hostage? The couple looked as if they'd stepped into
the lab straight from a leisurely morning dog walk.
She was wearing skinny jeans and had gathered her

yellow-blond hair into a messy bun, and he was sporting thick-rimmed black spectacles, the square, Clark Kent kind that young men wore these days with their fades and their manicured beards. There were no catsuits, no balaclavas, no bomb vests. Bendigo jolted when the man snapped at him.

"Get *the fuck* down!"

He set his coffee on the steel tabletop, hitched his trousers, and kneeled. When the woman came around him and gripped his chubby wrist, slid the cable tie around it, Bendigo got a whump of adrenaline in his belly. The zipping sound of the cable ties set Bendigo's teeth on edge. This was real. The young security guard on the floor looked to be unconscious. There was a big gash on his forehead, blood drying on his heavily stubbled jaw. He was snoring in that thick, vulnerable way Bendigo had seen once when he was a kid and his buddy got knocked out cold by a fly ball at the local park.

Bendigo's throat was suddenly dry as chalk.

"We don't keep cash here," he rasped. "This is a research and testing facility for—"

"We know, Gary. We know," the woman said. The sound of his name in her mouth ratcheted up the fear. Bendigo trembled as she took off his watch and set it on the table beside his coffee. She reached into his pockets, took his phone and wallet. Bendigo thought of dead bodies, the way their possessions were taken off like that and set down in a neat row on hard surfaces. Waiting for bagging and tagging.

"Who are you people?"

"I'm Elsie Delaney, and this is Ryan," the woman said. "You'll understand everything that's going on soon. I'm gonna help you get up now. I want you to go over there beside Ibrahim, and si—"

"No. Don't do that," Ryan cut in. "Don't sit them next to each other. Put him there."

"Oh, right." Elsie nodded. "I just thought they might want to be near each other. For support."

"They're fine," Ryan said. "We're fine. Go make the coffee. Take it nice and easy."

Bendigo stood shakily and let Elsie help him hobble to the side of the room, ten feet away from the security guard, Ibrahim. Every word the couple said was echoing in Bendigo's brain, as if they were talking in a tunnel. Sounds bouncing out and then rippling back into him. He kept picking over the interruption. The sharpness. *No. Don't do that.* Ryan was in charge here. Elsie was new at this. Maybe they were both new at this. He didn't know which he preferred—inexperienced hostage-takers or experienced ones. A droplet of sweat ran down Bendigo's jaw.

Elsie went and made the coffee. One cup for her. One for Ryan. They sat steaming, untouched, on a nearby table.

"Listen," Bendigo began. "I'm not—"

"No talking." Ryan was setting up a laptop on the steel bench, beside Bendigo's coffee and watch. "That's the rule. You sit tight. You shut up. You speak only when you're spoken to."

Bendigo shut up. He worked the cable ties between his wrists, feeling useless and embarrassed and guilty somehow, like a kid plonked down in the naughty corner. There was one tie around each of his wrists and a third between them, linking them together. That was good. It gave him space to maneuver his shoulders, turn his arms, didn't require the tightness that a single band around both wrists would. They'd thought about some things, these two. Other things they were working out as they went.

They drank the coffee. Two sips each, eyes locked over the rims of their cups, mouths downturned, as if they were forcing down poison. Telling themselves, each other, wordlessly, that they were fine.

Then Elsie went to one of three huge duffel bags on the floor and started unpacking objects—shiny black U-shaped bike locks that she hung off her arm like enormous bracelets. She walked away with six of them, disappearing through the double doors by which Bendigo had entered. Out of another duffel bag, Ryan was heaping electronic equipment on the tabletop—more laptops and a tangle of cables, two iPhones, and huge battery packs. Bendigo heard a groan, looked over, and saw that the young security guard was waking, dragging his head on the linoleum, trying to sit up. He flopped back down. Ryan had followed Bendigo's gaze and shrugged a shoulder, unsmiling.

"We don't want to get violent, but we will if we have to," he said. His eyes bored into Bendigo's. "You see that, right?"

"Yes," Bendigo said.

"Just do what you're told and you'll be fine."

"What is this all about?" Bendigo asked.

Ryan looked away, didn't answer. He sipped from a water bottle he'd taken from the second duffel bag. Bendigo also spied the corner of a box of food poking out of the zippered flap.

Rations. This was a long-term engagement. The way Ryan sipped delicately at the water and screwed the lid back on carefully filled Bendigo with foreboding. They were conserving their water in a building filled with sinks.

Elsie returned, gathered up more bike locks, then dashed away. Ryan tapped and poked at the laptop, pulled up a bunch of gray windows divided into boxes. They looked like CCTV feeds.

When Elsie returned, there was a tight pause, the couple watching each other, their faces grim. Elsie took a deep breath and exhaled hard.

"Are you still all right to do it?" Ryan asked.

"I think so."

"It has to be the mother," Ryan said. "People get on board with it right away when it's the mother."

"I know. I know. I remember."

Ryan took up one of the phones. He pointed it at Elsie, and Bendigo saw the white light next to the camera flick on.

CHAPTER 2

The bottom of Saskia Ferboden's computer screen was wearing a tutu of yellow sticky notes covered in her lacy handwriting. As the chief of police put the receiver of her desk phone down in its cradle, she took a note from the very corner of the screen, one that simply read "Hoss." She crumpled the note and dropped it into the wastepaper basket next to her desk. There was nothing more she could do for Charlie Hoskins right now. The undercover cop, one of her own, was reportedly sleeping off the aftereffects of his unplanned marathon swim across the Californian coastline. The Kaiser Permanente nursing staff had informed her that his "levels" were back up, which was "pleasing." Whatever that meant. He'd also consumed "solids." That was good. Saskia came from a family of dog breeders; some of their German shepherds formed part of the ranks of the LAPD dog squad. She knew from tending to puppies all her girlhood that the runts that were going to make it were the ones who ate. Hoss would be okay.

She flipped through the remaining sticky notes, deciding what to tackle in her regular Sunday-morning check-in before she went to enjoy her day off. Saskia hated to start her Monday already sandbagged with unfinished business. The rest of the sticky notes related to the twelve men Saskia had in custody, each and every member of the Death Machines that her strike team had been able to round up in the ninety-six hours since she received that breathy phone call from Hoss telling her that Operation Hellfire was over. Last night, Saskia had toured Men's Central Jail, wanting to go and look at their haul. She'd felt a heavy sense of disappointment. Twelve wasn't nearly enough, and none of the big fish were there. Dean Willis, Franko Aderhold, and Mickey Randal, the top trio, had disappeared after their attempt to make shark food of Charlie Hoskins had failed. Those members of the outlaw biker gang who were left for Saskia's team to scoop up were either too stupid to heed the warning from their superiors that a raid was coming, or not worth the effort by those same superiors to be forewarned.

Next Saskia peeled off the sticky note that read "Rookie." She'd gotten confirmation from Van Nuys station that the rookie officer who had caused the whole shit fight, whatever her name was, had been canned two days earlier. She crumpled and trashed the note.

The chief got up, raised her hands as high as she could, felt and heard a crack in her mid-back as something shifted there. Through the windows of her office on the ninth floor of the Civic Center, the downtown skyline was hazy. She was heading for the door to take a little stroll around the bullpen when the phone rang, and she walked back to her desk to pick it up.

"Ferboden."

"Sass, I've got Jason from the *LA Times* on three," said the switchboard manager.

Out of habit, Saskia gave the specific groan she reserved for reporters who called her directly, but because it was Jason, she pushed the button to let the call through. She'd been out drinking with Jason a couple of times over the years when big cases had made it through the courts, and once, they'd ended up at a karaoke bar in Chinatown, him with his shirt off, her with too many Negronis on board. There were confidences to maintain.

"Sass?"

"Hello, Jason. How's every little thing?"

"A bit better than for you, I imagine."

"Yuh." Saskia blew out a sigh, heard it crackle on the line. He must have been calling for an update on Hoss. "The fun never stops."

"Are you on your way there now?" Jason asked. "I must have just caught you."

Saskia felt a ripple of something up her weary spine. "Sorry? Am I on my way to . . . ?"

"The lab?" Jason said.

"What are you talking about?"

There was a sickening pause.

"Oh, Jesus." Saskia heard Jason's breath quicken. "Maybe they've . . . Maybe they've only sent it to us so far . . ."

"Jason, I don't—"

"Go to your email," he said.

Saskia walked around the desk and woke the computer, dread blooming in the center of her chest, sharp petals of trepidation. She only had to wait a second or two before an email arrived from Jason. She opened it, clicked on a file. A video began to play. A woman in her forties with a messy blond bun piled high on top of her head. She was lean, sharp-angled, the tension in her throat and jaw making her appear more sinewy than she probably was. She was vaguely familiar to Saskia. The chief scanned the video as quickly as she could, noting the edge of a steel-topped table beside the woman, a wall covered in laminated signs above a steel sink. A commercial kitchen? Laboratory? There was something on the table. The edge of a laptop, maybe. Some cables.

The woman was holding a piece of paper against her chest, her hand spread over the back of it, like a child with a precious toy hugged to her heart.

"Hello," the woman said. Her voice was trembling. She cleared her throat, and her next words were harder, more resolved. "My name is Elsie Delaney."

Saskia's knees went. She sank into her chair.

Elsie turned the paper over. "This is my daughter Tilly Delaney."

Saskia looked at the photograph of the child. She'd seen the image a hundred times, and yet still it made her jaw twitch. The wide smile. The apple cheeks and chocolate-brown ringlets. The ice cream held out like a microphone toward the camera.

"On this day, *two . . . years . . . ago*"—Elsie's eyes were narrowing now, her hands shaking as anger pulsed through her—"Tilly went missing from Santa Monica State Beach. In the seven hundred and thirty days since her disappearance, the police have done *nothing—absolutely nothing*—to find her and bring her home to her father and her sister and me."

"Oh, Jesus," Saskia said into the phone, which was sweaty now against her ear. "Jason, is this a suicide video or what? I don't want to watch a—"

"Just watch," Jason said.

The video shifted. Whoever was holding it, filming Elsie, panned around the room. Saskia could see it was indeed a laboratory. Bare steel tables. Sinks. Tabletops crowded with machines and scientific equipment. Her eyes raced over the screen, taking in details as fast as she could. Like Elsie's face, the images were triggering something in Saskia's brain, but she didn't know just yet why the place was familiar. Finally, the camera settled on a pair of men. A young man was lying on his side, wearing a uniform of some kind. White collared shirt, epaulettes, black trousers. There was an older man with a potbelly sitting on the floor, looking rattled and dejected, leaning up against the side of one of the steel tables. The hands of both men were behind their backs.

Elsie Delaney's voice carried on as the camera panned. "My husband, Ryan, and I have taken over laboratory 21 of the Hertzberg-Davis Forensic Science Center. And we intend to . . . *to do a lot of damage here* . . . if our demands are not met."

"Christ!" Saskia gripped her hair with one hand, the phone clamped hard against her ear with the other. "Oh, *fuuuuuuck*!"

"We want our daughter brought home to us within twenty-four hours," Elsie said.

Saskia's cell phone started vibrating on the desk. She glanced at the screen and saw a name: Ike Grimley, the mayor of Los Angeles.

"We just want our daughter. That's all," Elsie concluded. The camera returned to settle on the mother holding a picture of her child. Saskia could see there was a gun in her hand now, held down by her side. Like thousands of mothers of missing children who had gone before her, Elsie's eyes were big and wet, and full of a potent, poisonous combination of terror and rage.

"We don't want to hurt anyone," Elsie said.

Saskia swallowed hard.

"But we will, if we have to."

The video ended.

Ten minutes of silence. Bendigo counted them off on the clock on the wall. Then Elsie Delaney exhaled hard, obviously wanting Ryan's attention. The man with the thick black glasses didn't look up from the phone screen he was bent over. Bendigo found himself analyzing their every facial expression and body movement, the tone of their voices, the way Elsie's hair was starting to cascade down from that messy bun and the way Ryan chewed his nails. How in control of all this were they? How ripe for being overthrown?

Elsie huffed again, and Ryan put a hand up without raising his eyes from the phone screen.

"I know," he said. "I know."

"Nothing at all yet?"

"No, nothing at all." Ryan's thumb was dancing over the screen. "I'd tell you, El. You know that."

"But it's not as though we've sent them a goddamn pitch for an article," Elsie snapped. "It's a fucking ransom video!"

"Chill." Ryan looked up at her, his eyes dark. "Just chill, okay? They need time. Someone's got to watch the video. They've got to decide if it's a joke or not. They've got to take it to their boss. Then *they've* got to decide how to respond. And that's just a bunch of reporters at the *Times* offices. The video has to make its way through them and get to the LAPD, where the same process starts again. It's going to take more than thirty seconds to get a response."

"It hasn't been thirty seconds, it's been ten minutes."

"Elsie, come on."

The security guard on the floor sat up suddenly, startling Bendigo. The young man went from limp, snoring, stringless puppet to fully animated human being in a second, sitting there looking baffled, blood smeared messily across his forehead.

"What the fuck?" The young man shuffled onto his knees, trying to wrench his bound hands apart. "Wh-what's happening?"

"Just stay still," Bendigo said. "You're okay, buddy. You're okay."

The security guard took in Elsie and Ryan, who were poring over the screen of his phone. "Where are we?" he asked.

"You're in one of the labs." Bendigo sighed. "Just . . . Your hands are tied, young man. Don't wriggle around like that. You've got a head injury and you're probably concussed."

The security guard went still. Now that he was upright, Bendigo could see the ID badge clipped to the front pocket of his shirt. A grainy photograph, and a name in bold type. IBRAHIM SOLEA.

Ryan put the phone down on the tabletop. Whatever the two hostage-takers had been watching for or examining, it was apparently over. They embraced, Elsie leaning her head into the hollow of Ryan's collarbone, Ryan cupping the back of her neck with his big hand.

"We're going to find her," Ryan said. "We're going to find our baby. No matter what."

"I know," Elsie said.

The four people in the lab all jolted as a buzzer sounded somewhere. Bendigo knew the sound. It was the after-hours buzzer at the front of the building. Ryan and Elsie stepped back from the edge of the table, and Bendigo could see on the laptop screen that there was a woman standing at the after-hours access door off to the side of the main entrance. He squinted, barely able to make out the notebook clutched in her arms.

"Who the fuck is that?" Ryan asked no one and everyone, his eyes suddenly huge and wild. He turned to Bendigo, angled the laptop screen so the old man on the floor could get a better view. "Answer me. It's a Sunday. No one's supposed to be here but you and him. Who the fuck is that?"

Bendigo felt a chill ripple in his chest. Ryan and Elsie knew he'd been coming in over the weekends, doing extra hours, trying to work through the backlog. Had they been watching him?

"Who is that?" Elsie pressed.

"How am I supposed to know?" Bendigo asked. "There must be five hundred people who work in this building. Why don't you just hit the intercom and ask her who she is?"

Ryan thought about it. But maybe he saw the plan in Bendigo's eyes, the tightness in his throat as he prepared to scream. Because, in the few seconds since she had hit the buzzer, Bendigo had already decided that was what he was going to do. He was going to suck in a huge breath, and when Ryan opened the intercom, he was going to howl with all his might for the woman to run. Ryan gave a mean smile and shook his head.

"I'll stay on these two," he told Elsie. "You go and bring her inside. Three hostages are better than two."

CHAPTER 3

LEE: Ranchos Palos Verdes Parks and Recreation, Ranger Lee.

HOSKINS: Hey, Lee. How are you?

LEE: Good. Good. How can I help, sir?

HOSKINS: My name is Charlie Hoskins. I'm a detective with the LAPD.

LEE: Oh. Okay. Yep?

HOSKINS: The guys at Central put me through to you. They said you might be able to help me with a person I'm trying to track down.

LEE: I'll do what I can.

HOSKINS: Last Wednesday, there was a rescue down near East Beach. Guy got washed into the bay, and a woman dragged him out of the water. I don't know if you heard about that?

LEE: I did! I did hear about that! Yeah. Wow. Incredible!

HOSKINS: Right?

LEE: A couple of the guys, the regular surfers, they were talking about it.

HOSKINS: Have you got a report for that incident, or . . . ?

LEE: No. Look, Detective, we don't have

lifeguards down there this time of year. Best
we got is a few land-based rangers like myself
and my team patrolling that area, watching
out for illegal campers and drunks.

HOSKINS: Right.

LEE: If someone got into trouble in the water
and someone else helped them out, well,
unless it was reported here to the ranger's
station, there's no way we'd know about it.
Except through chatter with the locals, like
I said.

HOSKINS: So she wasn't a lifeguard, then? The
woman?

LEE: Well, not one of mine, at least. I've got
two lady lifeguards on my team right now,
and one's in Italy on vacation and the other's
my wife. I reckon she would have said something about pullin' some guy's naked ass out
of the water.

HOSKINS: I see.

LEE: She must have known what she was
doing, whoever she was. To be out there
like that in the first place, I mean. It's not a
friendly bay. And to bring the guy in all by
herself? He wasn't a small guy, so I heard
from Flick and Zero.

HOSKINS: Who?

LEE: Yeah. Flick and Zero. They were the two
surfers who helped her out.

HOSKINS: Okay.

LEE: I don't know their real names, before you
ask. No, wait. Zero's real name is John, I
think.

HOSKINS: Don't suppose you could give me
John's number?

LEE: I could probably do that. I'll just, uh. I'll
just see if I can find . . .

HOSKINS: Thanks.

LEE: Who was the guy? Can I ask that? Was
    he just some idiot who got washed off the
    rocks, or . . . ?
HOSKINS: Something like that.

Charlie Hoskins flipped the switch on the electric
razor and felt the vibrations shiver through the bones
of his hand. He took a moment to enjoy the sound
of the device buzzing loudly around the tiny hospital
bathroom. For five years, he'd been dreaming of this
moment. Taking off the mask. He set the teeth of the
clippers to his left sideburn and raked them up over
his temple. In the sink, his hacked-off ponytail lay
limp in the dampness like a small, wounded creature.
As he shaved, more strands rained softly down.

He worked the clippers close over his head, edging
around an already shaven patch bordering stitches
that secured a long, vertical wound there. The jagged
split was where Franko had beaned him on the crown
of his skull with a section of lead pipe. As he shaved,
Charlie saw a flash of that moment: Dean standing
in front of him, holding his attention while Franko
snuck up from behind. He remembered those last
few seconds of Operation Hellfire. The horror wrap-
ping around him, hard and sudden like a surprise
bear hug, as he watched Dean's mouth spread into a
knowing smile. The jig was up. Game over.

The gang had found out who he really was.

The memories assaulted him as he shaved his beard.
Charlie had seen the distant, sparkling strip of lights,
the nighttime coastline, tilt sideways as the pipe hit
his skull. Then he lost his legs and the deck of the
boat smashed into his chin. He'd felt so small, the
ocean spreading out endlessly all around the boat on
which he lay.

Oh god, he'd thought as he felt Franko's hands
around his ankles, dragging him across the deck toward
the lower deck hatch. *Oh god. Please. Please.*

Not now.

Not out here.

Charlie had learned early in his time on the job not to try to force the memories away. Slamming the door shut on traumas only gave them power. Instead, it was best to let them have their time. He finished shaving his head and beard, and the pictures of the night when he'd almost died at sea gently settled.

He tidied up, tucked the clippers back into the bag of supplies his friend Surge had sent him, and took out a clean set of clothes. He slipped off the hospital robe and put on jeans and a black T-shirt. Charlie's body was groaning and complaining in a dozen different places, stitches pulling and bruises aching and tired muscles straining against the effort of making his escape. He wanted to lie back down in the hospital bed, submit to the strangely soothing chorus of bleeps and rattles and mumbling intercom announcements, but it wasn't safe here. There was a Beretta at the bottom of the bag, a burner phone, a set of car keys. Everything he'd asked for, down to the make of the gun and the extra clip. Surge was like that. Meticulous. Reliable. The painkillers and antibiotics Charlie had been prescribed sat on the bedside table in paper bags marked with the logo of the hospital's pharmacy. Charlie scooped them all into the bag and zipped it up, went into the bathroom.

On the phone, he called the switchboard and asked to be transferred to the nurses' station at east wing's ward C. In time, he heard the distant peal of the landline only fifty yards from where he stood.

"Ward C nurses' station. This is Lori."

"Lori, it's Tom down at security," Charlie lied.

"I'm sorry, who?"

"Tom Edgeworth, hospital security. Is the head nurse, Allison, there?"

"No. Um. No. Sorry. She's not on right now. Can I help?"

"You've got a couple of cops up there in ward C, haven't you?" Charlie asked.

"Ah. I'm not sure I should—"

"My logbook says you've got two police officers up there watching the door of a patient who's under protection."

"Yes," Lori admitted. "Yes, we do."

"Can you get one of them on the phone?"

Charlie went back into the main room, waited. Soon, outside the door to his room, he heard a conversation playing out, the nurse, Lori, having carried the cordless handset to the two patrol officers manning Charlie's door. He sat on the bed and struggled to pull on a pair of boots, his ribs creaking, the phone clamped between his ear and shoulder. The boots were too tight, but they'd do.

"Hello?"

"It's Tom Edgeworth here." Charlie took the Beretta from the bed and slipped it into the waistband at the back of his jeans. "I'm one of the security guards at the admin building."

"Okay . . . ?"

"You're up there protecting some kind of special patient, aren't you?"

"Uh, maybe. What—"

"I just thought I should bring it to your attention that there's a suspicious-looking character who's just entered the elevators, heading up toward ward C. I'm tracking him on the CCTV in front of me here. Might be nothing. Just thought I'd warn you—"

"Yep. Yep. We're on it."

"I'm sending two of my guys up behind him. Maybe you should—"

"We'll intercept him here."

The patrol officer outside the door hung up. Charlie went and listened. He counted ten seconds, then opened the door and looked down the hall. The two uniformed officers were heading toward the nurses' station: alert, heads up, their movements cautious, like a pair of apartment dogs who've heard footsteps on the stairwell. Charlie sighed, shook his head, and slipped out of his hospital room, heading the other way down the hall toward the fire escape.

He clocked the girl following him at the edge of smoker's row. Charlie was walking, head down, stride quick, past the circular driveway at the front of the hospital and toward the main road when he saw her out of the corner of his eye. She burst out of the automatic doors of the hospital's entrance and jogged up the driveway, past the row of patients and visitors chomping worriedly on cigarettes and flicking butts into the sad hedges. Then she slowed her step, tracking him, waiting for the right moment—for what, he didn't know. Charlie watched her in the reflection on the front windows of a little café as he crossed Normandie Avenue. She was too young and pretty to be Death Machines, but he didn't like to make assumptions. He ducked quickly left off the sidewalk on 257th and into a shopping mall, blinking away green spots on his vision left by the sunlight as he passed a doughnut shop and a nail salon. He took the ramp to the underground parking lot and waited until she'd reached the bottom. Then he stepped out from behind a pylon and grabbed a fistful of her T-shirt, used it to just about lift her off the ground.

"What *the fuck* do you want?"

"Oh, shit." Her soft hands grabbed his, her whole body hanging back in the shirt like a turtle in a shell. "Oh, god. I'm sorry. I'm sorry. I'm—"

"Why are you following me?"

"Please let me go. You're hurting me."

Charlie dropped her. The girl straightened her shirt, fussed with the edge of it to buy time while her mouth trembled and her eyes sprang with tears.

"I'm Lynette Lamb," she finally confessed as if it

would mean something to Charlie. He stood there trying to put this all together: the girl, the name, the apparent impending emotional meltdown. Whoever she was, she was waging an internal war against oncoming waterworks and losing. Her face was flushing red, and the hands that swiped at her eyes were shaking.

"That name means nothing to me, honey," Charlie said. "If you're a reporter looking for an interview, you're fresh out of luck." He started to walk off.

"I'm not a reporter. I'm the rookie," she said.

Charlie stopped. Around him, the parking lot seemed to shimmer with energy. A car horn blared somewhere. An engine revved. He found that his back teeth were locked. When he turned back, Charlie found the girl's teary eyes were big and full of meaning.

"I'm the one who got you found out," she continued.

"You?" He looked her over, head to toe. Then he squinted. *"You?"*

"Yes, me." She seemed to gain some ground in the battle against her tears out of sheer indignation. "What's that supposed to mean?"

He tried to answer, couldn't. He was too tired.

"What?"

"You look young, that's all."

He scratched at the stitches in his scalp and tried to think of an exit strategy. "Listen, I'm sorry I grabbed you. And I'm sure you're sorry you almost got me killed. So let's just say we're square, Miss Lamb. Sound good?"

She opened her mouth to answer. He didn't let her.

"See ya," he said.

He was almost at the corner of the lot where the car Surge had left him was supposed to be when she spoke again, still, amazingly, on his heels.

"I'm not sorry that I almost got you killed," she said.

Charlie stopped.

He turned.

"It wasn't my fault," Lamb continued. "I did nothing wrong, okay? Absolutely nothing. I went out on the town with my friends, celebrating a professional triumph, which I was perfectly entitled to do. I took a man home to my apartment, which I was also perfectly entitled to do. And I fell asleep with that man inside my apartment, leaving him unsupervised, which I was *perfectly entitled to do*."

"I can't believe what I'm hear—" Charlie started, but it was her turn to power on over the top of him, performing a speech she'd obviously rehearsed.

"That Brad Alan Binchley *chose* to use *my* computer and *my* police log-in to hack into secure files is not something *I*, or *any other rational person on the earth*, could *possibly* have anticipated!" Lamb spat the words, tapping her chest to the beat of them.

Charlie watched her. The boom gate of the parking lot went up and down, letting drivers out into the sunshine. The girl took in a long, shuddering breath, and he noticed for the first time how tired and rumpled she looked. Her hair was greasy, and her shirt was stained. He guessed she'd been sitting in the hospital's main waiting area, hoping he would appear, since the moment she'd learned of his fate. It had been nifty work, finding out what he looked like from police records. A good guess which hospital he had been admitted to. A far-fetched notion that he would appear in her line of sight at the front of the hospital if she waited long enough. And now this Lynette Lamb character was throwing all her chips in on a wild, impossible wager that he'd agree to hear her out on whatever it was she was trying to say. Charlie couldn't marry her strange courage at tracking him down and confronting him like this with her sheer inability to keep her emotions in check. He looked at that little trembling chin and felt downright uncomfortable.

"I'm sorry about what happened to you, Detective

Hoskins," Lamb said, rising to her full height, which wasn't much, to conclude her speech. "But I didn't do it to you."

Charlie allowed her a few seconds to enjoy her moment. Then he asked, "Are you done?"

"Yes."

"Good, because I gotta go."

"You're not going anywhere." She'd won the battle for now, was dry-eyed and at his side as he fished the car keys out of the side pocket of his backpack. "I need your help."

"Oh, you need my help?" Charlie laughed, clicking the button on the fob and seeing the taillights of a silver Kia light up in the corner of the lot. "This just keeps getting better."

"They fired me. Did they tell you that?"

"No, but I'm not surprised."

"I didn't even get a single day on the job."

"Less surprising again."

"So now that you've heard . . . you know." She gave an exasperated sigh, waved her hands. "Now that you . . . that you understand where I'm coming from on all this, you can help me get back in."

Charlie put a hand on the driver's-side door of the Kia and used it to hold himself up while he laughed. He hadn't had a good laugh in days. It made everything hurt.

"Oh, wow."

"What? What's 'wow'?" Lamb snapped. "Why are you saying 'wow'?"

Charlie sighed, raked his fingers down his stubble. "Look, Miss Lamb. It's like this. You bringing a random dude home from a nightclub and him turning out to be a patched outlaw biker who was only using you to access top-secret police files? Yeah. You're right. It's pretty unlikely stuff. There's no way you or anybody else could have seen that coming."

Lamb looked heartened.

"But you've just spent three minutes demonstrating to me"—Charlie gestured back at their path across the parking lot—"the myriad ways in which you're not suited to this job."

"*What?*" Her voice was so high and loud with outrage it made his eardrums pulse.

"You're all wrong for this job."

"No, I'm not. I'm—"

"You've come running for help at the first sign of disaster rather than handling all this yourself," Charlie said. "And you've chosen the exact wrong person to run to. I'm tired, okay? I'm also hiding out from those members of the Death Machines who weren't rounded up when Operation Hellfire collapsed. Because of you—of what you *didn't mean to do, but nevertheless did*—I've got a metal plate in my head and enough painkillers on board to kill a racehorse. I'm the last person on the planet who's willing, or able, to help you right now."

He popped the driver's-side door and threw the backpack in, then pointed at the new tears rimming her long, dark lashes.

"And this is the fourth time you've almost burst into tears in this single conversation," he said. "That's not cop material. Okay? You understand? *You're. Not. Cop. Material.*"

He slipped into the car and slammed the door, then watched in dismay as she rounded the hood. She opened the passenger side before he thought to hit the auto lock and slid into the seat beside him.

"Please, go away!" he moaned.

"No," she said, wiping her nose on the back of her hand. "Me crying right now is a physical response to heightened emotion that I usually have control over. It doesn't mean I shouldn't be taken seriously."

Charlie snorted. "It doesn't?"

"No, it doesn't," she said. "I worked hard on the crying thing at the academy. I got ahold of it."

"You did?"

"Just shut up." She spoke through gritted teeth. "You're going to help me."

"No, I'm not. I'm—"

"You're going to help me, or I'll call the police right now." She brandished a cell phone.

Charlie's smile was widening all the time, the absurdity starting to tickle something deep in his grisly old heart. "Lamb."

"Not one minute ago, you admitted, in my presence," Lamb said, "that you are currently under the influence of a narcotic substance, a quantity of which you yourself described as being capable of 'killing a racehorse.'"

Charlie watched her.

"Therefore, you are legally prohibited from operating this vehicle," Lamb went on, pointing to the keys, which were sitting in the ignition. "And, at present, you are doing just that."

Charlie leaned his head against the seat and folded his arms.

"Does saying things like 'at present' and 'you yourself' make you feel like a cop?" he asked her.

"I will dial 911 right now."

"Oh no you won't."

"Oh yes I will."

She began to dial. Charlie stopped smiling and thought about the potential danger. He reached out and took the phone from her and ended the call, then tossed the device over his shoulder into the back of the car somewhere.

"You're starting to annoy me now, Lamb," he said. "So I'm just going to sit here and close my eyes and wait for you to go away."

He reached out and flipped the radio on, settling back into the seat with his eyes closed. She started prattling on again, but his focus was drawn away by the smooth, official tones of the broadcaster.

"—*this morning, as police respond to a hostile situation currently unfolding at a testing facility at the
Hertzberg-Davis Forensic Science Center.*"

He put a hand up to silence her, but she'd heard it,
too. Police. Hostile. Hertzberg-Davis. Charlie felt a
tremor of warning reverberate through the core of his
body, the territorial alert instinct that wakes a man in
his home in the dead of night at the sound of a foot-
fall on his porch. They were in the lab. *Their* lab. He
found the dial and turned the volume up.

"—*to a large police presence assembling outside
the facility. It is believed two armed persons entered
the building at approximately 6:50 a.m. and are currently in communication with LAPD officers on the
scene. It is not known yet whether—*"

"Shit," Lamb said.

"Shit," Charlie agreed. He turned the engine over,
flapped a hand at Lamb's door. "Get out. I've gotta
go."

"You're not going anywhere."

"I'm not kiddin' around this time. I'm serious." He
shoved at her. "Get out."

"You can't drive!"

Charlie threw open his door and went around the
hood, his thoughts tangled up in the Hertzberg-Davis
report. Two armed persons. The same desperate voice
he'd heard in his mind on the boat in the middle of
the ocean was speaking again. *Not now. Not there.
Please. Please.*

Everything he had on the Death Machines was in
that lab.

All his samples. All his work.

Five years.

He yanked Lamb's door. At first, he thought it was
the force with which he'd grabbed the handle that
had burst the glass of her window. But Charlie had
been in enough shoot-outs in his time to know what
close-range gunfire looked like when it popped and

flashed off a car's glossy surface. Lamb screamed and he heard the pop again, and a second bullet whined off the roof of the car an inch or two from his hand. Charlie looked over his shoulder and spotted the shooter advancing determinedly toward him between the parked cars, gun out, ready to fire again.

Lamb was already scrambling across the car into the driver's seat, trying to tug him into the car at the same time, her scream transforming to shouts. "Get in! Get in! Get in! Get in!"

She was tearing out of the parking space before he could shut the door behind him. Charlie gripped the handle above his window and the back of her seat, and tried not to slide into her as she jerked the wheel sideways and sped down the lot toward the boom gate. Screaming tires. Crunching suspension. The boom whacked open against the brick wall, hollow and useless. Glass was tumbling sideways on the floor at Charlie's feet. Another shot took out the back window of the Kia, raining glass cubes onto the leather upholstery. Charlie yanked his door shut, twisted in his seat, and tracked the shooter, a guy in a black hoodie, as he sprinted across the lot, probably making for a pickup car waiting somewhere on the street.

"What the fuck!" Lamb was gripping the wheel, hunched over it, eyes wild. They roared down the street toward the PCH. "Who was—"

"Just drive," Charlie said.

She raced toward a gap between a van and a food truck stopped at the traffic lights. With a confidence he could only guess the source of, she stomped on the accelerator. The mirrors on both sides of the vehicle smashed off. Charlie jammed his boot into the footwell to stop himself sliding again as Lamb swung the car onto the PCH, heading east.

The pickup car was a black Mustang, illegal tint and huge mag wheels. Flashy and stupid. Death Machines. The driver wasn't as confident about the gap between the trucks and leaped the sidewalk instead with a spray of sparks. Charlie watched the Mustang in the rearview, weird relief that the gang had indeed come for him, as he'd known they would, competing with anger hitched high in his stomach. When simply watching the car that pursued them felt impotent, he turned back in his seat, looked at Lamb, and saw she was flushed in the cheeks but tearless and quiet. Somehow the blubbering kid he'd met in the parking lot had been traded out for a woman whose face was rigid with focus.

"Take the 110 north," he said, regretting the words as soon as they were out of his mouth. His mind was torn, fragmented, wanting to shake the tail but also desperate to get to the situation at Hertzberg-Davis. The 110 would be jammed, even on a Sunday morning. Lamb ignored him, careering across an intersection toward a small road off the side of the highway overpass.

A golf course yawned beside them. That was smart, Charlie thought. Little roads. Undulating hills. Lots of cameras. Tight groups of trees by the edge of the road, blocking upcoming hazards. It was a big, winding maze for them to get lost in. Lamb took the entrance gates at a fast but sensible speed, glancing in the rearview for the following car. By the time she'd rounded the first bend between the manicured hills, scaring the crap out of a group of old-timers chatting around a golf cart, the follow car had fallen back. Charlie and Lamb waited, winding through the course, slower and slower, until the Mustang turned off and disappeared.

They didn't speak until the Kia bumped onto a sandy side road connecting the golf course to a brushy slab of vacant land behind Harbor College.

"Oh, man. It worked," Lamb breathed, easing back a little from the wheel. "I hoped they'd get spooked by the golf course. Too many people, you know?"

"You did good," Charlie conceded. He pointed ahead. "Just stop here. I'll let you out. You can get a cab from the highway."

She ignored him again, following the back roads toward the Harbor College parking lot.

"Lamb, pull over."

She chewed her lip, cautious, watching for the Mustang as she drove.

"Hello?" Charlie leaned forward, trying to catch her eyes. "Paging Lynette Lamb."

"I hear you. I'm just ignoring you."

"Well, don't," he said. "Pull over."

"You need to get to Hertzberg-Davis." She glanced both ways at the edge of the lot before pulling onto the 110. "Whatever's going on there, you want to be involved."

"What I want and where I'm going are none of your damn business," Charlie said. "I—"

"You can't drive there by yourself," Lamb said. "I'll take you."

Charlie didn't fight her. He didn't have the time or the energy. His head hurt, the new addition to his skull feeling like a vise clamped around his brain. He took out his phone and dialed one of only three phone numbers he had burned in the surface of that dried, overworked lump of gray matter. It was the same number he'd dialed on the beach four days earlier. He didn't expect his boss to pick up now. Her cell would probably be at risk of overheating and blowing up in her hand with calls, texts, and emails from all manner of police and media. But he left a message anyway.

"Sass," Charlie said. "It's Hoss. I'm coming in."

CHAPTER 4

They watched the doors, the three of them, the world beyond its simple frame seeming to Gary Bendigo like a terrifying, foreign landscape being consumed by a gathering tempest. He could hear what he assumed were Elsie Delaney's steps, steady and hard, marching back up the hall toward the lab where he and Ryan and Ibrahim waited. The footsteps were getting louder and louder. Also approaching and increasing in volume were the shuffling, unsteady footsteps he assumed belonged to the woman who had hit the buzzer at the side door of the building. Rising alongside those footsteps was the sound of her high-pitched, unanswered protests and questions. Behind those noises, the peal of police sirens and what Bendigo guessed was the rhythmic whump of a chopper. A wall of noise was coming toward the door. Bendigo was so tense and so alert for the women to arrive that the icy microseconds before they appeared seemed almost physically painful.

Then they were there, Elsie dragging the woman into the room by her bicep, releasing her in front of Ryan. The woman did the same awkward, hesitant quarter turn back and forth that Bendigo had done when Ryan told him to get on his knees, not completely sure yet that this wasn't some kind of joke or mistake.

"Who are you?" Ryan asked as Elsie bound the woman's wrists.

"Oh god." The woman swiped at her short blond bob, causing Elsie to scramble for the wrist that had just slipped from her grasp. "I'm, uh. I'm sorry . . . I think you've got the wrong person here."

"You're exactly where you're supposed to be. So just stay calm and tell me who you are," Ryan said. His voice was gentle and might have been effective if he hadn't then taken up the gun and pointed it at the woman's chest. The woman was panting, open-mouthed, like an injured bird, her eyes flicking from the gun to Bendigo to Ibrahim. There was no sign of the notebook she had been carrying.

"I can't do this," the woman said.

"Just say your name."

"It's-it's-it's-it's Ashlea Pratt." The woman glanced again at Bendigo, held his eyes for longer this time. "I'm a reporter from the *LA Times*. I came to talk to-to-to . . . to *him*."

She jutted her chin at Bendigo, sharply, as if the move were going to get her freed, the responsibility passed to him for whatever the hell this was. The doctor sagged in his binds.

"What do you want to talk to him for?" Ryan asked.

"The backlog," Bendigo sighed. He watched Elsie Delaney shove the female reporter onto her butt against the steel table he was hunched beside, maybe three yards away from him. "Here I was thinking the *Dateline* asshole who ambushed me last week was an outlier. Guess the *Times* is after me, too."

"What's the backlog?" Ryan demanded.

Bendigo resigned himself. "We test rape kits here for the police and sheriff's departments. Once upon a time, there was a significant backlog here, okay?

Thousands of untested kits were just sitting in storage, and no one was getting through them. But there are laws against that now. There are oversight boards. That stuff doesn't happen anymore."

"So why's she here, then?" Elsie pointed at Ashlea.

"Because—" Bendigo shook his head. "Urgh. Look. She's here because modern journalism is a farce, that's why. This lab is a little behind in its testing again. Which is a natural, predictable, and solvable phenomenon. In any workplace, there are ebbs and flows. Peaks and troughs in productivity and outcomes. But that's not much of a headline, is it?"

"How far behind are you?" Ryan leaned an elbow on the table behind him, a smirk on his face, like someone chatting at a bar and not a man trying to compete in volume with the orchestra of police sirens outside the building in which he stood.

"Are we really doing this right now?" Bendigo snapped.

"Hey." Ryan shrugged. "I'm just interested in the other ways you people have managed to fuck up your rather simple job and destroy human lives in the process."

"What do you mean, 'other ways'?" Bendigo asked.

"Look, can I just say something?" Ashlea's face was stiff and colorless. "You have to let me go. I really, really have to go. I have a family. I have a . . . I'm . . . My mom's expecting me for dinner tonight."

"Well, our apologies, Miss Pratt," Ryan said. "We didn't plan for you to become part of this. But you are. So them's the breaks, I guess. Your mom will survive. Just sit there and be quiet."

Ashlea was quiet for no more than an instant.

"What's happening here?" she asked. The young reporter was still trying to put it all together—the guns and the duffel bags and the zip ties around their wrists. "Why are you doing this to us?"

Ryan and Elsie didn't answer. They'd turned to the

laptop screen, which Bendigo couldn't see now. He imagined they were watching police cars swarming the parking lot, the first responders taking up their positions. The cell phone Ryan had used to film the ransom video started to buzz. They ignored it.

"Let me paint a picture for you," Bendigo said to Ashlea instead. He kept his voice low, but refused to whisper. "These two lunatics lost their daughter a couple of years ago. They think the LAPD have botched the job finding her or that they didn't try hard enough or something. Whatever the case, they're dissatisfied with the LAPD. So they had the bright idea of bursting in here and taking us hostage as a way of putting a firecracker up the ass of the police."

"What?" Ashlea said. "*What?*"

"Yeah," Bendigo replied. "That's what I said."

"Where . . . Where *is* their daughter?"

"That's the whole point, darling." Bendigo lifted his brows. "They don't know."

"I mean, is she dead?" Ashlea huffed. "Was she abducted? Did they see an abductor? Were there witnesses? Why didn't the police—"

"Ashlea," Bendigo soothed. "Ashlea, Ashlea. I don't care. I don't care where the child is." Bendigo looked to the captors, felt Ryan's icy gaze wandering over him. "It has nothing to do with me. I'm a fucking hostage right now. I'm a hostage in my own lab."

"It has more to do with you than you think," Elsie muttered.

"Who's that?" Ashlea leaned forward.

Ibrahim, who had been watching all of this unfold in silence, gave a nervous nod of greeting.

"That's Ibrahim. He's a security guard." Bendigo looked over at the young man. "We haven't had a chance to discuss it yet, but I'm assuming the Delaneys clubbed him and dragged him in here just before I arrived at work this morning."

"I didn't see them coming," Ibrahim admitted.

"Are you okay?" Ashlea asked him.

"I'm fine. I'm fine." Ibrahim straightened, and Bendigo saw the young man's biceps and triceps strain against the fabric of his shirt for an instant. "Thanks for asking, ma'am."

Ashlea took a few moments to try to take it all in, swallowing hard, her feet in their shiny high heels shifting uncomfortably on the floor in front of her, finding no traction. Then she looked back at Bendigo.

"You called them lunatics," she said.

"I assume that's what they are." Bendigo felt his lip twist with bitterness. "This isn't how normal people get what they want. What they're doing, it's basically terrorism."

"Have they threatened you?" Ashlea's voice broke over the words. "Are they . . . are they saying they're going to hurt us?"

"They're not gonna hurt us." Ibrahim had shuffled up to his full height, sitting cross-legged on the floor. "It's okay, ma'am. We're here. We're all together. We'll be okay."

"I admire your optimism, Ibrahim." Bendigo smiled. He nodded at the couple poring over the computer screen. "But if I had to guess, I'd say the next stage of this little stunt will involve those two demonstrating to the police that they're serious."

CHAPTER 5

Someone got Saskia a fold-out chair, but she didn't take it. She knew, from decades of working leadership roles in crisis situations, that the tiniest gestures would communicate to her team whether she was confident about a resolution or not. She stood in the sunshine outside the little white tent someone had dragged out of nowhere and erected, and refused coffee and water when it was brought her way. To sit and think and drink coffee and keep hydrated in the shade was long-term, comfortable behavior. Standing and moving and talking: that was action, and action was confidence, the kind of confidence the top dog of the Los Angeles Police Department was expected to display. This was a short-term operation. Get in. Kill the threat. Get out.

There were a lot of people to whom Saskia needed to convey this confidence. Eyes watching, measuring. At the edges of the parking lot, a physical ring of squad cars stood nose to tail, and armed patrol officers stood with their guns trained on the front doors and the windows of the Hertzberg-Davis Forensic Science Center. Beyond them, at the gates to the facility, journalists were already assembling. They lined the outer cordon with vans, cameras, mics, long, snaking cables, and anxious faces. They were far enough away that

Saskia couldn't see individual facial expressions, but she knew their cameras could see hers. Overhead, two police choppers circled, one keeping an eye on the building, the other patrolling the cleared airspace for any brazen sweeps by press helicopters wanting an aerial shot of the operation. Saskia's team of specialists busily loaded fold-out tables under the tent with equipment, their work taking place behind a protective wall created by three parked SWAT BearCat vehicles. Saskia watched as laptops were flipped open, heavy-duty suitcases were dumped and unclipped. Boots clunked on the dusty asphalt, people bumping into each other in their haste, apologizing. They'd find their rhythm soon.

Two men approached her—one she knew, one she didn't. Leonard Franklin, head of LAPD SWAT, jammed a tablet rimmed in heavy rubber tactical casing in front of her, the screen lit with the image of a blueprint. The huge, boxy, white special tactics officer had put on some pounds around the belly since Saskia had seen him last, and he was wearing cologne, which told Saskia a girlfriend had probably cut his usual six hours in the gym down to a more reasonable four. The leaner Black man with him nodded to Saskia in greeting. Saskia took the tablet from Franklin and nodded back.

"This is Ronnie Curler." Franklin jabbed a thumb in Curler's direction, his eyes on the tablet in Saskia's hands. "FBI negotiator. I've already argued for your lead on this, ma'am, so you can thank me for that whenever you like."

"Thanks." Saskia rolled her eyes. "Nice to meet you, Agent Curler. Have you made contact with the suspects?"

"Not yet. They're not answering," Curler said. "Standard. Expected."

"This is the lay of the land." Franklin pointed to the screen with a huge gloved finger. "They're on the ground floor, in the forensic biology and DNA lab. They've secured every external door to the building from the inside with bike locks. They're solid steel U-bolt-style locks—take about five minutes to cut through with a grinder."

"Okay," Saskia said.

"Those automatic glass doors at the front of the building are still showing as functional," Franklin said. He turned and pointed. "And inside, through this reception area, there's another glass automatic door, which still looks to be online. They've bike-locked this internal door here, which cuts off that whole right wing of the building. So this is their sandbox."

Saskia looked at the blueprint. The area Franklin was calling the Delaneys' "sandbox" encompassed four laboratories, a small kitchen area, and two bathrooms. An internal stairwell led to the first floor of the building.

"Stairwell's open?" Saskia asked.

"Yes." Franklin nodded.

"That's good," Saskia said. "We've got two possible paths in: the front doors and the internal stairwell."

"Means shit if you don't have line of sight," Franklin grunted.

"Yes, I know." Saskia smiled. "But it's better than nothing. What do we know about the room they're in?"

"It's thirty by thirty feet," Franklin said. "Access points are the internal door, an air-conditioning vent, three sinks, and these windows here." He swept a hand over a row of six windows covered by gray roller blinds, fifty yards from where Saskia stood. "Special ops is looking at getting a worm camera up one of the sinks, or a robot in through the air-con vent, or both. Either way, we expect to have a visual and mics in the room within the hour."

Saskia looked at the windows Franklin had pointed out. Six gray slabs of glass, framed in aluminum, completely nondescript and with no sign of movement within. She knew that at that moment, these six windows were being splashed across emergency news broadcast screens nationwide—six tall, wide boxes reflecting the crowded outer cordon and the sunny sky buzzing with choppers. More interesting visuals would punctuate the coverage, probably. The SWAT teams suiting up by the gates to the parking lot. Footage of herself, and her inner team, strategizing by the tent. Happy snaps of the hostages before the fateful morning they were taken, likely ripped straight from social media, and press conference photos of the Delaneys and their missing child. But for now, those six windows were drawing Saskia's gaze, and those of the men and women around her, as they tried to imagine what was happening inside.

"Cut the power to the building," Saskia said. "The water, the gas, the air-con, everything. I want them dead in the water. They'll be using the CCTV to track our movements. Make sure you kill the Wi-Fi."

"With respect," Curler said. "My advice is not to make them too uncomfortable yet, ma'am. We'll want that leverage for later. And in terms of the CCTV, I advise you leave the cameras on for now. Let them watch us. Let them know we're not making any crazy moves. We want to establish communication, then—"

"The water's got to go off." Franklin held up a gloved hand, a huge stop sign. "I need the drains."

"The Wi-Fi, too," Saskia said. "To lock down communications. Keep it in-house."

"But there's a rub here," Curler said. "A major one. I've just been speaking with our contact for the lab itself. The general manager under Gary Bendigo, who is one of the hostages. She's telling me that there are dozens of fridges in there, each of them crammed full with—"

"Biological samples." Saskia huffed a sigh. Her stomach plummeted. "Right. Of course. All our DNA.

All our samples. They're all in temperature-controlled storage."

"So we need to keep the gas and electricity."

"Consider the water and the Wi-Fi gone." Franklin turned and made a hand signal to someone over Curler's shoulder.

"What are they packing?" Saskia asked. "Can we confirm whether the Delaneys have got anything more than the guns we saw on the ransom video?"

"Special Investigations is taking a good look at the video now, but they could have anything in those duffel bags." Franklin sighed. "I've got a couple of detectives rounding up friends, family, neighbors to talk about what they've been doing in the past few months. Whether they've talked about explosives or if they've seen any explosives inside the household."

"Good. We're going to proceed as if they've got a fucking nuke in there," Saskia said. "I want the bomb squad on the ground ready to go in as soon as we have access. We treat this as a high-grade threat until we know any differently. What are we doing to establish that there's no one else in the building?"

"A lot of the blinds in the upper-floor windows are open," Franklin said. "I've got snipers checking out what they can see, but that's useless if someone's ducked under a table or hidden in a closet. We've got to run back through the CCTV, count heads. Someone's on it."

Saskia turned to Curler.

"Talk to me about comms," she said. "That phone they used to shoot and send the video. Is that the only line in?"

"The Delaneys aren't answering their personal cell phones," Curler said. "If I had to guess, they probably left them at home, or they may have destroyed them to hide the trails of anyone who helped them with this. The phone they've got will have been purchased specially for the occasion."

"You said them not picking up so far is expected?" Saskia said.

"They won't jump right away." Curler nodded. "They'll make us wait."

Saskia stood, feeling quietly helpless as seconds and minutes ticked by without the situation being resolved, with no measurable steps being made toward bringing the hostages out safely. She looked around the tent. A young female technician was sitting at a laptop, a headset on, watching a blank audio feed with an icon of a phone unmoving at the center. As Saskia watched, the technician dialed. The phone icon jiggled but didn't turn green.

Just talk to us, you assholes, Saskia thought, looking back at the windows.

The phone rang and rang. Bendigo sat listening to its thrumming vibration through the steel table on which Elsie and Ryan had set up camp. A silent pall had fallen over Ashlea and Ibrahim, over the cold slice of the laboratory reserved for the hostages. Ashlea was twitching and opening her mouth now and then, about to begin more questions. But she fell quiet again and again, apparently cowed by the very number to be asked. Ibrahim sat dazed, either lost in thought or numbed by the blow to his head, staring at a spot on the floor just beyond his feet.

"Okay," Elsie said suddenly, glancing at her watch. "Okay. Next steps. Next steps. Should we bring them all here? Lay them out in a line, maybe, for when we connect again?"

Bendigo felt the attention of his fellow hostages zero in on the Delaneys. Ashlea cocked her head beside him.

"No, we need to leave them in the fridges until we need them," Ryan said. "Maintain their integrity."

Bendigo felt his chest tighten. His eyes drifted to the fridge nearest the door, the laminated instructional

placards almost entirely covering its polished steel surface. Lab 21. Fridge 21. Ibrahim seemed to sense his
dread, reached out, and nudged Bendigo's foot with
his own.

"What?" the boy asked.

Bendigo couldn't speak. Couldn't give life to the
wretchedness of the idea that had sprung into his head
by speaking it aloud.

CHAPTER 6

"So what can you tell me about the hostages?" Saskia beckoned Curler to start walking with her toward the gates to the parking lot, where a group of lieutenants was checking IDs and seeing vehicles in and out of the cordon. Movement. Action. Confidence. She'd spent too long poring over electronic maps and blueprints, watching laptops and phone screens for the Delaneys' answer. She needed to move. Curler followed her, his hands in the pockets of his slacks.

"Ibrahim Solea is a twenty-one-year-old night security guard here on the campus," Curler said. "He was born in the U.S., but his parents are Iraqi citizens. The security gig is a part-time job he started three months ago. He's a freshman in architecture on the campus."

"Okay," Saskia said.

"Dr. Gary Bendigo is the head of two major divisions inside the building," Curler continued. "The Forensic Biology Unit and the Forensic Chemistry Unit. He oversees a total of ten labs. He's sixty-five, divorced."

"And who's the woman?" Saskia arrived at the checkpoint and grabbed the crime-scene log from the lieutenant standing there, glanced over the list of vehicles that had gone in and out of the parking lot.

So far, the lot had been emptied of civilian vehicles, and there were three BearCats and eight police tactical units in the inner cordon. She handed it back. No mystery there. Saskia could see exactly who was coming and going, but the media needed to see her checking things, giving directions, staying on top of it all.

"The woman is Ashlea Pratt," the negotiator said. "She's a twenty-eight-year-old assistant writer with the *LA Times.*"

"What the hell is she doing in there?"

"Seems like she might have been chasing Bendigo for a story. First response units were about two minutes out when she got scooped in by Elsie Delaney at the front doors. Two students walking to the library saw it."

"Christ." Saskia felt like rubbing her eyes, working at the growing tension across the bridge of her nose. She didn't. There were cameras on her. "So we've got two kids and an old man in there."

"Maybe three kids," Curler said ruefully.

"What?"

"One of the first responders got Ashlea Pratt's mother on the line about ten minutes ago. She says Ashlea's been trying to get pregnant for some months now. She was supposed to go to dinner with her daughter tonight and was half expecting an exciting announcement."

"Great." Saskia chewed her lip. "Great. That's just fucking great. We need to lock down the boyfriend. He can't tell the world there might be a baby in there right now. If the world thinks there's a pregnant hostage, this will become an international sensation, not just a national one."

"There's no boyfriend." Curler held a hand up. "She's doing it on her own."

"Oh," Saskia said. "Well, now I feel old-fashioned."

"Join the club." Curler gave a half smile. Saskia

appreciated the look of it, the microscopic relief it brought that people could still smile while all this was going on.

"What about her colleagues at the *Times*? Do they know about the baby mission? Whether it's a yea or a nay?"

"We're not sure yet."

Saskia nodded again, her face hard, decisive.

"We proceed as if there's a baby," she said. "I'll let SWAT know that Ashlea Pratt is priority number one among the hostages. We negotiate for her release first, and if there's a breakout at any point, our goal is to get Ashlea to safety above the other two."

Saskia and Curler headed back to the tent to wait for the Delaneys to pick up. A news van that had chanced a pass at the gates was being turned away. It was a ridiculous attempt, but worth a shot. Saskia had seen stupider blunders at crime scenes in her time than allowing a vehicle full of reporters into the inner cordon, and the journalists inside the van would know that. All it took was one distracted boot or unsupervised rookie, and they'd get the scoop. History-making footage. Grisly audio. Muzzle flash or victims running, or a glance at precious documents spread over a table. Saskia had known reporters who'd posed as biohazard cleaners to get into victims' houses. As mourners to get into funerals. There were no rules.

That was what she assumed the silver Kia that approached the gate at high speed must have been—another reporter trying to beg or bribe or bullshit their way to a setup closer to the action than anyone else. The officers guarding the gate seemed to recognize the driver and let them through. When Charlie Hoskins hopped out of the front passenger seat and started marching toward her, Saskia had to remind herself where she was, what was happening.

She went to him. Saskia's world was fully upside

down by the time they came together. The bad guys were in the crime lab. Charlie Hoskins was out of the hospital. Nothing was where it should be.

"What can I do?" His cold gray eyes were already on the Hertzberg-Davis building, measuring, analyzing. Saskia was right back where she'd been ten years ago, when he was a boot and she was his LT. "Do we have a line in yet?"

"Hoss, what the hell." Saskia stumbled over her words. She was painfully aware of Curler and a young girl who had parked the car Hoss had arrived in and was jogging to his side. "You're . . . you're not supposed to be here. You're not supposed to be *anywhere*. You're—"

"Sass—"

"It's *Chief Ferboden* in public," Saskia said. "You're my subordinate. We've worked together for a long time, but you're going to respect the stars, especially today."

"Chief Ferboden," Hoss said. "Do not try to shut me out of this. Everything I have is in that lab."

"Yeah, you and every other cop in the state." Saskia wanted to laugh at the arrogance. "Here. I got this when I arrived. It's a rundown of exactly what's in storage in labs 18–21, the ground-floor labs, which the Delaneys now control." Saskia drew a folded sheet of paper out of her pocket and handed it to Hoss. "They've got ninety-nine biological samples in the fridges in those two rooms. That's without worrying about the evidence that hasn't been swabbed yet. Within that collection of ninety-nine are about fifty rape kits, twenty DNA swabs related to serious assaults and robberies, ten major cold cases . . . I could go on and on."

She slapped the paper in his hand, made it rustle satisfyingly, but he didn't drop his eyes to it. He was holding it, watching her, refusing to look down at the numbers. Saskia knew he had no reason to. It was just a list of codes, a printout of Dr. Gary Bendigo's "stock list," which someone had been able to extract from his staff account. The six-digit numbers would mean nothing to Bendigo, or his staff, or Hoss. But Saskia's people had run the codes against the LAPD bio-evidence submission protocols. She knew exactly which cases they related to.

"Chief, listen," Hoss began.

"No, you listen," Saskia said. "A month ago, a couple of detectives working cold cases sent new evidence to Hertzberg-Davis relating to the Malibu Mountains Killer. Twelve murdered girls, three sets of detectives, two case reviews, and almost four decades of work. All that might come down to a sample they pulled off a pair of underpants. That sample is in lab 21, where the hostages are. There are also samples in there from the double murder of a couple of patrol cops up in Encino. There's a serial rapist in there with eight assaults under his belt. Did you know the mayor's niece was assaulted at a college party a week ago? The fucking *mayor of Los Angeles,* Hoss. Guess where that swab is."

"It—"

"It's in lab 21." Saskia kept her voice calm, but she could feel her face and neck were growing red. "See, those cases I just listed? They're one-shots."

"My three samples are one-shots, too," Hoss said.

"Sorry," Curler cut in. Saskia hadn't even noticed him easing his way toward them. "'One-shots'? What are 'one-shots'?"

"You've got one shot at it," Hoss grunted, looking the negotiator up and down. "The test. By processing the sample and extracting the DNA profile, you'll destroy the evidence itself."

"There are no do-overs," Saskia said. "Usually with evidence samples, the item, whatever it is, is sent to the lab, processed to see if there are any biological samples that can be derived from it, and then it's sent back to evidence holding at whatever police station it originated from. So say you've got a bloody shoe. You send the shoe in, the lab rats get the DNA sample off of it, and then they send the shoe back to you in case you need it for anything else. Photographs. Comparisons. As an exhibit in court. Whatever."

"But in the case of one-shots, it's not a whole goddamn shoe you're having processed," Hoss said. "It might be a single hair or a speck of dried blood somebody scraped off a wall. The sample is too small to test multiple times."

"So if anything happens to *those* swabs, that evidence for that case is lost forever," Curler concluded.

Saskia and Hoss nodded.

"How many of the ninety-nine samples are one-shots?" Curler asked.

Saskia couldn't answer. She glanced at the list.

"Wait—" Curler smirked humorlessly. "They're marked on the list?"

"The one-shots have asterisks beside them." Saskia showed him.

"Why?" Curler asked.

"So the lab rats know to be extra careful with them, I guess," Saskia said.

"Shouldn't they be extra careful with *all* the samples? Isn't that their job?"

"Who is this guy?" Hoss asked Saskia.

"Ronnie Curler, FBI," Curler answered him. "I'm handling the negotiations."

"You know what I hate more than loony tunes threatening people with guns, Curler?" Hoss asked. "Cops standing around at active crime scenes, debating ethics."

"Noted," Curler said. "But my annoyance remains the same. If the Delaneys know what those asterisks mean, they'll know which samples are the most precious to us."

"So what are you waiting for? Get talking to them,"

Hoss said. "Find out if they know. Find out who told them."

The negotiator wandered away, his shoulders high and tight, having swallowed Hoss's directive, it seemed, with difficulty. Saskia was left standing in the sun with Hoss, speechless with dread. Nearby, the girl who had accompanied him hovered awkwardly, unsure whether to stay close to the Kia or come to Hoss's side.

"We have to assume the Delaneys have accessed all the ground-floor fridges," Saskia said. "So, if they blow up that lab, we're going to lose all the physical evidence relating to those cases, whether they're one-shots or not. But if they start destroying swabs individually . . ."

"Jesus." Hoss rubbed his eyes with his palms. "Everything I have."

"Don't tell me everything you have is in that lab." Saskia's voice was low and mean. "*All that anybody has* is in that lab."

Saskia glanced at the young woman again, who'd now gathered the requisite courage to come to Hoss's side. Saskia forced herself to take a real measure of the girl. For a moment, she tried to remember if Hoss had a teenage daughter.

"Who the hell is this?"

"Don't worry about her." Hoss waved at the girl. "She's a problem I'm dealing with."

"Actually, I'm not a problem that he's dealing with." The girl nudged Hoss aside and thrust her hand at Saskia. "I'm Lynette Lamb, Los Angeles Police Department graduated officer. Temporarily discharged but soon to be reinstated. I'm here to offer any assistance that I can, Chief Ferboden."

Saskia didn't shake the tiny palm offered. She felt her eyebrows rise as far as they could. She looked at Hoss as realization flooded over her.

"Is this . . . ?"

He nodded ruefully.

"You're shitting me." Saskia felt a bewildered, horrified laugh rise in her chest and get caught there, right behind her sternum. She was grateful. To laugh in front of the cameras at this moment in history would have been career suicide. "Is this a joke?"

"I said I was dealing with it," Hoss insisted.

Saskia caught the eye of a nearby patrol cop, beckoned him over.

"Get her out of my sight."

"Wait." The rookie tried to wrench herself out of the patrol officer's grip. "Chief Ferboden, if I could just have a moment to explain."

The patrol officer pulled the rookie away, murmuring gentle placations and instructions. Saskia took Hoss in a similar hold and started walking him toward the tent.

"What the actual fuck?" she said. "She came and tracked you down? The cadet who got you dumped in the fucking ocean?"

"Just forget about it. It's not important." Charlie pointed at the building ahead of them. "This is important."

"What does she want? Did she threaten you?"

"Boss, focus."

"Oh, I'm trying."

"So the only demand the Delaneys have made so far is what's on the video message?" Hoss asked. "For their daughter's disappearance to be solved within twenty-four hours?"

"Where did you hear that?"

"They played a clip of the audio on KYSS-FM."

"Urgh." Saskia closed her eyes. "Thank you, twenty-four-hour news cycle, for making my job nine times harder than it has to be. Yes, that's their only demand thus far."

"So who are you putting in as lead?"

"On what?"

"The Delaney case."

Saskia shook her head. "No one. That's . . . Hoss, we're not doing that. We're not touching the Delaney child's case right now. No way."

"Why not?"

"Because, *Charlie*"—she looked harder at him, worried now—"you don't hold the goddamn LAPD at gunpoint to get your fucking case reinvestigated. Nobody does. If we do a single thing to play ball with these psychos, we'll have every family member in the country with a case dragging through the system thinking they can get justice by sticking a gun in somebody's face."

"But what do we know about the case?" Hoss persisted, searching Saskia's eyes. "Look. This is extreme behavior we're seeing here. The Delaneys are not just impatient, they're fucking pissed. What did we do to push them this far?"

"What did *we* do?" Saskia squinted. "We didn't *do* anything, Hoss. We did our fucking jobs. The case was investigated and closed. It was given the attention it deserved."

"Do you know that? Have you looked at it yourself?"

"Are you . . . are you feeling all right?"

"I'm fine," he said.

"You've had a head injury. You should be in bed. You should be safe somewhere. The Death Machines are probably watching you on their television screens right now, and—"

"I just want to know what happened to the kid, Sass. Tell me that much."

"It was an accident. She drowned," Saskia said. "The girl went missing at Santa Monica Beach. She was five. The body was never recovered. But she was seen going into the water by herself, and she wasn't a strong swimmer. The parents have obviously got other ideas about what really happened. They think maybe she was abducted, and our detectives botched it or covered it up, and the lab made it easy for them to do so." She gestured toward the Hertzberg-Davis building.

"What do you mean, the lab 'made it easy'?"

"There was a swimsuit," Saskia said. "It disappeared from evidence testing. File says it did indeed arrive here at the lab, but then it vanished before anyone could definitively prove it belonged to the girl."

"Did it belong to the girl, though?"

"Hoss, I don't have time for this!"

"Just another minute. Humor me, please."

"It was the right size," Saskia relented. "The right style. It was found in the right spot. It was damaged. But it was never tested for DNA, so we can't know for sure. The Delaneys were furious, of course, when they were told the evidence was lost. Which is probably why, when they were trying to decide where to pull this little stunt, they came here."

"Why are they so sure she didn't drown?" he asked.

"No body. No closure."

"That's all?"

"I don't know, Hoss. Maybe they didn't want to believe it. Without a body, they could cook up all kinds of ideas about the girl still being alive." Saskia felt exhausted. "They're obviously crazy."

"They're crazy," Hoss agreed. "But are they right?"

"No, they're not right."

"Could they be?" he asked. "Is there a *chance*?"

Saskia's words fell away. His eyes wandered from her, fixed on the tall, skinny palms that slashed the LA horizon. Saskia had seen that look before.

"Don't," she warned him. "Just go home."

"Tell me more." Hoss looked back at her. "Was there ever a search of—"

"No." Saskia put her hands up. "No, no, no. You're not hearing me, Hoss. The Tilly Delaney case is irrelevant right now. This is not a missing persons investigation we're dealing with. It's a goddamn siege. We're treating this as a hostage crisis, because that's exactly what it is."

Hoss's eyes were defiant.

"*Don't*," she repeated.

"Just let me look into it," he said.

"Even if I wanted to let you do that"—Saskia shifted closer, her voice quiet and dangerous—"there's no fucking way that I could. If I set up a team on the Delaney case, I'll be giving in. I'll be siding with the Delaneys. I'll be sending a message to every single one of these cops out here that I believe these two crazies when they say the police got it wrong."

"But you can't offer them nothing," Hoss said. "You can't just refuse to even look into it. They'll start dumping evidence. You know they will."

"I'd rather they dumped evidence than my officers out here start a mutiny," Saskia said.

"Chief." Ronnie Curler had returned to the tent and was calling her over. "We've got contact."

Saskia went to Curler's side. She stood beside the negotiator as he pulled on his headset. The connection, represented by a circular icon on the laptop screen, had transformed from red to green. Saskia donned her own headset and listened to the soft, staticky sounds of the cold, wide laboratory coming through the line.

Saskia shut out the activity around her. The men and women assembling at the edges of the tent to watch her and Curler's faces as they reacted to the phone conversation. The still-confounding presence of Charlie Hoskins and the fired rookie at the back-left corner of the tent. Leonard Franklin by the BearCat, eyes locked on hers, waiting to spring into action at the slightest gesture. She closed her eyes and listened to the line. After several painful seconds, a voice responded to Curler's repeated greetings.

"Hello? Is someone there? Hello? This is Ronnie Curler from the FBI."

"We're here," Ryan Delaney said.

"Okay, good. You're coming through loud and cl—"

"We want to go to video. Can you accommodate that?"

Saskia's stomach plunged. Curler met her eye. She nodded.

"We can," Curler said. "Go ahead and switch over."

Saskia, Curler, and everyone around them looked at the laptop screen. Curler tapped the button on the screen to end the voice call and accept the incoming video call. Saskia heard a bleeping in her ears as the Delaneys appeared on the screen.

The phone had been propped against something on the steel tabletop. Saskia couldn't see the hostages, whom she presumed were still sitting on the floor by the steel tables. Elsie Delaney was standing beside her husband at the end of the table, holding a small test tube with a bright purple cap. Saskia recognized it as a potassium EDTA vacuum tube, used for storing DNA samples.

"Oh, Christ," she whispered to herself.

"Ryan, Elsie," Curler said, easing himself into a fold-out chair in front of the laptop screen. "We're here. We can see you. We're all very anxious out here, because we'd like to know that Ashlea, Ibrahim, and Gary are all right and in good health. Can you confirm that for me?"

"They're fine," Elsie said. She glanced to her right, off-screen, straightening her shoulders with resolve. "They're absolutely fine."

"We know from the video that Ibrahim was injured," Curler said. "Is he conscious?"

"He's conscious," Ryan said. "Now, we—"

"It's important that we get him some medical assistance," Curler interrupted. "Ashlea, Ibrahim, and Gary all have family members who love them and who are very, very worried. I want to talk to you about the possibility of us sending a medic in. Just to make sure everyone's all right, including yourselves."

"This isn't the negotiation," Ryan said.

There was a pause while Curler got his bearings again. Saskia felt the crowd around her shift. Even without the audio, they could see that Ryan was determined to dominate the conversation.

"We'll start that later. For now, all we're giving you is a demonstration. We're going to show you what will happen if you don't meet our terms."

"What kind of demonstration?" Curler asked.

Ryan slid an object into view from off-screen, positioned it right in front of the camera. It was a Bunsen burner and tripod. Saskia was taken all the way back to her high-school science days, looking at the little tripod, blackened from use, above the gas-powered valve standing a few inches tall. Ryan extracted a cigarette lighter from his breast pocket and lit the burner. They all watched, helpless, as Elsie Delaney twisted and pulled off the sealed cap of the EDTA tube, and extracted the thin white swab attached to the inner surface of the cap.

"This biological sample," Elsie said, her words stilted from over-rehearsal, "is related to LAPD case file 411–321."

Saskia turned and looked at Charlie. Wordlessly, he walked over and handed her the slip of paper she'd given to him: Bendigo's stock list from the lab. Saskia ran a finger down the list and found 411–321. The sample had been submitted to Hertzberg-Davis eight days earlier. She followed the row across the columns of information on the sheet of paper until she found the submitting officer. Lieutenant Kylie Whinlon.

Saskia knew the case. She felt her teeth lock together. She traced her finger along the row to find an asterisk in the very last column.

One-shot, Saskia thought.

"We understand this sample relates to a bank robbery," Ryan said on the video screen. Both Delaneys were looking at the swab, which Elsie was holding up in the thin light from the closed blinds. They looked like two jewelers examining the clarity of a diamond. "Two police officers and two tellers were wounded in a shoot-out at the Bank of America branch in Torrance. The suspects got away. This sample is from an internal doorknob, which police believe one of the suspects touched with their bare hands. It's the only piece of biological evidence relating to that case."

"Ryan," Curler said. "Listen to me now. Just take a breather here for a second. Before you do anything that makes this situation worse for you and Elsie, I want us to talk about—"

"Do it, El," Ryan said.

Elsie Delaney lowered the tip of the swab into the flame. On the laptop screen, the flame turned bright white as the cotton swathing burned, then the plastic tubing blackened, shriveled, and collapsed. Elsie Delaney was left holding a thin, useless tube cap attached to a deformed noodle of melted plastic. The sample was gone.

Saskia exhaled. She clicked the button on the side of her headset that allowed her to speak.

"You don't have to do this," Saskia said. "Ryan, Elsie, this is Chief Saskia Ferboden of the LAPD here. I'm telling you that you can stop this right now, before it gets any worse. Listen to us. Please. What you're doing is deeply, deeply wrong. We know you're angry, and we know you're upset, but you're—you're messing with the lives of other victims here."

It was like she wasn't speaking at all. Ryan and Elsie Delaney just watched the burner, gold light from the flame flickering and dying on their cheeks and foreheads as Ryan turned off the gas.

Then Elsie lifted her eyes to the camera.

"We'll destroy one sample from this lab every two hours, until you find our daughter," she said.

Ryan reached forward and ended the call.

CHAPTER 7

Lynette Lamb was numb with horror. When Charlie Hoskins marched over to where she stood at the side of the tent and put a hand on her shoulder, the weight of it felt impossibly light, as if he were made out of air.

"Oh god, the samples." Lamb felt as though she were trying to breathe through a closed straw. She looked at Charlie. "They're going to burn them."

"Congratulations, you've caught up." Charlie turned her away from the tent and started pushing her back toward the car. "We have to go."

"Was it a one-shot?"

"Lamb."

"That sample. The Delaneys said it was the only . . . Can it be replicated? Is there evidence still in holding somewhere? Or is it over now? Did they just . . . did they just—"

"They just fucked that case." Charlie nodded, pushing harder. "So we have to get moving. We have two hours before they do it again."

"How did they get that list?" Lamb looked over her shoulder at the hive of activity now buzzing under the tent. "Did they destroy one of the one-shots on purpose? How did they know that was the one and only sample from that case?"

"Not our problem," Charlie said. "Our problem is not getting caught up in that traffic snarl on our way out of here."

He pointed to the gates, to a queue of police and press vehicles blocking the road out of the parking lot. Lamb felt tingles of exhilaration rush over her skin as Charlie walked to the passenger side of the Kia. She climbed into the driver's side and turned on the car.

For the first ten minutes of the drive west and then north out of the pandemonium of the Cal State grounds and onto the 405, Lamb gripped the wheel and listened as hard as she could to the calls Charlie was making on his little burner phone. They didn't reveal much to the casual eavesdropper. Mostly, he called, relied on the receiver to recognize his voice, and asked if they'd done "that thing" he'd asked them to do. She assumed he was sending requests in the text messages he typed out between the calls, then going down the list after a few minutes, checking that what he wanted done had been done. When all the mysterious organization was apparently complete, he pulled a packet of cigarettes out of the backpack he'd brought from the hospital and sat back, smoking and watching the city go by.

Lamb hadn't felt so completely buzzed since the long walk from the Van Nuys station after her catastrophic first morning on the job. It seemed as if there were a thousand things she needed to do right now just to maintain her fingernail grip on Charlie Hoskins and the possibility that he would help her get back into the LAPD, but she didn't know what any of those things were. She was painfully aware that his next command might be for her to drop him at the foot of the rocky cliffs that surrounded them, or at the gas station they passed turning onto the 101 from the 405, or at a diner, and then he could simply walk away, and there was nothing she could do to stop him. Lamb couldn't cling to him forever like a desperate mollusk on a slippery rock, and without him she would be back exactly where she was on the fateful morning two days earlier when she'd learned that she had almost killed him: flailing wildly for what or who to cling to next.

On the Hollywood Freeway, still following his barely audible muttered directions while he scrolled through texts on his phone, she spoke up.

"Maybe it was just an unlucky guess," she said. "They said they knew that was a one-shot, but maybe that's because they have some kind of other insider information. Maybe they know an officer who worked on it. Maybe they don't know which samples are one-shots and which aren't, and they'll burn a few more, but they'll be recoverable. The detectives in charge of those cases—they'll just send the evidence for retesting after the siege is over, and everything will be fine."

"If you're going to display that level of optimism for the rest of the day, Lamb, we're going to have problems," Charlie said.

"Do you have samples in the lab?" she asked.

Charlie didn't answer.

"Are you going to tell me where we're going or what?"

"You don't need to know that right now."

"Yes, I do. I need to know everything we're planning, because I want to keep us safe, and I want to contribute." She looked over at him as the traffic slowed to a standstill. "Are we going to try to find out what happened to Tilly Delaney?"

"We are," Charlie said.

Lamb choked back an excited yelp, came out with a strangled cough instead.

"Or, at least, I am."

Lamb inhaled unsteadily.

"You're along for the ride until you figure out that this situation is just too dangerous for you, which I'm frankly amazed hasn't happened yet," Charlie said.

"Unless you missed that little bang-bang game we played with the Death Machines only minutes ago."

"You mean the one where I saved your ass? That game?" Lamb asked.

Charlie ignored her. "If we're lucky, you might instead just wake up to the fact that this whole job isn't for you," he said.

"Yes, it is."

"No, it's not."

She shook her head. "I want to be a police officer, Charlie."

"Why?"

"Because—"

"No, wait. Let me guess." Charlie smiled, watched the traffic ahead of them, the wide, sunbaked highway leading down toward the studios. "Somebody made your life a nightmare in high school, and now you're out to even the score with society's jocks and mean girls."

"No," Lamb said.

"Your dad was a cop."

"No."

"A loved one was murdered. Cousin. Grandparent. Sister. It never got solved, and you swore to avenge them."

"No."

"You grew up in a crappy neighborhood and dream of going back there and cleaning it up."

"Where are you getting all this stuff?"

"It's the uniforms." He nodded knowingly. He was slumped in the seat now, an elbow on the sill of the open window, his phone in his lap and his eyes fixed on the brown smudge of smoke haze hanging over the city. "If it's not any of those things, it's the uniforms. You see the uniforms, the structure, the rules and regulations and protocols. Cops have their own language. Codes. Signs. They all look the same. Act the same. You thought you were going to turn up at the station on day one and fit right in, and the lonely loser you'd grown so accustomed to being for your whole damn life would be no more. You'd be a cow, identical to ten thousand other cows, rolling right off the truck and into the bosom of the herd. Your particular brand of weird instantly camouflaged."

"You should be a psychologist," Lamb said.

"It's the same reason people join gangs."

"Uh-huh."

"So am I right? Is that the reason?"

She gave her best nonchalant shrug, but right on cue, the process began. Lamb felt the pain in her nose first. Then her eyes ached and her throat grew tight. She swiped angrily at her face.

"Oh, Jesus, Lamb."

She heard him laughing, didn't dare look. "I'm not crying."

"Yes, you are."

"Why is it so terrible for me to want that?" She swallowed a sob, felt it burn right down her throat like acid. She focused on the anger, the disappointment, the horizon of cars before her wavering and trembling through the tears. She swiped them away again. "I want to fit in. Doesn't everybody?"

"No."

"And I want to solve crimes. I want to use my brain." She tapped her temple hard. "I want to commit myself to something big and important. Yes, I want to make this city better and its people happier, and all those good, wholesome, justice-y sorts of things—"

"'Justice-y sorts of things'?" Charlie bent double and hugged himself with laughter.

"—but I also want a partner." Lamb glared over at him. "I want to go to work in cohesion with someone. We—you know—we could look out for each other. Bounce ideas off each other. Cover each other's asses. Policing is a dangerous profession, and when you work in danger, you've got to really care for each other."

"This is so cute." Charlie sighed, his hilarity finally receding. "Oh. Oh, this is so cute, I could just die."

"You have barbecues at one another's houses," Lamb went on, more to herself than to him now, changing lanes. "The whole team. Everybody bitches about the boss. You have nicknames."

"Look, I'm sorry to break your heart, Lamb, because you genuinely do seem like a very sweet person, but . . ." Charlie's words trailed away. He gingerly fingered the stitches in his scalp and looked befuddled.

"What?"

"Your name is Lamb," he said finally, shrugging. "You're going to get Chop."

"Chop?"

"Yeah. Lamb Chop."

"Well, that's boring." Lamb felt her shoulders sag.

"It is."

"I mean, why not Shanks? Why not Stew? Why not Souvlaki?"

"You want me to call you Souvlaki?"

"No, but—"

"That really rolls off the tongue. *Hey, Souvlaki, pass me that Taser, will ya?*"

"I don't know why I'm still talking to you at all at this point." Lamb sighed.

"The nickname thing, it's not beautiful and clever and romantic the way it is on TV." Charlie pointed to an off-ramp, and Lamb took it. "You'll get the shortest, simplest, most logical nickname available. It'll either be your real name cut in half, like Hoss for Hoskins, or some basic, meaningless association, like Lamb Chop for Lamb."

She wrung the steering wheel and felt dejected.

"If you're a Kruger, you'll get Freddy," Charlie went on. "Cash, you'll get Johnny. Oh, wait. I forgot.

You're too young to know who either of those people are."

"I know who Freddy Kruger is, asshole."

"For a good nickname, you've got to do something really spectacular." Charlie was leaning forward in his seat now, searching for their destination ahead on Lankershim Boulevard. "And somebody with a quick sense of humor has to be right there on the scene. And when I say 'spectacular,' I mean it. I knew an undercover once who was in a crack house full of gangsters when he got outed, and they all turned on him at once. Fought his way out using nothing but a broken umbrella. Guy's name was Peter McGenry. Guess what everybody calls him now?"

"What?"

"Peter McGenry."

Lamb turned into a driveway straddled by a huge royal-blue sign. Sharp gold letters glimmered as she followed traffic cones to the boom gates. UNIVERSAL STUDIOS.

"What are we doing here?" she asked.

He didn't answer. As Lamb crept forward behind two other cars making their way through the checkpoint into the lot, she hung her elbow on the window and looked up at a huge billboard affixed to the front of a towering office building. A slender, white-blond woman was leaning on the railing of what looked like a yacht, her hair wind-whipped away from her razor-edge jawline. She was glowering at the camera, her dark brows low and her upper lip almost imperceptibly tightened in a sexy scowl. Lamb couldn't tell what the billboard was for. It seemed to be just a picture of the actress silently challenging all who dared enter the lot.

"Urgh." Lamb shook her head.

Charlie leaned over. "What?"

"Viola Babineaux. Look at her neck. It's like her mother was a swan or something."

Charlie smirked. He gave his name at the entry booth, and their car was shown through onto the studio grounds.

Charlie gave Lamb directions through the lot toward studio 33. She was driving painfully slowly, her head on a swivel, watching movie-crew people walking equipment on dollies past the huge studio roller doors, execs doing breathlessly fast walk-and-talks with their underlings in the sunshine. She stopped the car altogether to watch a pair of men in cowboy costumes guiding a horse past a coffee truck surrounded by a crowd of people. Charlie had to urge her on.

The directions ended at a row of eight single-wide trailers parked diagonally in the middle of an aisle of warehouses. People were buzzing around the trailers importantly. A queue of actors in black leather attire waited outside one that was obviously a makeup trailer for touch-ups to grievous face and neck wounds. A pair of young women were beating anxiously on the door of the nearest trailer, tasked, he guessed, with rousing some precious star who was too drunk to function before midday. Lamb parked the car fifty yards from the trailers, and they got out.

The rookie asked him again what they were doing here, who they had come to meet, but Charlie didn't answer her. He liked secrets, surprises, comedic irony. It had made him a good undercover, his ability to tuck away interesting pieces of information for later use, or to restrain his emotional reaction and let matters unfold without intervention. A limousine pulled up behind their Kia, and Lamb scooted too close to his side. Her arm was unconsciously touching his.

And then Viola Babineaux was there. In real life.

The actress burst out of the limo like an angry horse kicking open its stall, almost clotheslining her assistant, who had jogged from the other side of the limo to open her door. The showstopping entrance, the huge sunglasses, the scowl—it was all classic Viola. Charlie felt some comfort that Viola's behavior hadn't changed in the five years since he had seen her in person, yet that comfort butted against the unsettling realization that she looked younger than she had on that occasion.

He was so caught up in her arrival that Charlie almost forgot to watch Lamb's reaction. When he saw it, his face spread into a grin so wide he felt the stitches in his scalp pull. All the blood in her body rushed up and flooded her face dark and purple, and then it rushed away again, leaving her sickly pale. She grew bug-eyed, the tendons in her neck taut as she took in the billboard beauty magically sprung to life.

"Viola." Charlie smiled. He put his arms out to hug his sister, but Viola ignored the gesture and came to a stop out of his reach, snapping into a hostile pose that was too striking to be accidental—hip slipped, leg out, arms folded.

"Well, look at you." She flipped her sunglasses up onto her head in a whip-fast move she obviously did hundreds of times a day. "You look like something a dog coughed up. I hope they paid you good to do this to yourself."

"It's nice to see you, too," Charlie said.

"You—" Lamb's eyes were flicking between Charlie and Viola. She was trying to speak, but her throat seemed to be jammed with something she was struggling to decide whether to hack up or swallow. "You—"

"This is my sister, Viola."

"No, that's—" Lamb's voice was low and hoarse suddenly. "That's *Viola Babineaux*."

"Check her Wikipedia page," Charlie said. "She was born Viola Beatrice Hoskins. She switched to Babineaux because she thought it sounded fancy. And, no, our mother wasn't a swan. She was a dental hygienist from Santa Barbara."

Viola was examining Lamb now with that scalpel-sharp gaze. "Who is this little person? She's adorable."

"It's a long story," Charlie said. "Viola, I'd like to get into how glamorous you look and how I've missed you and how even my covert duties with one of the nation's deadliest criminal organizations hasn't prevented me from watching your career over the past five years with a mixture of intrigue and awe—"

"Oh, please." Viola rolled her eyes.

"But I really need my stuff. I've got a case, and it's time-critical."

"He's only nice to me in front of other people," Viola told Lamb, who jolted when Viola spoke directly to her as though her words were charged with electricity. "Really, he's an asshole to me and always has been."

"Oh." Lamb nodded eagerly. "Okay. Okay."

"I hear nothing from him or about him for five years," Viola told Lamb. "Five *years*. All the cops will tell me is that he's busy. And then he pops back up with a bunch of texts giving me instructions about what to do for him. No 'Hello.' No 'How are you?'"

"I'm saying hello now," Charlie noted. "And I knew how you were. All I had to do was walk past a newspaper stand to know how you were. You go get coffee and it makes six papers and fourteen websites."

"I had to hear what happened with the boat from one of my lawyers, who has a brother who's a cop," Viola said.

"So what are you complaining about, exactly?" Charlie asked.

"See?" Viola shook her head at Lamb. "Asshole."

"Okay. Okay."

"Aren't you supposed to be recuperating?" Viola squinted at Charlie. "I thought this whole undercover thing was done now."

"It is."

"So what's the case?"

"Another long story," Charlie said. "*My stuff*, Viola."

"Christ! Keep your pants on." Viola stormed off, beckoning for them over her shoulder. Viola's assistant stayed behind with the limo while they walked the length of the row of trailers, drawing the gaze of every person in direct line of sight. As they emerged at the end of the row, Charlie discovered that, hidden by the length of the single-wides, his trailer had been tucked into the ninth parking space. The battered camper with its peeling pale blue strip running down the length was still covered in desert dust and cobwebs. The faded ladybug-patterned curtains still hid its precious contents. When he had last drawn them over its grimy windows, he had still been pretending to be an outlaw biker.

"*Et voilà!*" Viola flipped her sunglasses back down and gestured to the trailer with a wide sweep of her arm like she was revealing a game show prize. "Monsieur, your hunk of crap awaits. Took my guys six hours with a map, aerial photographs, a drone, and a goddamn psychic to find this thing in the middle of the desert, but it's here now and you owe me big-time."

"You're the best." Charlie nodded. "So when can we get it out of here?"

"Oh, no, it's staying right where it is," Viola said. "Security knows the situation. Or some of it anyway."

"No, this won't work."

"Yes, it will."

"No, it won't." Charlie stepped closer to his sister, saw himself reflected in the sunglasses, a bulbous caricature. "What happened to you putting it on your property in the Hills?"

"Well, Charlie, what happened is that I ignored that suggestion because it was completely insane. Do you have any idea who owns the land on either side of me?" Viola said. "That's Brad's place on the left and Britney's on the right. Scorsese has a bungalow just down the street on the same side. Even if I had

someone cover this piece of garbage on wheels in cam-
ouflage paint and palm fronds, it would still stick
out like a dog's balls up there. Here on the lot, you'll
blend in with the extras and the equipment techs and
the food people, and all the other freaks and weirdos
and clingers who hang around movie lots."

A group of crew members, wheeling a cart of audio
equipment past them, bristled as they went by. Charlie
felt another wave of exhaustion sweep over him.

"How do I explain this to people?" he asked.
"What if somebody comes along—a movie exec or
something?"

"The Universal people know I organized it, and
they don't ask questions." Viola smiled.

"What about them?" He gestured to the other trailers, the people milling around them.

"Make something up, Charlie," Viola said. "You
can tell them it's a set piece from a postapocalyptic
thriller in which toad-people rule the smoking ruins
of planet Earth."

"All right, all right." He patted her shoulder, which
made her grimace as if he'd smeared her with slime of
the toad-people. "Thanks. Thanks, Viola."

She gave him a lot ID and a swipe card, and he
lifted an arm to hug her, but she just groaned and slid
away like she usually did.

Charlie went to the trailer. He had to give the door
the necessary sharp yank to get it open. The smell
that enveloped him, of old dusty carpet and cigarette smoke, dropped his blood pressure immediately.
Lamb scuttled in after him as if she were being hunted
and sank with relief onto the pea-green corduroy recliner sitting just inside the door. Charlie saw her reflection in the shiny toaster as he drew two cups from
a shelf above the kitchenette. She put her hands to her
temples and mimed that her brain was exploding.

"Your sister is *Viola fucking Babineaux*?"

"That? That's the most shocking thing you've

learned today?" Charlie flipped the switch on the coffee machine. "Really?"

"She was just in that thing with Matthew McConaughey!"

"Yeah, he's our cousin."

"What?!"

"Come on, Lamb."

"Oh, Jesus. You had me. You had me going there." Lamb held her head. "Why haven't I seen anything about Viola Babineaux having a brother in any of the press?"

"You wouldn't believe what you can scrub from the internet if you pay the right people," Charlie said. "Anyway. Does your mama let you drink coffee?"

"Yes, but I'm fine, thank you."

"Wrong." Charlie opened a drawer and extracted a spoon. "You want to be a cop, you never turn down coffee or food. From anyone. At any time."

"Fine. Black, then."

He watched the machine boil.

"Viola Babineaux. Wow. Do you think I came across like an idiot?" Lamb murmured, peering out the gap in the ladybug curtains, presumably watching Viola and her assistant leave. "I should have said something about the Oscar. Or her foundation. I should have told her she looked nice. I just stood there saying, 'Okay,' like an idiot."

"I think she liked you," Charlie said. "You should tap into that. It only happens once every three hundred years. And Viola goes through assistants the way most people go through underwear. You could score some free travel."

"I don't want to be Viola Babineaux's assistant." Lamb turned back from the window. "I want to be a police officer."

He poured cold water into his coffee so it was cool enough to drink fast. As he leaned against the kitchen counter, Lamb sipped her coffee and looked around her at his belongings. The paperbacks crammed into the bookshelf, the colorful afghan hanging over her chair. The photograph of him and Viola as teenagers that hung on the wall by the bedroom door fixed her gaze.

"What is this place?" she asked eventually.

"This is my house now, I suppose." He drained his coffee and poured another. "I had an apartment in the gang. But that was fake. It was full of the things my character acquired. His clothes. His furniture. His ID. I kept this trailer throughout the assignment. It was parked out in the desert. I used to sneak out there now and then to do my paperwork, research, recordings, all that stuff. When the gig ended, I asked Viola to go find it and put it somewhere safe."

He didn't go on, didn't tell her that the trailer he'd bought for five hundred bucks two weeks before he went undercover was much more than a spider hole for his police work. It had become like an emotional recharging station during his years inside the Death Machines. He didn't tell Lamb that there were times after big weekends with the crew, drinking, fighting, doing cocaine, waking up twisted in the sheets with some woman or another on top of him and his head pounding and the skin grazed clean off his knuckles, that traveling to the trailer in the wide, empty desert had been the only thing that stopped him from going insane. He went to the trailer to remember, because to remember was to survive. He would look at the picture of himself and his sister, or hold the blanket his grandmother had crocheted, or finger through the cheap novels he'd owned since he was a teen, and remember that he was Charlie Hoskins: detective, not Chuck Hanley: criminal. He was not an ex-con, a drunk, a drug addict, a gang member, a manipulative and hateful human tumbleweed who had ended up unintentionally in the brotherhood of a motorcycle gang after meeting and befriending one of its leaders in prison. That was the lie, and the trailer was a sacred shrine to the truth.

"I'll be safe enough here," he said, turning to his phone as an alert pulsed through it. "The lot will be guarded and crowded day and night."

"So the gang," Lamb said. "They're just going to keep coming for you?"

"They're vengeful people," Charlie said. "And I was in the inner circle for a long time. It was like a family. These guys, they told me things that were embarrassing and secret and important. And now they know all those things are written down in reports somewhere in the police files. They're going to be read and analyzed by hundreds of police officers. What I did was the worst thing you can do. And then, just when they thought they had me, when they thought they were going to make it right, I slipped through their fingers. So yeah. They're pissed." He sipped his coffee. "And they're just going to keep coming."

Lamb looked as if she was struggling with something, words dancing on her lips, her eyes big and locked on his.

"What?" he asked.

"What did they do to you out there?"

"Lamb," he sighed.

"The guy who fired me, Harrow. He said you were tortured."

She woke them. The visions. They flickered, closed in. The near and dim wood paneling of the trailer became the swaying interior of the boat in the middle of the ocean. He was on his knees, zip-tied to a pole in the galley. Dean was cutting his clothes off with a big pair of scissors. He was naked and bleeding and shaking, and they were all talking about how long they'd held fantasies about having a cop to do whatever they wanted with. Charlie's stomach was rolling and clenching, because he'd heard the fantasies already, plenty of times. Business first. Dean was taking out his hunting knife and squaring up the Death Machines patch Charlie had tattooed over his heart, and they were all trying to decide how deep Dean should go to make sure he got all the ink out as he began to hack the emblem off Charlie's body.

And then suddenly the trailer was back, and Lamb was staring at him, and Charlie blew out air and shook his head like he could barely remember, and Lamb seemed to accept it, because he was a good actor, just like his sister.

"They slapped me around a little, that's all." Charlie drained his second coffee. "Sounds like this Harrow guy was being dramatic. I'm fine. You can see that I'm fine."

Lamb stared at him.

"You need to put all that stuff aside and focus on what we're doing here."

"The Delaneys." Lamb nodded. "So we're going to try to find Tilly? Or at least try to find out what happened. Won't that piss everybody off?"

"They're pissed off already," Charlie said. "The Delaneys have cooked up something amazing here. There are cases in that lab going back decades."

Lamb looked tired already, lost in thought.

"They've started soft, in a way," Charlie said. "The bank robbery in Torrance; I googled it in the car. Nobody died. Couple of gunshot wounds. But if they start canning evidence in murder cases or sexual assaults, they're . . ." He shook his head. "They're letting bad men stay on the street."

"What evidence do you have in there?" Lamb asked. "It's from your work in the gang, right?"

"Right."

"So just—what?—drugs? Gunrunning?"

"No." Charlie had to ease his breaths through his nose to stifle the anger. "Not just drugs and gunrunning."

Lamb backed off. She was learning which buttons to push and how hard.

"But Chief Ferboden told you to stay off the case," Lamb said. "I heard her."

"She doesn't need to know what we're up to. Not yet," Charlie went on. "Even though I don't agree with it. Sooner or later, she's going to realize that those two people in that lab aren't going to stop until they get what they want. Hopefully, when she decides she'll play ball with them a little, you and I will have something she can offer them."

"So you're going to go against the chief of police," Lamb said. "But kind of . . . not?"

"I've been going against Saskia, 'but kind of not,' for some years." Charlie gave a small smile. "She put me in with the Death Machines. Operation Hellfire was her baby."

"But how can we work on the Delaney case if we don't have any information to go on?" Lamb asked. "We'll need all the files. We'll need to know who to talk to."

"That's where this guy comes in." Charlie nodded toward the closed door of the trailer. He'd spied Surge's rapid approach through the gap in the curtains. A sharp thumping came upon the door, and Lamb got up and opened it. The huge man stepped up into the trailer, ducking his head to fit beneath the low, curved ceiling.

Surge, Charlie was happy to note, looked precisely five years older than he had when Charlie last clapped eyes on the giant, black-bearded ex-cop. He was tanned and flashing his big, bucked donkey teeth. Charlie tossed his coffee down the sink just in time for what came next—a painful bear hug. Lamb was so surprised by the six-and-a-half-foot, two-hundred-pound man's sudden presence that she backed up and then fell into the armchair. Surge's focus was all on

Charlie, his big, dark eyes creased at the corners with his smile.

"He's here! He's here!" Surge shouted, shaking Charlie's hand so hard his whole arm flapped. "Lock up your daughters. Big Bad Hoss is back on the prowl, baby!"

"Yeah, yeah, I'm back."

"Urgh!" the big man roared, crushing two handfuls of the air in front of Charlie's face with his huge fists. "I'm so happy to see you I could just *squeeze* the life right out of your body!"

"Please don't," Charlie said. "You bring the papers?"

"I got papers! I got guns! I got food! I got drugs!" Surge dumped a swollen leather satchel on the kitchenette, sending up a chorus of rattles from the plates inside the cupboards. "Photos! Phones! Cables! Cash! I got everything we need! I'm ready to work-work-work!"

The big man noticed Lamb sitting, stunned, in the armchair.

"And who's this?" he asked.

"Lynette Lamb," Charlie said. "She cries too much. Lamb, meet Surge. He's too enthusiastic."

Surge grabbed Lamb's hand, yanked her out of the chair, and gave her arm a shaking that traveled down her entire frame.

"Pleased to meet you, Lamb!" Surge grinned. "Let's find us a missing kid!"

CHAPTER 8

YAP: Shop.

MINA: Oh, hello. My name is Mina Delforce. I'm calling for, uh, Yap?

YAP: You got him.

MINA: Oh. Hi. Hi. Um, uh . . . A friend of mine, George Deerfield, told me to call you. He said you might be able—

YAP: Oh, you're Georgie's friend?

MINA: Yeah, that's me.

YAP: Right. Right. Shit. He told me what happened.

MINA: Yeah.

YAP: What a trip.

MINA: I know, right? Anyway, it's . . . You probably think I'm so weird, trying to track the guy down.

YAP: I don't think that's weird.

MINA: Okay.

YAP: I see a lot of weird in this job. You wanted to know if he made it or not. That ain't weird.

MINA: I mean, I think he would have made it. It's just . . . Why was he out there? What happened?

YAP: Right.

MINA: I haven't been able to stop thinking about it, if I'm honest with you.

YAP: Georgie said you tried the hospital?

MINA: Yeah, they weren't terribly forthcoming.

YAP: What did you tell them?

MINA: I just said I was a friend, and I wanted to check that he was okay.

YAP: Big mistake. Friends don't get squat.

MINA: They sure don't.

YAP: Should have said you were the sister.

MINA: I will next time.

YAP: So tell me about the tattoos, then. I'll see what I can do.

MINA: Well, he was pretty covered in them. There were a lot of, uh . . . eagles and things like that? Birds in flight? The American flag. Guns. There was a big cobra on his left arm. I remember that. Really thick black lines. Bold colors. The cobra was coiled around a knife. Some of the tattoos were sketchy. Kind of . . . faded into the skin, and blue?

YAP: Hmm.

MINA: Does any of that sound . . . ? I don't know . . .

YAP: So far, you're not telling me anything that's gonna set this guy apart from any other piece of American white trash. Had to be white, right?

MINA: Yeah.

YAP: Every second guy who comes in here wants tattoos like that. Some shops, that's all they do. The sketchy-lookin' scratch tattoos means either he's done time or he's the kind of shithead who would take free tattoos off somebody who bought a kit online. That's what all the kids are doing. Buying a kit from China for seventy bucks and fucking up each other's skin. Then they come in here and spend three thousand bucks for me to fix it. How old was the guy?

MINA: Forties?

YAP: Probably the time, then.

MINA: Okay.

YAP: You see any Nazi symbols on him? Burning crosses, lightning bolts, guys with helmets on . . .

MINA: No, no, nothing like that.

YAP: No Celtic shit?

MINA: No.

YAP: Black and white stars?

MINA: No.

YAP: Then I don't know what to tell you, lady.

MINA: That's okay. It was worth a shot.

YAP: Yeah.

MINA: Listen, can you tell me one thing?

YAP: What?

MINA: Why would a person cut a tattoo off?

YAP: Wait—one of the tattoos was *cut off*?

MINA: Yeah.

YAP: You sure?

MINA: Well, I mean, I think so. He had a huge piece of skin cut out of his chest. It was like . . . sliced out, in a crooked square shape. Maybe half an inch deep. And there had definitely been something there. I could see the edges of it.

YAP: Shit. That's hilarious.

MINA: What?

YAP: That's the first damn thing you should have told me.

MINA: Oh, really?

YAP: Yeah. Now I know exactly who the fucking guy is.

MINA: How?

YAP: Only two types of people cut tattoos off:
      bikers and gang members. So if he was white
      and covered in Americana, then he was a
      biker. And guess what? The cops just did
      a huge sting on one of the crews out here
      called the Death Machines.

MINA: Are you kidding me?

YAP: Nope.

MINA: Whoa.

YAP: These guys, they cut the tattoos off mem-
      bers who go against the club. Sometimes
      they burn them off. So, this guy, whoever he
      was, he probably snitched. He's probably the
      reason the whole crew went down.

MINA: Oh my god.

YAP: Listen, you sound like an all-right lady.
      And Georgie is a good kid. He's been coming
      to the shop getting decent ink for years.

MINA: Okay.

YAP: If I can give you any advice at all, it's that
      you should stop calling around about this
      guy.

MINA: Oh.

YAP: Yeah. Just forget you ever met him.

The energy bar thumped onto the linoleum between
Gary Bendigo's socked feet. He'd kicked off his shoes
half an hour into the hostage crisis and had been
considering asking one of the Delaneys to loosen
his belt. But he didn't want to give them anything,
even the barest notion that he should be grateful for
some kindness that they were providing him. Anger
was boiling in his chest and stomach, spreading out
through his shoulders and arms, and he knew that if
he didn't control it, he was going to be dealing with
serious neck and back pain in time, with his arms
twisted behind him as they were. Elsie Delaney took

two more energy bars from the plastic bag she had extracted from one of the duffels and dropped them at Ibrahim's and Ashlea's feet.

"How are we supposed to eat these with our hands bound behind our backs?" Bendigo growled.

"Don't get huffy," Elsie said. "We're only a few hours into this thing. I'm going to release you one at a time so that you can eat."

"Wait. Please, let me get this straight," Bendigo sneered. "You expect us to survive for twenty-four hours sitting on our asses on the cold, hard floor eating energy bars and listening to your vigilante bullshit, while you threaten our lives and degrade us like animals . . . without getting 'huffy'? I'm not huffy, Ms. Delaney. I'm fucking livid. I'm so mad I could scream."

"We should have drugged them." Ryan was watching the CCTV feeds on his laptop. "If you'd just let me drug them all, we'd be sitting here in pleasant silence right now."

"It's not really going to be twenty-four hours, though." Ashlea rolled her shoulders when Elsie released her wrists. She seized on her energy bar and opened it with trembling fingers. "I mean, that's all for show, right? You're . . . you're going to pick up the phone to the negotiator in a minute and, like, do a deal."

"For show?" Elsie Delaney rose, a water bottle in her hand. "No, it's not for *show*, Ashlea. We're serious. We're serious as a heart attack."

"But you can't, I mean . . ." Ashlea chewed nervously, her eyes flicking from Elsie to Bendigo to Ibrahim, who was shaking his head frantically, silently willing her to drop it. "You can't expect them to solve your daughter's disappearance in a *day*. It's . . . That's crazy. You said it's been two whole years with no result. So how can they—"

"It's been two years of no *activity*." Ryan took off his glasses and rubbed them furiously on the edge of his shirt. "A single solid day of looking at our daughter's case and taking it for what it actually was—an abduction, not an accident—and the police will realize that they fucked up. They'll find her. We're convinced of that. All it will take is for someone to wake up."

"If it were Chief Ferboden's kid, they'd have solved it in twenty-four hours," Elsie said. "If it were the mayor's kid—Ike Grimley's niece was raped. Did you know that? Her rape kit is here, in the lab." Elsie pointed to the fridge against the wall, from which the three hostages had watched her extract the sample from the Torrance bank robbery.

"In the twenty-four hours after the rape," Elsie said, "the LAPD had deployed eight detectives in a task force to solve that crime. They interviewed one hundred male students at the college she attended. They took more than eighty DNA swabs. They rounded up thousands of hours of CCTV. Can you imagine what that kind of manpower looks like? It looks like a goddamn army descending on a village."

"Tilly didn't get that." Ryan's jaw was flexing as his finger worked the laptop trackpad, going from camera to camera, watching the police activity outside. "We got two detectives and ten patrol officers. It was given a preliminary 'accidental death' ruling within two days. They gave our daughter *two days*, and then they gave up on her."

"How do you know all this stuff?" Bendigo asked. "How do you know what samples we have here? Where they're kept?"

"Wouldn't you like to know." Ryan smirked.

"So what happened to Tilly?" Ashlea asked. "How do you know it was an abduction?"

"Guys, can we just . . ." Ibrahim widened his eyes at Ashlea and Bendigo. "Maybe we should just stay quiet, huh?"

"Ibrahim would like you to stop encouraging the terrorists, please, Ashlea," Bendigo deadpanned.

"We're not terrorists," Elsie snapped.

"Oh yes you are," Bendigo said. "You're terrorizing us. I'm terrorized. These two? They're terrorized, too. You're using fear, intimidation, and violence against innocent civilians with the hopes of forcing an institution—namely, the police—to act in accordance with your wishes. That's goddamn terrorism in its purest manifestation!"

"Just tell us what happened." Ashlea's sole focus was Elsie. "I want to know what this is all about. I want to listen to you guys."

Bendigo sighed. Ashlea was obviously trying to connect with Elsie, woman-to-woman. Bendigo watched as Elsie bent and rebound Ashlea's wrists, this time in front of her. He understood Ashlea's plan. Empathize with the hostage-taker. Curry favor: reap the benefits. The plan was already working. With her hands bound in front, Ashlea could push back the strands of hair that had been hanging in her face and bothering her, and Bendigo watched enviously as she loosened the button that had been cutting into her waist on the side of her pencil skirt. Bendigo knew he could charm the Delaneys with a little flattery and sympathy, but he was too sullen, too filled with dread and frustration, to offer the Delaneys anything right now. Elsie freed Ibrahim's wrists so he could eat, then sat on the stool beside her husband.

"It was my fault," Elsie said. "I sent her to the beach. It was because of me that she was there that day. It was because of me that someone took her."

"She drowned," Soloveras said. He and Detective Dubois were sitting on fold-out plastic chairs in the secondary command tent, the one shielded from the view of the cameras on the hill by a pair of blue tarps tied together with twine. Someone had obviously dragged the retired detective off his boat to attend the Hertzberg-Davis hostage crisis, because his thin, sunbaked ankles descended into boat shoes and his weathered gray T-shirt was stained on the hem with what Saskia guessed was engine grease. Dubois had come straight from a gangland shooting in Culver City and was wearing the classic two-striper detective getup. His suit was rumpled, his hair was crazy, and there were latex gloves hanging out of the back pocket of his trousers like limp tail feathers.

"Take me through it," Saskia said. She had a summary of the Delaney case file in front of her. "I want to hear it from you two. Because, to me, this is your fuckup here today, gentlemen. Go ahead and convince me that it's not."

"She drowned," Dubois repeated, shrugging stiffly. "It's like this, okay? The mother sent her to the beach with her older sister. There was a huge age gap between the kids. Tilly was five. Jonie was fifteen. The older sister was pissed about having to entertain the kid for the day while her parents stayed home and talked out their marriage problems. The relationship between the girls wasn't great anyway, but this put the icing on the cake because Jonie had been planning to spend the day with her friends at the beach and then she gets landed with the baby last minute."

"The trouble started when the kid wouldn't go out back." Soloveras was rubbing the fine wisps of hair left on his bronzed scalp and looking longingly at the gates of the parking lot. The checkpoint. Freedom. "Jonie gave up on the whole thing and made a move to take the kid home."

"Wait, what do you mean, Tilly wouldn't go 'out back'?"

"Out beyond the breakers." Soloveras sighed. "The little girl was scared of the big waves, about being out that deep. So she made Jonie paddle around in the shallows with her. All Jonie's friends were out on their boards way out the back, where the teenage boys hung out. They were having a wild time, and here was Jonie, stuck with her little sister on the edge of the water playing puddle ducks. Jonie was bored and frustrated, and she kept asking Tilly to let her take her out the back. But the kid wasn't having any of it."

"So Jonie says, 'Fuck this,' and takes the kid up to the parking lot," Dubois said. "Jonie says they're going to take the bus home. They argue the whole way. Jonie's dragging her. People see it. Jonie stops in the public toilets on the edge of the parking lot. Tilly waits until her sister's in the stall before turning and bolting."

"She took off?" Saskia asked.

"Back toward the water." Soloveras nodded. "*Where she drowned.*"

"Wait, okay. Wait." Saskia put a hand up. Around her, the tent was rippling with activity: Curler pacing, waiting for the Delaneys to answer his calls, strategizing with his assistant. SWAT Commander Franklin was taking reports from different divisions around the scene. "How do we *know* the little girl went back into the water?"

"Because that's where *she wanted to go*," Dubois explained. "And that's where she was *seen* going."

"By whom?"

"Two witnesses, independently verified."

"How many people were at the beach?"

The detectives paused, glanced at each other. Soloveras crossed his legs now, his whole body a twisted monument of self-defense. "Hundreds. It was a nice day."

"And you relied on two eyewitnesses to confirm she went back into the water?"

"There was the swimsuit—" Dubois said.

"I'll get to that." Saskia held a hand up. "I'm trying to confirm the kid went back into the water. Little kid walking by herself back down the beach like that, alone, obviously upset. You'd think more people would notice."

"Probably people did." Dubois shrugged. "But it's Santa Monica Beach. Half the people there were tourists. Foreigners, out-of-towners. We couldn't track them all down. But we tracked two of them down, and they told us the same thing: that she went back into the water."

"How many witnesses saw her being dragged up the beach?" Saskia asked.

"I don't remember," Dubois said. "It was two years ago."

"A few," Soloveras said. "The kid made a scene."

"And only two witnesses noticed the same kid marching back down toward the water alone?"

"Yes." Soloveras barked the word.

"No body, though," Saskia said. "No remains at all."

"Lifeguards said she could have gotten sucked into the undertow." Dubois shifted in his chair. "It can happen. She gets rumbled, doesn't come back up. It's fast. Silent. Nobody notices. The body pops up a mile or two out. Happens all the time."

"So you put most of your efforts into that scenario." Saskia glanced at the summary in her hands. "You sent out the coast guard. You had volunteers walk the coastline."

"We had choppers, we had divers, we cleared the beach, we posted sentries," Soloveras counted off on his fingers, leaning forward. "We had members of the public out there in their own boats searching all through the night." His voice was rising. "If these assholes are trying to tell you we didn't do enough to find that kid, they're wrong. They're just fucking *wrong*!"

"What were your land-based efforts for finding her?" Saskia asked.

The two men glanced at each other again. Dubois

licked his teeth, simmering quietly, while his partner huffed and slouched in his chair.

"We had good intel, and early intel, that she was in the water," Dubois grumbled.

"I'm asking about your theories about what might have happened to her on land."

"There weren't any," Dubois said. "We didn't need theories. We had facts!"

"So you didn't lock down the scene immediately." Saskia flipped the first page of the summary. "You waited two hours to do that. A lot of potential witnesses left the scene."

The men were silent. Saskia scanned the document further.

"It was an hour before you had anyone make note of the cars in the parking lot."

"When she didn't turn up after a week, we looked at it," Soloveras said. "It's not as though we disregarded that scenario completely. There were kiddie-fuckers living in the vicinity of the beach. Of course there were. They're everywhere. So we checked them out. One of them was known to attend the beach frequently, and another two guys had residences within five miles," Soloveras said.

"How did you check them out?"

"We interviewed and alibied all four of them," Soloveras said.

"Did you search their premises?"

"We brought them in," Dubois said.

"But did you search their premises?"

"No."

"What about dashcam footage?" Saskia asked. "Social media posts from the beach around the time of the incident? What about the hotels and houses lining the beach? Did you check out the pier? Is it possible she went up there to look at the rides?"

"We got CCTV from the pier," Soloveras said.

"But nothing else?"

"She didn't go up to the pier," Dubois said. "We know that."

"How?"

"Because she went into the water."

Saskia held her head. "Are you telling me that you didn't hit the hotels at all? Did you walk the pier, or—"

"Let me tell you a story, boss." Soloveras's eyes were blazing and his smile was mean. "One of my first cases as a detective was a missing woman. Lady went hiking up at Mount Lowe. Disappeared. Left her bag under a tree, water bottle there, car keys, everything. I didn't get CCTV in that case. I didn't interview scumbags living in the area who might like to abduct a woman. I didn't go out looking for fucking aliens in spaceships that might have beamed her up. She went hiking and she went missing on that hike, so I searched the goddamn hiking trail. I did that because it made *sense*. When they found her body, her husband thanked me. He sent me a goddamn bottle of scotch."

Saskia watched the retired detective. The muscles across his lean chest were twitching with anger. When Soloveras didn't go on, Saskia shrugged.

"Why are you telling me this?"

"Because that's what we've done here!" Soloveras snapped. "The kid went missing in the water, so we searched the fucking water!"

Saskia had to take a moment to compose herself. Even hidden as they were from the cameras, from the world, there were other officers in earshot.

"You searched the water, Soloveras, because you wanted to believe the girl went in there," Saskia said evenly. "You wanted to believe that, because a kid drowned means an investigation closed in ten days, a footnote in the local newspaper, and a potential nightmare case avoided. A kid abducted? Now, that's a different story. A kid abducted means days without sleep, a task force, an inquiry, media appearances, public pressure, an all-around pain in the balls. No one wants to catch a stranger abduction case where the victim is a kid, especially someone who's a month out from retirement, as you were, Soloveras. So what you did is you got two witnesses who said they saw the kid going back into the water and you seized on them. And you, Dubois"—she turned on the second detective—"you were lazy. You were happy to follow Soloveras into a half-baked, knee-jerk assessment of the crime because you were overworked and underpaid and you didn't give a fuck about Tilly Delaney."

Dubois's mouth dropped open. Soloveras, too, looked like he'd been sucker punched.

"Your laziness," Saskia said to Dubois, "and your selfishness"—she turned to Soloveras—"might have killed a five-year-old, gentlemen. And today, it has ruined our chances of solving a serious crime. It might keep doing that, all day. It might mean rapists and killers get away and do what they've done already to more innocent people. And if the Delaneys have a bomb in there? Your laziness and selfishness might kill five people before we're through here. All because *you* wanted to retire. And *you* wanted to get home before dinner."

She looked at the men in turn. Neither spoke.

"Of course the Delaneys think she was fucking abducted!" Saskia snarled. "You didn't close that door for them. And with no body to tell them the girl was dead, they were taking *any door* that led to hope of finding their baby alive. Get out of my sight, both of you." Saskia rubbed her brow and waved them off. "Find a dark corner to crawl into until I need you again. And if you speak to the press, I'll have both your pensions stripped so fast you'll get whiplash."

She didn't look up as the shell-shocked men climbed out of their chairs. She was looking at the summary sheet on her lap, at the photograph of Tilly Delaney with her ice cream cone thrust at the camera.

"Where's Jonie Delaney?" she asked anyone who was listening.

"On her way in," Curler said from somewhere over her shoulder. "One of our agents picked her up at her high school."

"When she gets here, bring her straight to me," Saskia said.

"So you're telling me"—Bendigo snorted—"that you have *another kid* out there who you've just completely abandoned so you can come in here and cause a scene about losing the youngest one?"

The room fell silent. Elsie, who had been sitting on a stool by the steel tables, telling her story, let her hands drop in her lap. Ryan looked over at the old man on the floor, his face unreadable.

"Don't you see?" Bendigo reasoned. "You're going to do long, hard jail time for this. You're . . . you're *kidnappers*. You're *terrorists*. Even if you were to successfully force the police into producing your daughter alive in the ridiculously short amount of time you've given them, you're not going to see her or the other one. You're not going to walk away from this and be a happy fucking family again. The only time you'll ever hope to see your girls is visiting hours inside prison."

"We're already in prison, right now," Ryan said.

Elsie turned to him. She was thumbing a tear from under her eye.

"You don't get it. You don't have any kids. I can tell." Ryan sighed, shook his head. Beside him on the tabletop, the cell phone was buzzing, as it had been on and off since the police outside obtained the number.

"For the past two years, we've been in a glass box," Ryan said. "To our daughter Jonie, everything we've done and said for two whole years has been through the glass of this . . . this suffocating fucking cage." He looked around him as though he were seeing it. The close walls of a dingy, dirty, personal prison. "The moment we knew Tilly was gone, we were boxed up, Elsie and I. We haven't breathed free air in all that time. To Jonie, we might as well be locked up behind prison walls. There's this huge barrier between us. It's us, obsessed with finding Tilly on one side of the glass, and Jonie blaming herself for losing her on the other side of the glass."

Bendigo watched Ryan.

"If they find Tilly, we're just going to switch up this box we're in for a real one," Ryan said. "We won't even notice the difference, and neither will Jonie."

"So why do it?" Bendigo asked.

"Because maybe, in doing this," Elsie chimed in, "we could be giving Tilly *her* freedom. Maybe she's out there, right now, waiting for us to find her."

Bendigo hung his head, huffed a long sigh into his collar that he felt blow back hot and damp against his upper lip.

"She's not out there," he insisted.

"You don't know that." Elsie shook her head. "You can't know that. No one can, because the case wasn't treated properly. She might have been abducted. There were child sex offenders living in the area. The parking lot wasn't checked. The hotels, their cameras, they weren't checked. All that stuff? It means there's a chance."

"As long as there's a chance," Ryan said, "all of this is worth it."

Bendigo couldn't lift his head. It felt like it was stuffed with lead weights.

"Listen to me, very carefully," he said finally. "Your child is *deceased*."

He managed to look up and waited for the parents to take in his words. But neither Elsie nor Ryan moved.

"I saw the bathing suit." Bendigo tried to keep control of the volume of his voice, but it rose slowly nonetheless. "The garment came through my lab before it went missing. It was identical to the one you and your daughter Jonie described to the police. The one police were looking for."

"You saw it?" Elsie rose from her seat.

"I looked." Bendigo nodded. "It was a curiosity. A child's bathing suit, torn, damaged. It was something different. Most of what we deal with here is guns and cuttings of fabric. I notice anything different if it passes before me. A child's toy. A piece of art. A fork. A steering wheel."

"What happened to the swimsuit?" Ryan's eyes were fierce and fixed on Bendigo's.

"It went missing. It happens."

"Did you lose it?"

"No." The scientist shook his head. "I'm not a tech here. I'm a manager. I saw it passing through. I don't know what happened to it. Point is, I saw it. And it was damaged."

His words rang in the air.

"You have to take the emotion out of this, both of you," he said. "Be sensible. Be logical. Do the math. Do you know what the odds are that your daughter is alive somewhere, in someone's care, waiting to be rescued? They're just . . . they're just—"

Bendigo saw Ryan leap from his stool, but he didn't see his boot swing back until it was too late. The tip of the boot slammed into Bendigo's ribs, pain erupting and swelling in his abdomen, crushing his lungs, leaving him unable to speak or make a sound. Elsie was grabbing Ryan by the arms, trying to drag him backward. In the chaos, Bendigo was strangely detached, lying on his side, his eyes following Ibrahim as the young man slid onto his knees, then rose behind Ryan's back and bolted for the door.

CHAPTER 9

Lamb sat in the green corduroy recliner chair in the trailer and looked at the printed photograph of Jonie Delaney. It was a typical teenage shot, snapped unexpectedly at what looked like a family barbecue in the precious moments the girl had her guard down. She was half turned toward the camera, a drink in a plastic cup held out from her body, her elbow jutting into her hip and shoulders slightly hunched. She looked like a bird with its back bent against rain, her eyes dark and accusatory, lips parted, probably in protest to the shot being taken. Lamb felt a wave of sympathy for the girl as she sat quietly reading the case file on her lap. She imagined the lanky teenager scouring the Santa Monica shoreline, pushing between groups of strangers, searching frantically for the little girl she'd only moments before blasted with vitriol simply for existing, for being the four-foot-tall, sweet-cheeked, and chubby-limbed wall between Jonie and a fun day at the beach.

Surge and Charlie seemed to have reviewed the file at the exact speed Lamb had. Surge had taken up residence in the little booth attached to the side of the kitchenette, and Charlie still leaned against the counter, the file in one hand and a cigarette in the other, trailing smoke out of the tiny flip-open window above the kitchen cupboards.

"Say she didn't drown," Charlie mused. "What are the alternatives?"

"Abducted," Surge said, folding his huge arms. "For whatever reason. Abuse. Sale. Replacement child for someone whose own kid is dead. Weird, crazy belief that she's the second coming of Jesus. Strangers abduct kids for all sorts of reasons. And the public bathroom where Jonie Delaney last saw her sister is a great spot to do it from. It's right next to the parking lot. Suspect sees the kid, grabs her, stuffs her into the trunk of his car—presto! You're good to go!"

Lamb glanced at the map of Santa Monica Beach in her case file. The image was marked with official crime scene measurements, and there were handwritten notes made in the margins. She felt a strange exhilaration, staring at the image. The dusty, claustrophobic interior of Charlie's trailer was the last place she had imagined herself examining her first real crime scene map, but the excitement was the same. She was working on a case. She didn't know how long that would remain true, but for now, she was working on an actual case.

"So how do we pursue the stranger-abduction angle?" Charlie rubbed his stubbled jawline. "We've got to reinterview the pedophiles Dubois and Soloveras looked at in the area and make sure there weren't any around they didn't know about."

"That's easy enough as a starting point." Surge took out a small phone and started thumbing at it. "I'll map-search the whole area with Megan's Law for child sex offenders. See what sick fucks are living there now. Might be they lived in the area when Tilly went missing but they hadn't yet been caught for anything."

"We've also got to try to hunt down images of the

parking lot, see if we can match up any vehicles," Charlie said. "It was an hour before the detectives listed any license plates. That's too long."

"We'll also need to reinterview the two witnesses who saw Tilly Delaney heading back down the beach," Lamb offered. When the men turned to her, the floor hers for suggestions, she felt a tingling in her chest and arms. She hoped her face wasn't flushing red. "We have to know how sure they are about what they saw. Because if she did go back down the beach, then the abduction scenario still exists, but it changes. She might have been convinced by someone to walk farther along the beach and get into a car at one of the other parking lots."

"Listen to Lamb." Charlie smiled at Surge. "She's sounding like a real pro."

"I like your thinking, Lamb Chop! Keep it up!" Surge leaned over and put an arm up for a high five. Lamb had to rise slightly off her seat to reach the extended palm.

"What about Jonie Delaney?" Lamb went on, emboldened. "Is there a way we can talk to her?"

"Everything she has to say about it is right here." Charlie flapped his copy of the file. "They interviewed the kid for eight hours. I'd say that about covers it from all angles."

"But she's older now," Lamb said. "Maybe she had a change of perspective. Maybe she's wiser. I know it's only two years, but fifteen to seventeen is a big mental leap."

"You'd know." Charlie exhaled smoke over his shoulder toward the window. "You *were* seventeen about ten minutes ago."

"How old are you, Lamb Chop?" Surge jutted his chin at Lamb. "If you don't mind me asking."

"I'm twenty-one."

"Twenty-one!" Surge hacked a loud laugh, rocked back on his booth seat, which was creaking with the effort of supporting him. "Little Chop-Chop's only twenty-one! Right on! I loved being twenty-one. I bought my first car when I was twenty-one. It was a Durango! I rammed it into a tree! And look at you, trying to solve your first missing kid case at the same age. Nice work, little buddy. Nice work!"

"We'll see whether it's nice work or a complete waste of time." Charlie was looking back at his file.

"Oh, man," Surge said. "You're not giving her shit about joining the cops young, are you, Hoss? You, of all people?"

Charlie shot Surge a warning look.

"What do you mean, him 'of all people'?" Lamb asked.

"Forget about it." Charlie waved her off. "Get back to the case. That's all you've got to offer, Lamb?"

"No." Lamb straightened. "It's not, in fact. I want to know what the Delaneys were doing when their daughter went missing."

"They were fighting," Surge said. "About money, they said. He's a surveyor. She's a beautician. They're hardly rich."

"So let's check that out." She shrugged. "Can't hurt. We know they were in an agitated state. Maybe one of them left in a fury. Went to the beach. Decided to take the girls and run. The fact is that in most child abduction cases, it's not a stranger; it's a family member or someone the kid knows well. And familial kidnapping is often instigated by a fight between the parents. Maybe whichever parent went to the beach to take both girls only got Tilly. Then maybe there was some kind of accident, or a psychotic break, and Tilly ended up dead. The traumatized parent dumped the body and returned home in time to receive the panicked call from Jonie that Tilly was missing."

Lamb waited for a response from the men. There was none, so she went on.

"The file says Jonie and her friends searched for

Tilly for forty-five minutes before making the call," Lamb said. "The Delaneys lived in Sunkist Park. That's, what? A half an hour away? It's doable."

"It's a stretch," Charlie said. "But not completely crazy."

"I love the lateral thinking." Surge was nodding, eyes and grin wide. "That's some twisty shit right there! The last person the police are going to suspect is the parent who makes all the effort to hold up a goddamn forensic lab, just to find the kid that they *themselves* murdered."

"How are we going to source images from the scene?" Charlie asked. "We can basically count on any and all CCTV from the time having been deleted or recorded over. Some images were handed in from Facebook and Instagram at the time, but not many." He flipped the pages in his file. "Fourteen in total. Eleven from the beach, three from the pier. Nothing interesting on them."

"Looks like the images they did source were collected from the scene." Surge was following in his own file. "So Dubois and Soloveras's guys approached bystanders and asked for pictures from their phones. What they should have done was go public with a request for images. Get it on the nightly news."

"We could do that now," Lamb suggested.

"It's a good idea! But I don't like our chances," Surge said. "Ferboden would shoot that down. She wouldn't want the public knowing we're working on the case."

"What if we approached Facebook and Instagram, the companies themselves?" Lamb looked at Charlie. "We could just ask them to give us any and all images posted with geotags from the beach on that day."

"Another hard ask," Charlie said. "We've got twenty-four hours to solve this thing. A request like that is going to take months. And those companies aren't terribly generous with their users' information. We'd need warrants. Multiple." His eyes wandered the low, water-stained ceiling of the trailer as he thought. Then they landed on Surge, and the two exchanged another meaningful glance.

"What?" Lamb said.

"Nothing. All right, Surge, you're our man on the ground. You know your assignment," Charlie said.

Surge leaped from his crate, almost banging his head on the ceiling.

"Let's do this!" he roared, his fists balled and his muscles flexed hard against the seams of his shirt. "Come on, team!"

"You're with me, Lamb." Charlie tucked the file under his arm and stood. He beckoned to the rookie as he shouldered open the sticky trailer door. "Grab the car keys. We've got to switch rides."

He was gone in two seconds or less. Bendigo watched Ibrahim sprint across the lab and out the door, his shoes barely squeaking on the linoleum, his hours sitting on the floor, most of them with his wrists bound, hardly seeming to affect his speed or coordination at all. *Adrenaline,* Bendigo thought. The flight reflex. Ibrahim's conscious mind would have taken a back seat as his powerful, muscular body switched into survival mode, and he would have barely felt anything as he fled. The same superability that made rabbits scale twenty-foot walls to escape hounds. Bendigo guessed the young security guard might have been able to leap hurdles or climb stairs three at a time with that kind of necessity urging him on. The scientist wheezed on the floor, on his side, his thoughts hammering with a single word as he listened to the sound of Ibrahim's footfalls, and Elsie Delaney's in pursuit, as they receded up the hall.

Go! Go! Go! Go!

But the flight of fancy was short-lived. As a realist, not someone prone to temptations of faith, Bendigo was unsurprised when Elsie marched Ibrahim back into the room under the watchful eye of her pistol. There had been nowhere for Ibrahim to go; Bendigo knew that the second he laid eyes on the bike locks Elsie had extracted from the duffel bag that morning. She shoved Ibrahim down and roughly rebound his wrists behind him. Bendigo felt his cracked ribs burning as the young security guard slumped at his side, catching his breath.

"Nice try," Bendigo offered.

"Don't congratulate him." Ryan shook his head, staring down at Ibrahim in pity. "He's just bought you or Ashlea a world of hurt."

"What?" Ashlea yelped.

"Yeah, sorry, did I not mention that part of the arrangement?" Ryan asked. The cell phone was ringing on the tabletop, doing a halting dance across the steel surface. "If any one of you tries to escape, we have to hurt one of the others."

"Oh, don't." Ashlea's face crumpled. She drew her knees up to her chest. "Just don't, okay? You don't need to do this. You've got us locked up here in this miserable fucking place, we're tired, we're hungry, we're . . ." She struggled, tears streaming down her cheeks. She seemed unable to form the words, her mouth opening and closing, head shaking sadly. "We've done everything you've asked!"

"I've just smacked the old man." Ryan was ignoring her, speaking to Elsie. He gestured to Ashlea. "It'll have to be her."

"Okay, but—" Elsie drew a long, resigned breath. "Ryan, don't do anything crazy, okay?"

"Please don't hurt me!" Ashlea wailed.

"Don't hurt her," Ibrahim stammered. "I understand, okay? I wasn't thinking. I just reacted. I won't try anything again. I promise."

"We have to do it." Ryan shrugged.

"Hurt me, then. I'm the one who tried to run."

"Why won't you answer the goddamn phone?" Ashlea snapped. "The police are trying to talk to you! They're probably trying to give you what you want!"

"I'll just break one of her fingers," Ryan said to Elsie.

"No! Don't!" Ashlea cried.

Ryan took a step forward. Bendigo shot to his feet and stepped between him and Ashlea. He was painfully aware of himself. Of his inferior height, and strength, and eyesight, of his bound wrists, of the ten extra pounds encasing his belly as he pushed it up against Ryan's. He was aware of the stupidity of gallantry in a situation such as this. Heroes got shot. It was a tale as old as time. The taller, younger, stronger, fiercer man smiled, holding his gun at his side, and Bendigo tasted Ryan's breath on his lips.

"You're not going to touch that girl," Bendigo growled, despite it all. He was aware of Ibrahim scooting across the floor to huddle awkwardly with the crying journalist, the security guard murmuring gentle placations to his fellow hostage. "This, *none of this*, is going to get your daughter back. What you're doing here today is not only morally wrong, it's also not going to work."

"Well, I guess I'll just have to change tactics, then," Ryan said. He raised the gun and pointed it at the pair on the floor behind Bendigo. Before the scientist could react, he heard the blast of the weapon.

The effect of the gunshot rippled through the crowd under the tent. Saskia felt the distant pop like a punch to her sternum. She reached out immediately for Ronnie Curler, got his arm, which was solid as a tree trunk, propping him up against the table. It was her radio she wanted. The negotiator had grabbed it instinctively off the table by the laptop. Saskia took it and thumbed the talk button.

"All units, this is Command. Hold your positions! Hold! Hold! Hold!"

"We need to go in," someone said. Saskia glanced behind her. Leonard Franklin stood there, huge and imposing beneath the black cladding of his protective gear. "That was a gunshot. It's out of control in there. We need to enter immediately. My team is ready to—"

"No, I said hold. We're going to wait."

"But the hostages are—"

"I said wait!" Saskia barked. The barrel-chested, bearded SWAT officer rocked back on his heels slightly, his chin jutted in defiance. "Curler, call them again."

"They haven't answered in forty-five minutes." Curler had his eyes locked on the screen. "Respectfully, Chief Ferboden, I think we should go with what SWAT says. Make an entry and hope for the best."

"Get out of the way." Saskia shoved him. The negotiator backed up, and Saskia hit the call button again, watching as the screen flashed an image of a white telephone receiver jiggling back and forth. She could feel the dissent in the shade of the tent. The ring of men standing by, muttering, joking that it obviously required a "feminine touch" to get the call to magically connect, when Curler had been dialing the Delaneys nonstop for the better part of an hour with no success. Saskia was numb with anger and self-consciousness as the ringing phone symbol transformed into a round green bubble. For a second, she was too distracted to realize the couple inside the building had picked up.

"Hello?"

"He-hello." Saskia's throat was suddenly dry and hoarse. "Hello? Is this Ryan?"

"Yes."

"We heard a gunshot. What's happening in there?"

"Ibrahim tried to escape." Ryan's voice was flat.

Saskia could hear crying in the background. "I've warned the hostages that if it happens again, I'll kill one of them. Hopefully they realize that I'm serious. I just put a bullet into a steel cabinet right beside Ashlea's head. Must have missed her skull by a half an inch."

"I'm sure everyone in there is very scared," Saskia said gently. "But I'm glad you're talking to us again. Could you put Gary or Ibrahim or Ashlea on the phone? I just want to know that they're all right."

"I'm telling you they're all right. So you can believe me or you can fuck off."

"Ryan, you're not leaving us with much wiggle room out here." Saskia wiped sweat from her brow with the back of her wrist. Around her, dozens of people were staring at her, frozen in place in the tent or in the shade of the BearCats parked nearby. "I need you to tell me what I can do to secure the freedom of all or at least one of those hostages."

"The hostages are staying right where they are," Ryan said. "Until you find our daughter."

"I understand that you're—"

"What are you doing right now to find Tilly?" Ryan demanded.

Saskia licked her lips. They felt raw.

"Tilly's case is a very complex one," Saskia said. "It's also old. That's the truth. Two years is a lifetime in a criminal investigation. Even if we were to reopen the case, it would be incredibly difficult to make any kind of headway on it in the time you've allowed us."

"So you're doing nothing?" Elsie's voice came down the line, as hard and unforgiving as her husband's. "You're kidding me, right? You've got three people here who need you to do what we're asking or they're going to die. And you've got victims and their family members who need you to bite the bullet and admit that you were wrong about Tilly, or their own cases will go up in smoke."

"Elsie—" Saskia said.

"The first case we chose was a bank robbery," Elsie said. "The next case will be something a lot more serious, trust me."

"How the hell did they get that list?" Curler murmured to himself. Saskia glanced at him. "How do they know which cases are which?"

"Listen, Ryan, Elsie—my priority is those hostages," Saskia said, iciness slipping into her tone. "Do you understand? I don't care about the evidence you're destroying. You've got innocent human beings in there. Tell me what I can do to get them out."

Saskia felt another shimmer of emotion through the people around her. Glances, gestures, whispers. She was losing her grip on them already. Her people. She had started to notice it when she brought Dubois and Soloveras onto the scene to review their actions in the Delaney case. There was wonderment, confusion, in the officers around her. Surely she wasn't going to side with the Delaneys. Surely she wasn't going to let two maniac hostage-takers cause her to question the quality of the work done by two cops. Now she'd revealed she was going to let the Delaneys keep destroying the hard work of other officers if it meant delaying an entry and keeping the hostages safe. She was actively talking down the importance of the work of her colleagues.

Saskia was trapped. To approve an entry by a SWAT team might cost Ashlea, Gary, and Ibrahim their lives. To delay an entry would mean more evidence destroyed and cases lost. The only way to save the hostages and the evidence was to negotiate for the Delaneys to give up. But they weren't going to give up without their case being worked, and allowing their case to be worked would send the message to the world that violence against police got the job done.

"Please just tell me what I can do to get the hostages

out of there," Saskia said. "I can't reopen your case. But there must be something I can do."

Ryan Delaney snorted with derision on the other end of the line.

"Fifteen minutes," Ryan said.

Behind his voice, the laboratory was silent. Whoever had been crying was quiet now.

"Then more bad men go free."

CHAPTER 10

Charlie put a boot on the dashboard and rested his phone against his thigh, tapping an address from the case file into the map. They had exchanged the Kia for a Dodge Ram Viola had left for them in the studio security lot. He'd sunk down into the footwell of the huge black vehicle as they exited the lot, and Lamb had borrowed a black cap and sunglasses from someone. The security staff at Universal all seemed to have been briefed that he and Lamb were to be given whatever they needed at any moment, which made him feel vaguely uncomfortable, as if he were exploiting the studio. Viola surely hadn't told them the whole story, and as far as any of her movie friends had ever known, she didn't have a brother. He guessed she'd given them some line about him being a mega-important foreign actor, in town hiding from paparazzi. He popped his head up a few streets away from the studio and didn't see any obvious tails as they drove away from Universal.

"Head for North Hollywood," he told Lamb. "I'll direct you from there."

"Where are we going?"

"We're going to pay a visit to one of the kiddie freaks who was around on the day Tilly went missing." Charlie glanced at the file. "Dubois and Soloveras only called the persons of interest in the area. They didn't do home visits. That was fine in the case of two of the three. Clinton Sims was in jail on bad checks, and this guy, Mateo Hernandez, was in the hospital getting surgery on his back. But the third guy, Nicolas Rojer? He says he was visiting his mother. Doing some gardening for her."

"Doesn't make much of an alibi." Lamb listened, eager. "What mother is going to burn her own kid to the police? Especially on such a serious charge. He could have just fed her a line about what to say. So Rojer used to live near Santa Monica Beach?"

"Two-bedroom apartment, maybe three blocks back from the water," Charlie said. "Mom's got money."

"And now he's moved to North Hollywood?"

"Hansen Hills."

"Oh."

Something changed in Lamb. She tapped the steering wheel, her eyes locked on a queue for brunch forming outside a Denny's.

"What?" Charlie asked.

"Nothing."

"You know the area?"

"Nope," Lamb said. She straightened in her seat. "So you said when we left that Surge knows his assignment. I didn't hear you give him one."

"Don't worry about it. We'll get to it."

"Who actually *is* Surge? Are you guys usually partners?"

"No. He's just a very handy man to have around." Charlie shrugged. "A go-to guy, I guess you'd say."

"Is he a cop?"

"No." Charlie licked his molars, thinking hard now about how to worm his way out of the next few questions. Because the truth was, he hadn't thought much about Surge and Lamb meeting and what that might lead to. Now he felt boxed in to his seat as Lamb's gaze swung around inevitably from the Denny's to the traffic light flicking to green and then to his avoidant eyes.

"*Was* he a cop?" she asked.

"Yeah," Charlie said, admitting defeat.

"So what happened?"

Charlie eased a huge sigh, decided to just get it all out in the open and deal with the aftermath. "He got fired," he said. "On his first day on the job."

"*What?*" Lamb squeaked. Charlie didn't have to look directly at her face. He could see her agape expression in his peripheral vision, it was so dramatic.

"He was teamed up with an older cop, a sergeant, guy named Robinson," Charlie explained. "Robinson was real straight. By the book. Not creative. Their very first call was a traffic accident over on the 105, near Lynwood. Surge had been on the job for about two hours, all paperwork. They hadn't even gone cruising yet. Then they get the call. They jump in the patrol car and get to the scene, and it's a pickup truck that's hit the back of a semitrailer at high speed."

Lamb was listening, sitting rigid in her seat and leaning over the steering wheel, her hands gripping the plastic tightly.

"So the front end of the pickup is completely crushed under the semi," Charlie said. "The driver's a young guy. His foot is trapped, pinned under the collapsed engine bay. The truck is on fire, and so is the back of the semi. At any second, the whole thing could blow. Surge asks Robinson what they should do, and Robinson does what he always does: he plays it by the book. They can't get the guy out, not without endangering themselves and other civilians. So he tells Surge to clear the area to stop any citizen heroes from getting involved. Then they just have to stand there and let the guy burn."

"But—" Lamb shook her head. "What . . . That's it? Just let him burn?"

"The fire department was on the way, he said. Nothing they could do in the meantime."

"So you're not even supposed to try?"

"No," Charlie said. "That's protocol. And Surge soon realized why, when he disobeyed the sergeant's orders and went into the vehicle to try to pull the guy out. As soon as Surge got anywhere near the driver, the guy grabbed hold of him and wouldn't let go. He was on fire, screaming his head off, clawing at Surge like a crazy person."

"Jesus," Lamb said.

"Yeah."

"Drowning people will do that, too, so I hear." Lamb nodded.

They fell into tense silence. Lamb perhaps imagining Charlie in the sea. Charlie recalling it with terrifying clarity: the woman swimmer, whoever she was, twisting frantically in the water as he grasped on to her. Had she not kicked him, he'd never have let go. He knew that in his bones.

"So what happened?"

"Surge punched the guy out," Charlie said, grateful for the escape from his memories. "He was a big guy, too. Took a few solid slams to the head to get the job done. All this is being filmed by members of the public, of course. Every asshole in the country's got a camera on his phone." Charlie took out his cigarettes and lit one. "But when he finally gets free of the guy's grip, Surge figures he's made such a mess of this whole thing already, he'd better get the guy out somehow. So he looks in the back of the pickup and sees there's a big ol' chain saw lying there."

Lamb was so deep in the story she had to slam on the brakes to avoid hitting a family using a crosswalk.

"He . . . he didn't," Lamb said.

"Yeah," Charlie said. "He did."

"You're shitting me."

"I'm not."

"And the guy survived?" Lamb asked.

"Sure did," Charlie said. "He's still hobbling around out there somewhere, as far as I know."

"So Surge just got fired?" Lamb's mouth twisted. "I mean, no warning? No reprimand? No nothing?"

"He cut a guy's foot off!" Charlie laughed.

"But he saved his life!"

"Doesn't matter." Charlie shrugged again. "It just doesn't matter, Lamb."

"Was his chief pissed?"

"Yeah," Charlie said. "I wasn't at the station when Surge got back, but I heard from guys who were. They said you could hear the chief yelling at Surge from down on the sidewalk. The whole building went quiet to listen in. People stopped answering the phones. At some point, the chief goes, 'If you wanted to be a surgeon, you shoulda gone to med school!'"

"Whoa," Lamb whispered. "That's where it comes from. Surge. The Surgeon. I thought his name must have been Sergio."

Charlie choked out a smoky laugh. "Sergio. No, it's not Sergio. His name's Wyatt Hill."

"A pretty spectacular act, to earn a nickname like that." Lamb nodded. "I see what you meant."

"Yeah."

"But Surge still works for the cops. I don't get it. You said he was fired."

"Oh, he was. He is. He's not a cop. He just does things for cops now and again." Charlie glanced up at another billboard of Viola Babineaux as it sailed past the window. "A lot of guys at the station felt like Surge got a raw deal, so they'd cut him in on things if they could. You know. Grunt work. Security gigs. Concerts. Cleanups. Stuff like that. And the guy whose foot got cut off turned out to be somebody, too. Son of a big gangster from up in Pasadena. He was pretty grateful. So now Surge kind of works both sides, I guess."

"I wish someone from my station had done that for me," Lamb said, her eyes wistful.

"Done what?"

"Figured I got a raw deal and helped me out."

"Lamb, where are you sitting right now?" Charlie narrowed his eyes in disbelief. "What are you *doing*?"

"This isn't you helping me out." Lamb looked over, curiosity creasing her face. "This is you tolerating me until you can convince me I need to be doing something else with my life."

"Right." Charlie exhaled smoke out the window. "So that isn't helpful?"

"No, it's not."

"I think you'll find that it is," Charlie said. "When you're on a private jet to Paris with Viola and you're earning half a mil a year just to make sure the hotel carries the kind of shampoo she likes."

"I'm not working for Viola."

"Getting fired was what Surge needed," Charlie said. "He shouldn't have been a cop, either. He was too impulsive. Too creative. He couldn't follow rules. Sure, cutting the guy's foot off was the right thing to do, but that's only because it worked. A couple of miles down the road, he was going to do something equally as crazy and stupid, and he was going to get a bunch of people killed, including himself."

Lamb wasn't convinced. Charlie could see it on her face.

"Why do you think I'm even telling you this story?" he asked. "I'm trying to show you that people have been fired on their first day on the job before and survived and gone on to do what they were supposed to do. It's not the worst thing that could ever happen to you."

She thought for a while. "So what was I going to do a couple of miles down the road?" she asked. "If I'd been allowed to stay in?"

"You were going to get called a pig by some junkie

and burst into tears in the middle of an arrest," Charlie said. He didn't even hesitate.

"See, that's where you're wrong." Lamb shook her head vehemently. "Maybe I've been a little overly emotional the past few days, but that's only because my entire goddamn world just imploded. I'm capable of taking abuse from criminals and making good arrests and keeping my emotions in check. You'll see that."

"If you're not inconsolable about something within the hour, I'll eat my hat."

"You don't even have a hat."

"Go left here."

Lamb froze, then shook herself into action, swung the wheel toward the turn too late, and then chickened out, swerved back into her lane. Charlie watched the turn sail by, a pair of panhandlers on the corner balking at Lamb's driving.

"That was the turn," Charlie said.

"Where?"

"Back there."

"Oh. Uh. Sorry. Uh. You didn't give me enough notice."

"So go around the block."

"There are only strip malls down that way." Lamb was watching the rearview mirror, the tendons in her thin wrists straining. "The guy doesn't live there."

"I know. I want to grab something to eat. There's an amazing Cuban sandwich place down there."

"It doesn't have to be that exact one, though. Look. There are more food places farther on."

"It *does* have to be that exact one," he said. "I've been hanging out to go to this place. Biker gangs are racist assholes, and I've spent the past half a decade pretending to be one of them. That means steak, eggs, and burgers. The most exotic cuisine I had in all my time under was Wiener schnitzel. When this case is over, I'm going to hit every one of my favorite Chinese,

Mexican, and Cuban places, between tattoo removal appointments. Turn here."

She missed the second turn. Wasn't even listening now. "We're on the clock here! Let's just hit a drive-through."

"What's wrong with you?" Charlie squinted. Something in his gut was twitching at Lamb's sudden nervousness, her furtive glances at people on the sidewalk.

"Nothing, nothing. Urgh. I'll go. I'll go."

She got the job done, reluctantly, swiping weirdly at her long black hair and sweeping her gaze back and forth across the parking lot continuously as they drew into the space. Charlie would have been more disturbed by it all, but when he opened the door of the car, his nostrils were flooded with the smell of onion powder and grilled pork, and he was drifting across the lot with Lamb at his heels as if he were walking on clouds. The storefront was as he'd remembered it. Huge jars of lazy, green pickles lounging in brine on the counter, crowded with sauce bottles. A dark, narrow interior crowded with mismatched tables, old men in guayabera shirts reading newspapers in silence. He ordered himself a sandwich, heavy on the mustard, in a combo and nudged Lamb, who was watching a row of stores across the street and groaning quietly to herself.

"Order," he said.

"I don't want anything."

"Wrong again."

She went back to staring and groaning, her arms folded tightly across her chest. He ordered for her, and when the bags of food came, she snatched hers and her can of soda and was halfway across the parking lot by the time he had turned to step away from the counter.

"Come on, let's go, let's go, let's go," she was saying, juggling the can and the bag and the car keys, her head still on a swivel. He was about to confront her, to demand an explanation for all the squirrel-liness, when a small, round woman cut across him so sharply he stumbled to a halt. She rushed toward Lamb with her arms outstretched.

"Linny! Linny! Linny!"

Charlie looked in the direction from which she'd come and spied another small, round human shutting the door of a Ford Fiesta with a huge television box crammed in the back. The driver looked around, searching for his wife.

"Linny! What are you *doing* here?"

"Oh, Jesus, Mom," Lamb moaned as the small woman reached up and gripped her head, tugged it down to plant kisses on her cheeks. Charlie stood back and watched, his mouth stretching into a slow smile as Lamb's parents boxed her in against the side of the Ram.

"This is such a nice surprise!"

"Hi, Mom, hi."

"Look, Eddie! Linny's here!"

"There's my baby blue!"

"Hey, Dad."

Charlie watched all of Lamb's will to live drain out of her, her mouth and shoulders downturned, her knees sunk together. Her parents were almost identical: a foot and a half shorter than their daughter, dark-haired, with big, eager mouths and deep, earnest eyes. Lamb's father was sporting a handlebar mustache, and her mother was wearing a T-shirt with gold cursive script that read TOO GLAM TO GIVE A DAMN across her breasts.

"What are you doing here, Linny?" Lamb's father was taking it all in—hands on hips, the examiner of evidence. The Ram, the bag and soda in Lamb's hands, Charlie standing there watching from the end of the car space. "You should have told us you were coming!

Aren't you working? You said you had three days on duty."

"Yeah, you said you were working today." Lamb's mother was stroking her arm. "If you'd told us you had a day off, you could have come with us to pick up the new TV! We just got back. Are you staying with us tonight? We can watch *Succession*!"

"Oh, no, no, no, I just, I just, I just . . ." Lamb's words drained away and her jaw worked up and down soundlessly, her eyes lifting desperately to Charlie. He put his bag and soda down on the roof of the Ram and strode forward.

"She is working," he said. Mr. Lamb turned toward him, and Charlie grabbed his warm, pudgy hand and pumped it. "You must be Officer Lamb's parents. I'm her partner, Detective Sergeant Charles Hoskins."

Mrs. Lamb straightened, her chin up, making her round cheeks catch the light. "Oh. Ohhh!" She glanced at Lamb for confirmation. "You're her *partner*. Oh, wow. Wow! Eddie, this is Linny's partner!"

Mr. Lamb braced for his wife's enthusiastic backhand slap to the chest a good half second before it came, something Charlie assumed he'd been doing for decades. "I heard the guy, Fiona. I'm standin' right here."

"Well, say hello, then, for god's sake!"

"It's nice to meet you, Detective."

"We have a store, right over there." Mrs. Lamb thrust out an arm toward the row of stores across the street, her aim centering vaguely on a shoe store while her eyes inspected every inch of Charlie, lingering on his boots. "That's us. Eddie's Shoes. Linny didn't tell us she was working in the area or we would have invited you both to lunch. Oh, this is such a nice surprise. We've been dying to know how it's all going. She didn't even tell us she had a partner yet! We don't know anything about you!"

"Mom, please, just—" Lamb tried.

"I have so many questions." Mrs. Lamb clutched at her neck, flapped a flustered hand, her eyes wandering the skyline as she tried to organize them all in her mind. "Are you . . . Why aren't you two in uniform? Are you her permanent partner? Are you training her? Will it just be the two of you from now on? What happened to your head? You've been injured! Oh—I shouldn't have said anything. How rude. You look fine. Really. Really, you look great."

"Mom, please!"

"It's okay." Charlie put his palms up. "It's okay. I fell off my motorcycle about a week ago. It's no big deal. And Lamb's not in uniform because she made a big arrest this morning, and it was a bit of a wild one."

Charlie could feel Lamb's eyes on him. He didn't look, kept up the smile instead, holding her parents captivated. Lamb's father's heavy brows were knitted above his bulbous nose.

"What do you mean, 'wild'?" he asked.

"We pulled in a major suspect in a drug-trafficking ring over in Van Nuys." Charlie jerked a thumb west. "Guy didn't want to go down. Lamb chased him through a vacant lot and over a fence, and she ripped her uniform trousers right down the side."

"Oh my god, are you hurt?" Mrs. Lamb turned to her daughter.

"Did you catch the guy?" Mr. Lamb asked.

Lamb couldn't offer either parent an answer.

"She's not hurt. And yes, she got the guy," Charlie said. "We're just going over to serve a warrant on his spouse. She might be a runner, too, so I thought I'd match Lamb in civvies so we don't spook the target."

"Where does the spouse live?" Mr. Lamb asked.

"Hansen Hills."

"We live in Hansen Hills!" Mrs. Lamb gasped.

"You don't say." Charlie smiled.

"Don't you have spare uniforms in your locker?" Mrs. Lamb turned again to her child.

"They're in dry cleaning," Charlie said. "First set got smoked up when we responded to a house fire, second set got blood on them from a barroom brawl. It's been a big couple of days. But Lamb's rolling with it, aren't you, Lamb?"

"Yes," Lamb managed.

"I always tell my rookies: you need five uniforms on deck, minimum, at any given time." Charlie clapped Lamb's father on the back, sucked in a breath to inflate his chest, the reluctant boss handing out rare and hard-won praise. "It's a tough gig, but she's a tough kid. She's gonna be a great cop one day."

The parents gaped at their child, who was gaping at Charlie.

"Anyway," Charlie said. "We gotta head out."

"Four minutes." Mr. Lamb held a hand up.

"For what?" Charlie asked.

Mr. Lamb pointed at Charlie's feet. "Your boots are too tight. Those are Canlen-Morrows. Walmart, am I right? The bridge is notoriously narrow. You're wearing a twelve; you need at least a twelve and a half for a foot like yours. I can tell by the way you're standing. Four minutes in my shop, we'll get you something that fits proper, and you can be on your way. I have a nice pair of classic-cut Waybournes that—"

"Dad, *no*."

"I just got in a nice pair of—"

Mr. Lamb bent, presumably to feel Charlie's toe through the boot. Lamb grabbed his shoulder.

"No, I said." Lamb was firm. "We have to go."

"Another time, then." Mr. Lamb shook Charlie's hand.

"Yeah, sure," the detective said, smiling. "Another time."

Lamb bent and kissed her mother and hugged her father. "We're busy."

"Yes, you're busy. You're busy. Go." Mrs. Lamb all but pushed her daughter into the car. "Go get 'em, baby blue!"

They drove in silence for a long time, condensation beading on the outside of the soda cans as they jostled in the cup holders between them. In time, Lamb pulled over, and they sat at the roadside, numbed, watching a homeless woman wheeling a huge shopping cart full of blankets and garbage across four lanes of traffic.

"Shoes, huh?" he said eventually, because someone had to say something.

"Yeah," she replied. "They've owned that store for thirty years."

He nodded. Understood. There was nothing more regulated, predictable, safe, and secure than owning a shoe store. Steady business. Daily routine. Patterns of fluctuations in sales determined by school terms, and the meager mental entertainment provided by a sustained David-and-Goliath battle with superstores such as Walmart for loyal, inevitably local customers. Charlie had drifted away from the scene with Lamb's parents into an armchair-psychologist's analysis of the shoe store and how it probably drove Lamb's desire to seek a career in law enforcement, as an escape from the soul-destroying boredom that came with being the child of a couple of shoe store owners. But then he looked over and saw that Lamb's eyes were full of tears. He tried to hide his smile but couldn't.

"Don't do it!" he said, but it was too late. She had hurled herself at him, and her body was pressed against his, and he could feel swallowed sobs hitching in her ribs as he awkwardly patted her back.

"Why did you do that?" She was sniffling loudly in his ear. "Why the hell would you do that?"

"I don't know," he sighed. "It just happened."

He held her, stiff with discomfort, his broken ribs aching and his neck throbbing from the weight of her arms around it. He thumped her on the back a couple of times to encourage her to get off him, and eventually she did. Lamb drew back and ripped a handful of tissues from the front pocket of her jeans, swaddling her entire nose and mouth in them. He took his soda can from the holder and cracked it.

"You have to tell them eventually, Lamb," he said.

"I know. I will. I promise."

"Well, while you're in the mood for making promises," he said, "promise never to hug me again. I don't need to catch whatever you got that makes you act like this. I can't be starting every morning for the rest of my career weeping into my goddamn breakfast cereal."

"Okay. I promise. I'll never hug you again."

"Good," he said. He waved at the road. "Now dry your eyes, baby blue, and take the next right."

CHAPTER 11

The hostages sat numbly, tiny noises around the lab amplified in the wake of the gunshot. Bendigo leaned his head against the steel table behind him and watched Ibrahim and Ashlea, huddled together maybe five feet away. The young journalist had slipped down to rest against the security guard's blood-spattered shirt, her head rising and falling softly as he breathed. Bendigo could hear muffled sounds from teams of police officers outside the windows, talking, strategizing, moving about, no telling how far away they were. He could hear the fridges humming and his own heart beating in his ears. Some part of him also wondered if a buzzing he could hear, that seemed as if it originated behind his eyes, was in fact the tiny fluctuations in air particles still responding to the sound generated by the bullet tearing into the steel table against which the other two hostages sat. The sound had rippled through the table frame, probably reverberating out against the walls and back again multiple times, too minute for his brain to recognize, probably entering his bones in imperceptible micro-vibrations that would carry on for minutes.

He looked at the hole in the side of the steel table. Ashlea and Ibrahim had shuffled sideways a couple of feet away from it, closer to Bendigo, as though by moving away from the trace of the gunshot they could somehow move away from its occurrence altogether. Because, while Ryan had played it out to the police, and to the hostages, that the shot was a warning, Bendigo had been looking at the man's face when he pulled the trigger.

He hadn't looked when he fired.

That the bullet had missed Ashlea was pure luck.

And there was nothing a scientist hated more than luck. Bendigo wanted to know, *had* to know, the outcome of all this would be based, somehow, on his efforts. On strategy, and timing, and balanced actions and decisions. He couldn't rely on the efforts of the police. He couldn't rely on fate. He needed something about the equation to change, right now, because the trajectory he and Ibrahim and Ashlea were on only ended in demise.

Ryan hadn't cared, when he fired, if his bullet hit Ashlea or not.

That meant it was real. All of it. He and the other people in lab 21 might never leave the room alive.

On the wall across the room, the cheap plastic clock ticked away the seconds and minutes to Elsie and Ryan's next conversation with the police, their next probable destruction of evidence. Elsie sat at her stool beside her husband, examining one potassium tube in comparison to another, talking quietly with him.

Bendigo wondered silently, hatefully, about who within the building had told the Delaneys where they could find the specific samples they'd chosen to destroy, who had given them the list of anonymous inventory numbers attached to those samples. He knew for a fact that the samples they were talking about—the rape kit taken from Mayor Grimley's niece and the doorknob swab sample from the Torrance bank robbery—shouldn't have been anywhere near each other in the lab. One would require a

Chelex extraction technique to identify the DNA within the collected sample, while the other would need to undergo solid-phase extraction. One should have been in lab 20, and one should have been in lab 19. But both had been drawn, right in front of Bendigo's eyes, from the fridge against the north wall of lab 21.

Bendigo imagined that, after the Delaneys had dragged an unconscious Ibrahim into the lab, but before Bendigo had arrived, the couple had gone from fridge to fridge in labs 18, 19, 20, and 21, sourcing the exact samples they wanted from the list. They would have gathered them into a test tube holder and stored them in the fridge on the north wall of lab 21, ready for their two-hourly destructions.

In truth, Bendigo figured there were dozens of people who could have assisted the Delaneys. His lab was staffed by eleven full-time scientists, eight interns, and a rotation of five forensics students working on their doctoral studies. For chain-of-evidence reasons, these were the only people who had access to the samples. But the list that contained the sample types, the case numbers attached to those samples, and the names of their submitting officers was an electronic thing, which he knew could have been intercepted somewhere between his lab coordinator's computer, where it was created and maintained, and his own computer, or that of any of the other staff members who worked in the Forensic Biology Unit. That intergalactic pathway between clouds or databases or whatever the hell it was that stored the lab's administrative system might have been infiltrated by any number of people, maybe even the Delaneys themselves. He slumped against the table and sighed, working his fingers, trying to keep up the circulation in his digits. Time ticked away. The police called, and the Delaneys ignored them.

It was when he looked over again that Bendigo noticed Ibrahim watching him, waiting to catch his gaze. The young security guard glanced at the Delaneys meaningfully and raised his dark eyebrows, and Bendigo felt a prickle of excitement hitch in his throat as the guard shifted under Ashlea. Bendigo dropped his eyes to Ibrahim's bound hands, following movement, and saw that he was lifting the untucked back edge of his white uniform shirt. Bendigo saw the curve of the younger man's backside, the thick, striped band of his boxer shorts, and within them, the handles of two pairs of steel scissors.

Bendigo's stomach plunged. He met Ibrahim's gaze again, remembered the young guard's submissive walk back from his escape attempt out into the hall, the anticlimactic return that had made Bendigo burn with anticipated but nonetheless crushing disappointment. Ibrahim must have darted into another lab, found the scissors lying on a steel tray, maybe over in lab 18, trace evidence extraction. They looked like the kind of scissors the technicians used there to cut fabric.

The two men met eyes, and Bendigo nodded. Ibrahim eased one of the pairs of scissors out of the waistband of his boxers and lowered it silently to the linoleum beneath him. Bendigo watched as Ibrahim slid the scissors gently under the steel table, just out of sight.

"Okay, we have sound and a partial visual," Franklin said. Saskia followed the hulking SWAT commander over to a row of laptops positioned on a fold-out table under the second tent. Saskia had finally accepted a coffee from someone, but held it against her chest with her back to the east, where the army of reporters had gathered on the hill beyond the outer cordon. She bent and looked at a grainy image that at first reminded her of a collection of pale, morose abstract artworks she had once observed in a gallery. The image was divided in half, a hard, gray line separating a slab of pale gray from a block of a lighter shade of gray. As she watched, the image rotated, tiny imperfections in the view sliding across the screen as the camera shifted around. She saw a blue block slide into view, then disappear. A brown smudge did the same, appearing at the left of the screen and then disappearing at stage right.

"What the hell am I looking at?" Saskia asked.

"This is a three-sixty-degree view of lab 21," Franklin said, giving a short, frustrated huff. "Visible from a drain hole in the center of the room. The brown thing, the geeks think, is the leg of a stool. The blue thing is the edge of a cabinet."

"You're kidding me," Saskia snapped. "That's all we can see?"

"You'll forgive us, Chief." A nearby technician looked up from the laptop she was leaning over. Saskia recognized her as a member of the Special Operations Squad. "It's not as if we can send the worm camera up the drainpipe, out the hole in the floor of the lab, and four feet into the air. The Delaneys might notice a thing like that."

"Thanks for the long-suffering tone, Officer." Saskia smiled.

"No problem, ma'am."

"Does your magnificent worm camera have a mic?"

"It does."

"Well, that's something, at least," she said. "What about the robot you're sending through the air-conditioning vents?"

"It's slow going," Franklin said. "It's louder than the worm camera. The operators are inching it along the vent, trying to roll only when someone in the lab is talking. But there's not much of that going on. After the gunshot, the mood in there took a dive."

"What are they saying to each other?"

"Ashlea cried for a while, and Ibrahim comforted her. Elsie blasted Ryan for being so reckless." The

SOS technician tapped at her laptop while she spoke. "Guess the gunshot was a spur-of-the-moment decision."

"We need to exploit that somehow," Saskia said. "Right now, Elsie and Ryan are not on the same page on this thing. Not completely. We need to convince her she can't trust him, she needs to bail out."

Franklin followed her through the tent, through the space between two police squad cars at the edge of the tents and into the secondary command area hidden from press view. Ronnie Curler was bent over sheets of paper, a collection of blueprints of the Hertzberg-Davis building. Leonard Franklin dwarfed the FBI negotiator as he sat down. The men leaned back as Saskia took her seat, a move she knew was meant to signify that she had the floor, but one that nonetheless left her feeling as if she had been granted a probationary position at the grown-ups' table, where she'd have to prove her worth to have any influence at all on what was said. Curler at least offered a small smile. Franklin didn't.

"So where are we?" she asked.

"This noncontact game has got to stop," Curler cut in before Franklin could speak. "So far, the Delaneys have decided exactly when they speak to us and for how long. That's not going to help us build a rapport. We need to access the building's PA system and start talking to them, whether they want to hear from us or not."

"How do we do that?"

"From what Special Investigations is telling me, we will need to get an officer in here." Curler pointed to a large sheet of blue paper to his right. Saskia leaned over. It was an architectural drawing of the ground floor of the building, complete with electrical and sewage lines. "This is the reception desk. The main controls for the PA system are there. All we have to do is plug in."

"Wouldn't it be easier to get as close as we can to the lab windows and use a megaphone?" Saskia asked.

"Only if you want the press hearing everything we say to them." Curler shrugged. "Which could be strategically dangerous in the long run."

"How can we get a guy in here?" Saskia turned to Franklin.

"The Delaneys have secured these two doors, as well as this one, this one, and this one with bike locks." He pointed to the closest doors to the reception area. "The auto doors at the front and the side of the reception area work, like I said earlier. But they're not going to let someone just walk in. They'll start waving guns around. You know they will. And they're trigger-happy. So the thing to do would be to access the ground floor from inside the building, not externally. I've got a team on the roof already, waiting for your approval to start heading down the internal stairwell. We can distract the targets while an officer gets to the desk and hooks us up to the PA."

"What do you think?" Saskia asked, turning to Curler.

"That'll piss them off," the negotiator replied. "If they spot officers on their floor, they'll be angry. They'll feel betrayed."

"They won't spot them," Saskia said. "We'll do it the next time they take a video call with us. They'll have their eyes on our screen."

"It's risky." Curler sighed.

"But worth it. They're already angry. It's not as though we'll be undoing the hard work we've done building rapport. We have no rapport at this point."

"We'll fix that," Curler said. "These things take time."

"What's your suggestion for when we have the PA set up?" Saskia looked at him.

"You've got the teenage daughter coming in, right?" Curler asked.

"Should be here any minute," Saskia said.

"I suggest we put her on."

"Really? Jesus. I don't know if she'll be in any state to talk." Saskia pursed her lips, looking toward the vehicle checkpoint across the parking lot, where another press van was attempting to beg its way in. "Her sister's dead, and she'll be in her sixties before her parents get out of prison. As far as we know, this morning, Ryan and Elsie Delaney sent her off to study group as if it were any other regular morning, all the while planning this." She gestured to the Hertzberg-Davis building. "If anyone should feel betrayed today, it's her."

"We could work with that," Curler said. "I'm not interested in opening a dialogue between her and her parents. That's too likely to get out of hand. So I'll give her a script. The fact is, what the Delaneys have done here today has to have been so meticulously and obsessively planned, it's likely they didn't factor in their other daughter at all. They will have been completely consumed by the logistics of it. The difficulties. The challenges. Something like this would have taken months to put together. Maybe a year. And now it's D-day. You're right, they've betrayed Jonie Delaney shockingly today. And I'm hoping they might not have given much thought to that yet."

"So the kid's heartache might be just the right kind of log across the tracks to derail this train," Saskia said.

"Right," Curler said.

Saskia nodded, thinking. She caught something in Franklin's eyes. The huge SWAT officer was staring at Saskia, his gaze fixed on hers, narrow and full of menace.

"You're lookin' at me a certain kind of way, Officer Franklin." Saskia jutted her chin. "Out with it."

"I'm just trying to work you out, ma'am." Franklin plucked at his thick beard. "You're saying all the right things, sure. But you're giving us mixed messages here."

"I am?" She laughed, then glanced at Curler, who was sitting upright, arms folded, listening.

"What are you talking about, Franklin?" Saskia said.

"You told the Delaneys that you refused to reinvestigate their daughter's case," Franklin said. "Because you're on our side. You stand with the police. You're not going to let a couple of wannabe terrorists push us around, make like we're pussies in front of the whole world. You're not going to let them set an example and possibly endanger the lives of other officers who are just out there trying to do their jobs."

"That's exactly right," Saskia said.

"So what doesn't make sense to me"—Franklin pointed to the main command tent—"is you telling those same two criminals that you don't give a shit about the police evidence they're planning to destroy."

"I don't," Saskia said.

Franklin's nostrils flared. Saskia felt Curler's gaze on her.

"Are you serious, ma'am?" Franklin barked.

"Yes, I am," Saskia said. "My priority here today is the live hostages sitting in that lab with guns trained on their goddamn heads. If the Delaneys destroy any more police evidence, that'll be a real shame."

"A 'real shame'?" Franklin's eyes widened. He looked at Curler to see if the agent had heard. Curler didn't move.

Saskia gripped her chair, forced her tone to remain level. "The crimes that have samples sitting in the lab? They aren't in progress right now. That harm has already been done. What I'm focusing on are the three, maybe four lives *currently* in peril."

"You don't think you're going to put further lives in danger by letting the Delaneys destroy the best leads we have on the killers and rapists and fucking monsters who are on that list of samples?" Franklin was rising in his chair, swelling and expanding outward from his chest like an aggressive ape. "The *future victims* of those criminals are in peril right now. The piece of shit who killed those two officers in Encino is on that list! That sample is a one-shot. *We lose that sample, we lose that guy!*"

"The detectives assigned to those cases will just have to find their suspects by other investigative means," Saskia said. She could feel her jaw tightening. "Believe it or not, Commander Franklin, it is possible to solve crimes without the use of DNA. I know. I've done it myself, once or twice."

Franklin leaned over the table, his voice low and mean. "If the Encino double-cop murder is the next sample the Delaneys choose to destroy, ma'am, you're going to have every officer on this scene up your ass about it."

"Oh, I imagine I will," Saskia agreed. "But the Delaneys are just as likely to choose the mayor's niece's sample. And in that case, I'll have the goddamn mayor of Los Angeles up my ass. I'm surprised he's not here already." She looked around. "Must have stopped to kiss a baby."

Franklin leaned back in his chair. "I'm going to say this once, real clear." He glanced at Curler and stabbed a finger into the tabletop. "You're my witness, fed. Chief Ferboden, you need to approve a SWAT entry into lab 21. You need to approve it right now. I believe my team can extract the three hostages with minimal threat to their lives. We'll breach fast and hard, and snatch them up before anybody even knows what's happened. It's what we do. It's what we're good at."

"The answer is no," Saskia said. "It's too risky. We have guns at close quarters with the hostages and possibly an explosive device in play. Until we have more information, the plan is for Curler to negotiate with the Delaneys and to try to get a peaceful resolution."

Franklin rose from his chair, smiled a shit-eating

smile, and shrugged at Curler in a manner Saskia had seen men do ten thousand times across her career. *Women, huh? They can't be reasoned with.*

She rose and sidestepped the big man on her way to check in with the long-suffering tech in the other tent to see if the visual had improved. As she attempted to slip through the gap between the squad cars, Franklin darted in front of her, and she had no choice but to follow him through the gap and pass him when he stopped to wait for her on the other side.

As she passed, she felt his breath on her face as he muttered at her.

"They never would have caught the guy who fucked you up if he hadn't handed them a sample," Franklin said.

Saskia turned, rage flaring so fast and wild in her body it made all her muscles seize. For a moment, she was caught there, half twisted toward him, her fists bunched, unable to relax back into the controlled state she had been in before he'd uttered those miserable words. It was almost as if she were a slave to the momentum of her arm swinging up and across, her fist smashing into Franklin's wide jaw. Almost, but not quite. Because as she heard his teeth crunch together and watched the big SWAT officer stagger backward into a stack of chairs, Saskia felt the inevitable ripple of pleasure at a decision made and honored, no matter the cost. She shook her hand out, felt the knuckles crack, and glanced around at the shocked faces of the officers manning the command tents.

"Someone alert the second-in-command on SWAT," she said. "They just got a promotion."

CHAPTER 12

HOSKINS: Detective Sergeant Charlie Hoskins.
FLICK: Oh, hey, man, this is Flick. I got your message.
HOSKINS: Great. Great. Thanks for calling me back.
FLICK: No problem. I was in the water, that's all. Really trippy to hear from you.
HOSKINS: You weren't expecting the call?
FLICK: Nah. Nah. Nah. Although, Ranger Lee did say someone was calling around about something. A cop. But I didn't realize it was about that.
HOSKINS: Oh, okay.
FLICK: I was only half listening. Ranger Lee talks a lot. So, what did you need to know?
HOSKINS: Well, I'm trying to get any information I can about the woman who pulled the guy out of the water last Wednesday. I'm just trying to track her down, that's all.
FLICK: Did she do something wrong?
HOSKINS: No, no, no.
FLICK: Because from what I saw, she did all the right things. And it's, like, she was just some chick on her morning swim, you know? She didn't ask to get involved.

HOSKINS: We're not saying she did anything wrong. We'd just like to know her name, if possible.

FLICK: Hmm.

HOSKINS: You're skeptical.

FLICK: Yeah, well, you know, maybe it's just me. I got kind of a history with it. See, my cousin was in the gym once, and some guy had a heart attack on the treadmill next to him.

HOSKINS: Okay.

FLICK: The gym owners, they didn't know shit about, like, what to do and all. So my cousin, he jumped in and did CPR. He got the guy back. He was alive when the ambulances took him away. But he died later. Anyway, his family sued my cousin. They took him to court and everything.

HOSKINS: This is nothing like that.

FLICK: Yeah. You sure, though?

HOSKINS: I'm sure.

FLICK: So what do you want her for, dude?

HOSKINS: Uh . . .

FLICK: You there?

HOSKINS: Yeah, I'm here. I'm just thinking. Look, Flick, I'm going to level with you, okay?

FLICK: Okay.

HOSKINS: She pulled *me* out of the water.

FLICK: Whoa! You're the dude?

HOSKINS: I'm the dude.

FLICK: You're the duuude!

HOSKINS: Yeah.

FLICK: Shit, man! What the hell happened? What were you doing out there?

HOSKINS: It's a long story.

FLICK: Literally everybody I know wants to know what happened, man. Like, literally everyone.

HOSKINS: I know. But I can't really say. It's a police matter.

FLICK: Well, shit. That sucks.

HOSKINS: But finding her isn't a police matter, it's a personal one. I just want to know who she is. It's hard to explain. I just feel this kind of, uh . . . It's, like, a . . . drive . . . to find her. Or at least to know her name or . . . or something. All I know is that I need to find her.

FLICK: Man. That's deep.

HOSKINS: Ha! Is it?

FLICK: It's hellz romantic, too. Kind of.

HOSKINS: Well, I don't know about that.

FLICK: Now I sorta wish I *could* help you.

HOSKINS: What! You're saying you can't?

FLICK: Nah, man. I don't know anything about her. Never seen her before. Never seen her since.

HOSKINS: Oh, Flick. Flick. You're killing me here.

FLICK: Sorry, bro.

HOSKINS: So she hasn't been back to the bay since that day? No one's seen her?

FLICK: Not that I know of. I mean, I could keep asking around.

HOSKINS: And you didn't talk to her after I was taken away in the ambulance? You didn't catch her name?

FLICK: Yeah, sure, we talked to her. Me and Zero. We were all heading home; we walked her to her car.

HOSKINS: Okay.

FLICK: But I couldn't tell you anything about

it. I can't even think what color it was. And we didn't talk about anything, like, personal. It was sort of all, like: *Oh, shit, how about that guy, huh? That was random. I hope he's all right. Okay, bye!*

HOSKINS: Okay. Okay. Urgh. Well, what about John? I've tried his number a couple of times, left messages.

FLICK: Oh, Zero won't talk to you. He's even more paranoid than I am. Some of these guys out here, there's a reason they spend all day and night in the waves, you know what I'm saying? Like, they've had a hard time on the land.

HOSKINS: Right.

FLICK: If Zero had gills, he'd never go to shore. He doesn't like cops, and he doesn't answer calls from strange phone numbers.

HOSKINS: Right. Well. Thanks for talking to me, Flick. I'll keep trying.

FLICK: Oh, wait. Wait. Wait. Uh . . .

HOSKINS: Yeah?

FLICK: Her car. There was one thing. I think she had, like, speakers in the back, maybe? Yeah. She definitely had speakers in the back.

HOSKINS: You mean she had a sound system?

FLICK: No, like, she was hauling speakers around. Big black ones. They were the kind you'd see at a concert, maybe?

HOSKINS: Okay. No instruments? Just speakers?

FLICK: Just speakers. But her car was packed full with them, and they were sort of strapped in properly. So maybe she's, like, used to hauling them around. I don't know if that helps.

HOSKINS: It's something, Flick. It's definitely
   something.

Charlie ended his call and stuffed his phone in his
pocket, finished his cigarette while watching the sunlight glint off a small fishpond outside Nicolas Rojer's
apartment building. Lamb came and stood by him, her
copy of the Delaney file tucked under her arm, her eyes
following the little orange-and-white goldfish darting
and gliding beneath lily pads.

"What did they teach you at the academy about in-
terrogating a suspect?" Charlie asked.

She thought for a moment. "Make them comfortable. Establish common ground. Play off your partner
and find out which of you the suspect identifies and
connects with best. Use that connection to lead them
into talking. Let them talk, talk, talk, then circle back
and try to trip them up on their inconsistencies."

Charlie watched her.

"And try to offer a face-saving scenario, if you can,"
she added in closing. "Even if he takes it and admits
to something less than the charge you're going for, you
can use it as a launchpad to get him to admit what he
really did later down the track."

"I'd love to be interrogated by you, Lamb," Charlie said. "Sounds like a real picnic. I bet you'd serve
tea and little cakes."

"You have other plans for our guy?" She nodded
toward the apartment building.

"Yes, because we don't have twelve hours to play
besties with Rojer." He took out his phone and glanced
at it. "The Delaneys are going to destroy another piece
of evidence soon."

"We should watch." Lamb took out her own phone.
"Surely the news channels will pick up what it is.
They've already reported that the first sample destroyed
was from the Torrance bank robbery. There must be a
leak inside the inner cordon."

"I don't want to know what it is." Charlie pushed her phone down.

"Because you don't want it to be one of yours," Lamb concluded. "I overheard Chief Ferboden saying there are ninety-nine samples in play and you saying yours are in there."

"Yeah," Charlie said. "They are."

"None of them have been tested?"

"No. I submitted all three the day I woke up from being out at sea. I told some of Saskia's guys where to find my evidence stash, and they bagged and tagged them and sent them to the lab."

"Why did you wait so long?" Lamb was watching his eyes. "You were under for five years. Surely there must have been other chances to submit stuff for testing during that time."

"If this whole fiasco at Hertzberg-Davis has taught you anything, it should be that those lists of what samples are being submitted to the lab, and by whom and when and why, aren't secure," Charlie said. "The last thing I needed was to be two years in with the Death Machines and have some . . . some lab rat with a big mouth telling one of the crew that his DNA had just turned up on a sample. The next questions would be: 'A sample of what?' and 'How'd they get that?' and 'Who's the submitting officer?'"

"Right."

"I could have brought the Machines down for any number of things, from week one," Charlie said. "Drugs. Guns. Thefts. Assaults. But I wanted the murder charges. I waited, for five years, so I could get the murder charges. And they're solid murders that'll get them life behind bars. Nothing they could claim self-defense or provocation for. They were bad, bad killings that'll have the killers and everyone who helped them put away for serious time."

"Who did they kill?"

"Let's talk about it later. We're on the clock."

"So what's the plan for Rojer?" Lamb started walking to the elevators. "If not a twelve-hour picnic."

"I figure we just beat his head in with a phone book." Charlie shrugged. "I'll hold his arms. You go to town."

Lamb stopped walking. Charlie watched her trying to decide if he was serious. It took her too long.

"We're not going to beat him, Lamb."

She sighed with relief.

They slipped into the elevator.

"The plan is I'm going to feed him a bunch of bullshit about his alibi having already come undone, make him defend it or hear his new version of events, see if there's anything there. You're going to listen in and take mental notes while you search the apartment."

"I'm going to search the apartment?" She turned to him. "How?"

"Work it out, partner."

The elevator doors parted onto an open-air catwalk lined with doors on one side, railings overlooking the building's courtyard on the other. Charlie walked, found a beige door with a glossy gold number, identical to a dozen others they had passed. He watched as Lamb stood back from the view of the peephole, turned sideways to make herself a smaller target, just the way Charlie had been trained to do a million years earlier. He wondered if the teachers had shown her class the same footage they'd shown his, of a drug squad cop being shot in the stomach through a door while attempting to serve a warrant. He remembered the other cadets around him jumping in their seats at the blast.

Nicolas Rojer opened the door and stood there, slightly stooped and wide-eyed behind his steel-rimmed glasses. Wary and quiet. Charlie had seen a thousand people answer the door to the police that way. No greeting, just standing there holding the doorknob and waiting for bad news.

"Nicolas Rojer, I'm Detective Sergeant Charlie Hoskins." Charlie breezed in through the door without waiting for an invitation. "This is Lynette Lamb. We're here to have a chat with you. Can we come in? Thanks."

Charlie scanned the living room. It was typical of a single man living alone, unaccustomed to guests. Acceptably clean, but with clothes dumped in the hallway, dishes in the sink, a smattering of evidence of a quiet evening alone last night; a smudged wineglass on the coffee table, a prone dent in the couch, a remote control on the floor. The place smelled of strong deodorant and damp towels. Rojer's gaze followed Charlie as he walked through the room and took a small cane chair by the door to the kitchen.

"I thought you guys might come." Rojer gave a dejected sigh and followed Charlie, leaving Lamb to shut the door. "As soon as I saw it was Mr. and Mrs. Delaney on the news this morning, I figured any minute I'd get a knock on my door."

"Thanks for tidying up, then." Charlie kicked a newspaper aside to make room for his boots on the carpet.

"I've got nothing to say without my lawyer present." Rojer picked up the wineglass and did an awkward little dance around Lamb, who was hovering now by the kitchen door. "I was questioned about the little girl going missing two years ago. I told them where I was. That was it."

"Well, you were hardly 'questioned,'" Charlie said. "They called you, as I understand it."

"Yeah." Rojer returned from the kitchen, having deposited the wineglass, and retrieved the remote from the floor.

"So there was no hauling down to the station,"

Charlie said. "No cramped interrogation room. No detectives leaning over you. No cooling-off period in a holding cell, wondering if someone's going to tell the other perps in holding that you like to molest little girls."

Rojer coughed, thumped his chest with a fist. "No."

"Not that time around anyway," Charlie said.

Rojer winced, standing by the end of the couch. He was still stooped as if he were bracing for a sucker punch to the gut. His eyes traced the apartment for more things that needed tucking away, roving the furniture, actively avoiding Charlie and Lamb. He went to the window and slid it open, letting warm air in and the deodorant stink out.

"Not that time around, no," Rojer answered.

"I bet you get hauled in every time something happens to a kid within a fifty-mile radius of this address," Charlie said.

Rojer nodded vaguely.

"So let's try to avoid that this time. Stop tidying up. Sit your ass down."

Rojer sat obediently, sinking onto the couch too fast, bouncing a little. A symptom of jail time; excons sit hard and fast like dogs when they're instructed to. Charlie glanced at Lamb. She met his eyes and scratched the back of her neck.

"Uh, Mr. Rojer, would you mind if I used your—"

"It's down there." Rojer waved at the small hallway off the living room. His thoughts were racing, making his mouth twitch.

Charlie told himself not to be hopeful. Excited. All pedophiles are nervous around law enforcement. This visit would be a regular but no less terrifying routine for Rojer. The child molester would be accustomed to getting knocks on his door not only about kids attacked in a fifty-mile radius of his home but also those near misses when kids were grabbed but managed to escape. He'd be questioned whenever a report came in of suspicious activity: kids being approached, spoken to, watched. Rojer had probably seen dozens of cops in his apartment over the years, and some would be polite talkers while others threw his shit around, yelled at him, made threats. The knocks could come at all hours. Sometimes he'd be dragged out of bed and thrown on the floor.

Lamb put her case file on the coffee table and walked away. Charlie heard her lock the bathroom door behind herself.

"Tell me about that day."

Rojer shook his head, ran a hand through his lank brown hair. "I said already, not without my lawyer."

"You could just repeat what you told the police two years ago." Charlie shrugged. "You wouldn't be adding anything new. No need to involve the lawyer."

Rojer thought about it, silent, rubbing the thighs of his chinos.

"Yeah, I know that trick," Rojer said. "If I get it wrong, you'll jump down my throat."

"Why would you get it wrong if it's the truth?"

Rojer mumbled under his breath.

"If you want to do this with a lawyer, we'll have to go down to the station," Charlie said. "Make it formal. Right now, this is just an informal chat. But that can change. If you want. It's up to you."

Rojer didn't answer.

"You know how friendly it is down there," Charlie pressed.

Still nothing.

"What'll it be? Formal or informal?"

"Informal, I guess," Rojer relented.

Charlie examined him. He was a good-looking guy beneath the awkward-dad fashion choices and the serial-killer spectacles. Lean and muscular, with a good jawline and big, deep eyes. He had the floppy, semi-long haircut of teenage rock stars and romance movie heroes. The cheap sneakers and plaid shirt were probably a choice intended to remind children of their teachers and fathers. Rojer oozed vulnerable trustworthiness at first glance. Charlie took Lamb's copy of the Delaney case file from the coffee table and flipped through it.

"You said you went to your mother's house at 9:00 a.m. to help her remove some hedges from her front yard," Charlie read. "You were there until 5:00 p.m."

Rojer said nothing, but he nodded slowly.

"Pretty neat, the whole nine-to-five aspect of it."

"Well, she confirmed that with police." Rojer sighed. "They called her right after they called me. She got her times pretty close to mine, only she said I left the house at four. I figure she meant that's when I came inside the house to have coffee with her, not when I actually left. She must have glanced at the clock then." He was rambling now, looking down the hall for Lamb. "Got confused."

"She's elderly." Charlie smiled. "They're a pain, aren't they? You feed her something very easy to remember. Nine to five. And then she messes it up."

"I didn't feed her anything," Rojer said. "That's when I was there."

"It took eight hours to get the hedges out? That's a long time."

"Well, they were thirty-year-old hedges." Rojer braved a small, tight smile. "And there were twelve of them. Their roots were about three feet deep. You've got to get down there and get the whole root. The main root. If you snap it, you'll kill the plant."

"Right. So it was eight hours."

"Yes."

"And I suppose Mom fed you lunch."

"She did."

"Well, good for you. You have a nice, fat time frame where you were all tied up and occupied and miles from where Tilly Delaney went missing around 11:00 a.m."

"Mmm-hmm."

"You were virtuously toiling in the earth and not hunting for prey, as you've been known to do." Charlie scanned the papers on his lap. "Hanging around beaches and parks, pretending to photograph birds, getting shots of young girls instead."

Rojer swallowed. "I wasn't at the beach. I was at my mother's."

"This is an opportunistic crime, the Delaney thing," Charlie said. "A lot like your prior. You grabbed your victim in a shopping mall. Dragged her into a disabled toilet. We believe Tilly Delaney was exiting a toilet when she might have been grabbed."

"I wasn't at the beach," Rojer repeated. "I was at my mother's."

"Dangerous time to do it, in both scenarios. Broad daylight. Lots of people around. But that's part of the fun, isn't it?"

"I wasn't at the beach. I was at—"

"Problem is, that's wrong," Charlie said. "That's a lie. You weren't there that day, digging up your mother's hedges from nine to five. Not on the nineteenth. You *were* there. You *did* dig up the hedges. But that was the day before. On the eighteenth."

Rojer was watching Lamb as she exited the bathroom and walked back up the hall. At Charlie's words, he whirled around to look at the detective in the chair.

"Huh?"

"You were there the day before," Charlie repeated.

"No, I wasn't."

"Yes, you were." Charlie flipped the pages of the report. "We've got two neighbors on your mother's street who say you dug up the hedges on the eighteenth of October, not the nineteenth of October, the day Tilly went missing."

"Well, that's . . ." Rojer was sitting upright now,

the stoop gone, his back ramrod straight. "That's not right."

"Why were you digging up the hedges in the first place?"

"Because she . . . she was selling them." Rojer worked a hand through his hair again.

Lamb was hovering by the windows, looking out at the view of Hansen Hills, low and baking in the California sun. Maybe looking for her parents' house.

"My mother wanted to put a flower bed there instead of the . . . you know . . . the hedges."

"Did she pay you?"

"Did she pay me?" Rojer scratched his stubble. "No. Uh, yes. Yes."

"I bet you needed it. The money, I mean," Charlie said. "Not easy to get a job when you're a convicted sex offender."

"I shouldn't be talking to you without my lawyer," Rojer said.

"Do you mind if I—" Lamb started, gesturing toward the kitchen, but Rojer cut her off again.

"Yes. Yes."

"So the nineteenth," Charlie went on. "What were you really doing?"

"I—"

"Because we know you weren't digging up your mother's hedges," Charlie said. "So you can just give up on that right now. You can stop wasting time with it. My time. Your time. Lamb's time."

Rojer said nothing.

"We have confirmed with the buyer of the hedges that they were picked up from your mother's house on the morning of the nineteenth, and that you weren't there," Charlie lied. "We also have dashcam footage from a car passing your mother's residence on the eighteenth, at 10:17 a.m., showing what we believe is a figure with a shovel, and three-quarters of a hedge."

Rojer scratched his brow. His hand was shaking.

"We also know," Charlie went on, "that you deposited the check your mother gave you into your bank account the next morning. The morning of the nineteenth. Your bank records show that. So, again, I'll ask you: What were you actually doing on the nineteenth of October at 11:00 a.m.?"

The man on the couch wiped sweat off his upper lip with the back of his hand. Shook his head, but said nothing.

"Did you leave the bank and go to the beach?" Charlie asked.

Rojer was as still as stone. Charlie heard Lamb shut the fridge in the kitchen, bottles rattling as it sucked shut. He slipped the picture of Tilly Delaney out of the case file and put it on the coffee table in front of Rojer, spun it around so that it faced him. The man didn't move. His face was blank. Charlie leaned forward, took his gun from the waistband of his jeans, and used it to pin down the corner of the photograph of the missing child, which wanted to flap in the breeze from the open window.

Rojer sat silently, seconds ticking by, staring down at the picture of the girl with the rich, brown ringlet curls, thoughts churning over what Charlie hoped were not holes in his own bullshit. Because he'd risked so much already. He'd risked that Rojer's mother's hedges were picked up by the buyer the day after Rojer extracted them from the garden and not a few days later or that same evening. He'd risked that a passing car could conceivably record footage of the hedges from the street, and that they weren't hidden behind a fence or a wall. He'd risked that Rojer's mother had paid him by check, not in cash, and that he'd been desperate enough for the funds to bank the check first thing the following morning. Bullshit, bullshit, bullshit. The kind of spur-of-the-moment, improvisational lies that had kept him alive inside a gang of killers for five years, delivered with skin-saving confidence and not a shred of evidence. But the risky little details had rolled off his tongue, a wave of lies barreling on and on, gathering speed, and he was hoping Rojer would get swept away by them, or at least knocked off-balance. He was starting to believe that was going to happen, because the man on the couch before him began to slowly sink in his seat like a pricked balloon, losing inches all the time, until he was sitting against the backrest. His eyes lifted to Charlie and his mouth opened, and Charlie found himself holding his breath as he waited for an answer.

But before Rojer could speak, Lamb walked into the room and took Charlie's pistol from the coffee table. She actioned the weapon, flicked the safety off, and pointed it directly at Rojer's face.

"Where's the kid?" Lamb said.

Charlie rose slowly from the low cane chair, hearing it crackle and creak in the searing silence that filled the room. Lamb's aim with the pistol was dead straight, her gaze calm and focused, the way he'd seen her look in the car while the gunman pursued them from the parking lot minutes after they'd met.

"Lamb," Charlie said gently. "What are you doing?"

"I'm holding the suspect at bay," Lamb said. "Until we can establish where his victim is and get her to safety."

Charlie looked at Rojer. The convicted sex offender was watching Lamb's eyes, chewing his lips, his neck taut as he stretched to maintain eye contact with her high above where he sat.

"I don't know what she's talking about," Rojer said.

"Yes, you do," Lamb said. "Tell me where you keep them."

"Keep who?" Rojer said.

"Lamb," Charlie said. "Put the gun down."

"No, Charlie." Lamb glanced at him quickly. By

now, he had crept to her side, her outstretched arm level with his chest. "Trust me on this. Trust me."

Charlie thought about it. Then he reached forward and chopped Lamb's elbow down with one hand, causing her gun hand to flip up, point the weapon at the ceiling. The gun popped out of her fingers and into his at the same moment Rojer leaped to his feet. Charlie shoved him back down with a shoulder to the chest. Rojer bounced again as he landed on his butt on the sofa.

"Sit down, asshole," Charlie growled. He glared at Lamb. "Lamb, I'm going to invite you to go and wait outside while I finish this interview."

"No," Lamb said again. "I won't. He's got a kid right now, Charlie. I'm telling you, he's taking kids and—"

"*Outside!*" Charlie snapped.

Lamb's lip trembled, just for a second, and then her face turned to granite. She walked stiffly out. Charlie looked down at Rojer, who was wide-eyed and staring at his reflection in the television set.

"Lawyer," Rojer said.

Charlie found her pacing the catwalk outside the elevators, her head down and face mean.

"Listen—"

"No, you listen." She stuck a finger in his face. "In Nicolas Rojer's bathroom cabinet, I found an insulin pack. I also found a glucose monitor. And under the couch, where he was sitting, there was one of those . . . those . . . those"—she waved her hand—"foot circulation thingies."

"So?" Charlie said.

"So he has type 1 diabetes," Lamb said. "And in his kitchen fridge, there are eight bottles of Coke."

Charlie tried to decide how to react to this information, Lamb watching him all the time for that reaction. His fury had dissolved suddenly under the weight of sheer bewilderment.

"So the guy likes Coke." Charlie shrugged. "He shouldn't. But he does."

"They're not big bottles," Lamb said. "Like the kind you'd buy to have in your home and pour out into a glass whenever you'd like a Coke. They're the small kind. Like you'd have on the go. And there are eight of them. Eight."

Charlie waited.

"In his bathroom," she went on, "there were also pills in clear plastic containers. Tupperware containers. Unmarked. Some of the medication was in bottles, labeled, on the shelf in the wall cabinet. Other stuff was in the drawers in these containers. Just random pills. All the same size. I took a photo with my phone. Look."

"Oh, Lamb." Charlie held his head.

"Listen, listen, listen, before you discount me completely." Lamb grabbed his shoulders. "Did you notice the graze on Rojer's shin?"

"The *graze* on his *shin*?"

"Yeah. I bet you didn't notice that. Right shin. It was big. Chunky. A horizontal graze about three inches wide, with scrape marks below it. Like you'd get if you tripped up a step. And . . . and . . . and in his kitchen, beside the microwave, was a big flashlight. You know the heavy-duty kind with the handle on top? Really big. It was out, on the counter. Not put away in a cupboard. It was new. It still had the film on the lens. The . . . the . . . the sticker. You know, the sticker? So, he's out at night, he trips up a step and he thinks, *Fuck this. I'm buying a big old flashlight, and*—"

"Lamb." Charlie put his hands on her shoulders now. For a moment, they stood there, holding each other, searching each other's eyes.

"What?"

"I'm sorry," he said.

"For what?"

"For bringing you along. For not putting a stop to all this earlier. What happened in that room just now? That was bad, honey. We've lost that lead now. Rojer's not going to talk, certainly not today, certainly not to us. But it could have gone a whole lot worse. You could have blown his head off. And trying to find a way to explain how that happened, why you were there in the first place, would take me the rest of my natural life."

He let her go, walked away, and hit the elevator button. Lamb followed him into the elevator. Her face was slowly darkening from red to purple.

"Don't cry," he warned.

"Oh, I'm not gonna cry," she said. "If I lose control of anything right now, it won't be my fucking emotions. It'll be my fist. I want to smack you in the mouth so bad I could scream."

Charlie looked over.

"Nicolas Rojer is going out somewhere at night with a big flashlight and giving kids bottles of Coke laced with pills," Lamb said. "Then he's taking them somewhere and abusing them. That's the truth. You need to believe me. You need to stop treating me like a child. And if you ever call me 'honey' again, I'll do more than just smack you in the mouth."

Charlie said nothing. She turned to him.

"*I deserve to be here!*" she yelled. Her voice made his eardrums pulse.

He said nothing. He couldn't articulate his guilt. His disappointment. Because as he'd stood in Rojer's apartment beside Lamb, watching her finger apply light pressure to the trigger of the gun that was pointed at the suspect's head, he'd played out the shot in his mind and seen the devastation that would follow it. Rojer dead on the couch. Lamb having done that ultimate, irreversible thing, her life changed, the die cast, all because she wanted to be a part of his case. Because she wanted to prove herself. Because she wanted to convince him that she deserved a second chance at being a police officer. And in allowing her to come along with him and follow those hopeless desires, he'd put her in a situation she would never have been in as a rookie officer: a dangerous, close-quarters encounter with a suspect on their own turf, with no plan, no rules, no idea of her own authority, of the expectations of the scene. She might have blown Rojer's head off, or he might have reached into the couch cushions, come out with his own weapon, and gotten her first. Charlie hated himself for not forcing Lamb to go away at Universal Studios. Or at the golf course. Or earlier.

He exited the elevator and rounded the corner, watching his feet on the pavement, feeling miserable, because the truth was he'd had innumerable oppor-tunities to dump Lamb. But he hadn't. Because he liked her determination. He liked her inextinguish-able hope.

"Who's that?" Lamb asked.

Charlie stopped dead. He looked up, followed Lamb's gaze down the driveway of the apartment building to where the Ram was parked in the shade of a big Catalina cherry tree.

There was a man standing by the hood with a phone in his hand. He took a quick tour around the car, dialed a number on the phone, and walked off.

"Death Machines," Charlie said. He hadn't recog-nized the guy, but he was typical of the prospective members Dean and Franko seemed to have an end-less supply of—the kind of cannon fodder they used in wars with other biker gangs or as mules for drug hauls down to Mexico. Young, tattooed, edgy, and world-worn beyond their years.

Charlie backed up, and Lamb followed him. They walked quickly through the apartment complex court-yard, through an archway, across a garden, and into a sprawling parking area. This time, it was Lamb who

was watching her shoes, thinking hard, so it was Charlie who spotted the familiar figure ahead of them,
bobbing as he marched across the dry, cracked dirt of
a vacant lot.

Charlie grabbed Lamb's arm and pointed. "Rojer,"
he said.

Lamb's eyes grew wide.

They forgot about the threat at their backs, Charlie
grinding to a halt, Lamb beside him. They stood and
watched Rojer cross the vacant lot, lift the bottom of
a chain-link fence, and slip underneath. As he disappeared down an embankment toward a construction
site, Charlie heard Lamb's voice rattle in his frantic
mind.

"Did you see?" she asked. "He's got the flashlight.
He's got the flashlight with him!"

They pursued. Through the lot, under the warped
chain-link fence, down the crumbling, rocky embankment, side by side, their breaths rushing before long
as they tried to keep pace with Rojer. The tall, loping
figure walked at speed across a street, down an al-
leyway, through another fence, and into the concrete
foundation of an apartment building under construction. There was grass growing in the gaps in the foundations, vines crawling up the half-erected walls, their
curling fingers shifting in the hot wind. Rojer walked
through a doorway to what Charlie guessed would
have been the fire escape if construction of the building had not halted. Lamb and Charlie crouched by a
pile of rusting sheet metal and waited, giving Rojer
a head start down the stairs. Then they set off again,
Charlie in the lead, his gun out, taking the stairs two
at a time as silently as he could. At the bottom of the
stairwell, he followed Rojer's distant flashlight beam,
one hand out touching the concrete wall in the darkness. He paused, slid his phone out, and flicked it to
silent.

"Phone," he said to Lamb. She did the same.

They walked on. Charlie stifled a yowl when his boot hit a stair in the darkness, causing him to trip forward, his shin scraping against a sharp metal edge.

He growled in pain.

"The step, right?" Lamb whispered.

"Shut up, Lamb," Charlie huffed.

Fifty feet down the hall in the darkness, his shin throbbing, Charlie heard rustling, saw the bouncing, bobbing flashlight he'd been following had turned into a thin vertical slit. A door almost completely shut, but not fully latched. Charlie reached back, pushed Lamb against the wall. From within the room, Rojer's voice came, hard and breathless.

"Come on. Get up. Get up. Get up. You've got to get out. Get out now."

Charlie kicked open the door. It flew back and smacked into Rojer, knocking him sideways. A tiny room was revealed, barely bigger than a storeroom, three feet of space between the door and the edge of a fold-out cot. Charlie caught a glimpse of a dark-haired teenage girl rising drunkenly from beneath a twisted sheet, holding her hand up against the dim light of the flashlight that had clattered to the floor.

"What . . . what . . . what's happening?"

Rojer scrambled into the corner of the small room, trying to find his footing, his hands making black spidery silhouettes as he grabbed for the flashlight. Charlie kicked out in the dark, knocked Rojer down again, stomped and stomped until he heard cries of surrender.

He picked up the flashlight and turned around. Lamb was gathering up the girl, ushering her through the door.

CHAPTER 13

The squad car carrying Jonie Delaney drove through the checkpoint, into the Hertzberg-Davis parking lot, and straight up to the main tent. By now, Saskia had managed to find a couple of officers to erect a tarp over the side of the tent to shield the internal operations from view of the press gang. This had caused a reshuffle of cameramen and journalists on the hill, and shouts of protest, which Saskia ignored. She waited in the weird blue light of the tent as Jonie exited the car, escorted by a teenage boy.

Whatever Saskia had expected, the girl before her was not it. The seventeen-year-old was dressed in jeans and a T-shirt, and was dry-eyed and straight-backed, not hunched and shivering the way Saskia imagined another child in her position might be. Though her face was puffy, obviously from crying, she came forward and shook Saskia's and then Curler's hands. Her voice was low and clear.

"I'm Jonie." She glanced awkwardly at the boy beside her, a brown-skinned hunk with high cheekbones and big, footballer's hands. "This is my boyfriend, Tanner Court."

"I'm Ronnie Curler," the negotiator said as Saskia waved away the patrol cops who had delivered the teens. "And this is Saskia Ferboden. We're working on getting your parents and the people they have with them out of the lab safely. We really appreciate you coming in. I bet you're feeling completely numb right now."

Jonie nodded. "It's, like, I can't . . . I just can't believe this is happening. This can't be real."

"It's real," Saskia said. "But we're going to help you through it. We're going to tell you exactly what to do. You're not alone."

The word seemed to jolt the teenager. *Alone*. Her eyes, which had been focused on the distant building, likely on the six now-infamous gray windows of lab 21, shifted and refocused on Saskia.

"That's exactly what I am, though," the girl said. "I'm alone. First Tilly. Now Mom and Dad. They're saying they're going to blow the place up. That'll mean it'll just be me. Just me left."

"Don't talk like that, babe." Tanner wrapped a big arm around the girl's shoulders and shot Saskia a dark look. "You have to stay positive."

The girl gazed up at him, bewildered. She seemed to give a small nod.

"Let's refocus." Curler put his hands up. "The future, we can't control. The past, we can't control. Let's focus on what we *can* control. These moments right here, right now. We're all going to take a deep breath, let it out slowly, and do what's within our power."

The girl inhaled hard. For a moment, Saskia thought Jonie was going to let out a scream. She went stiff, her jaw locked tightly, the tendons in her neck straining. Then her eyes went to Saskia's, dropped, and flicked back up, examining all of her in one devastatingly quick appraisal.

"You," the girl said, pointing at Saskia's chest. "Can I just talk to you?"

"Ah—of course," Saskia said. "Let's go and sit in one of these tactical vehicles. We can have a little time off from everybody."

Saskia looked at Curler, who nodded back, taking up the notebook in which he had been drafting the script for Jonie to read. She led the girl to one of the BearCats and waved at a patrol officer on her way, making a gesture for coffee. The boyfriend, Tanner, turned in a little circle, looking completely out of place. Having probably decided that he was the last of anyone's priorities, he sank eventually into a fold-out chair.

Chief Ferboden helped the girl up into the huge tactical vehicle and took the bench seat across from her, so that they were knee to knee. The door clunked heavily closed behind them, sealing them in dimness. In what light the distant windshield provided, Saskia could see there were semiautomatics lining the walls, emergency rescue gear, headsets, gloves, and bullet-proof vests stored on narrow racks. The BearCat's interior smelled of gun oil and sweat.

Jonie Delaney sat for a moment with her head clasped in her hands, her fingers spread, her choco-laty curls showing between the digits. The same curls as Tilly's, short and spilling down like soft springs. Saskia waited to hear the girl sobbing. But no tears came. In time, the teenager raised her head and looked at Saskia, her eyes hard and determined.

"I have to tell you the truth." Jonie shrugged sharply. "I don't have any choice now. The only way Mom and Dad are going to stop all this is if they know the truth."

"What truth is that?" Saskia asked.

"I killed her," Jonie said. "I killed Tilly."

Saskia felt the hairs on the back of her neck stand on end. She glanced at the closed door of the BearCat beside them, thought about the officers outside rush-ing busily about. Then she thought about her phone in her pocket, its recording capability, her obligations now to launch straight into giving Jonie Delaney her *Miranda* warning. But what came instead was a plea to a child who had endured so much suffering already, who sat before her, completely at her mercy, waiting with her hands clasped in front of her like she was already cuffed.

"You don't mean that," Saskia said carefully. "You mean that you were responsible for Tilly's care that day and you feel as if you neglected her, and that caused her to be killed."

"No," Jonie said. "I mean that I murdered her. I got angry at her, and I killed her, and I hid her body. And the only way you're going to get my mom and dad out of the lab is if you tell them that."

Lamb looked at her watch. At any moment, according to their plan, the Delaneys were going to destroy another piece of evidence in the Hertzberg-Davis lab, approximately twenty-five miles southwest of where she sat on a low concrete wall at the abandoned construction site. Charlie Hoskins sat beside her, examining the graze on his shin and the spot where the sharp metal edge of the stair had cut right through the leg of his jeans. The two had been swept aside while LAPD responded to the scene in the underground parking lot. Charlie had called, and the officers had swooped in with aggressive shoving, barking commands. They'd taken custody of Rojer and rushed the nameless teenage girl into a squad car, then into an ambulance. Establishing Charlie's identity had taken some time. He had stories about being a two-stripe detective, but without a badge, that had gotten him nowhere. He and Lamb had been relegated to the concrete wall, where they had waited in the sunshine, watching the activity, each lost in their own thoughts.

Eventually, a detective who had taken charge of the scene approached them, and Charlie rose to shake his hand. Lamb rose, too, and stood beside him.

"Hoskins, is it?"

"Yeah."

"I've heard about you." The stocky, mustachioed detective stood back a little and appreciated Charlie, head cocked, curious. "You were on the Machines thing."

"That was me, yeah," Charlie said.

"Somebody said they thought you were in Bali."

"That was the story, yeah." Charlie glanced at Lamb. "My partner, Lamb."

Lamb felt a zing of exhilaration rush up her spine. She shook the detective's hand hard and fast.

"Joe Bailey, missing persons."

"Who's the girl?" Lamb asked.

"Angela Lu," Bailey said. "Fourteen. Went missing yesterday morning. I was dreading the outcome of this one. We had another high schooler vanish maybe a month ago. She was gone for seventy-two hours. Same MO. The kid skipped school to go hang out at the mall, was seen being approached in the street by a tall guy with longish hair. She was dumped in a park after he was done with her. No memory of what happened to her or where she'd been kept."

Charlie nodded. "So you'll run the rape kit from that one against Rojer? Confirm a link between the two."

"Sure will. Just as soon as the lab opens back up." Bailey cocked his head again, examining Charlie in that curious way. "We might be able to tag him with a couple of other near misses in the area."

"You didn't think to check him out previously?" Lamb asked.

Bailey turned to her now, skeptical. "He lives just outside the range we were initially looking at." He looked her up and down slowly, curiously. "We would have got to him. In time."

Lamb nodded.

"Funny thing about that," Bailey said. "Some of the guys are saying they know about Rojer. That he was in the mix on the Delaney case. And now, lo and behold! Here you two are. Questioning Rojer. Without notice to our investigators *and* outside your jurisdiction, *and* on the same day the Delaney parents take over the Hertzberg-Davis lab."

Charlie exhaled wearily through his nose, patted his pockets for cigarettes, and found none. "What can I say, Detective?" he asked.

"Well, you can say what you were questioning Rojer about."

"It's a need-to-know kind of thing at the moment," Charlie said.

"But is it about the Delaney case?" Bailey pressed.

"It's not our story to tell," Lamb cut in. She felt Charlie watching her. "Whether we were questioning Rojer on the Delaney thing or a completely unrelated matter, it wouldn't be strategic for us to disclose that right now. We have no comment to offer."

Bailey grinned, turned back to Charlie. "These young cops. They're all trained for television, aren't they?"

Charlie didn't answer.

"Just cut the bullshit," Bailey said to Lamb. "Is the Delaney case being reopened or not? Are we really second-guessing the work of our own officers because a couple of whack-jobs decided to go vigilante on us?"

"Asked and answered, Detective," Charlie said. He tapped Lamb's elbow and turned away. "Let's go, Lamb."

They walked, the silent agreement lingering between them that they would hail a cab a couple of streets away from the scene at the construction site. Lamb noticed Charlie clicking and flicking the fingers of one hand, his eyes locked on the pavement. They passed a homeless encampment cramped with tents, tarps, and makeshift plywood dwellings. Lamb breathed air heavy with the smell of human waste and alcohol, walking behind Charlie for a hundred yards before coming level with him again.

"Shouldn't we stay with the scene?" She jerked a thumb back toward the construction site. "Aren't they going to need us for the report?"

"We're not staying with any scenes today, Lamb. Ten years on the job, you get to make decisions like that. It's one of the perks. If they want details on how we snatched up Rojer, they can call us later. Jesus, I need cigarettes."

"What was all that about Bali?" Lamb asked.

Charlie stopped at a tiny bodega, ordered a pack of cigarettes, and raked the plastic wrap off the box as if he were unwrapping an EpiPen to save someone's life. "We needed the world to think I wasn't here. Saskia and I. Before I could go undercover. We needed cops *and* criminals to believe it, because they talk to each other. So I faked having a drug problem. I did a couple of lines in the station bathroom in front of the right people. Lost my shit at the lieutenant in the bullpen one day, in front of everyone. That kind of thing. Then we spread it around that I'd dropped off the radar. Quit and moved to Bali."

He lit the cigarette and inhaled deeply, eased smoke through his nostrils into the breeze.

"Why did you go undercover?" she asked.

He shrugged. "Why does anybody do anything?"

"That's not an answer."

"I need to make some calls." Charlie started walking again. "Someone needs to dig up the flower bed at Rojer's mother's place. See if Tilly Delaney is there."

"If you want my opinion," Lamb ventured, "I don't see it."

"You don't?"

"No."

"You just stuck a gun in the guy's face." Charlie laughed.

"I knew he was good for something," Lamb said. "But Tilly? No. I don't think so."

"Why not?"

"His previous victim," Lamb said. "The one he was jailed for luring into the disabled toilet? Case file says she was twelve. Then there are these two: Angela Lu and the other girl, the high schooler. They're in their teens. While the MO was similar—grabbing or luring a girl away in a public place—Tilly Delaney was five. That's a big age leap. The stats show child sex offenders don't tend to wander outside their desired age group."

"I love that. 'The stats.'" Charlie smiled. "I can see you lying awake at night in your bunk at the academy, reading research papers on pedophiles while all the other cadets are at the bar. Were you popular at the academy, Lamb?"

"I've never been popular," she said.

"Incredible."

"As I was saying." She gave him a side-eye that made him drop the smile. "If Rojer's killed before, it also makes it unlikely he would be keeping these girls captive and then releasing them. I mean, he's already gone that far. His fantasies and practices have escalated to murder. We know from the stat—ah. It's just not likely someone who kills during a sex act is going to suddenly back off and let his next victims survive."

"That theory is sound if Angela Lu and the other girl who went missing are the only markers we're working with," Charlie said. "There might be others, dead girls who we don't know about. Girls who bridge the gap between five years old and twelve."

"True," Lamb said. "True."

They walked in silence.

"So what do we do now?" she said eventually. "Until someone interrogates Rojer and digs up the garden bed, we're at a loose end with him."

"We just press on." Charlie was reading a message from his phone screen. He stepped out into the street to hail a cab. "We're heading Surge's way now. He's got something for us."

They slipped into the cab. It smelled of feet. Lamb restrained herself for a couple of miles of heat-shimmering landscape before she snapped.

"So is this the part where you apologize for what happened back there?" she asked finally.

"What?" Charlie looked over, broke into that husky laugh that made her teeth want to clamp together. "No, Lamb. It's not."

"I was right about Rojer," she said. "I was right about the pills. I was right about the Coke bottles. I was right about the flashlight. I was right about the step."

"You were lucky."

"*Angela Lu* was lucky," Lamb said. "Rojer's next victim was lucky. Me? I wasn't lucky, I was right."

"No, you were lucky," Charlie said, rolling down his window and leaning his tattooed elbow on the sill. "You put a bunch of bullshit, meaningless, insignificant little details together and deduced that a guy with a history of being up to no good was once again up to no good. And, okay. Sometimes, very rarely— I'm talking *never*—that kind of Sherlock Holmes shit actually works. Every other time, the guy's walking stick isn't dented because he owns a curly-haired spaniel. It's just dented because it's dented."

"You've read Sherlock Holmes?" Lamb asked.

"I was in prison for nine months. There was reading and jerking off and playing basketball. And I'm all thumbs on the court."

"Why the hell were you in prison?"

"It was the only way I could get in with the Machines," he said. He drummed his fingertips on the windowsill. "They cooked up a new identity for me and chucked me in a cell next to Franko Aderhold's. He was one of the top three major players in the club."

"So, what? You made friends with him and he just let you into the gang?"

"No." Charlie laughed again. "No, Lamb. I waited four months for an opportunity to prove my worth naturally. The last thing you want to do is walk up to one of these guys and announce that you'd like to be friends."

"How'd you do it, then?"

"Around my fourth month in, I got sick. I was in my cell sleeping it off, and I heard someone go into Franko's cell next door. Someone who wasn't Franko," Charlie said. "The guy's name was Matsukas. He was known for faking illnesses and staying back on the block while everyone else went to the yard so he could steal people's shit. I got up and dragged his ass out of Franko's cell, made him eat concrete. Franko appreciated the save."

"So from there you were buddies?"

"Not really," Charlie said. "Franko just said thanks, and that was it for another two months."

"Six months!" Lamb shook her head. "Six months undercover in prison, and that's before you're even in the gang!"

"You've got to have a lot of patience for this gig," Charlie said. "Part of the reason you're not right for it."

Lamb ignored the gibe. "So what happened?"

"I asked if I could use one of his cell phones. He'd have a cell phone smuggled in every now and then. I'd hear him using it at night. I knew Franko always made people use the phone right there in his cell, in front of him. So I made out like I was talking to a guy about moving a big load of heroin. That piqued his interest."

"So you got to be a prospect from there, right?" she asked. "That's how it works?"

"Look, it works like that sometimes," Charlie said. "If you have nothing to offer, you just come in off the street, and you want to be a gang member, then yeah. You're a prospect. You wash bikes and eat shit until you can prove you're worth something. But I was proving my worth pretty fast with this big heroin deal. They were coming to me to be a member. I wasn't going to them."

"But I don't get it," Lamb said. "The heroin deal. That's a crime. That's entrapment. You couldn't bust them for that."

"And I didn't."

"So you committed crimes while you were undercover." She looked over at him, her eyes big. "Actual crimes."

Charlie smiled. "Lamb, the *books* say that if you have to commit a crime to save your life while you're undercover, you do it. And that's the only time you do it. So if those guys sit you down and tell you to do a line of coke, and you honestly believe they're going to kill you if you don't, you're allowed. But from there, you're supposed to extract yourself from the threatening environment, go directly to a hospital, and alert your superior officer. After that, the whole operation gets shut down."

"Oh," Lamb said.

"How long do you think an undercover operation would last if anybody followed those kinds of rules?" Charlie watched the city roll by.

"About ten minutes."

"Exactly," Charlie said. "Those first few weeks out on the street running with the crew are all about proving you're not a cop. They want to see you doing drugs, doing beatings, doing stickups, doing their women. They'll get whatever they can on camera, too, so if they ever have to face you in court, they can say you spent half your time undercover high as a kite and buried in pussy. You didn't know your head from your ass, let alone what crimes were being committed."

There was a quiet in the cab while Lamb thought of the kind of life he must have lived for those five years, the things he must have done. The truth was, she'd been noticing that life written on his skin from the moment she met him, not just in the tattoos but in scars and burn marks and signs of bones broken and treated by dodgy doctors. Homemade stitches, crooked and wide. Charlie had come in from the cold, and it was clear he'd been more than just freezing out there, all alone, undercover with the Death Machines. He'd been dying and a new man had been growing inside him, and now the old Charlie, whoever he was, was in a silent struggle to kill that hidden man while he sat in the car beside her.

She watched his face, his distant eyes. "Sounds crazy," she said.

"You'd hate it."

"Why?" she asked, her hackles quickly rising.

"Because undercover work not only requires patience, it's about emotional control, too. And lying. Those big, earnest eyes of yours would give you away in a snap. And you've got to have subtlety. And you're about as subtle as a brick to the face, Lamb. Or a gun to the face, as you demonstrated back in Rojer's apartment."

"I'm not saying I'd be interested in doing it. And even if I were, I wouldn't be talking about doing it tomorrow," Lamb said. "I'm talking about one day. Down the track. After I have some experience working the streets as a police officer."

Charlie gave a resigned sigh, began a nod that morphed quickly into a headshake. Lamb ignored him.

"You're going to have to be as subtle as you can in a minute. When we get where we're going." Charlie glanced at his phone.

"Why?"

"Because you're not going to like who we're about to meet."

"Who are we about to meet?" Lamb asked.

"Turn here," Charlie told the driver.

CHAPTER 14

Saskia put her hands on the knees of her trousers, dropped her eyes to the steel-grille floor of the BearCat, and drew a deep breath. Visions were swirling before her of Tilly Delaney dead on the floor of a damp, dimly lit public restroom while other children frolicked on the sand only a hundred yards away. While cars pulled in and out of the parking lot, and people jogged on sunbaked paths, and the occasional cheerful dinging of bells on hired bicycles split the air, and the tumble of the roller coaster up on the pier competed with the crunching waves. Jonie Delaney was holding her face in her hands. But she wasn't crying. She wasn't talking. She was just sitting there, breathing slowly, her eyes closed.

Saskia took her phone out of her pocket, turned the sound down, called Curler, locked the screen, and slipped the device back into her pocket. She quietly recited the *Miranda* warning to Jonie Delaney. The teenager didn't move.

"Listen," Saskia said. "Any minute now, Jonie, your parents are due to call us. They're probably not going to like what we have to say. And they're going to destroy another piece of police evidence as a reaction to that. My tactical officers are going to use these moments while we converse with your parents to sneak

into the ground floor of the Hertzberg-Davis building and access the PA system. We're going to use that
PA system to send a message from you to your parents . . ." Saskia's words trailed off. She grasped at
what to say for a moment or two, watching the top of
the teen's curly crown helplessly. "That message can't
be 'I killed Tilly' if it's not the truth."

"It is the truth," Jonie said, her face still hidden.

"Tell me what happened," Saskia said.

Jonie dropped her hands to her lap. She stared at
them as she went from finger to finger, scratching at the
pale pink nail polish with a thumbnail so that it flaked
off onto the grille at her feet.

"She was an annoying little shit," Jonie said.

Saskia felt her eyes widen.

"That was the only way I could think of her." Jonie
looked at the door of the BearCat, tears finally forming in her eyes. "She was Mom and Dad's 'whoopsie'
baby. Mom told me she was pregnant with Tilly when
I was nine. She and Dad were all, like, 'Whoops! I
guess you've got a sister on the way!' They were
laughing with their friends about it, about how they
were going to have to go all the way back to square
one and lose sleep and take time off work and do
the breastfeeding thing and all that." Jonie shook her
head. "It was a big joke. Like, *Oh, man, are your tits
gonna be up for it after all this time? Ha ha!* Their
friends were all saying how annoying it must be that
they'd gotten rid of all my baby stuff. The crib and the
clothes. It was real funny to everyone."

"But not to you," Saskia said.

"Not to me," Jonie confirmed. "The biggest laugh
of all seemed to be that this time around they had a
free babysitter in the house twenty-four-seven. They'd
go for naps during the day on weekends and I'd be
stuck looking after a fucking baby instead of being out
with my friends. I missed sleepovers. I missed parties. I
missed camps. Sometimes they would get me to sleep

in Tilly's room with her if they had something important going on at work, so they could both catch a full night's sleep. I just . . . I've just always thought of her as an annoying little shit, and no matter how much people tell me how cute she was or how funny she was, I never saw it."

"So that's how it was that day?" Saskia said. "You were the babysitter again? Stuck with someone else's annoying little shit?"

"They were arguing about something. And it was like, 'Jeeves, take the child to the beach, will you? We have some things to hash out here.'" Jonie waved a regal hand, her mouth downturned, snooty.

"You felt like you were the help."

"I *was* the help."

"And during this trip to the beach, it all just came to a head?" Saskia asked. "All the times you'd been saddled with the baby?"

"Yeah," Jonie breathed.

"How?"

"Tanner was out there," Jonie said. "Everybody was out there, out the back, on longboards. Not surfing. Just talking. He wasn't someone who ever, like, hung out with our crew. You know? He was from the popular crowd. But he'd shown up to catch some waves alone, and for some reason, he'd come over. And I could see them all talking and laughing, and my friend Michelle was . . . She was putting it on him *so* hard. Like that would work. Like she had a chance."

Jonie laughed and shook her head.

"I kept trying to convince Tilly to go out there with me, but she was afraid of sharks," she continued. "Mom and Dad were watching *Jaws* one night, and she crept up the hall and watched for a while from the doorway without them realizing she was there. Traumatized." Jonie rapped on her skull with her knuckles. "Just traumatized. She didn't sleep for a week and a half."

"So what did you do?" Saskia asked. "When Tilly wouldn't go out back at the beach?"

"I couldn't stay there and watch Michelle Clayton fake-laughing over Tanner anymore." Jonie shook her head. "I dragged Tilly up the beach. She was like a wet fucking rat. Crying and squealing. Her hair was plastered all over her face because she'd just gotten rumbled by a wave."

"So she was still in her swimsuit?" Saskia asked. "And you were carrying the bag?"

"Yeah."

"And she'd just been hammered by a wave, had she?" Saskia said. "So she was wet and upset."

"See, she didn't want to be in the ankle-deep water with the actual babies, but she didn't want to be out the back, either," Jonie huffed. "She wanted to hang around in the white wash. Which was so stupid, because if I didn't lift her up over the waves, she'd get dumped. And by lifting her up over the waves all the time, *I* kept getting dumped. Neither of us were having fun. A big wave smashed her good, and she came up screaming. I was like: *That's it. That's fucking it!*"

Jonie swept a hand sharply, slashing the air.

"Before we could catch the bus home, I went to the toilets near the parking lot. I had my period, and I wanted to, you know." Jonie waved again. "I was in there for a while. My tampons were right down at the bottom of the bag and I couldn't find them, and then I thought, *Oh, man, I haven't brought any.* Blah-blah-blah. Tilly was wailing that she wanted to go back to the water, and I was threatening her that if she walked off without me, I was gonna lose my mind. She knew she had a moment to do it. I was stuck in the stall with my pants around my ankles and the bag emptied out on the floor."

"And she did do it?" Saskia asked.

"She tried to," Jonie said. "That's when I snapped."

Saskia watched the teen's eyes. They were locked

on her fingernails. On the paint flaking and chipping away, landing like little pink stars on the universe of her jeans.

"What happened?"

Jonie shrugged. "I bashed her head on the sink."

Saskia waited.

Nothing more came.

"And she lost consciousness?"

"She just sort of died." Jonie had almost cleaned off all her nails. She brushed the chips off her jeans, her eyebrows high but her eyes still downcast. "It was fast."

"What did you do with the body?" Saskia asked.

"I put it in a dumpster at the side of the parking lot," Jonie said. "Then I made like I couldn't find her. Walked up and down the beach calling her name."

Saskia realized she had been holding her breath. She let it out slowly, glanced at her watch. The interior of the BearCat was hot. She plucked at the collar of her shirt, thinking there would be sweat gathering there, but her skin was dry. She realized the heat was internal. A strange physical discomfort, almost fever-like, radiating from within her.

"You never told your parents what happened?" Saskia asked.

"No?" Jonie shook her head like it was obvious. "I didn't want to go to jail?"

"You think they would have told the police?"

"They would have had to," Jonie said. "They've been up the police's ass about this from day one. Calling. Going into the police station. Following the officers to their cars, yelling at them, making threats to go to the press. They've emailed senators and gone on radio programs and . . ." She threw her hands up.

"They've been unstoppable."

"They hired a private investigator guy." She rubbed her nose. "That was the scariest time. He was all over me. He searched my room while I was out. My computer. My phone. But he was only really interested in the case for a couple of weeks. He was hanging in there, making a show of it until my parents paid him the deposit and the progress payment, two-thirds of what he'd quoted for the whole job. Then he disappeared. Ghosted them."

They fell quiet. Saskia thought about the private investigators she'd dealt with in the past. Wannabe cops and failed cops, predators offering victims' family members access to the underworld of crime where the truth was supposedly denied to cops with uniforms and badges. They made their day-to-day money catching bail jumpers and insurance cheats, and waited for those big whales, like the Delaneys, who would front them tens of thousands of dollars to do a job they didn't have the skills for. Then they'd close shop, lie low for a while, and pop up again two cities over to do it all again.

"Go back for me," Saskia said to Jonie. "You said when you hit Tilly, she 'just sort of died.'"

"Yeah."

"What did you mean by that?"

"I mean, like, you know." Jonie wiped her cheeks with both hands, leaving little pink freckles of nail polish on her high cheekbones. "It didn't take very long."

"Describe it for me," Saskia said. "Did she just slump to the floor? Did she bleed? What part of her head did she hit on the sink? Was it the temple? Was it the back?"

"Dude!" Jonie's mouth was twisted. "Do we have to talk about all that?"

"The dumpster, then," Saskia said. "You said it was on the edge of the parking lot?"

"Yeah," Jonie said.

"What edge? The front edge? Nearest to the street? The back edge, facing the water? Or on the side?"

"I don't know."

"How close was it to the door of the restroom?"

"I don't *know,* ma'am! I've blocked it out!"

The door of the BearCat suddenly opened beside them. Curler was standing there.

"We can't wait any longer," Curler said.

Saskia waved over a patrol officer to take care of Jonie. The chief and the negotiator walked back to the main tent, both with their cell phones in their hands.

"Did you listen in?"

"Yeah," Curler said. "We'll deal with that in a minute. Right now, we've got bigger problems."

Saskia heard a dull ringing. The laptop on the fold-out table beside them began to peal. The technician sitting in front of it pulled on her headset, and Curler and Saskia turned to face the Delaneys.

From his position on the floor, Bendigo could see the two vials in Ryan Delaney's fingers. He could barely make out the numbers scrolling back and forth as the hostage-taker rolled the plastic tubes with his thumbs like a man with two cigars, waiting for the call to the police to connect. Ibrahim nudged Bendigo's elbow, and the scientist looked over.

"Man, can we switch places?" Ibrahim said, a little too loudly. He glanced at Elsie Delaney, who was sitting on the stool nearest to him. "My head hurts. I think I need a little lie-down, myself."

Bendigo nodded and shuffled forward, allowing Ibrahim to take his place. He scooted on his butt to where the younger man had been sitting, Ashlea placing her head on his thigh without so much as a glance to query his consent. The journalist was still crying quietly, now and then scooping at the rim of her lower lashes in that strange way women did to preserve their makeup. Bendigo chanced a brief swipe of his own fingers under the surface of the table against which he leaned, brushing the cold steel handle of the scissors Ibrahim had hidden there.

The call with the police connected. Elsie and Ryan

Delaney straightened on their stools. Bendigo knew this was his chance. He shuffled backward, his back flush against the cabinet, brushing the scissors again. After some effort, he managed to hook a finger around them and bring them into his fist. For a moment, he simply held them, imagining himself folding them open at that very moment, cutting the cable tie around his wrists, throwing Ashlea off, leaping forward, and stabbing the Delaneys to death.

He knew that his cold, clear vision of himself ending the Delaneys' lives was nothing more than fiction. That in reality there would be a vicious struggle, and the younger, stronger couple would probably overpower him before he could land any fatal blows. He knew that it wasn't as easy to stab a person as he or most people dreamed, the scissor blades cutting through the flesh smoothly and soundlessly as though through butter. There were bones to consider. Rubbery tendons. The placement of organs and the elasticity of the skin's surface. It would take a hard blow, probably all his strength, to force the scissors through the fabric of Elsie Delaney's shirt, through her flesh, between her bones, into her heart. And then there was the biggest consideration of all: whether Dr. Gary Bendigo felt he was really capable of killing a man. Or a woman. Even in defense of others. Even in defense of himself. But before all those rational thoughts came, he simply sat for a moment, holding the scissors, feeling a hateful triumph at his having secured some foothold of power in a situation that had, until then, completely dissolved every ounce of his free will.

"Ryan? Elsie? Are you there?"

It was the woman. Bendigo had heard the Delaneys talking about her. Saskia Ferboden, chief of the LAPD.

"We're here," Ryan said.

"What have you done in the past two hours to find our daughter?" Elsie demanded.

The voice that answered wasn't Ferboden's. "We've been very busy for the past couple of hours," a man said. The negotiator, Curler. "Our focus has been on making sure the loved ones of Ashlea, Ibrahim, and Gary are aware of the situation and reassured that their family members are safe. It's our understanding that Ashlea may need to get access to some medications soon or she will become dangerously unwell. So we'd like to discuss the possibility of Ashlea, or ideally all the hostages, being allowed to come out safely."

Ashlea sat up. Bendigo saw that her tears had left a heart-shaped spot of dampness on his trouser leg. With her hands bound in front of her, the young journalist swiped nervously at her cheeks.

"That's . . . that's true," she said. "If I don't get my meds, I—"

"Bullshit." Ryan shook his head. "Come on. *Come on,* you stupid fucks. We've made it clear from the outset we're not gonna play these games. We want one thing, and one thing only. That's for you to find Tilly. If you're not going to do that, we have no choice but to keep destroying evidence. And when we run out of evidence, we're going to have to get real creative up in this motherfucker. Do you understand what we're saying?"

"We're trying to decide between two samples," Elsie said.

Bendigo saw that her hands were trembling as she took the vials from Ryan.

"One of them is related to the murder of two police officers in Encino. The other is from a missing persons case." She held up the vial to the light, examined the cotton swab inside it. "A twenty-year-old woman named Mariana Navarro."

"Which one should we burn?" Ryan asked. He

stroked his short beard, the mock philosopher. "I kind of feel like punishing the police. Don't you, El? I mean, maybe we need them to understand how it feels to lose one of their own and to have *no power, no ability* to do anything about it."

"Don't do anything," Ferboden said. "Just talk to us, Ryan. Elsie. Please, before you do anything at all. There are options we are willing to offer you."

"Like what?" Elsie asked.

"Like an endgame scenario for all this that allows you to see your other daughter," Curler said.

Bendigo watched the Delaneys' faces harden. They glanced at each other.

"Look, guys, we *are* heading for an end to all this. Okay?" Curler continued. "Some way or another, you're going to come out of there. And Jonie is going to be out here, waiting for you."

The couple were silent. Bendigo felt a shimmer of hope in his heart.

"How is she?" Elsie asked suddenly. Ryan reached over and gripped her knee gently.

"She's devastated, of course," Curler said. "She's worried about the future. And we want to talk about that future. Ryan, Elsie, we're prepared to cut a deal, right now, to ensure one of you can have a normal, noncustodial relationship with Jonie in the years to come. If we can get Ashlea, Ibrahim, and Gary out of there safely today, I can see that being a possibility."

"'Noncustodial'?" Ryan smiled icily. "You mean, 'outside prison'? Why don't you just say it? Say the word *prison*."

There was silence from the laptop.

"You guys have got it all worked out, huh?" Ryan continued. "This is the divide-and-conquer strategy. We send out Elsie and a couple of the hostages, and we feed the press and the lawyers and the jury and the judge a story about how I made her come here today and do all this. We'll say she only did it because she felt her life was threatened. Elsie gets a ten-year sentence, she's out in seven with good behavior, and then she's free and she gets to see Jonie again. That's the offer, right?"

"Ryan," Ferboden said.

"Sounds nice, huh, El?" Ryan asked. "You want to take it?"

"I'm not interested," Elsie said. "I want our daughter found. We didn't come here to cut deals. We came here to make you find our child."

"What have you done in the past two hours to find Tilly?" Ryan asked again. "Because if your answer is 'nothing,' and it keeps being 'nothing' for long enough, the only way anybody will be leaving this building is in a body bag."

He looked at Bendigo. The scientist felt a sparkle of fury in his chest. He gripped the pair of scissors at the small of his back tightly.

"Have you done anything at all to find—" Elsie began. But a sound interrupted her, a short, sharp crack from overhead. Bendigo looked up, Ashlea, Ibrahim, Elsie, and Ryan all doing the same. The crack rang in Bendigo's ears, but no further sound came.

"What the fuck was that?" Elsie asked.

"I don't know," Ryan said.

Their gazes drifted back to the laptop screen.

"I think it's clear that we have to do this," Ryan said. He pointed at the vials in Elsie's hands. "Pick one, El."

There was a taut silence. Ryan lit the Bunsen burner. Elsie shifted the two vials to one hand and seemed ready to take the cap off one of them, selecting and then pinching the top between her thumb and index finger. Then Ferboden's voice burst forth from the laptop, high and desperate.

"Mariana Navarro was just a girl," she pleaded. "She was twenty. A kid. Not much older than Jonie."

Bendigo heard some muffled noises on the other

end of the call. Elsie and Ryan looked at each other. Then Elsie uncapped the other vial and took the swab from it. Bendigo and his fellow hostages watched the cotton tip burn. He used the distraction to shift up onto his knees and slide the pair of scissors into the waistband of his trousers.

"All we can hope," Elsie said, "is that the families of the Encino police officers forgive you."

"Bring our daughter home before we have to do this again," Ryan added.

He slammed the laptop lid closed.

CHAPTER 15

MINA: You there?

DORREE: Yeah.

MINA: I don't know what happened. It just dropped out. Anyway, so yeah, about fifty people? Sixty people? Not bad for a Thursday night. It was jumpin'. Wall-to-wall partiers. My ears are still ringing. And then about 2:00 a.m., there was last call and they were all set to start closing down when who walks in? *The Weeknd,* and his entourage, and about fifty more people. The place went *off.*

DORREE: I don't even know who that is.

MINA: Of course you don't.

DORREE: I don't even think *you* should know who that is. No one who's over thirty should know who that is.

MINA: Well, I do, and I met the guy, and it was great. He bought drinks for everyone. The whole bar.

DORREE: I bet the bartenders loved that.

MINA: Yeah, they were pissed. But the tips were good.

DORREE: I tended bar in college. It was not a glamorous job.

MINA: I know, Dor. I was there.

DORREE: What time did you get in?

MINA: I don't know. About four?

DORREE: Jesus, Minnie, when are you gonna get a real job and stop crawling into bed at 4:00 a.m.? That's not right. It's bad for your biorhythms.

MINA: You sound like Mom.

DORREE: Case in point, I'm listening to you cooking your breakfast at goddamn midday. You're not supposed to have eggs this late. Keep doing that and you'll get anal polyps.

MINA: I was wondering how long it was going to take for you to bring my anus into the conversation.

DORREE: Four years in food medicine and I can't tell you anything about anything.

MINA: Anyway, now you can listen to the TV, too, because I want to keep up with this hostage thing.

DORREE: Oh god, isn't it awful?

MINA: Are they gonna go in or what? Why don't they just go in?

DORREE: They must have a bomb in there or something.

MINA: Jesus.

DORREE: I read on Twitter about them having *another* daughter. Like, what is *she* doing right now?

MINA: Freaking the fuck out.

DORREE: That poor kid. She loses her sister and now th—

MINA: *Oh my god!*

DORREE: What? What?

MINA: That's . . . *that's him!*

DORREE: Who?

MINA: The . . . the . . . the—

DORREE: *Who?*

MINA: The guy! The guy I pulled out of the
water!

DORREE: What?

MINA: Put it on. Channel 6. Channel 6.

DORREE: Okay, okay!

MINA: Jesus Christ, that was him! I'm telling
you! It was him!

DORREE: Which one, Mina, for god's sake?

MINA: Wait until they show the footage again.
Just wait. Just wait. Urgh, come on. There.
There! Black T-shirt. Jeans. Talking to the big,
important-looking police lady with the stripy
sleeves.

DORREE: That's him?

MINA: I swear to god.

DORREE: You told me the guy you rescued
had long hair and a beard.

MINA: Well, maybe he . . . I don't know.
Maybe he cut it.

DORREE: Um.

MINA: Look at the tattoos. I've paused it. I'm
going to take a picture. Look, he's got tattoos on his arms.

DORREE: It's not him.

MINA: It's him, Dorree! Fuck! I'm telling you!

DORREE: You told me you found out the
guy was a biker or, like, a gang member or
something.

MINA: Well, yes. But—

DORREE: So what's he doing in the middle of
all those police people?

MINA: I don't . . . I don't know.

"What the fuck was that?" Curler's eyes were wild.

Saskia straightened, felt light-headed. She needed
water, coffee, food—to sit and think. The consequences
of what she had just done tried to push into her mind,
to plead with her to begin damage control. But there

was no time. The burning of the second sample had sent a ripple of electricity through the scene outside Hertzberg-Davis. There were people coming to the edges of the tent, techs and SWAT members, patrol cops and comms specialists, open-mouthed and stunned or hard-faced and glaring. Recounting of what she had said about Mariana Navarro was taking place in whispers behind hands.

"What was that?" Saskia shrugged. "That was a second unsuccessful negotiation. Let's do something to avoid a third." She slid a laptop toward her, stood over it, watching the playback the technician had been working through. The black-and-white body-cam footage was from the SWAT officer who had crept into the ground floor of the building and hooked up the PA system while the Delaneys were distracted. The cracking sound of static that had split the air in the Hertzberg-Davis building came as he plugged a feeder cord into the PA system. "We have a new communication channel in," Saskia said. "We have to do this right."

"I wasn't talking about the negotiation." Curler was standing too close to her, working his jaw, his molars quietly clacking. "I'm talking about the line you gave the Delaneys about Mariana Navarro. You just pitched for them to destroy one piece of evidence instead of another. They burned the Encino DNA sample over the Navarro one because *you* made a personal appeal!"

"It was a spur-of-the-moment thing." Saskia swallowed hard. "I just . . . I said what I felt."

"With respect, Chief, you shouldn't be saying anything. This is my negotiation."

"I know. I know."

"What if they start shooting the hostages?" Curler asked. "Are you going to let me know now who your favorite is so I have a sense of your preferred running order?"

"Curler."

"If these cops here today weren't pissed at you already—"

"Come with me." Saskia tugged his arm. They slipped between the cars making a barricade along the side of the tent and stood in the shade of a BearCat. Saskia watched as Jonie Delaney and her boyfriend, Tanner, were reunited, hugging, gazing quietly toward the building together. When they were alone between the vehicles, with some semblance of privacy, she spoke to Curler.

"Listen," Saskia said, tugging him closer by his lapel, her voice low. "I know the Mariana Navarro case."

"And?" Curler asked.

"And it belongs to an undercover of mine. Charlie Hoskins. You met him earlier."

"Ah, with the tattoos."

"Yes."

"Delightful chap."

"Hoskins went under with a biker gang five years ago. He was made last week, and the whole thing turned to shit." Saskia watched the teens in the near distance, trying to catch her breath. "We're sure that one of the top three leaders of the gang, a guy named Dean Willis, killed the Navarro girl. Hoss spent *three years* trying to get that sample, okay? He did some fucked-up shit. I couldn't let them burn it."

"And all that makes it okay for you to throw the Encino cops under the bus?" Curler said.

"That case is stronger." Saskia watched his eyes, pleading. "It's a double homicide of two white LAPD officers! For god's sake, you know how this works. They'll still make that case even if they lose the sample. Mariana Navarro was a Hispanic kid from Compton with a father in prison. She witnessed a drive-by out of her bedroom window, and despite everything she'd ever learned from growing up in gangland, she decided to help the police. Charlie Hoskins was the only hope that case ever had. He almost died trying to make it."

Curler licked his teeth, squinted into the sunlight. "They're gonna turn on you." He shook his head. "The whole team. Look at them. Look at their faces."

Saskia didn't look. "I know. I know."

"Saskia," he said suddenly. The insubordination shocked her, but his eyes took her somewhere else. "I like you. Okay?"

She couldn't respond.

"I like you as a person," he went on. "So I really don't want to see this whole thing collapse in on you. Knocking out the SWAT leader with the haymaker from hell was a questionable decision. And now—"

"He made a reference to my assault," Saskia said. Curler waited. It was a story she'd told so few times in her life, she didn't know where to begin telling it. How to capture what had happened in complete and logical sentences, when so much of the event defied words.

"I was twenty-three," Saskia said. "I had an internship at a fashion magazine over on Wilshire. Every morning, my roommate and I would ride into work in my convertible wearing practically nothing. Miniskirts. Tube tops. We'd passed this homeless guy a few times before on the way in, and he'd yelled at us. You know, called us names. We didn't pay much attention. It's Los Angeles."

Curler's eyes searched hers.

"One time, he approached the car," she continued. "I should have seen it as a warning sign. That he was advancing."

"What did he do?"

"He dumped a bucket of sulfuric acid in my lap."

"Jesus fucking Christ." Curler's hands flew to his head. Saskia didn't know what he'd been expecting, but it mustn't have been that. Then he did what every one of the people who knew Saskia's story had done the first time they heard it. His eyes roved over her, searching for signs of burns.

"My damage is all below the waist," Saskia said. "My friend got it worse. It sort of bounced off me and up at her, at her top half." The chief straightened, signaling the end of her little therapy session. "Point is, the guy fled. And if he hadn't dropped the bucket, they might never have caught him. His sample went into CODIS, and he popped up again a year later on the other side of the country."

Curler nodded, his face unreadable. Then he said, "Now *I* feel like punching someone."

"I'm telling you this because I want you to know." Saskia fixed him with her gaze. "I would love, *love,* to tell the Delaneys, 'Yes. I'll do whatever you want. Just don't burn any more samples.' I'd love to tell the SWAT team, 'Yes. Do it. Go in there. Blast those fuckers. Save the samples.' I know better than anyone how powerful a single sample can be. *I know it.*"

Curler watched her.

"But that's not my job here. My job is to get the hostages out alive."

"I get it," Curler sighed. All the anger had gone out of him. "I believe you."

Saskia said, "Let's get a recording of Jonie to play to them. And I'm not the negotiator here. I know that. I've overstepped my bounds. But I also think having any part of Jonie's script read 'I killed her' would be a mistake, even if we think that's true."

Curler leaned against the BearCat, nodding, rubbing his stubble with his hands. She could smell his cologne and the laundry powder in his shirt, even though there was sweat beading on his collarbones.

"I don't think it's true," he said.

"You don't?"

"No," he said.

"It's the dumpster thing," Saskia said. "I looked at the case file. There's no mention of dumpsters down on the esplanade. But there were trash cans. The type with the narrow openings and a hood over them, to stop sea-birds and homeless people from foraging in them. You couldn't fit a body in one. And Soloveras and Dubois had them searched anyway. Probably the only example of them going the extra mile in this whole case."

"Just because the dumpster wasn't mentioned doesn't mean it wasn't there," Curler countered.

"Why search the basically inaccessible trash cans and not search a dumpster?"

"Look," Curler said. "The dumpster thing isn't the reason I don't think Jonie is guilty of this." They looked at the teens holding each other, Tanner curling one of Jonie's ringlets around his big index finger. "There was so much detail in the first half of her story. About the tampons. About the friend trying to flirt with Tanner. About the kid watching *Jaws* from the hallway. If Jonie had snapped and killed her little sister, some of that level of detail would have come through in that part of the story."

"Could she have blocked it out, like she said?"

"I have some psychological training in trauma responses, but it's not my primary expertise," he explained. "Having said that, I feel that her mind would have obliterated the entire incident. Not just the killing but the whole morning at the beach. The brain isn't selective. It doesn't play the tape through perfectly and then say, 'Okay, we just want to delete minute seven to minute nineteen and preserve everything else perfectly.'"

"Right," Saskia sighed, her thoughts racing.

"And there was just . . . something about the way she said 'it,'" Curler said.

"When?"

"She was talking about the body," Curler said. "She said, 'I put *it* in a dumpster.' I just don't see her having that kind of . . . detachment . . . toward Tilly's body."

"So why would she be saying all this stuff?" Saskia asked.

"She may *believe* that she did it." Curler shrugged. "Those moments after Tilly vanished would indeed have been incredibly traumatic. Maybe her mind has inserted something there. Something that makes sense. It's just not real enough to have any detail to it or for her sister to appear in it as more than a placeholder. A cardboard cutout. An 'it.'"

"But why is she so calm about it? About all of it? I mean, she's so cold right now. I'd be in hysterics. Doesn't that lend credibility to her claim that she just snapped and killed Tilly? Maybe she's a sociopath. Maybe Tilly was always an 'it' to her. Curler, that teenager's parents are in that building right now holding three hostages at gunpoint, and I haven't seen Jonie Delaney shed a single tear yet."

They looked at Jonie. She was sitting now in one of the fold-out chairs, Tanner knee to knee with her, talking and gesturing as if he was explaining something to her, while she quietly nodded along. She smiled suddenly at something Tanner said, a broad and uninhibited smile like her sister's.

"I'd say she's completely disassociated from what's happening here," Curler said. "Her mind has compartmentalized it all. Gone into safe mode. Offered a simple-to-follow solution to something that it insists is a small and temporary problem. *Tell them you killed Tilly, and this little hiccup will go away. Everything will be back to normal.*"

"Will she stay like that?" Saskia asked. "Or is she about to completely lose it?"

"She's a teenager," Curler sighed. "Whether she's about to completely lose it is impossible to tell at the best of times."

"So let's get her on tape." Saskia turned and started walking back toward the tent, Curler at her side. "She might be right about one thing: maybe she's the key to ending all this."

CHAPTER 16

Surge was waiting for them outside the trailer at the end of the row of trailers, his eyes hidden behind sunglasses with small, round lenses that gave him the look of a gothic, meaty GI Joe. He was watching them approach across the Universal lot with his big arms folded and horsey mouth grinning around the butt of a cigar. Charlie noticed that the skin on the knuckles of both of his hands was grazed clean off and there was blood in between his chubby fingers. It wasn't a new look for his old friend.

"Hoss and Lamb! Hoss and Lamb!" Surge cheered. "Look out, folks! The dynamic duo is here!"

"Hi, Surge." Lamb smiled.

Surge jutted his chin at Charlie. "Have you heard about the Navarro sample?"

Charlie froze in step, one foot out, one foot behind. Lamb halted beside him, stilled by his grave energy.

"I've been avoiding it," Charlie said. He held his breath. "Did they burn it?"

"No." Surge exhaled cigar smoke through his nostrils like a steam train, smiling at Lamb. "And it was Ferboden who stepped in, so I hear."

Charlie felt his phone ringing in his pocket. He picked it up, glanced at the screen, and nodded to

Surge. Before Lamb could follow Surge toward his trailer, Charlie shook his head.

"Just give me a minute before you go in."

He answered the phone, walking out into the road between the row of trailers and the shady lots, out of earshot of his partners. In a nearby studio, the huge roller doors were up and crew were lugging couches into a set made up to look like a Christmas-themed family living room, complete with fireplace and tree.

"Sass."

"Did you just pick up one of the early suspects in the Delaney case?"

"Rumors," Charlie said. "They're flying around. I just heard one about you diving on the Navarro case hand grenade. Is that true?"

"Yeah," Saskia breathed. "They were going to burn it or the Encino double homicide sample. I made a little personal appeal. It stopped them destroying your sample, but everybody heard me do it. Now I'm waiting to get burned at the stake by an angry mob of police officers."

"Thank you, Sass."

"Don't thank me," Saskia snapped. "Thanks mean dick to me right now."

Charlie hung on in silence, thinking about Mariana Navarro. Franko Aderhold, his old neighbor on the cell block, had spoken about himself and his friend Dean Willis carving up a Hispanic girl named Navarro in the months after Charlie earned his trust in prison. Charlie had listened, deliberately nonchalant, half expecting the tale to have been a test to see if he was a bleeding heart about kids, or Hispanics, or witnesses. A year later, he had found himself invited on a mission with Dean and Franko to burn down an abandoned house Dean owned outside La Habra, because cops were sniffing around the place about a missing Hispanic girl. They'd sprung it on him: the burning, the full story about what had happened to the Navarro girl. Charlie had stood in the living room of the house with Franko, sloshing gasoline on the walls, knowing that under the carpet, only feet from where he stood, there might be a bloodstain that could prove Navarro had died there. He'd walked into the yard with Dean and Franko, watched the flames spread through the house, and in desperation had come up with the most bullshit excuse in history to go back inside. His car keys. He'd patted his pockets, called out a half-hearted explanation, and dashed back in. With flames licking the walls all around him, crawling up the ceiling and spewing black smoke, he'd dug up the corner of the carpet with his pocketknife, ripped up a slab, found the big, dark bloodstain exactly where Franko said it would be. He'd gouged madly for a splinter of wood from the patch, his fingers bleeding from gripping the carpet staples and his lungs filling with ash.

He hadn't known, as he left the burning house, whether Dean and Franko had bought his story about leaving his keys inside. He didn't know if they'd looked in on him, seen him digging up the carpet through the windows. He'd run out of the flames and heat and smoke wondering if he was running into a hail of bullets.

Charlie had put the Navarro splinter of wood and the blood trapped within it with the other biological evidence he'd squirreled away over his years undercover with the Death Machines. Keeping the evidence, rather than submitting it and having the lab test it immediately, was a policy Saskia had constantly pushed him to drop throughout his time under. But Charlie knew risking the occasional trip to an expensive, temperature-controlled private storage facility in Fairfax was a lot safer than having Death Machines DNA pop up in a lab while he was in with them. The Delaneys, civilians, somehow working out how to access the inventory lists from Hertzberg-Davis, had proven he was right to be paranoid.

"I can't guarantee the Navarro sample won't come up again," Saskia said. "It's a crazy little game of roulette we're playing with these fuckers, and there don't seem to be any rules."

"Except find their kid, and find her fast," Charlie said.

"So are you looking into it? Even though I asked you not to?"

"No comment," Charlie said.

"Hey, fuck you, too."

"What did you expect me to do, Sass?"

"I expected you to lie low until the gang forgets about you."

"That's never going to happen," Charlie said. "They're going to hit me or someone I care about, whether it's now or twenty years from now. So, while you're busy, and I'm busy, and Viola can't scratch her ass without eighteen paparazzi crawling all over each other to get it on camera, and Surge is—"

"You brought Surge in on this?"

"Wouldn't you?"

"Oh, *fuck my life*."

"The guy's a getter. He gets things. And speaking of, I've gotta go."

"Hoss, if I can't stop you working on this thing, you might as well do me some actual good," Saskia said before he could hang up.

Charlie started walking back toward the trailer, toward his partners, who were standing in the shade outside.

"Find out what the garbage disposal situation was on the esplanade at Santa Monica, would you?"

"Why?"

"Just do it," Saskia said. "Particularly the parking lot. Look for dumpsters."

Charlie hung up on Saskia Ferboden and presented

himself to Surge outside his trailer. He could hear a steady banging coming from inside the rusted old vehicle, as well as a muffled groaning that seemed to be causing Lamb deepening concern. Around them, the sunny lot was a hive of activity; the makeup trailer two spots down was now hosting a queue of female actors dressed as pirates. No one was acknowledging the ruckus inside the trailer. Charlie stepped up and pushed his way inside, feeling the desire for coffee and cigarettes burning at the back of his throat.

Brad Alan Binchley was bleeding and cuffed at the wrists and ankles to the stem of the table in the trailer's kitchen booth. He sat, essentially hog-tied, glaring viciously at the team as they entered. Charlie could see Binchley had been working at bashing the tabletop upward off the stem to try to free himself, but the trailer was vintage and had been sturdily built, so the tabletop was warped but still in place. Surge had shoved a sock in Binchley's mouth and duct-taped it in. Lamb crept into the trailer cautiously, took one look at Binchley, and let out a wail of surprise and horror.

"Lamb Chop, I think you might recognize this guy," Surge said cheerfully as he locked the trailer door behind him. He slid onto the bench beside Binchley, his jeans riding up, exposing his missing sock. Binchley winced as Surge elbowed him in the ribs. "I hear you two had a little bam-bam in the ham, am I right?"

"You fucker." Lamb was raising a shaky finger to point at Binchley. "You fucker! You *fucker*!"

"We don't have time for this," Charlie said. No one heard him. He popped open the window of the kitchenette and lit a cigarette, found his painkillers where he'd left them by the sink, and downed a handful.

"Do you have any idea what you did to me?" Lamb seethed at Binchley. "Do you have any idea what you did to my *life*?!"

"You want to punch him?" Surge grinned. He beckoned Lamb over. "I've punched him a few times already. It's fun. Come on! He's got a good, meaty face. Soft bones. I haven't broken his nose yet. I left that for you. What can I say? I'm a gentleman."

Lamb's fists were balled. She was thinking about it. Charlie tried not to pick at the stitches in his scalp and felt tired.

"Enough messing around," he said. "Un-sock this idiot and let's get him working."

"Why is he here?" Lamb sank into the green corduroy armchair, her fists still balled. "Where the hell did you find him? Isn't he supposed to be in jail?"

"I found him exactly where Hoss said I'd find him. He was at his ex-girlfriend's place in Anaheim." Surge was smiling as he unwound the tape from Binchley's head. A considerable amount of the biker's ponytail and beard were ripped free as the tape came off. He vomited Surge's sock onto the tabletop and wheeled on Lamb.

"Well, if it isn't my baby police bitch." Binchley gave a bloody smile.

Lamb made a disgusted noise.

"So nice to see your tight little ass again. I thought for sure you were just a memory for me now."

"Shut up," Lamb snarled.

"I guess you're upset because they fired you. They must have fired you, right?"

"That's right." Lamb's face was scarlet.

Charlie was surprised that there were no tears yet.

"They fired my ass. I'm out. Because of you. Because of *you*!"

"Oh dang!" Binchley laughed. "Poor li'l baby. You got fucked by me *and* the LAPD in the same week. And all you got out of it were marching papers and a couple of ground-shaking orgasms. Or, at least, that's what it sounded like to me."

"Hit him, Lamb." Surge beckoned her again. "Come on. Just once. Do it for me."

"I'm not going to hit a handcuffed man."

"It's the cheapest therapy you'll ever get," Surge reasoned.

"Binch, you're going to do some work for us," Charlie said, pulling down a coffee mug for himself. "We need your expertise with some computer stuff. You help us out, and maybe I'll make it so you get out of here without Lamb putting your balls in a blender."

"Oh, fuck you," Binchley scoffed at Charlie. "You snitching, lying, backstabbing motherfucker."

Charlie poured his coffee.

"You know what I'm gonna do for you?" Binchley spat blood on the table and a chip of tooth that bounced a couple of times before settling. "I'm gonna tell them to do it fast this time. Because they're coming for you, Hanley—oh, I mean *Hoskins*. Dean, Franko, Mickey, they're gonna—"

"Mickey's dead," Charlie said. "I killed him. On the boat."

The trailer fell silent. Lamb was watching Charlie's face. He could feel her gaze on him like a spotlight.

"That's how I got free." Charlie leaned on the counter and sipped his coffee, the cigarette between his knuckles trailing smoke. He kept his breathing low and steady, hoping the memories wouldn't come. Telling himself they were just words. "Dean and Franko left me alone with him. Big mistake."

"Yeah, it was." Binchley was fishing around in his mouth with his tongue for more shards of teeth. "They should have just popped you. Cold and clean. But they wanted to play with you. Mickey especially. Must have got overconfident." His mouth spread into a broken grin. "Did Mickey make you suck his dick? I always felt as if he might have been a bit fruity, that guy."

Surge looked at Charlie and raised a single dark eyebrow, an invitation. Charlie gave an almost imperceptible shake of his head. Binchley noticed the exchange and looked temporarily relieved.

"The fact that nobody filled you in on Mickey's death tells me everything I need to know about your current circumstances, Binch," Charlie said. "Let me guess. You haven't heard squat from anyone in the crew since the sweep. You're out on your own. The inner circle, wherever they are, has closed up. Anybody who isn't important is in jail or in no-man's-land, or on their way to getting popped as well."

Binchley scoffed again, but it had none of the strength it required. "You think I'm not important? It's only because of me that Franko and Dean knew about you in the first place."

"So where are they?" Charlie looked around. He cupped an ear. The coffee machine gurgled. "Sorry to break this to you, buddy," he continued, "but you're not important. You're not a genius, either. You might know something about hacking bank accounts and putting tracking apps on phones. But the smartest thing you ever did for the Death Machines was convince a drunk kid at a bar to take you home." He gestured at Lamb. "And any asshole can do that."

Binchley looked over at Lamb, his eyes dark. Charlie looked there, too.

"Let me tell you something about this asshole, Lamb." Charlie jerked a thumb at Binchley. "Might make you feel better. He's not a gangster. He's not a biker. He's not even a very good criminal. Binchley got in with the Death Machines the same way I did—by endearing himself to a patched member while he was in the can. Binchley was locked up for punching his girlfriend. Yeah. He punched a woman. He was so terrified when they threw him in county that he pissed his pants in the intake room."

"That's not even true," Binchley muttered unconvincingly.

"When he got to Men's Central, he decided he was

going to make friends with the guards for protection."
Charlie shook his head. "He did some snitching. Did
some ass-kissing. That was a dead end. The guards
don't give a fuck. Half of them are in league with the
inmates. So then he had two gangs after him and his
cellmate threatening to pimp his ass out. He went to
the Machines as a last resort, and they said they'd
protect him if he took the rap for a couple of un-
solved cases the police were hassling Mickey about.
He did two extra years in the can because he's pretty
good in a fight with a woman, but he's a coward
when a man wants to tango."

Lamb was watching Binchley with disgust, and
maybe pity, in her eyes. Binchley's neck was growing
red and goose-pimply.

"Dean and Franko," Charlie went on, "they let him
hang around. Even patched him because he was so
useful with the computer stuff. But he's not important.
He's not respected."

"You're wrong." Binchley smiled. "The trouble I've
caused in the past few days, there are guys inside who
will be itching to have me on board. Fuck the Death
Machines. I'm going freelance. The world's going to
know I penetrated the LAPD *and* their head fucking
lab. There are guys down in Mexico who will put me
up in a mansion for that kind of skill."

A bolt of energy hit the room. Charlie put his coffee and cigarette down, his skin tingling.

"What did you just say?" he asked.

Binchley was nodding now, the flushing of his skin
dying down, his confidence returning.

"I'm behind the Hertzberg-Davis thing," he said.

CHAPTER 17

Surge, Lamb, and Charlie looked at each other.

"Your fucking faces right now." Binchley laughed.

"What are you talking about?" Surge shoved Binchley in the shoulder so that he bounced off the side of the trailer. The whole vehicle rocked around the four people inside it.

"The lab thing that *inspired* the LAPD thing," Binchley said. He shrugged, grinning mischievously, a proud teenager lapping up the street cred for burning down the school sports equipment shed. "This couple came to me. Parents of a missing kid. Ryan and Elsie Delaney. It was the usual sort of referral I sometimes get. A layman, a non-tech type, starts fishing around on the internet looking for a hacker, and they get fed through the channels to someone who has the right skill set and who wants the money. Nobody wanted to touch this job because it was police-related. So it got passed on to me. I took a meeting with the Delaneys. They even had me over to their cute little house, served me coffee and cookies. They didn't tell me the whole idea, about holding up the lab and all—not at first. They just said they wanted the stock lists from the lab, and they gave me a date. Guess they wanted the list to be fresh for their big show day. Today. I figured they were going to go to the press, you know. About the lab losing their evidence or whatever."

"Jesus." Lamb held her head. "Jesus Christ."

"So I'm working on it," Binchley continued. "Takes me a couple of days. I'm poking around the shared network between the lab and the LAPD, trying to find a way in, but taking my time because I have this specific date. And then I get to thinking: What if it wasn't just *the lab side* that I could tap into? What if I could get into *the LAPD side* of the network, too? Just imagine the kind of shit that might be in there. Summaries of open investigations. Communications between officers. Lists of evidence in holding. I'd have the home addresses of every police officer in the state. I never *dreamed* I'd find notes on active undercovers. Not then. I just wanted to see what was there."

Charlie could feel his knuckles pop as he bunched his fists.

"So while I'm over there at the Delaney house, giving them a progress report," Binchley said, "they get all crazy because their teenage daughter texts them, saying she'll be home any minute. It's unexpected. They don't want her to see me. While I'm hightailing it out the back door, I see the girl come into the house. She's cute. I get a hard-on. I think, *That's it.* That's what I need. I need a piece of ass to get me through the do—"

Charlie had a fistful of Binchley's hair before Surge could stop him. He rammed the hacker's face into the surface of the little table. Surge's huge hand consumed Charlie's, the big man's shoulder pushing hard into his.

"*Eaaasy.*" Surge patted Charlie's shoulder with his other hand, a hard clapping that brought him out of the red mist of rage. "Eaaasy, Hoss, we don't want to break him. Not yet."

"I'm going to strangle you, you worthless little worm." Charlie ground the hacker's skull into the table, making the loose top lean in its twisted bolts. "I'm going to slit your fucking throat."

They pulled him off Binchley, Surge and Lamb together. Charlie went to the kitchenette window, sucked in the warm air, watched the people on the lot passing back and forth in front of the studios. It took long moments of silence for him to come back from the dark place Binchley's words had swept him away to.

"You need to help us," Surge said to Binchley. "Or, I swear to god, I'll let him do what he wants to do to you. They'll be scraping pieces of you off the ceiling of this trailer."

"Try it," Binchley said.

"Help us, or we will tell the Machines you flipped on them," Charlie said. "You might not be on their minds right now, but you will be if they think you've started helping the police bring them down."

"Say cheese, asshole." Surge grinned. He leaned in and took a selfie on his cell phone with a dejected-looking Brad Binchley.

They all waited while Binchley thought. Charlie busied himself making coffees for Surge and Lamb.

"What do you want?" Binchley asked eventually.

"You're going to help us find the girl," Charlie said. "The Delaney girl."

"How do I know you won't tell the Machines I flipped anyway?" Binchley shrugged. He looked at Lamb. "You're pissed. I've fucked up your lives. Using me and then fucking me over anyway would be the perfect revenge."

"You have no choice, Binchley," Surge said. "You help us, or you waste away here, chained to this table. I'm a patient man. I'll wait. This is the only offer that's available to you right now."

Binchley stared at Charlie. His mouth was twisted, defeated.

"I'm gonna take that as a yes," Charlie said. "Surge can fill you in on what you need to do. I'm gonna go in there for a while. I want to hear keys tapping or bones snapping out here."

Charlie stubbed out his cigarette, tipped what remained of his coffee down the sink, and went into the trailer's bedroom. He pushed back the ladybug curtains, popped open the little window over the bed, and looked out, but there was nothing to see. The people of the movie lot were carrying on with their business—trucks rumbling by carrying sound equipment, lighting poles, wiring. Execs marching busily. The banging and shouting inside the trailer would have been easy enough to explain away to anybody who came to the door—they were actors rehearsing scenes. Agents getting furious with clients. But no one was coming. No one was paying attention. Charlie had been skeptical about Viola's choice of nest for him, but she'd been smart about the security and the possibility of having to explain far-out behavior.

He slipped his shirt off and pushed open the curtain to the tiny bathroom annex, stood over the combination toilet-sink, and looked at the bandage over his chest wound. He needed to change the dressing on both his upper thigh, from where they'd taken the skin graft, and the hole above his heart. Spots of blood had appeared at the edges of the bandage over the ragged diamond shape northwest of his nipple. He opened the cabinet above the toilet and dumped supplies into the sink. He was in his boxers, one foot up on the toilet, peeling the patch off his thigh, when Lamb raked back the curtain and stood there, looking at him.

"Do you know how to knock?"

"How do you knock on a curtain?"

"You just . . . What do you want?"

"I want to talk about Binchley," she said, finally meeting his eyes. "This is kidnapping, what we're doing here."

"Oh, Lamb." Charlie turned back to the mirror and

wiped carefully around his chest stitches with antiseptic. "You don't find a missing child in twenty-four hours without doing a little kidnapping. If this is too edgy for you, feel free to go home."

Lamb didn't go home. She just stood there, staring at his body. He knew what she was seeing. The bruises. The swelling. His broken ribs were taped, and there were drag marks on his shoulder blades. He knew what she was going to ask before she asked it, and the anticipation made the muscles in his jaw draw down tight.

"What was all that about—"

"I didn't suck anybody's dick, Lamb," Charlie snapped. He turned to her. "You need to get off the fence and decide whether you're going to take responsibility for what happened to me or not. Okay? Because it's either your fault or it isn't. And if it's not your fault, then you don't need to know."

She drew a chestful of air. "It's not my fault." She pointed in the direction of the kitchen. "It's his fault. The damage Binchley has done in the past week alone is . . . It's inconceivable. It's because of Binchley that the Delaneys have been able to do what they're doing to their hostages. To the victims involved in the cases they're destroying. To all the cops who worked on those cases. It's because of Binchley that my career, my dream, is in the toilet right now. It's because of him that you were out there in the ocean, Charlie. Not me."

Charlie turned away again.

"But I still want to know," Lamb said. "I want to know what happened."

"Why?"

"Because I . . ."

"You what?"

"I *care* . . ." She spread her hands helplessly. "Is that okay? That I *care* what happened to you?"

Charlie finished with the stitches and ripped open

a new bandage, started peeling off the adhesive backing.

"You don't know me, Lamb," he said.

"Well, I want to," she countered. "You told Detective Bailey I was your partner."

"It was a shortcut," Charlie said. "I didn't have time to explain the whole situation."

"You could have said nothing," Lamb countered again. "But you didn't. You said 'partner.' And I know that, in your world, you're the only one who gets to say what we are. But I'm living in my world. And over here, that's not how it works. In my world, we're partners."

He sighed. He knew she was going to keep countering. Keep standing there, staring at him. Keep pushing.

"It was supposed to be a drug pickup," he said. "We'd done dozens of them. A plane from Mexico comes along, drops a package in the sea, gives you a GPS location, and you go grab the package. That's how they got me on the boat. I sent a text to Saskia, telling her where I'd be. That there'd be no cell service and that I'd text when I got back. It was all routine. Then, when we were out far enough, they turned on me."

Lamb watched him. He kept patching himself up.

"They knocked me down," he said. "They dragged me belowdecks. They tied me to a pole. They smacked me around a little, cut the tattoo off, said some angry shit. By this time, the anchor had swung, and the boat was across the current. It was rocky. Slippery, too, with all the blood on the floor. So Dean and Franko went up to raise the anchor, put a couple of revs on, get us steady. It was a two-man job. They left me alone with Mickey."

"What did he do?" Lamb asked.

"He pissed on me," Charlie said, smoothing out the new bandage over his heart.

"He *what?*"

"He pissed on me." Charlie looked at her eyes in the mirror. "The guy was an animal. And Binchley's right. Mickey was gay. It was his secret. I knew about it. He was particularly insulted and worried that he'd confided that in me while I was undercover and that I'd probably written it down in a report somewhere and now people were going to find out about it. A thing like that could mean he'd be the next one taking a little boat ride. Or a road trip. Or a joy flight, or however they decided to do it next time. He also would have been worried about Travis Bookman."

"Who's Travis Bookman?"

"A lover Mickey killed about a year ago," Charlie said. "Bookman wanted to go public with their relationship. Mickey shot him in the head in his apartment. I got a sample from that. I went to Mickey's place, swabbed the drain hole of the bathtub where he said he'd cut up Bookman. It's a long shot, and it's also a one-shot. That sample is at Hertzberg-Davis. I was working on getting a recording of Mickey talking about it, maybe a location of the body, when the operation went south."

Lamb was silent.

"So he was angry." Charlie started cleaning up. "When they left me alone with him, he kicked the shit out of me and then he took his dick out and pissed on me like I was a fucking dog."

Lamb's mouth was set in a hard line. Her eyes were dry.

"It was the wrong thing to do," Charlie said. "The piss ran down my arms and made my wrists slick. I slipped the binds, threw myself at his legs, and brought him down. I got his knife from his belt and stabbed him to death with it."

Lamb held his gaze for five long seconds. Charlie counted them. Then she dropped her eyes to the floor.

"You mind if I finish up here and we go back to finding that kid now?" he asked.

"Yeah," she said, nodding, sliding out of the annex. "Yeah."

She went. Charlie looked at himself in the mirror, at the tendons in his neck and chest and jaw that were flexing and twitching with the effort of trying to stave off the memories. But they were there, pulsing, inviting him in. He saw the knife handle sticking out of Mickey's pudgy eye socket, where it had finally gotten jammed. He saw the blood-splattered stairs to the middle deck as he crawled up them, the welcoming blackness beyond the guardrail. He knew exactly where he'd paused, naked, shaking, panting, weaponless, staring down the length of the vessel and considering whether to try to fight it out with Dean and Franko or try his luck in the water. Human sharks or the fish kind. Hypothermia or bullet wounds. He'd heard footsteps on the upper deck and then filled his chest with air, turned, and dived over the rail and into the abyss.

The memories had him. He went to the bed, sat down, and lay back, looked at the heat-warped ceiling. Sleep was his only available escape.

CHAPTER 18

Surge had his big, hairy arm slung around Binchley's shoulders when Lamb returned to the tiny kitchen. Binchley's wrists were unbound, and he was tapping at the keys, his brow sunk so low Lamb was surprised he could see the screen through his golden eyebrows.

"I'm telling you, it's not as easy as you're making out," Binchley was grumbling. "I can't just set a geo-locator and pick up every image that was taken that day, in that time period, in that area. Nobody can do that. I'd have to break into each social media server individually and search for what's there."

"So do that." Surge shrugged.

"You want me to break into Facebook, Twitter, and Instagram." Binchley turned to him. The two men were nose to nose. "In a day."

"In an hour, ideally," Surge said.

"You're kidding yourself. You're all kidding yourselves," Binchley sneered. "What you're asking is impossible. And I'm not gonna do anything while you're sitting here with your arm around me like we're on a fucking date."

"I'm just sitting close so I can make sure you don't do any of your special little *tappity-tap-taps* and call for help on this thing." Surge flicked his fingers at the laptop. "Not that you'd have anybody to call. But still."

"I can't focus," Binchley said. "You're breathing on me."

"Just forget I'm even here." Surge snuggled in closer.

"Get off me, man!"

"Surge," Lamb called.

The big man picked up his coffee and eased himself up from the narrow bench seat. The whole trailer rocked noticeably. He went to the curtain leading to the bedroom, and Lamb pointed to the limited view of Charlie's bare feet sitting still motionless on the ragged carpet at the foot of the bed.

"I think he's asleep."

"Leave him alone," Surge said. "He can have an hour. It won't kill us."

Lamb hesitated. Charlie's story in the bathroom had made all the hairs on her body stand on end. She felt an unfamiliar, calm violence stirring in her chest. It was as if a new power had been unlocked. A killer ability making itself known, machine parts clanking and clacking to life.

"You said you had guns." She turned to Surge. "When you arrived here. You said you had guns and food and supplies in the bag."

"Yeah. I've got Pop-Tarts. You like Pop-Tarts?"

"I want a gun," she said.

"Hmm, did Hoss say you could have a gun?" Surge asked, looking at her over the rim of his coffee mug.

"I'm qualified to use one." Lamb shrugged. "I got ninety-five percent in my marksmanship exam at the academy."

"That's not what I asked, Lambert, you cheeky, murderous little pickle."

"Surge."

"What do you want it for?"

"To protect my partner," Lamb said. She looked

up at the big man towering over her and casting a huge shadow across the entire kitchen area from the tiny lights embedded in the ceiling. "And to get the fuckers who messed with him and put them in jail. I'm not going to be able to do those things without a gun."

Surge's smile was huge. "I love your attitude, Lamb," he said. "I fucking love it! You bring it, Lambanator! Bring the fire and the fury! Bring the pain! Bring everything you got!"

He put his coffee down, gripped Lamb's arms, and shook her hard. Then he went to his bag on the floor beside the corduroy chair and handed her a gold-plated Glock 19. She held out the gun and marveled at it. She could see her own awestruck reflection in the polished slide.

"What in the—"

"Isn't it beautiful?" Surge smiled like a new father. "Good size for you, too."

"I'm not even going to ask," Lamb said. She checked the mag and chamber, made sure the safety was on, and tucked it into her waistband.

Binchley sighed dramatically. "Where do I send the images?"

"You've got pics already?" Surge asked, sliding in beside the biker again.

"I've got a small scoop of pictures from a geo-search," Binchley said. "I haven't hacked into anything yet. These are just what's available if you know where to look."

Surge took a laptop from the bag and flipped it open. "Send them to this laptop. Let me take a look."

Binchley's tattooed fingers were fluttering over the keys like a pianist's.

"God, this is great. This is great-great-great! I always believed in you, Binchley! I always believed in you!"

Lamb watched as Surge looped an arm around the biker and squeezed him into his side.

"We should say something about ourselves," Ashlea said suddenly. She shot upright from Bendigo's lap, swiping back her hair, a decision made. No one had spoken since the second swab burning. Ibrahim had been sitting at Bendigo's side, staring at his knees, probably wondering exactly what Bendigo was wondering. About what the plan was. About how they were going to free themselves from two hostage-takers with guns and possibly a bomb using only two pairs of scissors and the will to survive. Everyone looked at Ashlea. Outside, Bendigo could hear a chopper thumping as it passed overhead.

"What are you talking about?" Ryan asked Ashlea. His voice was low. Exhausted.

Bendigo sensed that the energy of everyone in the room had plummeted. He wondered if it was simply hopelessness, or if the police had decided to try microdosing them with something through the vents. Fentanyl, maybe. He'd read that dozens of people were killed in a siege in Moscow when police had tested that little brain wave.

"Look"—Ashlea turned to Bendigo—"we need to humanize ourselves. Make them see us as people. Make them realize we . . . we have lives and families to get back to."

She straightened and looked at Elsie and Ryan.

"My name is Ashlea Pratt. I'm twenty-eight. I . . . I have a cat named Romeo. I started a degree in law, but it bored me to death, so I took a summer internship at the *LA Times* and now I work there. This whole backlog story—I wasn't even supposed to be here. I wasn't supposed to take the assignment. But I was trying to get them to take me seriously, to give me something to write about other than social media trends. I'm supposed to go to Florida in a month with my mom. It'll be her first vacation since I was born."

There was silence, then Ibrahim burst out with a little laugh. They all looked at him, Ashlea frowning hard.

"I'm sorry, it's just . . ." He stifled a smile. "It's hard to sum up your whole life in just a few sentences, I guess."

"What's wrong with how I summed up my life?" Ashlea asked.

"Nothing." Ibrahim shrugged as much as his bound hands would allow. "I thought it was kind of cute. It sounds like a nice life, that's all."

"It is a nice life, and I have to get back to it," Ashlea huffed. "You try, if you've got something more meaningful to say."

"Uh, okay. I'm Ibrahim Solea." He glanced at the Delaneys. Nothing further came for a while. He looked at the ceiling, smirked. "I'm studying architecture. My girlfriend just dumped me for a guy who lives in her building. He's a personal trainer."

"Oh, jeez. I'm sorry." Ashlea's mouth twisted in sympathy.

"That's your story?" Bendigo said. He could feel his mood lightening infinitesimally. "'I'm Ibrahim and my girlfriend just dumped me'?"

"Well, I wasn't exactly finished."

"How did you find out?" Ashlea asked. "About the other guy?"

"We were at one of those rooftop bars downtown, watching the sunset," Ibrahim said. "She asked me to take a picture of her looking at the view. A text from him came through while I was holding the phone."

"Can you all just stop?" Ryan sighed. "We know you're people. We know you have lives. We don't care. This isn't about you."

"Why don't you tell us about yourselves?" Ashlea asked. Ryan and Elsie looked at each other. "Or . . . I don't know. Tell us about Tilly."

"Yeah, tell us about the girl you're going to kill us all for," Bendigo deadpanned. "Was she cute? She'd better have been. I don't want my life to have ended prematurely for some misbehaving little beast."

Ashlea kicked Bendigo's ankle.

He looked over. "What?" he said.

"I'm trying to build something here," Ashlea hissed.

"What are you trying to build? An affection for your captors?" he asked. "Isn't that going to make things unpleasant for you when they chance a peek through the curtains over there and a sniper blows their brains out?"

Now Ryan laughed. It was a mean sound.

"Or are you hoping Elsie isn't going to use you as a human shield when SWAT bursts through those doors," Bendigo continued, nodding at the door to the hall, "because she wants you to have a nice vacation in Florida with your mom?"

"I bet you have a miserable life," Ashlea said, slumping back against the table. "You sound like you do."

"I have a life with purpose," Bendigo said. "It's the best thing you can hope for."

"Divorced," Ibrahim said.

Ashlea chuckled, nodding.

There was silence for a while. Bendigo turned over their words in his mind, listening to the rumble and bumble of activity outside the lab. Vehicles moving. People shouting. What he assumed was the impotent positioning and repositioning of police teams around the building as officers became tired and were relieved, new angles were considered, equipment was added or removed from the scenario in preparation for a forced or unforced entry. Chess pieces being moved around a table with only one player.

Eventually, he said, "I am divorced."

He felt, rather than saw, Ashlea raise her head to look at him.

"My life isn't miserable, but it's featureless," Bendigo went on. "It's routine. It's boring. At least, it is for everyone but me. Because I enjoy the work that I do, and the work I do is meticulous and structured and orderly. I come here. I supervise the activities of my staff. I chart results, submit paperwork, fulfill clinical criteria, and meet strategic obligations. I don't do a lot of testing, because I'm mostly managerial these days, but I still do some. When a challenge presents itself, such as obtaining a viable sample from a particularly difficult derivation, I enjoy meeting that challenge."

"Is it sad?" Ibrahim asked.

Bendigo frowned. "Why would it be sad?"

"I don't know. The kind of stuff that would come in here, it would tell a story, I guess, wouldn't it? Like a . . . a bloody pair of shoes. Or a gun, or . . . Don't you look at the stuff in here and think: *Holy shit.* I mean, it's a crime lab, man. Everything coming in here would have a sad story behind it."

"You said you saw Tilly's swimsuit before it got lost," Ashlea said. "Didn't you wonder what had happened to the girl who wore it?"

"No," Bendigo said.

Ryan shook his head. Elsie's face was unreadable.

Bendigo continued, "How could I do my job if I were sitting here crying over every artifact that came through for testing? I'd never get anything done. And to involve myself emotionally in individual cases would be to compromise the integrity of the work. I might decide I want to test a baby blanket that comes in covered in blood before I test a gang member's torn bandanna, because I'm suckered in by the apparent tragedy of it."

No one spoke.

"That's precisely why Tilly's swimsuit went missing,

I suspect," Bendigo carried on. "Neither my staff nor I attached any special meaning to it. So whatever happened to it—whether it was accidentally discarded or destroyed or any number of other possibilities—it happened because of chance. Pure chance. It's not any more tragic than any other workplace mishap or oversight that might happen here. That goes for the rape kit backlog, too. It's a logjam. They happen."

He looked at the Delaneys.

"I suppose I am telling you something about myself," Bendigo went on. "The most important thing there is to know about me. It's that I am wholeheartedly against what you're doing here. You're trying to tell us that your daughter's case is more important than any other case we have here. More important than the cases you're compromising every time you burn a sample. More important than our lives. More important than any or all of the possible crimes being committed right now, while you have half the city's law enforcement bodies out there in the parking lot, trying to secure our freedom. I'm against that."

He waited, wondering if his point was taking root in the minds around him. It was Ibrahim who broke the silence.

"Di-*vorced*!" he said.

Ashlea blurted out a laugh. Bendigo knew it was stress-induced, hysterical, nonsensical. But it disgusted him just the same.

Bendigo sighed and made a decision. "I need to go to the bathroom," he said. "I've been trying to hold it. But it's urgent now."

Elsie raked her fingers up into her messy bun and scratched hard at her scalp as though trying to wake herself.

"I'll take him," she said. She picked up her pistol, took Bendigo's arm, and helped him to his feet. Bendigo clutched his bound hands against the scissors hidden in the waistband of his trousers.

CHAPTER 19

In the hall, the air seemed thinner. Colder, somehow. Bendigo got a rush of adrenaline, felt the shape of the scissors pressing into his fleshy backside, handles and point shifting against the fabric of his underwear as he walked. He imagined a dozen scenarios. The scissors suddenly dropping through his trousers, hitting the linoleum with a clatter, Elsie meeting his eyes. The animalistic surge of power. Fight for survival. The violent, fumbling struggle for them. Would she have the presence of mind and the capability to simply shoot him dead there, or would she indeed fight him for them? And if he had to punch her to gain the upper hand, could he? Was his aim to stab her or to use the scissors as a threat to gain control of the gun? And if he got the gun, was his aim to free the other hostages or simply to bolt? There was no plan and no reasonable way to form one when the hallway quickly became the bathroom, and the environment and the odds and all the infinite minuscule variables of such a potential plan were transformed instantaneously.

Elsie guided him silently to the aisle of stalls. He stood there, looking at the rows of open doors with his hands bound behind his back, befuddled and nauseous.

"You'll have to free my hands so I can . . ." He trailed off, strangely ashamed.

Elsie wore a similar mask of shame. Hers was more reasonable. She was holding a gun on him while he begged to be allowed to urinate standing and holding himself like a man. Her instructions made her cheeks redden, the shame deepening.

"Get down on your butt and you should be able to slip your wrists down under your legs and bring them in front."

Bendigo felt a flash of rage. Wondered if he needed that rage to do what he had to do. With the scissors. With the gun. He crouched and then sat on the cold, damp bathroom floor and shuffled his wrists under his backside, the cable ties pulling taut into his flesh. With his hands in front of him, he felt giddy with a new kind of power and balance. Another little victory.

"Go on, then," she said, motioning to one of the stalls. He went into the stall, unzipped, glanced back to see if she was watching. She wasn't. Bendigo reached awkwardly around himself, twisting hard, and took the scissors. He examined them in the pale light of the stall. They were paper-cutting scissors. Heavy steel, slightly curved tip. There was an acute angle to their married blades that would make stabbing possible with the right amount of force. He opened them, listened to the whisper of their blades parting and looked at the wide obtuse angle made by their cutting edges. This was the right idea. Less force needed. He quietly took a long strip of toilet paper, wrapped one cutting edge and handle together, and gripped the makeshift handle so that the scissors became a knife, one sharpened edge facing out.

"Are you going to—" Elsie started.

She was interrupted by the sound of Bendigo vomiting into the toilet. He gripped the scissors in one fist and the edge of the cistern in the other and emptied his stomach, then stood there, retching, feeling dizzy, thinking about Ashlea and her stupid cat and how utterly, ridiculously impossible his chances were of killing Elsie and freeing himself, let alone of getting back there and freeing the two kids. And that was how he thought of them. As kids. Ibrahim and Ashlea had gloriously smooth skin and bright eyes, and they laughed easily, even with death staring them in the face, and their heads were full of dreams and not dread. He was sure they were both on the cusp of big, thrilling, character-defining times. A young go-getter such as Ashlea would have a man and a baby and a foreign correspondent position in a couple of years, a Pulitzer in a decade, a patriarchy-smashing magazine, and a cute studio in Berlin a decade after that. Ibrahim was going to lock eyes with some beauty across the university chow hall or at some frat party any day now and forget all about the fiasco with the personal trainer, and the girl would challenge him, make him reach up, stand with him while they cut the ribbon on his first building. Or maybe they were both going to lead completely mediocre lives. Lonely lives. Lives tragically shortened by some less cataclysmic event than being taken hostage and murdered in a forensics lab. But they were only going to do that, any of that, if Bendigo saved them both using a pair of scissors wrapped in toilet paper. His knees were wobbly. He turned, sat on the toilet, kicked the door of the stall closed, and tried not to cry.

"She isn't a misbehaving little beast," Elsie said.

Bendigo wiped sweat from his brow. His throat was burning. "What?"

"Tilly," Elsie said. Her voice echoed off the tiles around them. "She isn't a bad kid."

Bendigo leaned his head against the wall of the stall.

"She was all about farms, the last time we . . . we saw her. The last time we knew her," Elsie continued. He heard a creaking. Imagined her leaning against the row of sinks outside, before the long row of mirrors. "I guess she's different now. Older. But she got obsessed with farms a few months before she disappeared. She wanted to draw them. Talk about them. Visit them. Wanted me to braid her hair in two long pigtails, wanted me to buy her a straw hat. She kept asking if she could have a cow. She saw this Billy Crystal movie where the guy has a cow as a pet and walks it down the street."

Bendigo had seen the movie on a plane once. He found himself smiling, despite it all.

"But mostly, she just wanted to be like her big sister," Elsie said. "The fixations came and went. Farms. Under the sea. Bugs. Trains. I'd just started reading her *The Chronicles of Narnia* at night, because my mother had read them to me, and she loved that. But the one thing that was constant was her . . . was her wish to be just like Jonie. She wanted to wear Jonie's clothes. Go into her room, touch her stuff. When Jonie was around, Tilly would sing songs she'd heard coming from Jonie's bedroom. She would memorize the words and she would sing them, acting all casual, as if she wasn't trying to impress Jonie. But the singing . . . to me, it was like a lost little bird calling in the night, waiting for an answer. Jonie was going through her teenage thing, and she didn't have time for Tilly."

Bendigo came out of the stall. He was so distracted by the story, by the struggle in Elsie's voice, that he forgot to hide the scissors in his hand. Elsie was indeed leaning against the sinks.

"I figured when they grew up they'd be close." Elsie shrugged. "There was time for them to 'get' each other eventually. And then, one day, there was no more time. It was over."

She turned. When she saw the blade sticking out from his fist, her face tightened. She raised the gun and pointed it at his chest.

"Where did you get those?" she asked.

Bendigo didn't know what she was talking about

for a moment. Then he looked down at the weapon in his hand.

"Uh, I . . . I . . . I didn't . . ."

"Put them on the counter."

He did as he was told. Closed the scissors and laid them down, put the now-snipped sheath of toilet paper beside them. Elsie strode forward to grab them, but as she came within range of him, something snapped inside his brain. A hold released. A switch flipped. He made a grab for the gun. Elsie swiped sideways at him with her elbow, struck him in the sternum, bent him double. They fell on the counter together, scrambled and fought and shoved and slid to the floor. He got the gun and butted her in the mouth with his clenched fists. She wrenched the pistol free of his bound fists, but it clattered out of her fingers and slid away. Elsie kicked at him with both feet, knocking him down, before crawling over and snatching the gun from the corner under the sinks.

Bendigo lay on his back, propped on his elbows, watching her breathlessly as she rose to her feet. The aim of the gun was on his head.

And the handle of the scissors was jutting out of her stomach.

CHAPTER 20

Saskia sat watching the teenager's face as she bent over the paper and recording device Curler had given her. In a quiet spot at the back of the tent, huddled together in a circle of fold-out chairs, Saskia, the negotiator, and the two teens had been recording the message Curler had written for Jonie into a handheld device. Saskia knew that, somewhere else in the police encampment, Ashlea Pratt's mother had arrived and been escorted into a different quiet corner to read a message written for her by one of Curler's associates. Saskia hadn't met the mother yet, but she'd seen the older woman being led through the checkpoint at the gates, two patrol officers sandwiched on either side of her, helping her walk. Her grief and horror had been visceral, even from a hundred yards away. She looked like a bombing victim being walked out of the charred blast zone.

Saskia turned back to Jonie. The teenager was blank-faced and watching the digital equalizer react as she spoke.

"I'm asking you to please listen to the police," Jonie was saying, halfway through her fifth run-through of the message, "and do what they say. They know how to get Ashlea, Gary, and Ibrahim out of there safely.

Mom, Dad, I love you. I need you both to come home safe. Please do this for me and for Tilly."

Jonie handed the recorder back to Curler. He tapped a button to shut off the recording. "I think we have what we need," he said.

"If I've done the recording, I probably don't need to be here anymore, right?" Jonie said.

Curler glanced at Saskia.

The teen looked at her watch. "I mean, I've got a geometry test tomorrow morning. If I leave soon, I could get back and finish with my study group."

Saskia opened her mouth to speak, but Curler put a hand on her knee.

"Jonie, we've spoken to your teachers. They're happy to hold off on the test, given the circumstances."

"So what am I doing, then, exactly?" Jonie swiped at her curls. "I mean, if they're just going to be sitting in there for the next two days or whatever, are we all just going to camp out here and wait?"

"We're hoping it won't be two days."

"I don't understand why you're not telling them I killed Tilly." Jonie shrugged sharply. "Like, why isn't that part of the recording?"

"It's . . . ," Curler began. "It's not as simple as that, Jonie."

"To me it is." The girl slumped in her chair. "If I were in charge of this thing, I'd let me just walk on in there. They're not gonna blow me up."

"Babe"—Tanner put a big hand on his girlfriend's forearm—"maybe just keep your voice down a little. People are staring."

"So what?" Jonie glared at him. "Hell, they need something to look at. Nothing's moved over there all morning." She gestured at Hertzberg-Davis.

Curler nodded toward Saskia. They stepped away, stood out of the teens' earshot by a bank of plastic tubs full of tactical equipment.

"What do you think?" Saskia asked.

"She's in a state of deep derealization," Curler sighed. "She's not with us."

"What does that mean, 'derealization'?" Saskia looked back at Jonie, who was joggling one knee up and down beside her worried-looking boyfriend. "Does she know what's happening around her right now or not?"

"She does, but she's detached from it," Curler said. "I've seen this before. I did some work with grieving parents during my first residency. I remember a father who lost his daughter in a hit and run. It happened right in front of him. She ran out into the street after a basketball. He said he felt in that moment as though he should be hysterical, screaming and panicking, but he couldn't be. He just felt a weird, cold determination to put her back together like she was a jigsaw puzzle. He said the whole thing felt fake. Like it had been staged."

"So Jonie's not hysterical," Saskia said, "because she doesn't feel as if any of this is real?"

"Her mind's not *allowing her* to feel like it's real."

"What does that tell us about whether she killed her sister or not? I mean, if something traumatic happens and she has this ability to just switch off and go through the motions, could she have done that on the day Tilly died?"

"Maybe. But the human brain is not a machine." Curler shook his head. "Just because it has ease doing something today doesn't mean it's because it's done it before."

Saskia saw a tall, lean woman in heavy tactical gear approaching. The woman presented herself.

"Chief Ferboden, Agent Curler." She snapped her heels together. Her accent was thick and Southern. "I'm Delta Hodge. Your new acting SWAT commander."

"Oh," Saskia said, feeling her stomach flip.

"I come in peace." Hodge held up a hand like a stop sign. "I can guess the kind of thing Franklin said to get himself smacked out. He deserved the hit. And I deserved the promotion. You're looking at the first Black, female SWAT leader in the history of American law enforcement." She thumped her vest with a gloved fist.

Saskia suppressed a smile. "Well, congratulations, Acting Commander." Saskia glanced at Curler. "What do you need from us?"

"I need to report news, good and bad," Hodge said. "And I don't have time to ask you what kind you want first. So here comes the bad news. Our tactical guys have had to pull the worm camera back from the drain hole in the floor of the lab for a hot minute. Ryan Delaney has been pacing since his wife took Bendigo to use the bathroom, and he got close to stepping on it. It was only sticking up over the lip of the drain by half an inch, but it's not worth the risk of them finding out we're listening. So, right now, we don't have an ear in the room."

"What's the good news?" Saskia asked.

"Good news is we've now got better eyes. Our robot is all the way to the air-conditioning vent. So we have a visual of the spot we're interested in."

Hodge pulled a small tablet from somewhere on her tactical cladding and presented it to Saskia. She and Curler bent close to look at the black-and-white feed of Ryan Delaney slowly pacing the floor of the lab between two large steel tables, the gun in his fist swinging by his thigh. Ashlea Pratt and Ibrahim Solea were sitting on the floor, leaning against a second row of steel tables. Both appeared to be eating, with their wrists bound in front of them.

It was the first time Saskia had seen the young hostages, outside of the photographs that had been provided to her by their colleagues and families. They looked impossibly small beyond Ryan, who paced in the foreground. No one appeared to be talking. Now and then, someone would glance toward what Saskia assumed was the door to the hall and the restroom beyond.

"There are some things in this footage that make us wonder." Hodge tapped a fingertip on the rubber edge of the tablet's casing. "We see three duffel bags. The picture isn't great, but we can discern that the third bag hasn't been accessed yet. It's full, and it's zipped up."

"So you're wondering if there's a bomb in there," Curler said. "So are we."

"We need to know if there's a bomb," Hodge said. "Or, at least, we need to know the likelihood. Because if there's no bomb, we'll be working toward a forced extraction. That would mean you hit the green button, ma'am, and we swoop in and pound the room with everything we've got, pull those hostages out of there, and try to resist the urge to shoot one of the Delaneys in the head. But if there *is* a bomb, us all rushing in like a football team at a free barbecue is the worst idea anyone's got."

"How big a bomb could fit in a bag like that?" Saskia asked. "One big enough to take down the building? Should we be worried about the teams you have positioned on the roof?"

"It's not a simple question to answer, ma'am." Hodge squinted. "Thing is, yeah, sure, you could fit a bomb that powerful in a bag like that. But are a couple of suburban parents going to have the know-how to build something so sophisticated? I don't know."

"Neither do I," Saskia said.

"More likely they've put together a pressure-cooker bomb or something similar out of household items," Hodge said. "It's not gonna bring down the building, but it could take out everyone in the room if you pack it right."

"I've got detectives trawling through the Delaneys'

online lives." Saskia glanced at her watch. "I imagine someone would have let me know by now if they'd found searches for bomb-making instructions on their phones or home computers."

"Well, we have another source we could ask," Curler said.

They looked over at Jonie and Tanner, who were sitting and leaning against each other on the fold-out chairs.

CHAPTER 21

OLI: Hello?

HOSKINS: Hey, is this Oli?

OLI: Yeah.

HOSKINS: Hey, it's Charlie Hoskins here. I'm just responding to your ad on Craigslist from a week ago. You had some speakers for sale?

OLI: Oh, man, sorry. Those are gone. I thought I took the ad down.

HOSKINS: Damn.

OLI: Sorry, man.

HOSKINS: Listen, urgh. This is going to sound weird, but—

OLI: *Just leave it in the back!*

HOSKINS: Sorry?

OLI: Nothing. Just talking to my cousin.

HOSKINS: I was wondering if you could give me a lead on who bought them. The speakers.

OLI: What?

HOSKINS: I know it's a long shot. But there's just nothing around like that at the moment. And I've got a certain budget. Those speakers were right in my range, you know?

OLI: Uh. I don't know. The guy's name was Simon? He was from Long Beach? That's all I remember. Dude hit me up through the app, so there was no number.

HOSKINS: Oh, right. You think you could—

OLI: Gotta go, man.

Charlie ended his phone call and lay back on the bed. He'd snapped awake but found his limbs so heavy, his chest so tight with urgent drumming that he hadn't been able to face getting up right away. He lay there and made a series of calls, sent a handful of texts, and was ready to stand in ten minutes. He stumbled out into the kitchen area and found Surge and Binchley sitting on the bench seat, shoulder to shoulder, working on separate laptops. Lamb was in the armchair, tapping away at her own. No one looked up. He asked a question that he wasn't sure he wanted the answer to.

"Have they burned anything else?"

Surge shook his head, eyes still locked on the screen before him. "You were only down for an hour and ten."

"Show me what you have," Charlie said. He slid into the bench seat across from Binchley. Lamb came over and sat next to him. Charlie had a flash of memory, of himself and Binchley and Dean and Franko crowding into a booth like this in a diner somewhere outside Vegas a couple of years earlier. Pancakes on the table. Bikes lined up in front of the building, the windows grimy with desert dust. They'd been trying to decide whether to rob a small-time casino run by Native Americans near Corn Creek. He looked up at Binchley, wondered if he, too, was remembering when they'd been on the other side of the mirror together. Two criminals, now cop and captive.

"Get ready," Surge said, whirling his laptop around to show Charlie the screen. "Because we've found our girl."

Charlie looked at the image. It was a selfie taken by a young couple sitting on a bright pink beach towel. He was bald and tanned. She was blond and slinky. In the background, Charlie could make out the figure of Jonie Delaney walking with a plain red beach bag, leading a smaller girl in a pink dress by the hand down toward the water. He could see it was the Delaney girls by their crowns of brown curls swept back from their fair faces by the sea breeze, the strap of Tilly's swimsuit poking up from the collar of the dress.

"Where is this?" Charlie rubbed his eyes, tried to clear the painkiller fog from his mind. "What time?"

"Okay, so, this blue spot in the distance? We think this is lifeguard tower number twenty." Lamb leaned over and pointed to a speck of blue on the horizon of the image. "And there's no pier in the background, obviously. That's the bike path on the left, and we have these trees . . . So we think this image was taken in front of parking lot number three, facing southeast. It lines up with what Jonie said in her statement about where she entered the beach."

"Time stamp says 10:01," Binchley piped up. "But that's when the image was uploaded to Facebook. Doesn't mean that's when it was taken. Could be they took it and uploaded it right away. Could be that they waited. I can't know without access to their phones."

Everyone looked at Binchley.

The biker lifted his eyes at the silence around him. "What?"

"Look at you, getting in on the mystery!" Surge hugged the man close. "You're using your talents for good for once! I'm so proud of you! Welcome to the team!"

"I'm not on the team, and you'd better get this fucker off me, pronto," Binchley snarled at Charlie. "I'm cooperating with you because I want to get out of here. He keeps hugging me and I'm going to lose it."

"You want to 'get out of here'?" Charlie looked at Surge.

"I may have renegotiated while you were asleep," Surge said. "We had some resistance, and I'm all out of stick. I needed carrot. I said we'd let Binchley go when he was through here."

"I'll never sell that to Saskia," Charlie said. "She needs to know he helped the Delaneys."

"Just let me handle it," Surge soothed.

Charlie stretched in his seat, cracked his stiff neck. "Confirming when and where the girls entered the beach is helpful, but it's not our priority," he said. "I want to see the parking lot. I want to see eleven o'clock, when Tilly disappeared."

"Wouldn't it be nice if we could just do that," Surge wondered aloud, fishing around on his laptop. "Just call up a moment in the past and see it from a hundred angles. We're heading there. One day everything will be recorded. Everything, everywhere."

"We get close to the moment," Lamb said. She drew up an image on her screen of a happy yellow Labrador sitting on the sidewalk, wearing a pair of sunglasses. The dog's leash ran up toward the camera, and Charlie could see the shadow of the person holding the phone. "This was taken right at the edge of the parking lot. Time stamp says 11:05."

She clicked on the image. A video began to play. The dog wagged its tail, mouth gaping and tongue jiggling. Charlie heard wind crackling in the phone's microphone, the same gentle breeze that had been streaking through the Delaney girls' hair as they headed down the beach. The camera swung around to reveal a woman in her thirties in a Dodgers cap. She was squinting in the sun, flashing a peace sign.

"Just chillin' with my fur baby!" she said. The video blinked off.

"If we take it back," Lamb said, rolling the cursor

back to the dog in the video, "we get some cars in the parking lot."

Lamb paused the video after a second and a half. Charlie felt a zing of excitement in his chest. He shuffled forward, looking at the slanted image of six cars parked in the front row of the lot, closest to the beach. It was a good camera. The plates were unblurred. Charlie flicked his eyes over them.

"Have you run these plates?" he asked. "Who are these cars linked to? Is Rojer there? Anyone from the suspect list? Any of the witnesses?"

"Slow down." Lamb touched his arm. "We don't even have all the images yet. Binchley is still trawling. It's only been an hour."

"An hour is an hour," Charlie said. "One more of those, and the Delaneys will burn another piece of evidence, maybe one of mine."

"We know," Lamb said.

"So what else is there?" Charlie pressed. "If we can find an image right now of Tilly Delaney heading back toward the water alone, that would be a game changer. It would shift our investigation completely."

"Yeah," Lamb said. "It would make things a whole lot faster. Easier. We could tell the Delaneys that their daughter drowned and everyone can go home." Her gaze was fixed on him. "Is that what you want?"

"I want to find the kid, dead or alive," Charlie said.

"Well, I want to find her alive." Lamb raised her eyebrows.

"And that's why you're not suited to this job." Charlie went back to the video, scrolled through it again. "Because that's not your job. Your job is to find the answer. Not to hope for a particular kind of answer and let it blind you to the rest of the possibilities."

"Isn't that exactly what *you're* doing?" she snapped. "By hoping that she drowned?"

He turned to her. "You think I *hope a kid drowned*?"

Surge's hand sliced down between them like a huge boom gate.

"Cut it out," the big man said. "Both of you."

"What do you want out of this case?" Lamb asked over the top of the hairy arm hovering between them. "Do you want to find a little girl, or do you want to save your samples?"

"What do *you* want out of this case?" Charlie asked. "Do you want to find a little girl, or do you want to prove yourself so you can be a cop again?"

"Hey!" Surge bellowed. His huge fist descended on the table, smashing down hard, making the laptops jump and his fresh coffee slosh over the rim of his mug. A half-eaten apple that had been sitting at the table's edge fell onto the carpet.

Charlie and Lamb and Binchley all looked at Surge.

"I don't like infighting," the big man said.

There was silence. Charlie pushed Surge's laptop back toward him.

"So what else?" he asked Lamb.

"That's it," she said. "That's all we have in terms of useful images. We got Jonie and Tilly arriving at the beach and a shot of six cars in the parking lot around the time of the disappearance. It's not a lot. But it's not nothing."

Charlie stared at his hands on the tabletop.

"Aside from the pictures, I've pursued something else," Lamb said. She opened her copy of the Tilly Delaney case file to the images of the bathing suit found washed up in the vicinity the day after Tilly went missing. Charlie had seen a thousand photographs like this one before, of twisted, shredded, or bloodstained pieces of clothing lying like the husks of dead creatures, alongside rulers for scale. The swimsuit looked tiny and shriveled in the glaring light from the forensic photographer's bulb.

"This swimsuit," Lamb said. "It could tell us something. Yes, the item itself was lost at Hertzberg-Davis.

But we have forensic-quality photographs that we can examine. I've sent them to a professor who dropped in to give a guest lecture at the academy while I was there. Dr. Novid Sadik. I stayed behind after Dr. Sadik's talk and—"

"We all know you were a nerd at the academy, Lamb." Charlie waved wearily at her. "Get to the point. Who's Sadik, and what does he do?"

"Water." Lamb gave Charlie a scathing look. "Bodies in water. Water damage to murder weapons, vehicles, articles of clothing. I want to know what he thinks these tears to the suit are. Are they bite marks? Are they from the seabed? How long does he think this particular swimsuit would have been in the water? And how likely does he think it would be for Tilly to have been eaten by a shark and for her swimsuit to have survived in this condition? The photographs are very good. He might be able to tell."

"It's worth trying," Surge said. "We know the swimsuit was Tilly's size. And that it showed up in the right place, according to the currents."

Charlie looked at the swimsuit. He jolted as Surge kicked him under the table.

Surge raised his eyebrows. "Good work, Lamb."

"Yeah, yeah," Charlie conceded. He was more focused on the strange, brown, bulbous creature on the chest of the swimsuit. It had huge eyes and was wearing a jaunty powder-blue porkpie hat.

"What is that thing?"

"Herbie the Millipede," Lamb said. "He's from a family of millipedes who live in Sydney, Australia. Popular kids' show. I think Disney just bought it. It was never revealed publicly that the swimsuit had Herbie the Millipede on it. So if there's a culprit and we find them, this could be our trump card."

"Maybe. How many Herbie the Millipede swimsuits are out there in Tilly's size?" Charlie wondered.

Neither Surge nor Lamb answered. They didn't

need to. Charlie shuffled sideways, hustled Lamb out so she freed him from the booth. He went to the trailer door, pushed it open, and sat on the top step. The movie lot was strangely quiet. There was no queue outside the makeup trailer. No execs walking by. An eeriness lingered in the air, of bad things past and bad things yet to come. He thought about Jonie Delaney pushing open the door of her toilet stall and finding herself unexpectedly alone. How the world must have tipped for her, the way it had for him when Dean smiled at him in that evil, knowing way on the boat and he realized he was suddenly alone, too. A cop alone among criminals.

"We've got to go, Lamb," Charlie said eventually. "I've set up some meetings for us. Surge, get Binchley onto the plates in the parking lot. I want to know owners, and I want to know if any were sold in the months after the kid went missing."

"Are you really gonna talk about me like I'm not sitting right here?" the biker asked. "You're all drinking coffee and eating snacks and talking about me like I'm a goddamn printer. You just push buttons and I spit out what you want. This is bullshit."

"Oh, I'm sorry," Lamb said gently. "You're not feeling *used,* are you, Brad?"

"Yeah. I am."

"Well, *welcome to my world, bitch*!" Lamb roared.

There was a pause, and then Charlie heard Surge break into laughter. In time, Lamb joined in.

Béndigo just stood there, looking at the scissors embedded in Elsie's stomach. The handle was sticking out of her abdomen on the right-hand side, just beside her ribs, about where Bendigo knew her gallbladder would be. Elsie was just standing there, too, the gun in her hand, her palm flattened against her belly beside the scissors. Her new appendage. The fabric of her white linen T-shirt was grotesquely pulled in around the base of the blades in a way that made Bendigo think of upholstery buttons. He gagged again, covered his mouth with his palm.

"I'm so sorry," he murmured. The absurdity of it all caught him, the way it had when he'd first walked into the lab. How did a person apologize for causing another to be impaled on a pair of scissors? "Is it . . . is it . . . ?"

Elsie raised the gun, pointed it at him. Her face was white.

"Go back to the lab," she said.

"Should I help you walk?"

"Go!"

He went. She walked behind him, slightly bent, her hand still flattened against her belly, unwilling to touch the scissor handles, yet unable, it seemed, to pull her hand away. Ryan was pacing the lab when Bendigo entered the room. He seemed to sense something was amiss from the expression on Bendigo's face. When Elsie entered, his eyes dropped to the scissors. He put his gun slowly on the tabletop.

"What . . ." He twitched, glanced at Bendigo, back at the scissors. "What . . ." Ryan rushed to his wife.

"Don't touch it!" she screamed. Ryan fluttered helplessly around her as she eased herself onto a stool by the table crammed with equipment. "Just leave it. It's not bleeding. If we don't pull it out, maybe—"

"How did this *happen*?"

"It was—"

"It was an accident," Elsie cut Bendigo off. Ryan's jaw was slowly tightening. His dark eyes lifted to the scientist, rapidly filling with rage. Elsie wiped her bloody lip. "Ryan? Ryan? It was an accident!"

"Where did the scissors come from?" Ryan asked. Bendigo didn't answer. He stood cowering beside where Ibrahim and Ashlea were sitting together, clutching each other. When Bendigo didn't answer,

Ryan went and got his gun, leveled it at Ibrahim, then Ashlea. "Are you armed, too? Either of you?"

No one spoke. Bendigo watched the scissor handles and the fabric gathered around them moving slowly in and out as Elsie breathed. There was no blood. Not yet. The lack of blood made everything worse, somehow.

"Take off your clothes," Ryan growled.

Bendigo had to refocus, had to make a deliberate effort to comprehend what the man had said. Even when he grasped its meaning, he couldn't make sense of the command. "What?"

"Take your clothes off." Ryan's growl rose in viciousness to a snarl. Spittle flew from his lips. "You're gonna hide weapons? Try doing that without your clothes. Take them off. You two as well. Do it. *Do it!*"

"Ryan." Elsie seemed tired suddenly. Impossibly, miserably tired. "This isn't what we came here for."

"*Take your clothes off!*" Ryan barked. Bendigo held firm.

It was Ibrahim who broke the pulsing silence.

"It's okay. It's okay. We'll do it," the younger man said.

Bendigo watched. Ibrahim slipped his shirt off, revealing the kind of muscular torso Bendigo could remember having himself as an early teenager and no later. Ibrahim unbuckled his uniform belt. No scissors clattered to the linoleum. Bendigo guessed the young man must have secreted them somewhere else in the room, perhaps under the bench. Bendigo tried unbuttoning his shirt, but his fingers were numb. Ashlea was sniffling as Ryan turned the gun on her. She peeled off her top, her face pained. Ryan's glasses fogged as he went back to Elsie, staring helplessly and impotently at the scissors.

"What the hell do we do now?" he asked.

"We'll ask them to send a medic in," Elsie said. Her

voice was low. Quavering. "They offered that earlier. We . . . we can exchange one of these guys for a medic."

"What's a medic going to do?" Ryan asked. "You've got scissors in your fucking . . . *organs*, Elsie! There are things in there. Important things. Aren't your kidneys around there somewhere?"

"They're at the back," Bendigo ventured. A sudden wave of courage was swelling inside him. An opportunity he could grasp at. "I'd be more worried about the liv—"

"*Shut the fuck up!*" Ryan bellowed. He walked over and stuck the pistol right in Bendigo's face. The older man stared down the dark barrel to where he knew the bullet was waiting. Begging to be released. To enter his brain. To end him. "You say one more word—"

"You'll have to give up," Bendigo said anyway, talking into the abyss. "If your wife's not in an emergency room in an hour, Ryan, she'll be dead."

Ryan was panting. Sweat rolling down the sides of his neck into his collar. Bendigo could see his pulse hammering in his jugular.

"You don't know that. You're a DNA guy. You're not a doctor."

"She's going pale," Bendigo said. "Look at her face. Is that shock, do you think? Or is it internal bleeding? You're not a doctor, either, are you, Ryan?"

"You shut your mouth." Ryan's sweaty finger was sliding on the trigger.

"What happens if you find your daughter, but your wife's dead?" Bendigo asked, keeping his eyes on the gun. "Will it all have been worth it?"

Above them, a *crack* sound. Then a staticky kind of hushing that made Bendigo think of rainfall. Everyone looked up. The voice that came from above them was loud and made them flinch. Bendigo followed it to its source: a speaker in the corner of the room, nestled against the ceiling like a spider.

"Mom, Dad. This is Jonie," the voice said. *"I'm outside the Hertzberg-Davis lab right now. The police have asked me to record this message for you. I'm asking you to let the hostages go and surrender yourselves safely. I'm asking you to please listen to the police and do what they say. They know how to get Ashlea, Gary, and Ibrahim out of there safely. Mom, Dad, I love you. I need you both to come home safe. Please do this for me and for Tilly."*

"Oh my god," Ryan whispered.

Bendigo watched the man's face. Watched the resolve flicker in his eyes. A struggling flame. Breaking point reached. He lowered the gun and stood there, waiting, watching the speaker in the ceiling for more. Elsie wiped long streams of tears from her eyes. In time, the cracking sound came again, and the whooshing, and the recording began to replay.

"Mom, Dad. This is Jonie. I'm outside . . ."

"Ashlea!"

Elsie's shout drew Bendigo away from his imaginings of the teenager outside the lab, in the police encampment, recording a plea to her parents. He looked to Elsie, then followed her gaze to where Ashlea was sitting with her arms folded awkwardly across her front, trying to hide her swollen breasts and her obviously pregnant belly.

"Something's happened," the technician said. She was a different woman from the one who had been manning the live feedback when the siege started. Saskia was aware of police, SWAT, and sheriff's employees swapping out all around her. Taking breaks. Trying to ease the pressure. It made sense; the idea was to keep everyone sharp, refueled, ready to rush in at a moment's notice and save the hostages. But Saskia was also aware that the breaks meant opportunities for those police employees to spread rumors, discontent. As she stepped up behind the technician, Saskia could sense anger hovering all around the young woman sitting in the chair. It was like a bubble of hot air. Saskia leaned into it anyway, ready to be burned if she had to be.

"Show me," she said.

The technician showed Saskia a clip taken from inside the lab by the robot in the air-conditioning vent. Ryan Delaney pacing. Ibrahim and Ashlea sitting on the floor. She watched Bendigo enter the room, the scientist seeming smaller somehow than he had been when Elsie escorted him to the bathrooms a few minutes earlier. Saskia watched Elsie Delaney enter the room. Her gun was by her side, her hand clutching at her stomach. She eased herself onto a stool, her back to the camera, and Ryan raged, swinging the gun around, pointing it at Bendigo, at the two hostages on the floor. Even without sound, Saskia could see the terror in the room. The way the hostages flinched at Ryan's movements. She realized Curler was standing beside her when he spoke.

"Bendigo must have made a move in the bathroom," Curler said. "Punched her, maybe."

They stood watching as the footage played. Ibrahim and Ashlea pulled off their shirts. Bendigo fiddled with his shirt buttons.

"Why are they getting undressed?" Saskia looked at the image of Ryan barking at the hostages. "Is he making them strip?"

"Maybe he's trying to humiliate them." Curler shrugged. "You hit my wife, you lose your clothing privileges."

Something wasn't right. Saskia sensed the situation inside the lab had shifted. On the screen, all the residents of the lab looked up at once.

"This is the moment we played the recording," the technician said.

Saskia watched. Every person in the lab was frozen. Then they all turned to Ashlea, who was huddled into herself, crying.

"What's this?" Saskia wondered aloud.

"They've all changed," Curler said. He pointed to Ryan. "His shoulders are down. His head is up. You don't think—"

"Oh god," Saskia breathed. "She's got her shirt off. They've noticed she's pregnant."

"So she *is* pregnant?" Curler said.

"I guess so. Look how they're reacting to her. It's because she has her shirt off. She must be showing."

Saskia asked for the tape to be rolled back. The technician gave an icy sigh. Saskia and Curler watched.

"I'm sure that's what it is," Curler said gravely.

"We need to get the jump on this. Make sure they see it as an out, rather than an opportunity to make more demands," Saskia said. "Let's call them. Strike while the iron's hot."

The technician dialed. Saskia watched the little phone icon jiggling. It remained gray, unanswered.

"Fuck," she growled. "All right. Curler, let's hook you up to the PA system."

"With respect"—Curler put a hand up—"I say we wait. Let the recording from Jonie marinate with them a little. Let them take in this new information about Ashlea. We're trying to play on their sympathies. If we blast them with too many messages at once, we might undermine our own efforts."

"All right, well, while we're playing gentle mind games with these lunatics, I want some progress on our not-so-gentle approach," she said. Hodge, who had been leaning against a nearby table, strategizing with her second-in-command, sensed she was needed.

She walked over, and Saskia led her to Jonie and Tanner, who were still seated in the back corner of the tent.

"I really need to get out of here," Jonie said as Saskia sat down. There was nonchalance in her facial expression but a tautness to her voice. Saskia wondered if the reality of the situation was finally breaking through. "I'm done. I did what you asked me to."

"Can't we just, like, go somewhere nearby?" Tanner asked. The boy gestured vaguely to the press camp. "We won't talk to them. We promise. I just think Jonie needs to lie down or something."

"Jonie, if your parents respond to your message the way we hope they will, we're going to need you here," Curler said. "It may be that your presence is the deciding factor in getting a peaceful resolution to all this."

"You're also not done," Hodge said.

"Who are you?" Tanner's whole body tensed in the chair, making it creak.

"My name's Delta Hodge. SWAT commander."

"Whoa." The teen was a small boy for an instant, open-mouthed and disbelieving. "You're the commander? Like, the boss of the whole thing?"

Hodge ignored him and turned to Jonie. "I want to talk to you about your parents' behavior, Ms. Delaney, over the past year or so but particularly the past three to four months. I want you to think hard and give me all the details that you can. Nothing is too small."

Jonie looked distracted. She was watching an ant crawl across the asphalt at her feet.

"You with me, ma'am?"

"Huh? Yes."

"I can also help," Tanner said, perking up. "I've been around the house a bit since Jonie and I have been together."

Hodge ignored him again. "I'm not gonna beat around the bush here. We want to know if your parents have a bomb in that lab. So we'll start simple.

Have you seen a bomb or anything that looks like a bomb in your family's household or car recently?"

Jonie smirked. "No?"

"Any weird things in weird places? Kitchen items in the garage? Car parts or tools in the kitchen?"

Jonie thought. "No. I don't think so."

"Have either of your parents bought any electronics recently?" Hodge asked. "Cell phones. Toasters. Blenders. Pressure cookers. Any trips to the hardware store to buy cleaning chemicals or wire?"

"I can't remember anything like that." Jonie looked at Tanner.

"Neither can—"

"Have your parents displayed any signs of suicidal ideation?" Hodge cut Tanner off, only her eyes shifting sideways to take in the boy. "Increased drinking? Moodiness? Sudden weird calm? Selling or giving away their possessions? Closing bank accounts? Have you seen any long, handwritten letters being composed by either of them? Or have either of them talked about wanting to be with a deceased loved one or friend?"

Jonie watched the ant. It was heading for her shoe.

"Weird calm," she said. Everyone was silent. "The past couple of weeks," the teenager continued. "They've been weirdly calm in the lead-up to the anniversary. I guess . . . I guess they finished planning all this. All they had to do was go through with it. There was no more to worry about. They'd worked it all out."

Saskia watched Jonie watching the ant crawling up her shoe. The girl's chest was rising and falling as her breath began to quicken.

"We should stop this now," Curler said.

"And they always talk about being with Tilly." Jonie raked shaking hands through her hair. "But they talk about it happening here. In real life. Not, like, in heaven. I don't know why we don't just tell them that's not possible."

"Jonie." Curler reached forward.

"Because *I killed Tilly.*" Jonie lifted her eyes. They were suddenly hard and wild, her pupils tiny. "They'd come out of there if they knew. They'd stop all this. Just tell them. Just tell them. Just tell them. I killed her! *Why won't you just tell them that I killed her?*"

Jonie was on her feet like she had been launched out of her seat by a mechanical force. She tried to rush between Curler and Hodge. It was Hodge who put an arm out and scooped the teen into an embrace before she could sprint for the edge of the tent, for the no-man's-land of open asphalt between the police encampment and the Hertzberg-Davis building.

"Just tell them that I killed her!" Jonie screamed. *"I killed Tilly! I killed Tilly! I killed Tilly!"*

CHAPTER 22

"Is this awkward?" Lamb asked. Charlie tore his eyes off the flat, royal-blue horizon and looked at her. The ruthless Californian sun was blazing off the cars in the lot behind them, a sparkling sea of light dancing on Lamb's neck and shoulders.

"Is what awkward?"

"You and the sea. Together again." Lamb gestured to the beach yawning before them. White sand. Crunching waves. "After your last little . . . exchange."

Charlie smirked. She was right, but he wasn't going to tell her that. The very sight of the ocean rolling into view of the panel van they'd borrowed from somewhere on the Universal lot had indeed made him queasy. Made him wonder for the thousandth time since he woke in the hospital about the woman who'd looped her strong arms around him, dragged his deadweight toward the shore. *I've got you.*

He shook away the seductive whisperings of curiosity about the woman in the water and turned to the brick toilet block at the edge of the parking lot.

"Let's get a quick look in here before our witnesses arrive," he said. "Not that it will tell us much."

It was cool and dark in the little building by the sea. Spray-painted tags on the ceiling and walls, the smell of disinfectant and urine and seawater. Spatter of something unwholesome on the polished steel mirrors. The distant squeals of tourists from the roller coaster on the pier penetrated air vents beneath the concrete ceiling that doubled as studio apartments for spiders. Lamb and Charlie stood together, looking at a row of three steel sinks bolted to the wall, each aligned with a stall. Rickety, heavily painted doors. Lamb went into the stall nearest the door and sat on the toilet, her jeans still on. Charlie watched her sitting there. She closed the door, and he heard the latch. He raised an eyebrow.

"Should I wait outside?" he asked.

"I'm just researching."

"Looking for dents in the walking stick?"

"Maybe they're just dents, maybe they're from the spaniel," Lamb said. "But you can't find out unless you take a look at them."

She opened the door again, went into the next stall, repeated the sequence until she'd sat on every toilet with the door shut. Charlie waited for her to finish, shifting wet sand under his boot on the concrete.

"It's possible," Lamb concluded finally, closing the last stall door behind her.

"That Jonie Delaney did indeed go to the bathroom here? That from here she lost track of her sister?" Charlie asked. "You're a genius, Lamb. Case closed."

"No. It's possible that Tilly was abducted from here," Lamb said.

"Why?"

"We've been in here for four and a half minutes." Lamb looked at her watch. "No traffic. Not so much as a close pass by the door."

"So?"

"So it's a good spot," Lamb went on. "To grab a kid from, I mean. These restrooms don't get much use because they're ugly and old and there are much nicer ones a hundred yards away on the pier. And the parking lot is just there. You grab the kid, stuff her in your trunk or the back seat or whatever, and off you go."

"The height and the angle of the cars would shield her from view. No one would see her from the hotels and the pier." Charlie nodded. "You do it fast enough, no one looking up from the beach will see you, either. And if they do, you just pretend she's your kid and she's having a tantrum about going home. We know she was upset."

"Stranger abductions are opportunistic," Lamb said. "Rare, because they're usually the culmination of impossible conditions. The perfect storm. An offender carrying an urge that has, over time, become almost irrepressible. A catalyst event that tips the offender over, puts them into the red zone of actually acting on their urges. A victim who presents themselves—vulnerable, available, and in a scenario that the offender deems to be a low enough risk."

"I see you aced your 'abduction' exam at the academy," Charlie said. "You sound as if you're reciting from your notes."

She paused, and then seemed not to be able to help herself. "It can be incredibly helpful to recite your study notes aloud."

Charlie rolled his eyes and walked out into the sun. Green light blasted his vision. He examined the rows of parked cars. Then he turned and walked to the end of the lot, Lamb at his side, gazing at the distant esplanade before the strip of hotels and bars. A couple of tourists were pedaling a tandem bike along the path across the street. The cyclist on the front, a bearded guy with a crown of curly hair, ducked to avoid low-hanging palm fronds, leaving them to smack the second rider in the face.

"No dumpsters," Charlie said.

"We're looking for dumpsters?"

"Sass asked me to. I thought it was weird. I mean,

why would there be dumpsters down here? There are trash cans everywhere. Dumpsters live in alleyways behind big establishments that generate a bunch of garbage. They're a repository for the contents of trash cans that need to be emptied regularly because they're stuffed full all the time."

"They don't belong at the beach," Lamb agreed. "Trash down here would be sporadic. Seasonal. Balanced out across all the trash cans."

"But just because there are no dumpsters here now doesn't mean they didn't have them here two years ago." Charlie shrugged. "For whatever reason. Maybe there was a concert or an event at the beach we don't know about and a dumpster was left over or pre-placed here."

He took out his phone and snapped a picture of the contact details of the municipal garbage collection printed on the side of the nearest trash can. The can itself was cylindrical, three openings in the top of it big enough to accommodate a soda cup or a box of fries and not much more. The three holes were sheltered by a little steel bird-deterring canopy. Lamb was scanning the heads of a group of people traversing the sidewalk between the parking lot and the sand. Charlie had warned her in the car on the way here to be cautious. If the Machines could put it together that he was working on the Tilly Delaney case and that he might go and visit Nicolas Rojer, it followed that they might suspect he would visit the spot where the little girl disappeared. Charlie should have been as vigilant as Lamb, if not more, but a reluctant sort of dread was keeping him focused on the Delaney mystery instead. He knew, deep down, that the Machines were never going to stop trying to find him. That they were a new but permanent threat in his life now. He'd just spent five years with his ears pricked for danger at every passing second—an odd tone, a strange glance, unexpected questions. And even that hadn't saved him from the boat.

When Lamb saw Olivia Zaouk and Leanne Browning walking toward them, she tapped Charlie's elbow and pointed. The two women seemed like what they were—acquaintances introduced, and reunited, by unfortunate circumstances. They walked side by side, but a little farther apart than friends; Zaouk, the younger woman, tapping out a text on her phone, and Browning, older and with softer edges, walking with her arms folded, looking out to the sea.

"Olivia." Charlie stepped up and shook the younger woman's hand. She was tall and willowy with dark eyes. "Leanne. Thanks so much for meeting us so quickly."

"You're all over the news," Olivia told him, her eyes wandering over his tattoos. "They keep showing a clip of you outside Hertzberg-Davis." She turned toward Lamb. "You, too, I think. You're in the background."

"I wish I'd had time to do my hair," Charlie said.

"Are you working on the case?" Leanne Browning's arms were folded so tightly her paisley top was pinched in the middle, exposing her bra. "Do you think, you know, we're going to be called back in to give statements about what we saw, or . . . ?"

"I don't know what's going to happen in the next twenty-four hours." Charlie held his hands up. "I just need to hear again what you told police two years ago. And if there's anything else you can remember."

Olivia opened her mouth to speak first, but her phone pinged, distracting her. Leanne brushed aside her straight auburn hair and pointed toward the edge of the parking lot.

"I had dropped my son at a medical appointment, and I wanted to come down here and look at the water while I waited for him," she said. "I was sitting in the car, listening to the radio, and a little girl came out of that doorway right there. The women's bathroom. She turned and walked toward the water. She was in a huff. Bottom lip poked out."

Leanne made a face, her mouth downturned, jaw thrust forward. Lamb squinted in the sunlight bouncing off the parked cars.

"Do you remember what she was wearing?" Lamb asked.

"No, but I remember the curls," Leanne said. "My brother was about to have a kid, and he's got those same big, soft, brown ringlets. I've always been envious of them." Leanne ran her fingertips through her hair again. "Seeing the girl walk by made me wonder if his baby was going to be born with the same hair."

"So she came out of the doorway and headed directly down toward the water." Charlie pointed. "Was she moving fast or slow?"

"Fast," Leanne said. "Like she was storming off."

"Pretty much what I saw," Olivia chimed in. "Only I was farther down the beach, coming back up this way. I wasn't parked; I was staying at the Marriott."

"You saw a girl matching Tilly Delaney's description heading back down the beach toward the water?" Lamb asked. "Alone?"

"Alone and kind of angry," Olivia said. "With the big curls."

"Did she pass you?" Charlie asked.

"Yeah."

"Neither of you thought the situation looked strange?" Charlie asked. "Little girl like that? Alone and upset."

The women thought, Leanne staring at her shoes, Olivia tapping her phone against her thigh.

"Not really?" Olivia shrugged her lean shoulders. "I mean, I guess I just figured she was heading *to* somewhere, you know? She was marching very determinedly down toward the water, so I thought maybe she was going back to her parents to tell them something had happened to her, or . . . I don't know." She looked helplessly at Leanne.

"'Very determinedly'?" Lamb asked.

"I guess?" Olivia said.

"Why were you staying at the Marriott?" Lamb asked.

"It was my anniversary with my boyfriend." Olivia gave a sheepish smile. "I bought him a turtle."

"You had a turtle in the hotel room with you?" Lamb said.

"Well, it was only the size of a cookie. Nobody noticed me bringing it in."

"So you're certain about the date?" Charlie pressed.

"I'm certain because I watched all the police cars and stuff arriving from our balcony." Olivia pointed to the tall, tan-colored hotel diagonally across the street from the beach. "Daniel and I came down to check out what was happening, and I met Leanne, and she—"

"I was giving a statement." Leanne took over. "Soloveras was the officer's name."

"So you were still around?" Lamb frowned. "Jonie Delaney said she searched for Tilly for forty-five minutes on her own before she called police. If police arrived quickly, that's still about an hour before you'd be asked for a statement by Soloveras."

"Well, I didn't just stand here the whole time." Leanne gestured to the esplanade behind them. "I walked up there. I bought a coffee. I think I went into a store and looked at some magazines. My son would have been about an hour or so at his appointment."

"Then you came back here, to the car, and noticed all the activity," Lamb said. "You realized you'd seen the girl they were looking for, so you told Soloveras that?"

"I did."

"Did you two talk after you'd both given statements down here at the beach?" Charlie asked the women.

"Yeah, for a little while." Olivia nodded, looking at the older woman. "It was just, like, 'Oh, I saw the girl they're searching for,' 'Yeah, I did, too.'"

Charlie and Lamb exchanged a glance.

"Did you notice each other at the moment when Tilly walked out of the bathroom?" Lamb asked. "If you both saw her, maybe you saw each other, too."

The women looked at each other.

Leanne shrugged. "Not that I recall."

"Okay." Charlie turned toward the ocean without thinking. The very sight of the cold, blue horizon slicing across the sky sent electricity through his brain. He refocused on the women before him. "So neither of you saw Tilly Delaney actually enter the water?"

"No." Olivia shook her head. Leanne did the same.

Charlie and Lamb thanked the women and walked back to their panel van. He got into the passenger seat. He was relieved to shut out the sound of the roaring waves and the crying gulls as Lamb started the clattering engine.

"Lay it on me, Lamb," he said.

"They've influenced each other's stories," she said.

"Probably." He clicked his fingers, restless, thinking. "Probably. It's always a shame when witnesses get together."

"So either one of them saw Tilly, or both of them did," Lamb said. "But if my instincts mean anything—"

"They don't, but go on."

"—I don't believe that *neither* of the women saw Tilly."

"I agree," Charlie said. "Too weird to have two complete strangers make up a story like that."

"Unless they're not complete strangers," Lamb mused.

"Or they've got a good reason for making it up." Charlie looked up the trunk of a huge palm tree that was standing directly in line with the hood, a sentry looking out over the sea. "Soloveras and Dubois were looking for witnesses to say Tilly went back toward the water. They actively pursued them. It wouldn't be the first time a cop has put a story in a witness's head."

"Both Leanne and Olivia gave recorded statements down at the station, after their statements on the scene," Lamb said. "Let's listen to those and compare them to—"

The impact of the car into the back of their panel van was so hard, so sudden, no sound registered in Charlie's brain. A wave of silent, agonizing pressure swept him, knocked him forward into the dashboard, Lamb's body moving in almost slow-motion synchronicity, forced and bent and crushed around the steering wheel and dash in a blow that knocked the breath out of her. Charlie felt that breath on his face. Felt the windshield collapse down over him. The front of the car dipped down as the hood hit the base of the palm tree three yards from where they had been parked, giving him the impression of a roller coaster cresting, descending, g-forces crushing his organs. When the force was spent, he and Lamb slammed back into their seats, both too shocked and winded and blinded to contribute to the screaming of onlookers outside the vehicle. Charlie looked up and saw through the pain fog that the trunk of the palm tree was headed toward them. He reached over and grabbed Lamb's head, and shoved it down between her knees a half a second before the trunk of the palm tree collapsed the driver's-side roof above her.

"Oh god! Oh god! Oh god!" she wailed.

"Come on." He dragged her through the foot-high gap left between the ceiling of the cabin and the center console. "Come on, Lamb! Come on!"

They fell onto the asphalt together as the car that had rammed them screeched backward for a second attempt. Charlie got a glimpse of a familiar face through the windshield. Lamb had rolled off him and was dragging him behind a rack of bikes as the door of the ramming car popped open and Franko Aderhold stepped out and started firing. Bullets pinged off the bikes, chains, the curved, steel racks, exploding a cheap helmet in a puff of plastic and Styrofoam. Charlie saw through the hissing smoke from the panel van's crushed engine that some bystanders were running for their lives while others were lingering, frozen in place, watching the carnage as though they'd accidentally wandered onto an action film set and were trying to figure out how to exit without ruining the shot.

When Franko paused to reload, Charlie whipped out his own pistol and fired through a hollow in the briar patch of bikes and racks and locks in front of him. Franko ducked behind a parked car. Charlie followed Lamb in a crouching run to that same car, and he dove without hesitation under it, dropping and skidding his gun back toward Lamb, hoping she'd know what to do. Franko was rising from a crouch when Charlie grabbed his ankle from under the car and yanked with all his might, using his whole body to snatch the ankle sideways and under the vehicle, dragging leg and knee with it, sending Franko crashing awkwardly onto his side. Charlie was despairing as he glanced back and saw his pistol was still on the ground at his feet when he heard Lamb screaming, "Down! Down! Down! Drop the gun! Drop the gun!" and saw Franko drop his pistol, his back on the asphalt and his hands up, his stubbly chins bunched as he took in the young woman standing over him.

Charlie saw Lamb snatch up Franko's pistol. He crawled out from under the car, picked up his own weapon, and went around the hood, arriving at Franko's head. He smashed the butt of the gun on the older man's nose and flipped him onto his stomach.

"Oh, how I've been dreaming of this, Franko." Charlie laughed, putting a knee into Franko's right kidney and hearing a satisfying groan of pain. "I've been lying awake for *years* thinking about this, you old, fat fuck!"

"Get off me! Get him off me! Somebody! He's hurting me!"

"Don't waste your police brutality game on me." Charlie pulled a pair of handcuffs from his back pocket and snapped them onto Franko's sweaty wrists. "You're gonna need that on the inside."

"We're LAPD," Lamb was saying, holding her hands up, trying to settle a crowd of bystanders that was slowly becoming emboldened now that the gunfire had stopped. Every one of them was filming with their phones. "It's okay. It's okay."

"You want to know what is so glorious about this moment, Franko?" Charlie leaned on the big man's back, gripping a handful of his leather vest. The Machines logo embroidery clenched in his bloody fist was giving him an almost sexual burst of furious triumph. "I know how hard you took prison the last time, because I was stuck in a cell beside you for a fucking *year.* I know how *miserable* you were in there. I am just . . . Look at me." Charlie showed the big biker his outstretched hand. "I'm shaking, I'm so happy right now."

"You'd better shake, because I'm gonna kill you, you dirty little bitch." Aderhold was drooling blood on the asphalt from his smashed mouth and nose. "You think our playdate out on the boat was bad? Just wait. Just wait."

"Yeah, I'll wait." Charlie got up and spat on the man on the ground, told himself that was enough. But it wasn't enough. Something took hold of him. It was the sea air, the sound of the waves, the memories of those first few hours in the water with the big searchlight from the boat sweeping the blackness for him. Going under, dragging and pulling the curtains of cold water around him, rising when his chest was crushed and his eyeballs were about to pop out of their sockets, hoping somehow, ridiculously, that he could keep emerging to breathe without that light falling upon him. Franko and Dean had cut circuits of the water, hunting him, for so long that Charlie was sure the game must have been to simply exhaust him and run him over, let the motors make chum of him. He came out of the memories and found that he was stomping on Franko's head, Lamb dragging him off, her arms hooked under his and her shouts making his eardrums quiver.

"Charlie! Jesus! You've gotta stop!"

"I'm done." He walked away, struggling to catch his breath. "I'm done. I'm okay. I'm done."

Lamb led him back to the panel van a few feet away, pushed him against it, stood there with her arms folded, watching him regain himself. The palm tree was lying embedded in the van like a hot dog in a bun, and the sight of it made him laugh. Franko was cuffed on the ground. People were filming.

"What the hell are you laughing about?" Lamb asked. There was blood running from a big laceration in her left ear, making a straight line down her neck into the collar of her shirt. "You're gonna make the news for kicking the shit out of that guy, you know that?"

"Worth it." Charlie smiled.

CHAPTER 23

ZAFFER: Los Angeles Police Department,
Central Booking. This is Officer Zaffer.

MINA: Oh, hi. My name is Mina Delforce.
I was hoping someone could help me.

ZAFFER: Okay.

MINA: It's not an emergency. I'm just trying to
find someone who I think might be a police
officer.

ZAFFER: Who you think *might* be a police
officer?

MINA: Uh. Yes.

ZAFFER: What's the officer's name?

MINA: See, that's the thing. I don't know. I'm
trying to find out.

ZAFFER: Ma'am, what is this call in relation
to?

MINA: He . . . It's not a complaint or anything.
He . . . he just . . .

ZAFFER: Ma'am?

MINA: He helped me on a case. Uh. On my
street. I called him and, um . . . and I wanted
to connect with him and maybe say thank
you.

ZAFFER: Comments, concerns, and queries
about police performance can be made using

a contact form on the LAPD website. If you
have a pen, I can—

MINA: Well, I don't know his name.

ZAFFER: Do you have a case number for your
incident?

MINA: No.

ZAFFER: Then, ma'am, I'm afraid you'll—

MINA: I saw him on the TV. He's down at
Hertzberg-Davis right now. He must be helping out. That's why I thought he must be—

ZAFFER: Why you thought he must be a
cop. But you said you *knew* he was a cop.
Because he helped you on a case.

MINA: Uh . . .

ZAFFER: So do you *think* he's a cop? Or do
you *know* he's a cop?

MINA: Um.

ZAFFER: I think I understand. Let me see
if I'm getting this right: you were watching news coverage of the scene down at
Hertzberg-Davis and you saw a guy you
thought was cute on the screen, and you
figured he must be a cop, so you called here
trying to find out who he is so that you can
contact him. Is that right, ma'am?

MINA: No. No. It's not like that at all.

ZAFFER: Have a nice day, ma'am.

MINA: I'm not—

"When were you gonna tell us?" Elsie asked. Bendigo
looked over at Ashlea, who was still huddled around
her swollen belly like a kid trying to hog a favored ball
in the schoolyard. Now that he could see the shape of
her body, he wondered how she'd concealed it from
them all. But the top she'd been wearing, now discarded on the floor at her feet, had been flowy and
cinched under the breasts with a little string, and he

supposed, under the circumstances, they could all be forgiven for missing the subtle presence of the fourth hostage in lab 21. Ashlea's breasts were threatening to fall out of the top of her bra and were threaded heavily with blue veins.

"Never," Ashlea said.

"They might have let you go earlier!" Ibrahim barked. His anger was so sharp, so sudden, that it drew Bendigo's gaze. "Are you crazy? You could have been out of here hours ago!"

"I haven't told anyone at all!" Ashlea snapped back. "I've waited fourteen weeks to tell my own goddamn mother. Why should these two get to know before she does?"

"You've got to let her out of here." Ibrahim's entire body was poised like he was going to leap up and fight Ryan if he argued with him. "There's a baby in there. She . . . The stress could . . . You know! She has to go!"

"You should have told us." Elsie was speaking to Ashlea like they were alone. Like the lab, the other hostages, the police outside had all evaporated. And they were just two mothers. "We would never have kept you here."

"How could I have known that?" Ashlea shook her hands. "Maybe it would have changed things the other way. Maybe you'd have kept only me. A baby is worth twice what they are as hostages." She waved her hand at Bendigo and Ibrahim.

"We're not monsters," Elsie said. Her voice was weak, breathy.

Bendigo wondered if the shock of the scissors in her stomach was wearing off and the pain was setting in.

"We would have let you go the instant—" Elsie continued.

"He fired a gun at my head!" Ashlea pointed at Ryan. "Without looking!"

"Enough," Ibrahim said, his eyes pleading with her. "Enough. Enough. Just take her out."

"She has to go." Ryan's voice was smaller, calmer than Bendigo had ever heard it. He turned to Elsie. "You both have to go."

The hostage-takers looked at each other. Bendigo chewed his lips, told himself there would be another time. But he couldn't stop himself from speaking. Couldn't let the opportunity pass while he sat silently.

"End this," he said. "Let us *all* go."

Bendigo's words made Ryan stiffen. His upper lip pulled tight as he looked at his wife.

"Take Ashlea out," he said to Elsie. "Use her as a shield. Do *not* let her go until you're safely inside the police camp."

He stood, went to her, took her face gently in his hands, and kissed her forehead. Bendigo watched as they paused together, foreheads touching, eyes closed, their faces taut with pain.

"We'll find her," Ryan said.

"We'll find her." Elsie nodded.

When they parted, Ryan stepped away, but Bendigo could tell he was ready for what was to come next. Antsy. Restless. Eager to make a move. Elsie must have noticed it, too, because she sat watching him, waiting, but he was locked off to her now. Stony-faced. Planning. She eased herself up carefully, still bracing her stomach and the scissors there with her hand as her eyes went dim with dread.

"Go, Elsie," Ryan said. "I'll be okay."

"What are you going to do?" Elsie asked.

He helped Ashlea to her feet and she pulled her shirt on, then he walked the two women to the door.

"They have to know this isn't a win," Ryan said.

He touched the back of her hand to get her attention. She was standing there, thumbing her phone, reading a message from Charlie Hoskins about there being no dumpsters present on Santa Monica Beach but that he promised to check into it, when Curler brushed his fingers against her skin. Saskia felt a pang of hot shock in her chest. Half of it was the unexpected warmth and tenderness of the touch, a rueful excitement. It had been a long time. But the other half was a whip-fast right angle in her emotions that came after when she followed Curler's gaze across the parking lot toward the checkpoint and saw the mayor of Los Angeles, Ike Grimley, stepping out of a shiny Tesla. Somewhere nearby, in a huddle of officers, Saskia heard a low chuckle, murmured words.

"Oh, you in trouble now, bitch."

Saskia looked over, but the officers turned inward. Since she had intervened and caused the Encino police homicide sample to be burned by the Delaneys, the dissenting whispers had grown minute by minute into undisguised glares, murmured warnings, ranting displays that were as yet too bold to be directed at her or carried out in earshot but were nevertheless deliberately performed in her line of sight. Mayor Grimley marched over to Curler and Saskia with his phone out, the screen toward them, and Saskia got a closer look at his manicured hands and gleaming cuff links than she would have liked when he shoved the phone under her nose.

"Would you like to tell me what this is?" Grimley asked.

Saskia had to step back to take in the video. Curler leaned in to watch a clip of Jonie Delaney screaming that she had killed her sister, then being wrestled back by Delta Hodge. Saskia had a strange sense of rewinding in time twenty minutes to when the incident had actually happened. She looked around. Nothing much had changed in the tent since that moment. There was an untouched coffee standing on the fold-out table that someone had brought for Saskia, a coffee she knew in her bones had been spat in. And

Jonie Delaney was gone—dragged off, sedated, resting and, Saskia presumed, on her way to the local hospital to a secure ward to sleep off the effects of that sedation under police protection.

Saskia dropped her eyes to the text below the video, the scrolling banner. The mayor was playing the video from the *Los Angeles Daily News* website.

"It's a video." Saskia sighed. "Taken by someone inside the police camp, evidently. It shows a traumatized teenager having a mental breakdown."

"Hell of a coward we got somewhere!" Curler raised his voice, looking around him at the officers milling about. "To film something like that and shoot it over to a global news outlet!"

"Why is she saying she killed her sister?" Grimley asked. His narrow, wolfish face and furious eyes hadn't left Saskia's. "Is there anything to that? Or is she just being crazy?"

"There's . . ." Saskia thought about lying. Didn't. "We're checking it out."

"So she confessed to you?" Grimley said. "She told you what happened?"

"Mr. Mayor, with all the respect that I can possibly muster right now," Saskia said, "this is a police matter, and I would ask you not to intervene."

"Oh, wow." Grimley dropped the phone. "Really? *I* shouldn't intervene?"

Saskia felt her neck reddening.

"Because I'm hearing there's been a bit of that going around today, Chief Ferboden!"

Saskia heard a laugh from nearby. The group of officers turned away, their eyes on their boots.

"Jonie Delaney's confession does not appear to us to be credible at this time," Curler said. "Until we can find something that lends it credibility, we—"

"Tell those people"—the mayor pointed at the distant lab—"that their daughter's death was an inside job. End this thing. Now."

"Mayor Grimley," Saskia said through her teeth. "I thank you wholeheartedly for your operational advice. I'll take it under advisement. But whether or not I apply it is entirely my decision."

"Look." Grimley edged closer. Saskia could smell mint gum on his breath. "I've met with my lawyer this morning already—"

"Oh, is that why you're so late?" Curler murmured.

The mayor narrowed his eyes at Curler. "—and he's telling me the fact that my niece's sample has been handled *at all* by the Delaney couple is bad news for her case. Okay? Are you hearing me? Do you understand? Her case is already in hot water. I'm going to have to go through back channels to even *find* the guy who assaulted a member of my family. Then I'm going to have to try to prosecute him without an admissible DNA sample. And that's *if* the sample even survives the next few hours!"

Saskia watched the mayor's lips stretching taut under his gray mustache. His too-close, fast-moving, peach-pink and utterly punchable lips.

"*If* it's destroyed," he went on, "we'll have *nothing*!"

"Do you think you're telling me anything that I don't know already right now, Mr. Mayor?" Saskia asked. "How do you figure your situation is any different from that of the other families with samples in that lab?"

"My situation is different," Grimley said, smiling at Saskia, "because if they destroy that sample, *I'll destroy you*."

Grimley turned away, tried to storm off, almost ran headfirst into Tanner Court, who had been meandering sulkily around the police camp since Saskia forbade him to go with Jonie to the hospital, in case he was needed here. The boy twisted sideways to let the mayor through. Saskia only realized she had been holding her breath when it rushed out of her, sending tingles of relief across her scalp.

"Fuck." Curler exhaled in unison beside her. His face was tight and mean. "*Fuck.*"

She took out her phone and scrolled the news sites. The Jonie Delaney outburst was on the front page of all the major outlets. Saskia had known her career was over all morning. If punching out a SWAT commander hadn't done it, intervening against the Encino police officers' DNA sample would have. It was possible, she consoled herself, that things were set to fall apart even before the Delaneys took over the Hertzberg-Davis lab. What happened to Hoss shouldn't have happened. She shouldn't have trusted him to know he was safe to go off radar with the Machines when he was so immersed. He'd almost died. That was on her.

But she also knew that a decimated police career wasn't the end of the threat when it came to Mayor Ike Grimley. The guy had a penchant for vengeance, and a personal vendetta from him would mean Saskia would have to move to Utah to be employed as anything more than a Chili's restaurant manager ever again. The sense of loss, current and pending, made her feel weightless.

"It doesn't matter what's in the lab," she said, speaking to no one, to everyone, to herself. "It could be anything. DNA samples. Millions of dollars. Bags full of diamonds. I can't put objects before human lives. I have to help the hostages. That's my only job."

"I know," Curler said.

Saskia had forgotten he was standing there beside her.

"I'm with you."

Saskia almost leaned into him for a hug. The gratitude, and longing, was that strong.

The laptop at the fold-out table nearby started ringing. Saskia walked there, unable to feel the ground beneath her feet.

Ryan Delaney appeared alone on the screen.

"We want to send Elsie and Ashlea out," he said.

"Okay." Saskia nodded. "Okay. Good."

"But you're going to have to pay for it," Ryan said.

Lamb was quietly contemplative. She was gripping the steering wheel, now and then glancing over at Charlie incredulously as he smoked in the passenger's seat, with an elbow out the window, like they hadn't just bested a one-ton palm tree and a vicious gang leader in a fight for their lives. He figured she was upset at having left another crime scene without volunteering to sit for a report or hand over to the attending patrol cops. Still caught up in the policies and procedures they would have drilled into her at the academy with all the heaviness of priests yelling at Sunday school students about lying to their parents. The blood on Lamb's neck was drying and cracking. The Honda coupe that Surge had managed to source for them in a mere ten minutes in downtown Los Angeles stank of fish and was littered with woodchips. It made Charlie wonder how many hot cars the ex–police officer had lying around the city, whom they were used by, and how long it would be before he and Lamb needed another one. When she put the car into gear, the whole stick had come off in her hand, a metal tube with an eight ball attached to it that someone hadn't installed properly.

Charlie snapped when Lamb glanced over at him for maybe the sixth time in a single block.

"You look like you want to have some kind of outburst, Lamb," he said. He rubbed his aching skull and felt the pull of exhaustion on his bones. "You haven't cried in a couple of hours. Have you reached capacity? Do you need a handkerchief?"

"I'm not going to cry," Lamb said. "My pending outburst is about you kicking the shit out of a man just now in front of a dozen civilians. That was fucked up."

"It won't make the news. Not with the Hertzberg-Davis thing going on."

"I'm not worried about it making the news. I'm worried about you doing it again."

"Am I being a little unpredictable for your tastes, Lamb?" Charlie asked.

"Frankly, yes."

"Well, while we're getting all worried about things," he said, "should I start worrying about the gun you're hiding from me?"

Lamb scoffed.

"I know it was a bit Wild West down there on the beachfront"—Charlie sucked on his cigarette—"but, I swear to god, while I was crouched behind those bike racks, I saw a glimmer of gold out of the corner of my eye. It came from right where you were crouched. You know who likes big, ugly, gold-plated guns, don't you?"

Lamb didn't answer.

"Surge." Charlie looked over. "Surge likes those."

Lamb had shrunk two inches behind the wheel.

"When I crawled under the car, I slid my gun toward you," Charlie continued, exhaling out the window. "But you didn't pick it up. Then, lo and behold, you somehow get Franko Aderhold to drop his weapon just by asking him to. How'd you manage that?"

No answer.

"What am I gonna see if I look up that civilian footage of the shoot-out on social media, Lamb? Am I gonna see you standing there with a big gold gun?"

"I don't know where this whole idea that I shouldn't have a gun came from," Lamb huffed. "I'm qualified to have a gun. I have a license. I'm an excellent shot."

"This is not your day, Lamb. With everything that you have going on right now, it's not your ideal day for walking around with a gun. Especially near me. I set the rules in this partnership, and my rule for you is, 'No guns.'"

"Did you say 'partnership'?"

"No."

"All right, all right, all right. This line of inquiry is a nice little diversion from what *I* was trying to get at." Lamb tapped her chest. "Which is that you stomped Franko Aderhold half to death just now."

"What's your point?"

"My point is that you're acting like your time under, and how it ended, was no big deal. That you're not emotional about it. But it was. And you are."

"Am I?"

"Yes," she said. "Maybe too emotionally volatile to be on this case right now."

"You're right," Charlie conceded. "Maybe we should just go home, both of us. Weep into a bucket of ice cream and watch *Legends of the Fall* and leave all this kid-finding stuff to the experts."

Lamb tried not to laugh. She failed. "You're such an *ass.*"

"I'm not an ass, I'm a hero." Charlie's phone started ringing. He took it out and looked at the screen. Unknown number. He declined the call. "One of the top three Death Machines leaders is dead. One's in custody. Just one more to bite the dust."

"And then it's over?"

"No. But I'll feel less emotional about it."

"Why did you do it?" she asked. When he didn't answer, she pressed on. "Why let the whole police force believe you had a drug problem and had to be shipped off to Bali? Wouldn't that ruin your reputation?"

"Yes."

"So why do it?"

"Because that's what it took to get into the Machines."

"Charlie." Lamb gave an exasperated sigh. "I'm asking you why you went undercover. Why did you sacrifice yourself like that? You left your whole life to become one of them. It almost killed you."

Charlie tapped his finger on the windowsill, thought about coming up with something to deter her or convince her that it was all just a job. Something Saskia had asked him to do. The natural progression of detectives who knew how to act and could convince criminals to trust them.

"I'm restless," he said. "Okay? I get restless. I've been a cop for a . . . a long time. And I like it. It keeps me occupied—the puzzles, the chase, the game. But soon enough, that starts becoming a problem in your life. You can't keep a girlfriend because you want to be at work all the time. You want to be at work all the time because you know that every minute you're on the job, you're inching closer and closer to whatever it is you're trying to do—catch the guy, solve the riddle, find the victim, stop the catastrophe before it happens. When you're home, you're just . . . wasting time. You think about work while you're around your girlfriend, and you become distracted and aloof. Because her problems can't measure up to yours. You're trying to take her seriously when she's telling you about her best friend ordering a fucking hair straightener off the internet and it being a knockoff and not the real thing . . . Meanwhile, you're still thinking about the woman you arrested the night before for pimping out her own eight-year-old to guys on Craigslist."

"Jesus," Lamb said.

Charlie hardly noticed. "Your apartment is a shithole because you're never there," he went on. "You can't watch TV because all the stories are too perfect. The people are too pretty and too kind and too understanding. All your friends are cops, so when you socialize, the job is all you talk about. It gets into you. Into your blood." Charlie tapped his wrist, his veins. "In the end, you have to make a choice. You either spend your whole life trying to find that balance, trying to crawl back to normality in the hours between shifts, or you give in and throw yourself fully into the arms of the job."

Lamb gripped the steering wheel.

"I did that," Charlie said. "I gave in."

They rode in silence for a while.

"I asked Saskia if she had any undercover work because I knew it would mean I could be a cop twenty-four-seven. Even when I slept," he said. "It's not just me, either. Viola is the same. She decided to be Viola Babineaux, and that's what she is now, all day and all night. She goes to the doctor, it's Viola Babineaux going to the doctor. It's a whole thing. They have to shut the building down. She has to have an assistant and a security guy on her. She loves it."

"What were your parents like?" Lamb looked over, tried to read his eyes. "How did you both get this . . . obsessive?"

"Lamb, I thought you were hooked on being a cop, not a therapist."

"I *am* hooked on being a cop," she said.

"Well, maybe you should find a therapist, then," Charlie said. "Because I just sat here telling you how being a cop took over my life the way heroin does for junkies and you didn't even flinch."

"I'm not even going to fight it." Lamb shook her head vehemently. "I don't want balance. If I could be a cop even when I slept, I would."

"I don't get it." He sank down in his seat, put his boots on the dash. "I don't get it, Lamb. This thing you've got for being a cop—it can't just be about not wanting to become the kind of person who can clock a guy who needs better arch support at half a mile."

She drew a deep breath.

"My parents got held up," she said.

Charlie felt a smile growing on his face. "Someone robbed Eddie's Shoes?"

"It was bad." Lamb shot him a warning glance. "The guy was obviously on something. He had a woman's scarf wrapped around the lower part of his face, but he was tweakin' hard. He walked in just after opening and waved a gun around, made my mom and me get on our knees while my dad emptied the register."

"How old were you?" Charlie asked.

"Nine."

"Wow. Okay."

"The guy took two hundred bucks from the register and grabbed a pair of snakeskin ankle boots from the display window at the front of the shop. They were Everglades python. Ethically produced. Hand stitched. They had a cashmere blend insole, which—"

"Lamb."

"Anyway, my dad called the cops, and two officers came. One didn't even come into the store." Lamb's mouth twisted bitterly. "She just stood out front, talking on her cell phone. The officer who came in, he listened to my dad's story and made a few notes in his little palm-size notebook, but I was watching really carefully, and the guy didn't flip the page."

She looked at Charlie for some reaction that he clearly wasn't giving.

"He didn't fill more than *one page* with notes," she pressed.

"He didn't care that someone had stuck up Eddie's Shoes?" Charlie tried not to smile.

"The man stuck *a gun* in my *parents' faces.*"

"I get it. I get it."

"My parents kept calling and calling," Lamb said. "But nothing happened with the case. My mom wasn't right for a while afterward. A few months. She had nightmares. My dad had cameras installed. Eventually, they both let it go."

"You didn't, though."

"No, I didn't," Lamb said. "I was determined to do something about it. I changed the route of my walk home from school so I could go past a homeless encampment, in case I spotted the guy there. I used the school library to search eBay to see if the guy was trying to sell the snakeskin boots online. I used my pocket money to buy all the local newspapers, to see if he'd listed them in the classifieds. I waited until my parents weren't home, and I called every pawn shop within a ten-mile radius of Hansen Hills. The hunt was . . . It was exhilarating. It made me feel powerful and sort of . . . vengeful. If those stupid cops weren't going to find the guy, I was. I was nine years old, and I was going to show them how the fucking job was done."

Charlie was laughing with delight.

"There was one pawn shop over in San Fernando that wouldn't answer the phone," Lamb said. "I got convinced the boots were there. I never lied to my parents. Ever. But I told them I was helping out with an event for the chess club and staying behind at school one afternoon, and I caught the bus over to San Fernando to see for myself."

"Oh, Lamb." Charlie's heart felt warm and full. "Were they there?"

"You bet your ass they were," Lamb said. "Right in the window, just like they'd been in our store."

"So what happened?"

"Well, I marched right into the store and took the boots down from the shelf and checked the manufacturer's serial number on the heel against the one listed in my dad's intake list, of course," Lamb said. "And once I had the evidence, I went and told the guy behind the counter that the boots sitting on display in his front window were stolen property. I said I was going to call the police."

"And what did he say?"

"He said, 'Get the fuck out of my store.'"

Charlie grinned. Lamb swiped at her lashes.

"So what did you do?"

"I went home and cried all night," Lamb said. "I

was too embarrassed to tell my parents what had happened. I let it go."

"Oh, *Laaaaamb*."

"Point is, I knew then that I was made for this job."

Charlie didn't respond. His phone was buzzing again. He answered the call and knew from the volume of the voice alone that it was Viola.

"Why am I hearing that you have a bloodied, chained-up man in that trailer on the Universal lot?" she barked.

Charlie held the phone away from his ear. "Because we do."

"What the *actual* fuck?"

"I said I wanted a home base," Charlie said. "You gave me one. What I do with it is my business."

"This is not like you using my locker at school to keep lizards, Charlie," Viola sneered. "This is my *career*."

"You got paid a half a million dollars last year to wear a hat to a lunch meeting. I think your career is gonna be fine, honey."

"Who's the guy?"

"Just some criminal."

"Who's the other guy? The one who answered the door and gave some bullshit story about rehearsing a scene?"

"Surge," Charlie said.

He held the phone down in his lap for a while, waiting for Viola to run out of steam. Lamb's lips were pursed. He lifted the phone again.

"Get your ass here to the Mulholland house," Viola said.

"I'm busy."

"I know. You're working on that missing kid case, right?"

"Right."

"Yeah, well, I found the kid," Viola said. "She's here. You can thank me later."

CHAPTER 24

All across the police encampment, Saskia could see personnel crowded around laptops and tablets, some with headsets on, listening to Ryan's call. The camp was sickeningly silent and had been since the ambulance took Jonie Delaney away. Tanner Court was standing by a cooler full of water bottles, watching the Hertzberg-Davis building, chewing his nails, strangely vulnerable-looking in the aftermath of being told he could not accompany Jonie in the ambulance. On the screen, Ryan Delaney put his gun on the steel table. It made his laptop shudder so that the image of him that Saskia, Curler, and the technician were watching wobbled slightly.

"I'm going to burn this," Ryan Delaney said. He held up a test tube, rolled the thin plastic object in his fingers so he could read the label. "It's case number 533–821."

Saskia felt a minor sense of relief. Payment for losing Elsie would be an extra burning, it seemed. She glanced at Curler, who snatched up the stock list and handed it to her. She didn't recognize the case, but noted it was a one-shot. There was no denying it. The Delaneys knew which samples were the ones that, if destroyed, would be unrecoverable. That meant someone had explained the concept of one-shots to them.

Someone inside the lab. She tried to push those curiosities from her brain and listen to the hostage-taker in front of her.

"Okay," Saskia said. "Okay. We understand. We—"

"From now on," Ryan continued, "I'm going to burn a sample every half an hour."

"*What?*" Saskia's mouth fell open. An audible ripple of shock went through the crowd around her. "Ryan, that wasn't—"

"That wasn't the deal?" he asked. "You're right. The original deal my wife and I presented to you was that we would burn samples every two hours until you find our daughter. So far, you haven't responded to that deal. And my wife's no longer here with me. So I'm changing things."

"Ryan, let's take a minute here," Curler said. The negotiator's lips seemed impossibly dry. He licked his teeth, watching Ryan lower the tip of the swab into the Bunsen burner flame. "Because you're right. You're completely in control of this situation. You've made a choice—the right choice—to send Ashlea and Elsie out. You can keep making those good and sensible choices now."

Ryan lifted the singed and blackened tip of the swab, held it close to the camera lens, made it do a slow ballerina twirl in his fingers.

"It would be really helpful for us to have more information about what's happening in there," Curler continued. "About what *exactly* the new deal that you're giving us entails."

"You want to know if there's a bomb in here," Ryan said.

"Yes," Curler said. "And we're being honest with each other, right? We're putting it all out on the table. We need to know exactly the kind of danger Ibrahim and Gary are in right now. Our only concern is for the safety of everyone in that building. Including you, Ryan."

Ryan smiled. "How cute."

"If you've made an improvised device on your own, it's possible that it will detonate without you intending it to," Curler said. "So please tell us if that's what we're dealing with. What's in the third duffel bag, Ryan?"

"How do you know how many bags are in here?" Ryan lifted his eyes finally from the blackened tip of the swab in his fingers.

Saskia felt her throat tighten. "Our analysts have examined the videos you've sent so far," she cut in. "There are three bags, right?"

Ryan didn't answer. The whole police camp seemed to hum with tension.

"The only person whose safety I care about right now is my youngest daughter," Ryan said. "What have you done to find Tilly since I spoke to you last?"

"Just tell him," someone hissed.

Saskia looked toward the noise but couldn't discern which nearby officer it had come from. More murmurs of dissent seemed to ease through the air, but Saskia couldn't tell their origin.

"*Why the fuck don't they tell him?*"

"*Your other daughter did it, man!*"

"Where are Ashlea and Elsie?" Saskia asked. "Can we expect them to come out soon?"

"They left here about three minutes ago," Ryan said, twisting the gas to turn the burner off. Saskia watched as his hand rose to the laptop's lid, sheltering the camera lens like a fleshy awning. "If anything happens to Elsie, I'll change the deal again."

Ryan slammed the laptop shut. Saskia watched the automatic glass doors of the Hertzberg-Davis building, the darkened reception area beyond. Seconds passed, then minutes, the tension pounding between her ears.

She sought distraction to latch on to. An island in the turbulent sea. Next to her, Delta Hodge was following Tanner Court with her eyes as the boy paced the side of the tent. She reminded Saskia of an eagle she'd seen in a documentary once, the huge bird of prey tracking a rabbit across a distant riverbank. Unmoving. Lethal. One of her team came and gave her a progress report, and Hodge gave the slightest nod in response, still tracking the boy with eerie stillness.

"You don't like that kid, do you?" Saskia asked Hodge.

"Reminds me of some fuckboy I used to know." She finally stole her eyes away from the teen. "I got three snipers set up and two grab teams in position. I'll join them when we have a visual on the women."

"Sounds good," Saskia said.

Saskia and Hodge stood side by side, watching the doors of Hertzberg-Davis. It was Curler who shattered the silence in the tent.

"There they are."

Saskia saw a figure emerge from the darkness, Ashlea Pratt taking awkward, slow steps toward the inner doors. Her pale hands were raised, shaking visibly, on either side of her face. As the automatic doors slid open, Saskia expected a wave of shouts and activity from the press camp on the hill. But there was no sound. Even the choppers overhead seemed to have been muted. Saskia saw a pale hand on Ashlea's shoulder, then a slice of Elsie Delaney's face came into view.

Saskia was surprised to see Hodge crouched with her team at the edge of the police camp. She hadn't felt the officer leave her side. She recognized the SWAT commander's arm waving her team of five officers forward. There was another team at ninety degrees to the first, ten pistols in total aimed at the pair, more guns on the hill, on nearby buildings, wherever Hodge had hidden them.

The women walked, Elsie almost stepping on Ashlea's heels, their bodies all but touching. Saskia couldn't see a gun, but she had to assume it was jammed into Ashlea's spine. Saskia's mind fought to stay in the moment, in the agonizing seconds ticking by. But she couldn't tear her thoughts away from that—from the hidden gun pointed directly at Ashlea's back. At the baby inside her. The world watched silently as one mother led another out into the sunbaked no-man's-land between the doors of Hertzberg-Davis and the waiting SWAT teams. The young journalist's tear-filled eyes flicked from one team of SWAT officers to the other.

"Don't shoot! Don't shoot! Don't shoot!" Ashlea's whimpers came across the space to Saskia loud and clear.

"Slowly! Slooooowly!" Hodge's low, hard voice echoed across the empty lot. "Alpha team, hold! Hold! Hold!"

Saskia didn't even realize she was gripping Curler's hand until he tore it from hers, his whole body flinching at the sound of the gunshot. It seemed as if the glass door fifteen feet behind Elsie shimmered in the air, suspended, before it dropped like a curtain. Elsie's head whipped around to see the impact of the shot that had missed her by less than a foot. Ashlea and Elsie dropped into a crouch together. Both SWAT teams flattened on the asphalt, their guns still raised, Hodge's scream ringing across the parking lot.

"Hold fire! Hold fire! Hold fucking fire!"

"Who the *fuck* is firing?" Saskia looked instinctively toward the hill, but she had no idea where Hodge's snipers were. When she looked back, the SWAT officers were descending on Ashlea and Elsie. Ashlea shook off the man trying to lift her off her feet and carry her out of harm's way. She was pointing frantically at Elsie, who was squashed under two officers in tactical gear.

"She's hurt! She's hurt! Get them off her!"

A pop. A crash. Voices shouting. Ryan was standing well back from the window, positioned so he could see the parking lot through a crack in the blinds without being spotted by the snipers. From the floor, Bendigo saw the impact of whatever had happened outside hit Ryan so hard his whole body jolted. For a moment, Bendigo's brain told him Ryan had been shot. That the bullet had somehow defied the laws of physics and entered his body without penetrating the glass or the roller blind. But the hostage-taker recovered, clapped a hand to his mouth, a moan of shock muffled by his sweaty palm.

"They shot her!" he cried.

"Who?" Ibrahim asked. His voice was high and soft, full of terror. Any and all possibilities related to the sound they had heard being a gunshot were going to be bad. Cataclysmic. Bendigo wanted to freeze time permanently, to delay ever finding out what horror awaited him next. Schrödinger's bullet.

"Who's shot?" Ibrahim insisted. "Who's shot?"

Bendigo heard a scream among the frantic voices outside.

"She's hurt! She's hurt! Get them off her!"

"They . . . shot . . . my wife . . ." Ryan's words were gulped. Inhaled. Like the very ability to speak had left him. Bendigo dropped his eyes to the gun in Ryan's fist. Was now his moment? Was Ryan so distracted, so incapacitated by what was happening outside, that Bendigo could end all this in a single, calculated move? He got to his knees. Ryan walked stiffly to the table, seized a cell phone, and dialed. Bendigo's courage faltered. He slid back down next to Ibrahim and spoke while Ryan was on the phone, his voice fast and low and near to Ibrahim's ear.

"Where did you hide the second pair of scissors?"

"You shot her! You fucking shot her! She was surrendering, and you shot her!"

Ibrahim's eyes were locked on Ryan. "We can't do this, man. We can't kill them. Those scissors sticking out of Elsie . . . I-I-I can't do a thing like that. I don't know how you did it."

"Is she dead?"

"I didn't do it." Bendigo sighed. "It was an accident."

"I can see now what's going to happen as soon as I surrender. Your people are going to take me out."

"Listen." Ibrahim inched closer. His breath was sour. Exhaustion. Hunger. The heat and the long hours of terror roiling in his stomach. "The cops have it out for these two. Okay? They want revenge. They're gonna bust in here as soon as they can, and they're going to blast anything that moves. They don't care about getting us out of here anymore. Okay? This is about nailing Elsie and Ryan for destroying all those cases."

"We can't think like that." Bendigo shook his head.

"We have to think like that!" Ibrahim's pupils were huge. A terrified house cat outmatched in a fight with a cougar. "We're gonna get caught in the cross fire here, man. I've seen what cops do when you piss them off like this. And it'll all be inside this lab, away from the cameras. They can say whatever they want about what happened in here."

"We can turn this around," Bendigo said. He'd never heard his own words sound so phony emerging from his mouth. So false. "We can get Ryan to back down."

Bendigo and Ibrahim were distracted by a noise. It was Ryan, marching to the fridge by the door, the huge steel machine from which he and Elsie had drawn all the samples they had burned so far. They watched as he snatched up a handful of vials and started popping the caps off each one in turn.

CHAPTER 25

A coyote was calmly traversing the rocky landscape beneath one of the cantilever houses on Mulholland as Charlie emerged from a hairpin turn halfway into the Hills. Lamb had been up into the hills behind LA a couple of times in her life, as everyone born in California probably has, either to ogle celebrity mansions or on school excursions to the observatory. When she was in high school, an emo boy a few grades above her had mumbled an invitation to go with him one night to see the Sharon Tate murder house, and Lamb had been so stunned by the offer she'd ignored its painfully bleak theme and accepted. They'd ended up talking awkwardly in his car for a half an hour outside the fenced-off, bare slab of land where Charles Manson's crew had murdered a bunch of people decades before Lamb was born. When the atmosphere and the paint-thinner vodka and hazy moonlight failed to have any amorous effect on her, Lamb told the boy she had period cramps and walked home. The boy had never acknowledged her existence again.

Charlie took over driving. His familiarity with the area was apparent from the speed with which he rounded the tight corners and flew down the narrow streets crammed with expensive cars and construction

vehicles. He wedged the car into a driveway Lamb
would not have noticed, the entrance to the property
a mere dent in a huge wall covered with thick ivy.
Charlie leaned on the horn, huffing at the security
cameras settled on top of the wall like gulls.

"Come on," he sighed. "It's not like she doesn't
know we're coming."

A sharp blast of music made both of them jump.
Charlie scrambled for the cell phone that was pumping out "Bad Case of Loving You" by Robert Palmer
from the change well under the radio.

"What the hell is that?" Lamb asked.

"Surge," Charlie sighed. "He gives you a phone, he
always sets a ringtone for himself. The man's a come-
dian. Yeah?"

The speaker was so loud Lamb could hear the bear-
shaped man on the other end. "I'm gonna send you
some more images. They're weird."

"Okay," Charlie said. "What else?"

"I nailed down the six license plates from the video,"
Surge said. "No Rojer. No Rojer relatives. Nothing interesting about the owners of the vehicles. I got one
guy who was arrested for an aggravated assault on his
wife, but that doesn't mean much in this context and,
besides that, it was fifteen years ago. Far as I can tell,
a sale of one of the cars went through four months
after Tilly went missing, but it was a woman selling
the vehicle to her sister. So . . . not something you'd
do if you wanted the vehicle out of your life because
it was full of evidence."

"Keep at it," Charlie said. "This is good, fast stuff.
How's Binchley?"

"I fed him."

"Why?"

"Because he was bringing me down," Surge said.
"He's a very negative person when he's hungry."

Lamb found herself smiling.

"I also checked up on the dumpster thing," Surge

said. "A lot of the garbage workers down there were pinch hitters. Students and migrants. It's a shitty job. Long hours, heavy labor. So most of them have moved on, but I might have a lead on a guy who worked the waterfront that month."

"Good," Charlie said. He and Lamb watched the solid slab of ivy before them part into two gates, revealing a long, flagstone driveway. "Good stuff."

"Listen, you two see the latest from the lab?"

"What latest?" Lamb asked before Charlie could.

"It's all over the news," Surge said. "Sorry, Hoss."

Charlie hung up, swiped the call away, and opened a Google search page. Lamb leaned over. Charlie's thumb hovered as he tried to decide which headline to click on.

Shots fired outside Hertzberg-Davis siege.

One hostage freed in dramatic shoot-out.

Ryan Delaney revenge video follows shooting.

Police insiders tell of new Delaney threat.

Charlie selected a headline. Lamb watched the empty driveway before them as he read aloud.

"*LAPD officials are not commenting on whether a sniper shot that hit a glass door at the Hertzberg-Davis forensic laboratory minutes ago was deliberately fired or whether the gunshot came after tensions among members of law enforcement reached boiling point.*" Charlie's reading was muffled as he chewed his fingernails. "*Hostage Ashlea Marie Pratt and her alleged captor Elsie Ann Delaney were approximately fifty yards from police, in the midst of a dramatic surrender, when the shot was . . .*"

His voice trailed away. Lamb's thoughts were crashing into each other.

"Elsie's in custody," Charlie said. "Fuck. *Fuck!*"

Charlie punched the dashboard. Lamb held her head, afraid to hear more.

"This is good, isn't it?" Lamb said. "One hostage and one perpetrator are out. We're nearing the end."

"They shot at his wife," Charlie said. He shook his head. "This is gonna piss him off."

"What's the revenge video?" Lamb asked. "What was that all about?"

"*Ryan Delaney responded to the shooting with a video sent directly to the* LA Times," Charlie read. He clicked a link.

Lamb leaned over again. They watched as Ryan Delaney appeared on the screen, holding a fistful of swabs over the Bunsen burner flame.

"There are five samples here," he said. His lip curled viciously, his eyes reflecting the flame, blazing gold. "I'll send the ID numbers after this video. This is what you get, you stupid, useless motherfuckers. You shoot at my wife, I *fuck your cases*!"

"Five samples," Lamb said. "Five samples at once."

"One of mine will be in there," Charlie said. "It has to be. We know they already got the Navarro sample out of the fridge."

They sat back in their seats, watching the breeze trace its fingers up the walls of the thick, green hedges ten feet in height that lined the driveway.

"We've got to call Chief Ferboden and find out what's going on," Lamb said.

"I don't want to know what's going on." Charlie stepped on the accelerator. The car lurched up the long, ornate drive. "I don't want to feel any more helpless than I do right now. Let's stay on track here. We've got to find the kid and end the siege."

The house was as Lamb had imagined it from what she'd seen in glossy magazines and "at home with" specials on the Oprah Winfrey Network. Huge, white, sprawling. A network of gaping spaces accented with matte black glass, shimmering water features, or strategically placed blocks of pale pine. In the foyer, which was as big as her parents' store, there was a full-size horse carved from white marble, wearing a lampshade for a hat. No other furniture.

Viola Babineaux opened her own door, stood back, and took in their appearance with her manicured brows hanging low over her wolfish blue eyes.

"What happened?" she asked, looking at Lamb. The surreal and paralyzing intimidation Lamb had felt at first meeting Viola swelled again, threatened to choke off her words or bring tears to her eyes, but she straightened her shoulders and pushed it away hard.

"We had a little disagreement with a palm tree," she said, giving a pleasant smile. "We're fine."

"Where's the kid?" Charlie asked.

"Through here." Viola motioned. Charlie walked off with a speed and confidence that told Lamb he was immune to the gallery-like reverence the enormity of the house commanded. Lamb caught up to Charlie in a bowling alley–size space she guessed served as a living room. On a long, low couch, a girl was sitting, facing away from them, taking in the panoramic view of the lush gardens behind the house. Charlie stood staring at the back of the child's head. The crown of chocolaty ringlet curls.

Tilly Delaney's curls.

Lamb stopped beside her partner, her brain screaming a single, high note of rattling exhilaration.

When the child turned, sensing their presence, Lamb heard that thrilled cry strangled into silence as surely as if a bird were being throttled. The girl was about nine or ten, taller and fairer than Tilly Delaney had been, and her face was instantly recognizable.

"Ruby Monacco," Lamb said. Another little surge of intimidation hit her chest as she recognized the child actor. Lamb had watched Ruby Monacco run and fight and cry alongside Nicolas Cage and Harrison Ford and Brad Pitt in half a dozen or more movies, and now she had stepped across the screen into Lamb's real world. The otherworldly sensation was interrupted by Charlie barking at Viola.

"Is this a joke?"

Ruby got up and turned to them all.

"What? No?" Viola gestured to the child. "You're looking for the kid, right? The one on the news. Tanya Delaney. She was supposed to have been on Santa Monica Beach on the nineteenth of October. Well, Ruby called me a couple of hours ago and said it was her."

"It was you?" Lamb asked.

Ruby nodded. "Yes," she said. "I was there that day. I have proof."

"You said you had Tilly here!" Charlie hadn't taken his eyes off Viola. "You said, 'I have the kid. You can thank me later.' This isn't the kid! This is one of your fucking movie star friends!"

Charlie's phone pinged in his pocket. Lamb's did, too. She pulled it out. Surge had texted them a photograph of a Japanese man leaning against a brick wall before a sprawling beach. In the background, a small girl was walking with her head down, her brown curls spilling out from beneath a wide-brimmed, panama-style hat.

Have found this kid, Surge's message read. *Tilly? But clothes not right.*

"My understanding is"—Viola held her hands up—"that Ruby here was on Santa Monica Beach that day. The day you're talking about. So wherever your missing girl was, she wasn't there. It was Ruby."

"She *was* there." Charlie's face and neck were dark with anger. "Haven't you been paying attention? Haven't you read the articles? We *know* Tilly Delaney was there at the beach that day! That's where she went missing from!"

"Ruby, you must have been there at the same time," Lamb said. No one heard her.

"Charlie, I haven't *read* the *articles*!" Viola's voice had risen to meet his. "I haven't been paying attention to it! I've been busy. All I know is that you were looking for Tanya Delaney on the beach and Ruby was on the beach, and they look the same, and—"

"It's *Tilly* Delaney!"

"Whatever the fuck!"

"Okay, stop," Ruby said. The little girl pressed her palms together, the corner of her perfect cupid's-bow lips pulled tight in a disbelieving smirk. "You guys need to just chill, okay? I don't do raised voices."

Charlie pinched the bridge of his nose and groaned. "Oh god."

"Everybody sit down." Ruby gestured to the couches.

Charlie went and slumped onto one of the sofas while Viola and Lamb perched carefully on another. Beyond the huge windows, a big red parrot settled into a towering tree as though joining the meeting.

"I knew it was something about a missing kid on a beach." Viola's jaw was jutted, defiant. "I just took the call from Ruby and put two and two together and rang you. Which I didn't need to do. Because I'm busy. But I wanted to help you. Maybe I got it slightly wrong. But you need to show some *fucking gratitude* for once in your miserable life."

"Let's just figure this out," Lamb said. "Ruby, we're so grateful to you for making contact with us. You've saved us a lot of time. We just got some images through from our analyst of that day at the beach, and we would have been very curious to know who the girl in the pictures is, if not Tilly." Lamb took out her phone and showed the others the pictures Surge had sent. "So this is not a waste of time. And, Viola, we are indeed very grateful."

Viola rolled her eyes and muttered to herself.

"Ruby, did you happen to see Tilly Delaney or her sister, Jonie, at the beach that day?" Lamb asked.

"No," Ruby said. "Not that I recall. But I was keeping my head down and trying to go unnoticed, so I wasn't paying specific attention to other people.

Hence the big hat and sunglasses. I bought them at the hotel lobby."

"You were trying to avoid being recognized by members of the public?"

"Yes." Ruby smiled. "See, I wasn't supposed to be at the beach at all. I'd snuck away from my handler. He thought I was at a meeting with my agent. And my agent thought I was in the room with my handler."

"Why did you have to sneak away?" Charlie asked, his voice finally back at normal speaking volume.

"Uh, because I was eight years old?" The girl laughed.

Lamb felt her own eyebrows rise. She understood Charlie's question. The girl before them, Lamb had to remind herself, was only ten. But her vernacular, her poised and confident gestures, the way she commanded the room, made that fact hard to accept. Lamb guessed it was no accident. That her parents, who likely had control of the child's earnings, would have Ruby accompanied by a team of tutors as she traveled the world taking prestigious movie roles. The smarter and more articulate she was, the easier it would be for her to take on the roles of a ten-, eleven-, or twelve-year-old, to keep ahead of the child star's eternal nemesis: time. Ruby settled on the couch, the tiny chairperson of the meeting, Lamb and Viola on the left of her and Charlie on the right.

"I had other reasons for needing to be discreet," Ruby said. "I'd been forbidden from going down to the beach because I was in the middle of filming *Kokio*, and if I got a tan, it was going to be a nightmare for the makeup department."

"I saw that!" Lamb blurted. She shielded her eyes when everyone turned to her. "Good . . . uh . . . good movie."

"I was also hiding from a stalker," Ruby said.

"A stalker?" Charlie glanced at Lamb. "What stalker?"

"This is why I felt I should make contact." Ruby put her palms out, smiling at Viola. "It may be that I can assist in your investigation by providing you with a suspect."

She talked. They listened. It was a tale that dove into freezing waters and deepened so gradually, so stealthily, that Lamb didn't realize she was struggling with the dread it inspired until she could hardly breathe. It began as it usually did for Ruby. With an excited, gushing, poorly constructed message in her fan email account. He was a farmer from Wyoming. There were no pictures, initially, just a description of open, icy fields and forests and a little house where he lived with his son and a variety of oddball pets.

"I wasn't supposed to answer more than twice," Ruby said. "That was the policy. But there was a lot of activity on Instagram around the *Stranger Things* kids and how they answered fan mail and how that humanized them. I needed some humanizing. I'd just been snapped wearing stilettos at Paris Fashion Week, and that didn't go down well. My publicists wanted to reframe my image a little. I answered Jacob's email."

"What did you say?" Lamb asked.

"Just the usual. The stuff I'd been taught to say. 'Thanks so much.' 'Your support means a lot.' Blah-blah-blah." Ruby waved her hand.

"But it went on?" Charlie said.

"It went on. He wrote back saying how surprised he was that I'd replied at all. He sounded nice to me. Unassuming. Really kind of stunned. So I was flattered. He seemed like a sweet dad who worked hard for a living." Ruby shrugged. "He wrote back telling me about his son, Harrison, and how smitten the kid was with me. Jacob wanted to know whether he should let Harrison watch *The Upgrade*."

Lamb watched Ruby's face. She saw flashes of the child she really was in her eyes, the regret and embarrassment and terror of being in trouble. The child inside was tangling and twisting around the surreal vision that she was: of a ten-year-old girl, wearing jeans that cost more than Lamb's car, calling other children "kids" and grown men "unassuming."

"I continued the conversation with Jacob on my phone," Ruby said. "My publicists didn't know about it. My relationship with my father was becoming strained at the time due to the whole Scientology thing. Jacob listened. And his stories about the farm and the animals were nice. They all had their little eccentricities. He rescued a goat that he found abandoned on the side of the road, and I felt like I was there to see it. Finding her. Healing her. Helping her trust again."

"I've seen videos like that," Lamb said. This time, she didn't shield her eyes when they all looked. "Somebody finds a kitten in the middle of the road. Or they lure and trap a wild and frightened dog. There's nice music. Lots of shots at the vet. The befores and afters."

"Yes!" Ruby nodded eagerly, her eyes big and locked on Lamb. "Yes. They're addictive, aren't they?"

"Oh yeah."

"See?" Ruby gestured to Lamb. "She gets it."

"It was the story that drew you in," Lamb said. "This was a good man. A rescuer of animals. An honest single father who cares about his son. I bet the wife was dead."

Ruby froze. "She was!" she said. "Jacob's wife. I asked what happened. You know. Eventually. After a few months."

"What was it? Car accident?"

"Plane crash."

Lamb looked at the parrot in the tree outside and hated the world and all the weirdos in it for a small moment.

"Did Jacob ever send you a photograph or a video of himself?" Charlie asked.

"No," Ruby said. "He said he was camera shy."

"What about the son? How old was Harrison supposed to have been?"

"He was five. I did receive a picture of a kid sitting on a couch once. But that was after a lot of pushing. Mostly it was just pictures and videos of the animals."

Ruby paused and rested her face in her palm. When a few moments had gone by and she hadn't continued, Lamb shuffled forward, clasped her hands, tried to present an understanding front.

"So it got sexual," she said. "Right?"

"No!" Ruby blurted. Her sudden laughter tinkled around the huge room. "No, it wasn't sexual, ma'am."

Lamb sat back, feeling her face redden.

"I might be ten years old, but I know what grooming is." Ruby's brows were knitted, that curled-lip smirk returned. "My people were schooling me on that when I was still in diapers. Jacob didn't want dollies. He wanted money."

"'Dollies'?" Lamb frowned.

"Nude images of young female children," Charlie said. "The male ones are 'teddies.'"

"He started out saying his car had broken down." Ruby huffed an exasperated sigh. "He was desperate. One of his horses was sick and he couldn't haul the trailer to the equine vet. He sent me a video of the horse, Maurice. He was in agony. Kidney stones. It was an emergency payment. He walked me through the process, how to send it via PayPal. I told no one."

Silence in the room.

"Jesus, this is embarrassing." Ruby rubbed her brow.

"Hey, you got duped by a predatory asshole," Lamb said. "It just happened to me a week ago."

"And she's twice your age!" Charlie quipped.

"It shouldn't have happened to you this early in life, Ruby." Lamb ignored her partner. "But it was going to happen sometime."

A phone started dinging somewhere. Lamb, Viola, and Charlie watched as Ruby dug a cell out of a tiny handbag and looked exhaustedly at the screen.

"No," the girl muttered, swiping the screen and silencing the call. "You can wait."

"How much money did you end up giving him?" Charlie asked.

"Not a crazy amount. A hundred thousand?"

Lamb inhaled sharply. She was the only one in the room who reacted at all.

"Over what time frame?" Charlie pushed.

"A year?"

Lamb eased her breath out silently.

"So you . . . you have those kinds of funds to move around on your own?" Lamb asked.

"My parents have control of my savings accounts," Ruby explained. "But I have a monthly allowance of thirty thousand dollars."

Lamb nodded as casually as she could.

"It wasn't all animal-care emergencies." Ruby examined Lamb from the corner of her eye, her jaw tight, the gasp obviously having shifted something in her. "There were other things. I wired them some money so Jacob and Harrison could come out to the premiere of Let It Burn that summer. Harrison had a panic attack about his mother's death in a plane crash while they were boarding, so they couldn't come."

"What was the biggest amount you ever sent?" Charlie asked.

Ruby thought. "Maurice's surgery was about eleven grand in total."

"When did you realize you were being played?" Viola asked. Something in her tone told Lamb that Viola was speaking from experience.

"August," Ruby said.

"Two months before Tilly went missing," Charlie said.

"I was tired of all the games. The stories about

why they couldn't come to meet me, or why I couldn't get another photograph of either one of them, were wearing thin. Then Jacob sent me a video that he said he had taken, but in the video, there was a reflection in a pane of glass, and I could see it was a woman holding the phone. I trapped him in the lie, and things got aggressive."

Ruby took the phone from beside her, swiped through to a series of messages, and handed it to Lamb. She scrolled through the texts, which were completely one-sided, a tower of pale gray blocks of text.

> Fuck U mouthy betraying little BITCH
> YOU STINKING ROTTING WHORE
> i know where to find u. I know people to send
>   after u who will enjoy making u there pretty
>   little baby doll punk.
> U will answer these messages or i will upload
>   the whole thread to Reddit RIGHT FUCKING
>   NOW!!!!!!

"He says he'll 'upload the thread'?" Lamb said.

"Our entire conversation," Ruby said. "Everything I'd told him over the past year or so. I'd trusted him. I'd bitched to him about my parents, my agents, the network, the studio. Powerful people in this town." She gave a helpless little shrug, nudged a tear from the corner of her eye with a small, pale knuckle. "It would have been the end of me."

Saskia Ferboden could see the muscles covering the back of Delta Hodge's skull shifting beneath her close-shaved hair as she roared at the three men in front of her. Two of the snipers were heavyset, muscular types whom Saskia couldn't imagine being very stealthy as they set up their strategic positions to end lives from afar. The last was small and wiry, with a small goatee and thin, wincing eyes.

"Who the fuck fired?" Hodge was demanding. The strap of her helmet was clutched in her gloved fist, and Saskia joined Curler out of swing range of the heavy, blunt instrument. "Who was it? Was it you, Marsh? It was you, wasn't it?"

None of the snipers spoke. Their faces ranged from blank to defiant. Saskia saw no remorse there, which made a chill settle deep in the marrow of her bones.

"It's not like I'm not going to find out who it was!" Hodge snarled. "I know your positions! There's going to be a fucking investigation! Specialists are going to come down here and figure out which one of you it was, so tell me now!"

"Hard to figure out a thing like that," the little guy said.

"What?" Hodge barked.

"Well, there are variables," he went on, glancing at the other two for encouragement. "Line of sight. Ricochet. Air pressure. Wind resistance. I mean, I kinda felt like a big gust of wind came just as the shot was taken. You might not have felt it or noticed it, Commander Hodge. You being on the ground and occupied with the extraction and all."

"Then there's human error." One of the big snipers picked up the trail, smiling. "I mean, I'm not one hundred percent sure which covert post I was manning just now. All this drama is messing with my emotions. I think I was at the Echo post up there on the north face. But before the shift change, I was at Juliet. I mean, maybe I'm mixed up, right, guys?"

"Maybe whoever fired did it accidentally," the little guy continued. He turned to the others. "Or maybe he did it deliberately. But whatever the case, maybe the stress of it all blanked it right out of his brain."

Hodge sucked air between her teeth.

"You're all stood down," she said in a voice so icy it reminded Saskia of a snake's hiss. "Get off my scene."

Curler was watching the revenge video on his phone. Saskia leaned over and watched it again. It was the third viewing for her, probably the same for Curler. The stock list he held in his hand was crinkled and dog-eared from overuse.

"The Navarro case," he said. He was holding the list now beside the itemized case numbers Ryan had sent to the press. "It's in there. It's burned."

"Shit," Saskia breathed. She felt hollow inside.

"So is the Compton rapist," Curler said. "The case he burned just before the surrender; that was an aggravated burglary. But the mayor's niece isn't there. Neither is the Malibu Mountains Killer. That's something."

"Is she dead?" Hodge's voice was hoarse, her eyes still blazing as she came to join the others. "Elsie Delaney. What's the update?"

"Elsie and Ashlea just arrived at LAC." Saskia looked at her phone. "Elsie's been admitted to surgery, but no, she's not dead."

Hodge didn't react. She was eyeing Tanner Court again, the teenager slumped on the chair in the corner with his head in his hands. "What's the plan here? Is Ryan answering the phone?"

"No," Curler sighed. "We're still pumping the recorded message from Jonie, but things have gone quiet in there. We can only assume Ryan's going to keep to his threat and burn another sample in"—he glanced at his watch—"eleven minutes."

"We need to question Elsie Delaney," Hodge said. "Talk to her on the fucking operating table if we have to. I can't move my ground teams any closer until I know if there's a bomb in that lab or not. We're at all entrances to the ground floor, and we're on the roof. If I can get confirmation that there's no bomb, I can move a team down the inner stairwell and to the entrance to the hallway."

"Elsie Delaney might be in surgery for hours." Curler shook his head. "We don't know how deep those scissors went. Whether they hit a major organ. It's Ryan we have to focus on."

"That's bullshit." Hodge lifted the helmet and jabbed Curler in the chest with it. "You got one of these sickos *in hand*. Forget the fucking surgery. Hold off on all medical treatment until she tells you what they're packing!"

"That's inhumane and illegal," Curler said politely.

"So is holding a pregnant woman at fucking gun-point!"

"Stop, stop, stop." Saskia put a hand on Curler because she didn't dare touch Hodge. "He's right. We've got to focus on Ryan. But I've got someone I can maybe send to sit on Elsie until she's awake enough to talk."

CHAPTER 26

LAMPUGNALE: Yeah?

HOSKINS: Hey there. Is this Jay?

LAMPUGNALE: This is him. What do you need?

HOSKINS: My name is Charlie Hoskins. I actually got your number from Bill Spavey down at O'Reilly's. He said you're the manager there at the Eight Straight Club?

LAMPUGNALE: Yep.

HOSKINS: Look, I don't want to take up much of your time. I know you're busy. But I've just moved down from Frisco, and I'm looking to get a job—

LAMPUGNALE: Let me stop you right there. I got a full deck of bartenders here already. Besides which, I never hire off the phone. Last time I did that, the guy turned up and he was blind.

HOSKINS: Blind?

LAMPUGNALE: Yeah, blind.

HOSKINS: Oh.

LAMPUGNALE: You ever seen a blind bartender? Because I have.

HOSKINS: I'm looking for a job, but it's not tending bar. I was wondering who handles your sound down there.

LAMPUGNALE: The sound. Ah.

HOSKINS: I'm completely rigged for audio and visual. I got lasers and strobes and all that. I know you guys do live music all weekend. Tuesdays, too. If you're not happy with your current sound guy, I was thinkin'—

LAMPUGNALE: We're very happy with her.

HOSKINS: Oh. Well. Shit.

LAMPUGNALE: Yeah, shit for you, pal. And for the record, we don't do any of that laser bullshit. This ain't a gay bar. You should have done your research.

HOSKINS: You're right. You're right. I should have.

LAMPUGNALE: Take it from me, man. You want a job in this town? Get off your ass and actually walk into some bars and talk to managers face-to-face. And don't bother looking for work as a sound guy on this side of Pacific Avenue. Mina and Scott have got it covered from here all the way up Magnolia, pretty much.

HOSKINS: Mina.

LAMPUGNALE: Yeah, she's good. She's always on time. Doesn't mind getting off her ass, that one. And it's a cute ass, too, which helps.

HOSKINS: How do you know I don't have a cute ass?

LAMPUGNALE: Ha! Oh, man. That's funny.

HOSKINS: Listen, I get it. Everything you're saying. I get it. I just . . . ah. To be honest? I'm . . . I'm scratching around here. My wife just kicked me out. I've got four hundred

bucks to my name right now. I've got a trash
bag full of clothes in the car with my audio
rig. That's it. It's, like, I can sell the rig or I
can try to use it to get my life started again.
If you're starving, you don't sell your fishing pole. You catch fish. You know what I'm
saying?

LAMPUGNALE: Jeez, this is a tale of woe.

HOSKINS: It is.

LAMPUGNALE: It's not that I don't *care*. I
just don't have anything for you, man. Not
right now anyway.

HOSKINS: Well, maybe you do.

LAMPUGNALE: Yeah?

HOSKINS: Maybe you could put me in touch
with this Mina. Maybe I can, you know, join
forces with her or something. Or at least get
a picture of what she's covered and what's
available.

LAMPUGNALE: I'm not giving out her number.

HOSKINS: No, that's cool. What about her
email? Or you could just tell me her full
name, even, and I'll just look her up like
anybody else would.

LAMPUGNALE: It's Mina Delforce. But that
had better not come back to bite me.

HOSKINS: It won't.

LAMPUGNALE: Uh-huh.

HOSKINS: D-e-l-f-o-r-c-e?

LAMPUGNALE: That's it.

HOSKINS: Okay. Okay. I'll just google her.

LAMPUGNALE: I notice you're not interested
in Scott's number. He covers just as many
venues as Mina does.

HOSKINS: Well, you said Mina has the cute
ass, so . . .

LAMPUGNALE: Oh, wow. Ha ha! Funny guy
   we got here.
HOSKINS: You've got to laugh sometimes or
   else you'd cry.

Lamb met Charlie at the bottom of a floating staircase the size of a highway ramp. He ended his call and
stood there before her, tapping through messages. She
did the same, the two investigators face-to-face but
mentally miles apart. They left their digital worlds
at the same time and returned their phones to their
pockets like gunslingers holstering pistols.

"We've got to run this down," Charlie said. "It's a
solid lead. If this Jacob guy was pissed at Ruby enough
that he'd write those kinds of things to her, he might
have been pissed enough to try to grab her out in public. Could be that he was at the beach thinking he'd
give her a little scare so she'd continue ponying up the
cash. Maybe he got Tilly Delaney instead, and things
went from bad to worse."

"But Ruby said when she refused to answer the
threatening messages, they just trailed off to silence,"
Lamb said. "I mean, it sounds to me like Jacob got
bored and gave up. Cut his losses and moved on to
his next victim."

"Could be. But a hundred grand is a hundred grand.
It's the kind of money that makes you change things
about your life. Start living differently," Charlie said.
"Would he want to go back to square one with a new
victim?"

"I don't know."

"Neither do I."

"Maybe he wanted to appeal to her in person, in a
nonthreatening way," Lamb said. "You know. Apologize. Win her back."

"Either way—"

"We've got to run it down."

"How do we do that?" Charlie wondered. "I guess we get whatever videos and photos Ruby has from Jacob and we send them to Surge. Binchley can use them to try to find a digital trail."

"We don't need to send them to Surge," Lamb said. "I know how to do a reverse search for images and video."

"Look at you." Charlie's eyebrows popped up. "Little millennial tech genius."

"You're only a decade off. I'm Gen Z."

Charlie watched Viola approach from the living room. The animosity between the two seemed to have reduced to a simmer. "Thanks for this, Viola."

"'Thanks for this, Viola,' and 'Sorry for being such a jerk, Viola,'" Viola corrected. "'Having me as a brother is a heavy cross to bear, but you bear it with grace and poise, Viola.'"

"Would you ask an eagle to apologize for taking wing?" Charlie grinned.

"Yes." Her gaze fell on Lamb. "And you. You need to change. I can lend you something."

"Oh, no, I'm fine." Lamb brushed down the front of her bloodstained shirt. "I can get by. We—"

"It's okay for Charlie to be disgusting." Viola took her by the arm. "He's always disgusting. And he's wearing black. But you look like you just killed somebody. Come on."

Huge rooms. Art-filled hallways. A gaping and sparse bedroom styled in pea green and gold. Lamb edged around another horse lamp to follow Viola into a walk-in closet the size of a small restaurant. Viola rummaged through drawers until she found a T-shirt and jeans and tossed them into Lamb's lap.

"You really don't have to do this," Lamb said. "I can wash them and get them back—"

"Please." Viola flapped a hand at her. "I feel sorry for you."

"Oh, I'm okay. It's just superficial."

"You obviously haven't looked in a mirror," Viola said. "There's a triangle sliced out of your ear. You look like a cartoon rat." She was rummaging in another drawer. She pulled out a pack of cleansing wipes and came and sat beside Lamb on a plush ottoman. Lamb tried not to stare at the actress's unnaturally smooth skin as she wiped at Lamb's ear and neck. "I wasn't talking about that, though. I was talking about Chuckie."

"He's fine."

"No, he's not." Viola pulled another wipe from the pack, tossed the bloodstained one on the carpet in front of them. "He pokes people for fun. Particularly when he's feeling down. Whenever a girlfriend left him, I used to fly out of the country; otherwise, he would be over here making my life hell."

"He did say he'd had some trouble keeping a girl in his life." Lamb nodded, thinking about the string of famous boyfriends Viola had been documented with over the past decade in all the city's worst tabloid magazines.

"This undercover thing, I assume, has made him a real dick."

"Well . . ."

"What's he poking you about?"

"Joining the cops so young."

Viola froze. Her eyes, full of sudden mischief, flicked from Lamb's ear to her eyes.

"He has a point." Lamb shrugged.

"Okay." Viola's mouth spread into her brother's same wide, uninhibited grin. "I'm gonna give you something delicious, Lamb. You can thank me later."

Lamb slammed the car door when she got in. It wasn't enough to draw Charlie away from his focus on the case files he'd been reading on his phone, PDF copies Surge had sent him after their physical copies of the case were lost in the last borrowed car.

"In her original statement," Charlie said, zooming in on the text, "Olivia Zaouk says nothing about Tilly being in an aggravated or upset mood as she walked back down toward the beach. No mention that she was 'stomping away' or that she seemed like she was in a hurry. Then, today, she busts out with 'very determinedly' to describe the girl's gait. You picked up on that, too, right?" He looked at Lamb. "Unusual turn of phrase for such a young woman."

Lamb had a weird look on her face. Charlie put the phone down.

"What?"

"You joined the LAPD at *thirteen*?" she barked.

Charlie covered his eyes, let his fingernails rake down his stubble. "Urgh. Why did I leave you alone with Viola? Why, why, why?"

"Because you forgot she was there when you were signed up to the LAPD," Lamb said, her voice sick with menace. "*At thirteen!*"

"Look." Charlie turned the car on and put it into gear, felt rigid with annoyance at his sister. "It wasn't like that."

"It wasn't?" Lamb said. "Because Viola seemed pretty sure."

"She's right about my age." Charlie pulled out onto Mulholland and started heading downhill. "I was thirteen. I was sitting around in the hall outside one of Viola's acting classes with my mother. Two people in suits walked up and asked my mom if I was a young actor. She said I was. I didn't argue. I figured if they were talent or modeling scouts and I was about to get hired for something, it would really piss Viola off."

"But they weren't talent scouts," Lamb said. "They were LAPD."

"Detectives," he conceded. "One of them was Saskia Ferboden."

"She wanted you to lure pedophiles for her," Lamb said.

"It wasn't like that," he repeated.

"What was it like, then?"

"All I did was hang around in a big, empty sting house waiting for these guys to show up," Charlie said. "Saskia's team would find the guys online, invite them to the house. They'd make sure the mark saw me through the window, then they'd let him in. The moment the guy's feet hit the carpet, they'd arrest him."

"You were working for the LAPD, Charlie."

"I sat in a house, and I made a couple of phone calls. That was it. It wasn't police work. It wasn't even sanctioned. Saskia got in a lot of shit for using a real kid on her stings, and the fact that we got so many arrests with the gag didn't matter one bit."

"It was police work."

"No, it wasn't."

"You get paid for that job?"

"My mother did."

"And what did it say on the paycheck under 'Employer'?"

"Lamb, I was never in danger. I never got near the guys. Viola's making it sound like they gave me a gun and a Taser and sent me out on patrol before my balls had dropped."

"My point stands," Lamb said.

"What point?"

"That everything you've complained about since you met me, every *shred* of evidence you've presented to suggest I shouldn't be doing this job has been *bullshit*." She folded her arms. "*I'm* too emotional? You just beat a guy half to death in front of a crowd of people! *My* instincts are terrible? You stared Nicolas Rojer right in the face and had no idea he had a victim locked up somewhere nearby. *I'm* too young for this? You joined the cops at *thirteen*!"

"Lamb," Charlie said.

"What?!" she bellowed.

He didn't answer. After a block, the smile had taken over his face. "I can see you're quite upset about this . . ."

"Oh, Jesus." She fell back into her seat. "I'm gonna kill you before the day is through. Or I'm gonna hold you down while your sister kills you."

"And your instincts are still in question." Charlie glanced over as Lamb's phone started ringing. "You've been working cases for half a day. You haven't had the time to build—"

"Hello?" Lamb flapped at him. "Dr. Sadik? Hi. Hi. Thanks so much for getting back to me."

Charlie waited. On the bridge over the Cahuenga Pass, a falcon was perched, looking for highway pigeons. Charlie was getting uncomfortable at how much listening Lamb was doing. How smug her face looked.

"Can you just repeat that last bit, please, Doctor? I want my partner to hear you." Lamb had leaned over into Charlie's personal space, tapping the Speaker button. A guy with a thick Balkan accent came on the line.

"Sure. I was just explaining," Sadik said, "that I've examined the photograph of the swimsuit closely, and I've had my analysis of it reviewed by my colleague here at the lab. I believe that the tears I'm seeing in the fabric of the suit are distinctly characteristic of a manually operated implement."

"Someone cut up the suit," Lamb said, watching Charlie, her eyes bright with victory. "That's what you're saying? They cut it up to make it look like the suit had been torn naturally."

"I cannot comment on the intentions of whoever made these incisions," Sadik said. "But I can tell you that the cuts in the swimsuit are not consistent with animal predation, nor with the fabric having been torn because it was tossed around in the ocean. They're too precise, too methodical. The alignment of the direction of the severance of each strand of fabric suggests to me the use of scissors."

Lamb finished the call with Sadik, clasped her hands in her lap, and looked over at Charlie.

"I'm sorry. I interrupted you," she said. "You were saying something about my instincts?"

CHAPTER 27

"Three minutes," Ryan said. The hostage-taker had been fiddling with the clasp of his silver watch since his wife exited the lab. Squeezing the catch, pulling the release, snapping it back into place. Bendigo sat and wondered about the watch. About how many broken and scratched and blood-spattered watches in little labeled baggies had come through his lab over the years. The watches of perpetrators. The watches of victims. The watches of innocent suspects. Ibrahim's strange question about whether the items that came through the lab made Bendigo sad was playing again in his mind. It competed with the recorded message from Jonie Delaney, which was still cycling through the PA system. Bendigo thought he could hear Ryan's watch ticking down to the next burning, and at the same time, he knew that was impossible given the distance he sat from the man and the ambient noise. And yet, there it was. The *tick-tick-ticking* in his ears.

"I need to go to the bathroom," Ibrahim said.

"Yeah, sure." Ryan smirked. "Because that went so well last time."

"I'm not lying, man. We've been in here for hours. I'm gonna piss my pants."

Ryan took an empty water bottle from the table

and tossed it at Ibrahim. It bounced off the young man's chest and rolled onto the floor.

"Fuck, dude," Ibrahim whined. When Ryan made no moves to relent, Ibrahim took the bottle and shuffled a few feet down the length of the table. Bendigo turned away, trying to give the security guard as much privacy as the circumstances allowed. Ryan was rolling three test tubes between his fingers, trying to select one. He glanced at the stock list on the table, the list of assigned officers and case numbers matched to the tubes in his hands.

"Where did you get the stock list?" Bendigo asked.

"Where do you think?" Ryan said. "How do you get access to anything restricted in life? You break in, or you pay."

"Who did you pay?"

"A hacker," Ryan said. "We found him through an ad we posted online. He was connected with a biker gang. He found a way into your system and was willing to wait until we said we were ready to go. We wanted the most up-to-date lists, obviously. While he was waiting, he sourced us our guns."

"Did he help you build that bomb?" Bendigo nodded at the third, unopened duffel bag. Ryan didn't bite.

"The biker wouldn't have been enough," Bendigo said. "You must have had someone here in the lab to help you. Some . . . some low-life hacker couldn't have known about our processes. Which samples are the most valuable. Which fridges they would be kept in."

"Elsie and I watched the lab for a few days." Ryan nodded. "The comings and goings. We noticed a young woman, followed her to a bar, got to talking to her. She was an intern about to finish her placement at the lab. This place completely turned her off a career in forensics." Ryan glanced around. "She said the staff here were jerks. Particularly the lab manager."

Bendigo said nothing.

"Elsie and I played like we were auditors trying to get information on the lab, on its processes. We paid her a couple of grand. Between her and the hacker, we shelled out five grand, tops. That was it. That's what it cost to do this."

"But even with the lists . . . how did you translate the inventory numbers and their assigning officers to real cases?" Bendigo asked. "The list only tells you the number of the sample, where it's held in the lab, and who submitted it. It doesn't say what the crime is. The intern couldn't have told you that."

"Yeah. That took a little more digging," Ryan said. "We thought about running the same operation again. Just finding a young, stupid cop and paying them to match up officers who submitted samples to the lab to cases assigned to those officers. But we couldn't risk it. It's one thing to expect a sophomore to stay quiet about something sketchy. It's another thing entirely to expect a cop to do it."

After some difficulty, probably sheer inhibition, Bendigo could hear Ibrahim was having success emptying his bladder into the plastic bottle. He cleared his throat and spoke up.

"So how did you do it, then?"

"The internet." Ryan shrugged. "How else? Elsie had a real talent for it, actually. Like with the Malibu Mountains Killer. That one was easy. Elsie found an article from March saying the LA County sheriff's station in Malibu was assigning some of its cold case officers to reopen the investigation. Then comes another article from September, saying officers had submitted a new item of interest for testing. The cold case officers' names are listed on the sheriff's website. We just had to match the name to the sample submitted in September."

"This all took a lot of time," Bendigo said. "A lot of effort. You sound proud."

"This has been our saving grace," Ryan said. He was suddenly full of passion, sweeping his hand over the lab. "You don't understand. Planning this, researching this, joining the dots, running the contingencies, and rehearsing the setup—this is the only thing that has stopped Elsie and me from going *insane*."

"It *stopped* you going insane?" Ibrahim asked. His jaw was jutted, tight and mean, the bottle of dark piss sitting on the floor beside him, capped. "I got news for you, buddy. You and your wife are fucking certifiable."

"You would be, too," Ryan said, "if someone took your child and you couldn't find a single human being willing to help you find her."

"You didn't think about directing all this effort toward finding your kid yourself?" Ibrahim snapped. "While you were sitting on your asses at home googling police officers you could fuck over, you could have been walking the streets looking for Tilly."

"We did walk the fucking streets!" Ryan stood up. The gun was in his fist, the tendons of his wrist straining. "We spent the first *year* walking the fucking streets. We both quit our jobs. We lived on our savings while we knocked on the door of every bottom-dwelling scumbag, every human parasite, every crooked cop and phony witness and conspiracy theorist and snake-oil-peddling psychic this city has to offer! We tracked sex offenders down on the Megan's Law website. We followed them. There was a guy in Pasadena who said he had information on where Tilly was being held, and he'd only tell us if Elsie sucked his dick while I watched!"

Ryan's breathing had become rapid. Bendigo nudged Ibrahim's foot with his own. A warning to back off. The young security guard didn't look at him. For a moment, the air in the lab rang with potential violence.

"I didn't let her do it." Ryan lowered himself back

onto his stool. "In case you give a shit. She was prepared to do it, and I didn't let her. How do you think that conversation went?"

Ibrahim didn't answer.

"We had a psychic send us a pinpoint on a map." Ryan shook his head. "It was out in the desert. We dug for hours, the two of us. Shovels in the hard earth. Our hands blistered. Sweat pouring down our faces." He glared at Ibrahim. "Nobody gets to tell me we didn't make a fucking effort."

Above them, Jonie Delaney's message droned on. Ryan wiped sweat from his brow.

"*Mom, Dad, I love you. I need you both to come home safe. Please do this for me . . .*"

"Must have been lonely, being Jonie Delaney all this time," Ibrahim mused. "Your sister gone. Your parents digging holes in the middle of nowhere or sitting around trying to figure out what they're gonna hit the security guard in the head with on the morning of their big stunt."

"Ibrahim, shut the fuck up," Bendigo hissed.

"You can talk, man," Ibrahim hissed back. "You been givin' it to them all day. It's my turn."

The cell phone on the steel table began to ring. Ryan glanced at his watch. He was past due for the next burning. Bendigo assumed it was the police calling, wanting to try to negotiate again, to stop the new half-hour sacrifices before they began. But when Ryan's eyes moved to the phone screen, his brow deepened.

"Who the hell is this?" Ryan asked himself. He lifted the phone and answered the call.

Bendigo and Ibrahim watched, silent, frozen again by the unpredictability every second in the lab brought.

"Okay," Ryan said to the caller, "I can . . . I can do that."

With a few taps of the mouse, Ryan had transferred

the call to the laptop on the table. Bendigo shifted up onto his knees so he could watch the screen. A video icon flashed up, and Ryan opened it.

On the screen was a huddled blob of fabric in a brick room. Bendigo could see a hank of dark hair being gripped by white fingers. A man was curled into a ball, sobbing, trying as hard as he could to tuck himself into the protection of the corner of the room.

"Please, please don't hurt me!" the man cried.

Ryan, Bendigo, and Ibrahim watched the screen. A voice came over the line, a different one from the man on the ground.

"Ryan Delaney, I want you to meet Clinton Sims," the voice behind the camera said.

Ibrahim and Bendigo looked at each other, blank. But Ryan cocked his head.

"Sims was a convicted sex offender living in the area of Santa Monica Beach the day your daughter was abducted," the voice on the call said.

Ryan watched the image, one hand on his gun and the other clasped around his throat as though trying to soothe a blockage there.

"I have brought Sims here to question him about his movements on the day your daughter went missing," the voice said. "And, in return, I want to ask you to do something for me."

"Who the hell is that?" Tanner asked.

Saskia was so focused on the laptop screen in front of her, she hadn't noticed the boy walk up and join the huddle made by Curler and Hodge and the technician who had been supervising the feed from the lab. On the screen, Saskia could see Ryan Delaney locked on his own laptop screen, his hand around his throat. Bendigo and Ibrahim were on their knees, watching the video. The audio was a mess, the mystery caller competing with the piped recorded message from Jonie Delaney.

"Turn the recording off." Saskia waved at the officers manning a nearby tech table. "Turn it off! Turn it off!"

It took long, icy seconds for the recording to stop. When it did, the voice on Ryan's laptop was twice as clear.

"I have brought Sims here to question him about his movements on the day your daughter went missing. And, in return, I want to ask you to do something for me."

"Jesus," Curler breathed.

"Who is that?" Tanner repeated. "Who's the caller? How did he get the number to call Ryan on?"

"Would you back the fuck up, boy?" Hodge wheeled on Tanner, chest bumping the boy back with her heavy tactical vest. She popped him in the shoulders so that he almost fell over backward. "You ain't part of this team! Your job is to sit in that chair over there and keep your goddamn mouth shut!"

"Clinton Sims," Saskia said, her mind reeling. "He was one of the four known offenders questioned about Tilly."

The group went silent as Ryan Delaney began to speak.

"Is that really Sims? What . . . what have you done to him? Is he hurt?"

The caller responded with a small laugh.

"Of course he's hurt. I'm not the police. I don't give pieces of shit like Sims coffee and doughnuts when I want answers. I get answers with my fists."

Saskia could see Ryan's chest rising and falling with excitement. He wheeled on Bendigo and Ibrahim, obviously having gotten so tied up with the call he forgot to watch his hostages. But Bendigo and Ibrahim were also so compelled by what was happening on the laptop screen that they hadn't moved.

"Did he . . ." Ryan began. *"What's he saying? Is he saying he took Tilly?"*

"He denies taking your daughter. And I believe him. But I won't stop here. I'll keep looking for Tilly, but only if you do what I ask."

Ryan was shaking visibly. He was quiet. Thinking.

"The police aren't doing what you ask, Ryan," the caller said. *"They're not meeting your demands. I am. I'm on the case. Now you need to reward me."*

"What do you want?" Ryan asked.

"I want you to burn a specific sample for me," the caller said. *"I'll tell you which officer submitted it. You should be able to find it on your list."*

"Motherfuuu—" Curler's own throat seemed to cut him off. He looked at Saskia. "This can't be real!"

"How did he get that number?" Saskia asked. No one answered. She raised her voice, looked at the officers at the tech table, the groups assembling at the perimeter of the tent. "How did the caller get that fucking number?"

"It's not Clinton Sims," an officer said. He was staring at his laptop. "Clinton Sims is locked up in Bakersfield on a drugs charge. It's right here in the system."

"And he was alibied in the original investigation anyway," someone added.

"I don't give a rat's ass where Clinton Sims is or isn't!" Saskia barked. "Ryan Delaney obviously believes this vigilante motherfucker. I want to know how he got Ryan Delaney's cell phone number! No one should have that number except the officers on this scene. How and where did he get it?"

More silence. On the screen, Ryan Delaney moved, snatching up the stock list.

"Tell me the officer," he said, his voice trembling. *"What's his name? I'll find it."*

Curler put his hand on Saskia's shoulder. She turned on him, and he put his phone under her nose. She looked at the screen. It was a Reddit thread.

Ryan Delaney phone number inside hostage lab. Call now! Fuck LAPD management!

"Someone's leaked it," Curler said. "That's the only explanation. It's revenge for our handling of the burnings."

Saskia felt her entire being harden. She tasted sourness at the back of her throat.

"Whoever leaked that number has directly endangered the hostages inside that lab," she growled. "If we can't connect with Ryan Delaney because that number is inundated with calls, we can't negotiate for those two innocent lives still stuck inside that lab. If someone calls and tells Ryan Delaney they've got Tilly and they'll let her go if he shoots one of the hostages, he's going to do it. You get that, right? You all get that?"

The silence in the tent was hard and hot as forged steel.

"I will find who did this," Saskia said. "In the meantime, that's a wrap for everybody here. Let's go. Everyone. Swap *the fuck* out."

She swept a hand. No one moved. On the laptop screen, Ryan Delaney was burning another DNA sample. Hodge and Curler waited for Saskia, watching her, allowing her some time to back away from the line.

She didn't.

"I want this whole camp rotated." Saskia pointed at the nearest group of officers. "You. You, you, and you. You fuckers over there? You, too. Get out. All of you. Get out."

"Chief," Hodge said. "Just hang on a minute. You can't swap out a whole roster of cops all at once. It's one thing for me to change out three snipers, but—"

"We're doing it," Saskia said. "Somebody get me the staff coordinator. I want a round of replacement officers on deck in ten minutes. You guys leaked footage from inside this camp!" She raised her voice to address every officer in earshot. "You shot at my fucking suspect while she had a hostage in hand! *Two* hostages!

Now you've opened a channel of communication between Ryan Delaney and every criminal in Los Angeles who has a sample in that lab. You're all done!"

The sound of a phone ringing shook Saskia so hard she grabbed Curler by the bicep before she realized what she had done. The ringing was coming from the nearby laptop where she had been communicating with the Delaneys, but it was higher and softer than it had been all the times they communicated. Everyone froze. She realized the ringing was coming from inside the lab.

"Jesus," Curler sighed. "Who's calling them now?"

The sample sizzled and burned, the plastic tubing blackening and curling quickly. Bendigo watched as Ryan held the sample to the laptop's camera, turning it for the caller to view.

"Good. Good," the voice said. "I'll be in touch again soon."

The call blinked off. Ibrahim hung his bound hands over his bent knees, shaking his head sadly.

"You're a fucking fool," he said.

Bendigo felt his heart thumping in his ribs. The hostage-taker had been overcome with a strange, eerie calm. He was sitting, looking at the burned sample in his fingers, turning the tube around and around.

"You have no idea if that really was Sims, or whatever his name was," Ibrahim said. "The dude was probably faking it. How could he have tracked down this Sims guy so fast? What was the charge connected to the sample that he asked you to burn? Do you even know?"

Ryan glanced vaguely at the stock list beside him.

"No," he said. "It's not one that Elsie and I researched. We didn't research all ninety-nine samples."

"So you don't even know what crime you just covered up," Ibrahim said. "Dude. You could have just set some . . . some child rapist free. Some killer."

"I don't care," Ryan said. "If the police wanted to protect that case, they should have found my daughter. That guy, whoever he was? *He's* done more to find Tilly in one morning than the police have in two years."

"You just *think* he has!" Ibrahim snarled. "You're an idiot! You're a goddamn idiot! You keep pissing them off and they're gonna come in here and blow us all away! Don't you get it?"

Ryan's phone rang.

Bendigo shook his head. "This'll be some other degenerate calling to have his sample destroyed," he sneered. "I wonder what he'll promise you. Are you going to start burning samples for money next, Ryan? *Donate five grand toward the search for my daughter, and I'll dump your sample. For the next hour only—two samples for the price of one!*"

"Hello?" Ryan answered on the laptop.

"Oh my god, he picked up," a thin female voice hissed on the line. There were voices in the background of the call. "He picked up. Put him through. Dave! Put him through!"

A click, and a second voice came on, Ryan watching the screen, the gun in his lap.

"Ryan Delaney, are you there?"

"Who is this?" Ryan asked.

"My name is Manny Crawford; I'm a radio host with TroothFM. We're an independent station based in Culver City. I don't know if you've heard of us."

Ryan burst into high, hard laughter. Bendigo and Ibrahim looked at each other, their faces taut with disgust.

"Is this Ryan Delaney?"

"Yeah, yeah, it is." Ryan laughed. "You've got Ryan in the lab. I'm comin' to you live, baby!"

"Ryan, let's . . . let's talk." Bendigo heard Manny the independent radio host's voice hitch with tension. "I want to make it clear that this station and its produc-

ers have no intention whatsoever of interfering with
the current police efforts to get you and the hostages
out of there safely. We just—"

"Oh, for god's sake!" Bendigo roared. "Get off the
line, you vile, worthless piece of garbage! We're pris-
oners in here!"

"Ryan, is there anything you want to tell the world?
Anything you want us all to know? The whole city is
watching you, Ryan. We're all watching what's happening there at the lab. Tell us something. Tell us, ah,
tell us—"

"I'll tell you something," Ryan said. He was standing now, gripping the pistol, tapping it against his thigh
as his thoughts raced. "Sure. The LAPD are going to
find my daughter today."

"They are?" Manny's voice crackled on the line.

"Yeah." Ryan's smile was hard and cold. "They
have to. They *have* to. Because it's just like you said,
Manny. The whole city is watching. The whole world,
probably. There won't be a single person in America
today who doesn't know what Tilly looks like. It's
working, what I'm doing here. And I hope that inspires people. I hope it inspires everyone who's got
a loved one's case decomposing in a box in a police
warehouse somewhere. Don't take *no* for an answer.
Make them listen. Make—"

"Hang up the phone!" Bendigo rose to his feet.
"Hang up the fucking phone!"

The line went dead. Ryan looked at the screen, at
the little phone icon slashed through with a red mark.

"That guy's going to jail." Ibrahim shook his head,
his teeth gritted. "He just . . . he just gave a voice to a
fucking terrorist. He just interfered in . . . in them saving us . . ."

"Maybe I should start making my own calls," Ryan
said, still smiling. "I wonder if I could get on CNN."

The phone started buzzing again.

"Don't you dare," Bendigo growled.

"You're right." Ryan wiped sweat from his brow. "It's time to stop talking. I'm sure they got my message. Those radio people and the cops outside."

"The cops outside?" Ibrahim asked.

"Yeah." Ryan took his seat at the table again. "There's one reason and one reason only that they turned off the recording of Jonie's message. Or didn't you notice?" He pointed at the ceiling. "They turned it off in the middle of my call with the guy who had Sims. It must have been interfering with their ability to hear what my new friends were saying."

"What?" Ibrahim looked around.

"They've got a mic in here," Ryan said. "They're listening to everything we say." He stood and took up his pistol again. "Absolute silence."

Bendigo swallowed. He drew a deep breath, released it, and then drew another. He had to force the words through his lips as they stalled on his thick, dry tongue.

"I won't be quiet," Bendigo said. "I have something to say. I should have said it at the beginning. But I'll say it now. Because this has to end. All of this. It has to end."

Ryan and Ibrahim turned toward him.

"I know where the swimsuit is," Bendigo continued. He straightened, stood tall. "I was the one who hid it."

CHAPTER 28

"You're never going to believe this," Lamb said. The phone in her hands bobbed as Charlie took the speed hump in the hospital parking lot too fast. The headlines swirled before her. "Someone's leaked Ryan's number online. He's burning samples on command."

"I don't want to know." Charlie jammed the car into a random space near the underground entrance to the hospital. "Don't give me any more details about what's happening at the lab. Unless the hostages are freed and it's all over, I don't want to hear it."

"Did you take the advanced psychology elective at the academy?" Lamb asked as they exited the car.

"No."

"I just thought you might have found the class on anxiety types useful," Lamb said, jogging to keep up with him as they approached the automatic doors. "Particularly, anxious avoidant."

"In my day, they had no advanced psychology unit at the academy." Charlie skidded to a halt to review a map on the chipped and battered wall. "Criminals are idiots or psychos or both. That's all we needed to know."

"You actually said, 'In my day,'" Lamb pointed out.

"Stop psychoanalyzing me and hustle." He waved at her phone, taking off again, signs and fluorescent light tubes passing overhead as they marched. "You're supposed to be using your techno-magic to find Ruby Monacco's stalker."

"I am. I am." Lamb followed Charlie across a crowded waiting room, one eye on her phone screen and one on the back of his heels. "I've sourced two videos. They're both ripped straight from Instagram accounts."

"Different accounts?"

"Yeah."

"So those accounts have followers, right?" Charlie stopped at the intersection of two halls to look at her. "Like on Twitter? Can you cross-reference the followers and—"

"Find a profile that follows both accounts." Lamb nodded. "Charlie, I said I'm on it."

He paced, catching his breath. She leaned against a wall and tapped away, selecting a list of followers from an Instagram account, holding her finger while the text highlighted.

"This isn't good, any of this," he said, beckoning her. They turned right toward the Ear, Nose, and Throat Department and doubled back. "The cut-up swimsuit. There's only one reason someone would deliberately slice up a kid's swimsuit. Only one reason why that sliced-up suit would be exactly where those searching expected to find Tilly if she drowned."

"Because someone wants the world to believe she drowned," Lamb said. "I know."

"And there are only so many reasons why someone would want that."

"Charlie, I know."

"Do you?" He stopped and looked at her. Pushed her phone down. "Because we're heading for a resolution to this thing, Lamb. And that resolution is looking less and less like it's going to be a happy one."

She watched his eyes. For a moment, the whole hospital moved around them, two stones in an ebbing river. A patient was wheeled by on a gurney. Visitors chattered, wandering.

"I'll be okay," she said.

"No, you won't." Charlie laughed humorlessly. "No one is. The first time you see a dead kid on this job, you fucking lose it. And you never quite get it all back."

She watched him, listening.

"And I think you're too young for that to happen to you just yet," he continued. "But I also know that trying to shake you off right now would be a waste of my time. So I'm going to simply invite you, again, to back away. No one will know. There'll be no pride lost. I know I've been giving you hell, but I won't have fun with it. Not this time. You just say the words, and you're tapped out, no questions asked."

Lamb held his gaze. The words that came from her were steady and true and from the very deepest parts of her soul.

"Not on your life," she said.

"All right." He turned away. "Keep hitting the tech. The secure ward is up this way."

They breezed past a desk staffed by busy nurses. Charlie skidded to a halt in a hallway blocked by officers, the man at the forefront a figure Lamb recognized. Detective Joe Bailey raised a radio to his lips and smiled.

"Yeah, they just got here."

Lamb saw the wind go out of her partner for a moment before he sucked it back in and straightened.

"Bailey."

"Hoskins and Lamb." Bailey's mustache tilted with a crooked smile. "Security said you were coming up. You were too fast for them to pass on my message: you're not welcome on this ward."

"Oh, come on," Lamb snapped before Charlie could. "Don't waste our time. We're on the clock here. Those sample burnings you are so angry about are only going to stop if we get to an end point with this thing. You got two choices. You can step aside now, or you can step aside five minutes from now, when Chief Ferboden calls and tells you to do so."

"Funny thing, that." Bailey glanced at a couple of patrol cops stationed in the hallway with him. "Some of the guys are receiving calls fine, and some of us are getting certain calls and not others. The radios seem to be acting up, too. I wouldn't be surprised if it was hours before a call from Central Command came through here."

"Look." Charlie sucked air through his teeth; Lamb could see he was on the edge. "I know you're pissed that we're looking into the Delaney thing. But it's happening. It has been happening all day. Five minutes with Elsie Delaney isn't going to make a lick of difference to you, but it'll mean worlds to us and maybe to a missing child."

"Sorry. Elsie Delaney is still in surgery." Bailey shrugged. "Got a pair of scissors in her guts, so I heard."

"Jonie Delaney, then," Lamb said. "We know she's back there."

"Now, hold on," Bailey said. "You want me to allow you access to a fragile minor who's been admitted here after she suffered a very public mental breakdown? Maybe you two need to take a breather in a padded room yourselves, because—"

Lamb just managed to catch Charlie's fist before it hit Bailey's face. She shoved his arm sideways, using all her body weight to slam her partner into the wall. The two patrol officers behind Bailey rushed forward, but he stilled them with a raised hand. Lamb bounced Charlie off the wall and used the momentum and his unsteadiness to march him backward a few paces from the officers blocking the hall.

"Don't don't don't don't," Lamb soothed.

"He has no authority to keep us out. None."

"I know." Lamb shoved him back by the shoulders. "But you hit him and he'll have the authority to put you in cuffs, and then I'll be on my own out here."

They walked back toward the nurses' station, Charlie's shoulders high and tight.

"We're not dead in the water," Lamb said. "I'll keep hunting Ruby's stalker. You try to raise Chief Ferboden on the phone. If we play them the call on speaker, they can't deny they've heard it."

"I'll try to get her," he murmured, tapping furiously at his phone screen. "In the meantime, maybe I'll call in some reinforcements."

They slid down the wall and sat on the ground, the entry to the ward strangely void of visitors' chairs. Down the hall, Bailey and his team watched them, chattering pleasantly, the drone of hospital announcements and the hum of activity in the ward beyond drowning out their words.

Ibrahim got to his feet beside Bendigo. The two hostages stood before their captor, Bendigo feeling queasy and unbalanced with his decision. He lifted his bound hands and adjusted the collar of his crumpled shirt, pulled the hem down. If he was about to be shot, he wanted to take it like a man. But Ryan didn't raise the pistol. He just stood there, cautious, his face blank.

"You're shitting me," Ryan said.

"It was two years ago, October. Around this time of year, people here start organizing the Christmas festivities. I hate Christmas. I'm your classic bah-humbug type. I'm an atheist, but it's more than that. It's the commercialism, and . . . I'm rambling. I'm sorry." He drew a breath. "This Christmas was particularly annoying, because some of the female staff at the lab had decided to make a big deal of it. There was a whole heap more emails coming through about the . . . the theme. The decorations. What people should wear.

Who was going to play *fucking* Santa." He shook his head, disgusted, defeated. "We're grown adults, and this is a professional environment, and my inbox is being cluttered up with emails written in purple font, ostensibly addressed to magical helper elves."

"Get to the point," Ryan said icily.

"I snapped." Bendigo glanced at Ibrahim. "Some of the female staff brought party supplies into lab 18 and set them on a table in there to go through them. I was walking past, and I saw the box of foreign objects being unloaded, people wearing civilian clothing, no one adhering to lab protocol. I lost it. I walked in and verbally unleashed on them. This is supposed to be a sterile environment. It's a forensic laboratory."

The men waited. Bendigo wiped sweat from his cheeks with his wrist, with difficulty.

"Well, of course you had the dramatics after that." He drew a shuddering breath. "The crying and the calls for my resignation, the written complaints to the heads of department and the ensuing official reprimand. Point is, in my initial outburst, I grabbed the items the staff had unloaded and spread all over the table, and I shoved them back into the box. I took the box to a storage cupboard on the first floor and I dumped it there."

Ryan's eyes were huge, drifting over Bendigo's face, searching for deception. The older man could feel that hard gaze inspecting his every muscle twitch, the way his mouth formed his words, the darkness behind his pupils.

"You can put the rest together," Bendigo said. "I must have scooped a sample bag into the box by accident. There was a lab tech who was behind on his roster, and he must have come in early that day to get started. He was assigned to the swimsuit, and it was up next, and it was in lab 18. He must have had the swimsuit on the table the women chose. Whatever the case, we discovered the item was missing, and I was so cowed by my reprimand, so conscious of the department breathing down my neck, that I didn't reveal what I had done."

"Where's the swimsuit now?" Ryan could barely form the words. "Did you destroy it?"

"No," Bendigo said. "I left it where it was. Once I had confirmed it was in the box and that the error was my own, I shoved the box right to the back of the storage cupboard and left it there. The women never asked me for their box of supplies back. I assumed they were too afraid. And they probably assumed I threw it out."

Ryan stood, trembling gently, his teeth clamped tight.

"You're lying," he said.

"I'm not," Bendigo said. "I'm not. I promise I'm not."

"Why the hell didn't you tell us this morning?" Ibrahim asked.

"Because I didn't want to be shot!" Bendigo turned to him, tears burning in the corners of his eyes. "I-I-I'm afraid to be shot now! This man has every right to kill me. This whole situation is my fault. They might have . . . they might have found your child, Ryan, if not for my selfishness. My cowardice."

No one spoke.

"I told myself that the sample didn't matter. That the girl had drowned," Bendigo whispered. "I suppose I'm not the only one who was prepared to believe that. Sometimes, over the years, I've been able to forget about it. But at night, sometimes I wonder . . . I wonder if it might have been the item that changed everything. I've wondered if I should get the sample out again. Place it somewhere. Have it discovered." He heaved a huge sigh. "You don't know how many times I've gone to that cupboard and put my hand on the knob and not opened it."

Ryan raised the gun to Bendigo's face. Bendigo winced but didn't cower. He felt a tiny spark of pride at that, and grasped on mentally to that fleeting sensation, knowing it might be the very last emotion he ever felt.

He waited.

The shot didn't come.

"Show me where the box is," Ryan said.

Bendigo opened his eyes. He swiped at the tears on his cheeks. He nodded eagerly.

"I'll do it," he said. "But only if you let Ibrahim go."

CHAPTER 29

ERLAN: Whoa! Now *this* is the craziest thing
   to have happened in a while. That can't be
   you, Mina, can it?
MINA: It is, unfortunately.
ERLAN: *Shiiiiit!* How the hell are you, girl?
MINA: Don't do that. Don't try to be all
   buddy-buddy with me like we're pals. You
   know I would only resort to calling you if I
   was absolutely against a wall.
ERLAN: Ah, now, that rings a few bells for me.
MINA: Are you still a cop, or have they
   washed you out for being a complete fucking loser?
ERLAN: No, I still serve and protect, loser
   nature and all.
MINA: Surprising.
ERLAN: What do you want? Someone bothering you? You want me to come stomp some
   heads?
MINA: No, no one's bothering me. I'm trying
   to find someone who I think might be a cop,
   or someone who works with the cops. Like a
   specialist or an undercover or something.
ERLAN: Huh! What for?
MINA: It's a long story.

ERLAN: I've got time, Meenie.

MINA: I really don't want to get into it with you. And you shouldn't be sitting around chatting to me anyway. Don't you have a new girlfriend?

ERLAN: I do. I do, actually. And she's going to know this call happened. She checks all my calls.

MINA: Oh, gee. I wonder why.

ERLAN: She can even find the deleted ones. She's, like, an expert.

MINA: Uh-huh.

ERLAN: So if I'm going to get into trouble for this anyway, I want to make it worth my while. Tell me what you need this cop for. What happened?

MINA: I rescued him.

ERLAN: You what?!

MINA: He was in the water off Palos Verdes. I've been going out there after my shift sometimes, you know, if the sun is up. It's really nice out there.

ERLAN: Oh yeah. I remember. You've always been a mermaid.

MINA: He must have fallen off a boat or something, because he was in trouble and I dragged him in.

ERLAN: By yourself?

MINA: Yes, by myself. What? I dragged your blacked-out ass all the way up the steps into our apartment that time after Roxy's party.

ERLAN: Meenie, you're a complete badass, you know that?

MINA: Just help me find the guy, okay? I have a picture. I'm going to text it to you now.

ERLAN: You know, they don't give away medals or bravery awards for that kind of shit anymore. Not to normal people anyway. If

you're a kid, maybe, because it's a cute news
story. Besides that, you'd have to lift a flam-
ing bus off a group of pregnant orphans.

MINA: I'm not looking for a bravery award,
you idiot.

ERLAN: Well, what do you want him for, then?
You want a thank-you?

MINA: No, I just . . .

ERLAN: What?

MINA: When we were out there in the water
together, we sort of . . .

ERLAN: What?

MINA: I don't know how to explain it to you,
Erlan.

ERLAN: Just try. Come on.

MINA: It was as if we were the only people in
the world. Everyone was gone. It was just us
out there in the sea. I kind of felt, like, if I
could just get him to shore maybe . . . uh . . .
maybe he'd be okay but also . . . I'd be okay.
With everything. It was like him finding
me out there in the water, and us coming
together, was a test.

ERLAN: A test?

MINA: Do not laugh at me about this.

ERLAN: What happened to you in the last ten
years, Meen? You've gone all mystical.

MINA: I *really* haven't.

ERLAN: I've heard stuff like this before, about
people walking in the woods and meeting a
deer and seeing the meaning of life in its eyes
or something, but I didn't think it would
happen to you.

MINA: I'm hanging up now.

ERLAN: Don't. Don't. I'm just fucking with
you. I get it. I totally get it.

MINA: If I can just be sure that he's all right,
then . . . I don't know. Or even if I could

just know who he is and why he was out
there . . .

ERLAN: Send me the picture.

MINA: It should be there already.

ERLAN: Okay, I'm putting you on speaker. Oh.
Oh, *shit*!

MINA: What? What?

ERLAN: That's Charlie fucking Hoskins!

Saskia Ferboden gripped the edge of the desk. She felt
Delta Hodge jolt beside her as she held the earpiece
in her ear, listening to the feed from the laptop.

"Jesus," Hodge said.

"He's gonna let him out in exchange for the swimsuit." Saskia looked at Curler, who was watching the
feed on an iPad.

Around the tent, the remaining police officers from
the roster of dismissed staff were handing over their
posts to their replacements. Saskia was so excited, she
swept her gaze over the officers, expecting the same
elation. But she was met only with hostility. The swift
and bumpy emotional ride from rage, as they'd listened to the radio host's call with Ryan, to this new
revelation from Bendigo left her feeling nauseous. She
wanted, more than she had at any time that day, to sit
down. But she didn't.

"We need to get ready. We need to have an extraction team in place," she said.

"Already on it," Hodge said. "I've got a team on
standby and three new snipers all set up."

"First floor, storage cupboard," Saskia said, beckoning toward Curler. The negotiator passed her a blueprint of the Hertzberg-Davis building, and she spread
it over the comms table. Saskia ran her hands over
the smooth blue paper. "We're looking for a storage
cupboard. Where is your internal team right now,
Hodge? Have you still got men inside the building, or
did they retreat after they accessed the PA system?"

"There's one team still stationed on the second floor." Hodge pointed to the level-two section of the blueprint. "Tell me what your plan is, and I'll get them into position."

"I don't know what my plan is," Saskia said. "I have to think. I have to think."

"Ryan's going to send Ibrahim out, and he'll probably use the distraction while we get Ibrahim to safety to go up to the first floor with Bendigo," Curler said. "So you have to decide if you want Ryan and Bendigo to actually reach the storage cupboard or if you want to try to surround them and cut them off, I suppose."

"I can set up an ambush on the first-floor hallway," Hodge said. "We let Delaney and Bendigo walk in, and then we jump on them. That's one option. But my preferred plan, ma'am, if I may offer it, is to keep the first floor completely clear of police personnel, and we let Bendigo and Delaney go in on their own."

"Why?" Saskia asked.

"So my sniper has a straight shot," Hodge said.

Saskia felt her stomach plunge. She looked back at the forensic building towering behind her.

"All the blinds on the first floor are open, ma'am," Hodge continued. "They're not automatic. Delaney isn't going to be able to cross the offices up there to pull the blinds down by hand without coming into my sniper's firing line. The only innocent life we would be risking would be Gary Bendigo's. But he might be worth the sacrifice, if it means we can take Ryan Delaney down cleanly."

"I don't want to take Ryan down," Saskia said. "I want a casualty-free resolution to this."

"Yeah, and I wanted a Mustang for Christmas, ma'am, but my girlfriend got me a bracelet." Hodge raised her eyebrows. "Sometimes you gotta ignore the sugarplum fairies dancing in your head and take what you can get."

"I appreciate the advice, Hodge, but—"

"Look, ma'am"—Hodge showed Saskia the palms of her battered leather gloves—"if we were ever gonna talk our way out of this whole fiasco with Ryan Delaney, I feel like that would have happened by now. This guy here? He ain't no cut-rate negotiator." She slapped Curler's chest so hard that he winced. "If there's a logical psychological strategy y'all haven't tried, I can't think of it. As far as I can see it, that man in there is gonna exit that building in a body bag, just like he said. You just have to decide what you'll risk to make that happen."

"I don't agree," Saskia said. "Maybe if we let him get to the storage cupboard, let him get the sample bag with his daughter's swimsuit in it, it'll be enough to make him surrender."

"He wants you to find his kid!" Hodge said. "That's what the ultimatum was this morning! Find the kid. Bring her home. Dead or alive. An evidence bag isn't going to make him throw up the white flag."

"This morning, he had his wife there with him," Curler said. "He's tired now. Beaten down. He'll be hungry and dehydrated, and he will have run through all his supplies of adrenaline for the next goddamn decade. I think Saskia's right. The whole reason Ryan and Elsie Delaney chose the Hertzberg-Davis lab to stage this thing in was because that's where the swimsuit got misplaced. The swimsuit is a symbol. It was mishandled, just like their daughter's case. Maybe finding the suit will change something in Ryan. Give him hope."

"So you want me to keep my teams back?" Hodge asked, folding her muscular arms. "What about the snipers? Do I call off the shoot-to-kill order?"

Saskia looked at the map. The tiny blue boxes and grids and lines representing the halls, labs, cupboards, and annexes of the building. She visualized Ibrahim and Gary and Ryan in there, human lives held in peril simply by the refusal of one of their number to let them get to safety. She couldn't ignore the fact that, already, Ryan and his wife had allowed one of the hostages and her unborn child to go free. That they were not merciless. She didn't know if maintaining an order to shoot Ryan dead on sight at the very first opportunity meant she herself was without that same mercy.

"We got a visual!" someone yelled.

Hodge gripped her radio. The three commanding officers turned toward the building. In the dark beyond the automatic doors of the reception area, someone was moving.

"Let's just get Ibrahim to safety, and we'll think about shoot-to-kill orders later," Saskia said. "One step at a time."

"What's the third sample?" Lamb asked.

Charlie had to drag his mind out of the dark place where it had been swimming to answer her. He'd been thinking about those hours out in the ocean, floating on his back and looking at the stars, trying to talk himself into flipping over and continuing the hellish kicking and pulling toward what he hoped was land. He'd watched the tiny pinpricks of light up there, in the black velvet dome of sky, and told himself the same thing he'd told himself every day waking in his bed in his shitty apartment for five years undercover: that this would end. That he wouldn't be suspended here forever, rolling on the waves, neither dead nor alive, just like he hadn't been suspended for eternity in the Death Machines. Neither a good nor a bad guy. Operation Hellfire had ended badly, yes. And maybe in a couple of hours he was going to succumb to hypothermia, or something in the depths would rise up and eat him alive. But it wouldn't go on forever. Nothing did.

"The what?" he said.

"You said you had three samples in the lab," Lamb

said. She was still tapping and swiping on her phone, scrolling through photographs. "The Mariana Navarro sample. The Travis Bookman sample. What's the third one?"

Charlie leaned his head against the wall, watched a nurse walk by, scowling. The nurses clearly weren't happy about them sitting on the floor, but if they felt like that, Charlie figured they should have put out some chairs.

"Dean Willis has only got one good eye," Charlie said. "His right. He lost sight in the left one in an accident. He killed some people. It was revenge for the eye."

"What kind of accident? What kind of revenge?"

"I need coffee." Charlie glanced down the hall toward a vending machine between where they sat and the blockade of officers preventing them from entering the secure ward. "If I can't smoke in here, I'm gonna need coffee. Snacks. Lamb, you're the rookie. Go get your superior officer some snacks."

"I'm not a rookie," Lamb said. "I'm not a police employee, remember? Tell me about the sample."

"When you get me snacks."

"Charlie."

"There was a robbery." Charlie let his head thump back against the wall. "A liquor store in Anaheim. Dean had nothing to do with it. He just happened to be there, buying beer. The young Black guy who robbed the place, James Elliott, didn't even have a real gun. It was a painted water pistol. The kid was sixteen. Guy behind the counter didn't care. He pulled out a Magnum and tried to blow Elliott's head off with it. The kid ran. The bullet hit a bottle of Cognac, and a shard of glass got Dean right in the eyeball."

Lamb glanced over, horrified.

"Dean just killed the counter guy. Popped him clean while he was getting into his car outside his brother's house maybe a month later," Charlie said. "That's about as kind as it gets for Dean. He likes to play with you, like a cat. He used to say, 'You only get to kill them once.'"

"What did he do to Elliott?"

"He made Elliott carve up his own parents," Charlie said. "It was a dark, dark thing. Dean was telling the family he'd let the kid live if he did what he was asking him to do to the parents. So, the parents encouraged him to do it. *Save yourself, son.*"

"That's . . ." Lamb's mouth worked soundlessly while she tried to come up with the right word.

"Horrifying," Charlie said.

"Yes."

"He's a creative guy, our Dean."

"Did he kill Elliott?"

"Oh yeah," Charlie said. "Not fast. Dean and some other guys worked on Elliott themselves for a while. The kid had a heart attack, eventually, which cut the party short. I got Dean on tape talking about it, but I also managed the impossible of all impossibles—I got Dean Willis away from his favorite pocketknife for an hour."

Lamb watched Charlie. He felt her gaze, wondered if all these stories were turning her off being a cop or encouraging her. He was too tired to know the difference.

"It was risky," he said. "But I had to separate Dean from the knife. All the other guys in the room that night, they would have dumped their knives after the murder. I knew that. But Dean would have held on to his, because it was his favorite. His father gave it to him. He kept it on him at all times. Took it to the bathroom with him. Slept with it under his pillow."

"So how did you get it?" Lamb asked.

"I bumped Dean off the back of a pickup truck," Charlie said. "We were loading guns and supplies. Dean liked to go hog hunting. I was standing up there in the truck bay with him, and I saw my shot. I turned around real fast and bumped into him, knocked him off the truck, made like it was an accident. He fell and broke his wrist."

"You can't take your knife into the x-ray machine." Lamb smiled, nodding.

"I made like I was sorry as hell for causing him to fall," Charlie said. "Drove him to all his appointments. It wasn't hard to act the part. I was sorry. Sorry and scared. Even a pure accident like that can get you murdered by these guys. They're fucking psychos. Anyway, I took the knife apart, swabbed the insides, scraped out the little ridges and grooves and indentations on the surface of the blade under the wooden handle. Put it back together. Gave it back to Dean when he was out of the x-ray appointment. Hopefully that sample will be safe from the Delaneys out of sheer statistics. I can't be unlucky enough for the Delaneys to choose all three of my cases out of the ninety-nine."

"So you looked," Lamb said. "You saw the news reports of the cases Ryan has burned so far. You know you lost Navarro and Bookman."

"I was trying to be less 'anxious avoidant,'" Charlie said. He turned and widened his eyes at her. "So! About those snacks!"

She went. He sat there thinking about the recording he'd made of Dean talking about the Elliott murders. Dean had been having one of his "confession sessions" after a big night at the clubhouse. Charlie'd had some back-warmer whose name he didn't know sitting in his lap, whispering dirty things in his ear. He'd ended up guiding her hand down into his jeans to keep it from trailing up inside his shirt and hitting the mic.

Lamb came back, still looking at her phone screen, one fist full of candy bars.

"Okay, let me tell you where I am," she said. "The picture of the five-year-old blond kid on the couch that

Ruby was sent—that's a no-brainer. It was just on a mommy blog. Likely just came from a Google search. But the videos—I checked out the accounts they originated from. One of the videos is from a gay couple in Utah who run an animal sanctuary. That's the sick horse. The other video, the one of a goat, is from a woman in Kentucky who owns an emu farm but who keeps a couple of goats as pets."

Charlie started tearing open a Clark Bar.

"The animal sanctuary account has about six thousand followers, and the emu farmer has about two and a half thousand," Lamb said. "I selected all the names in both accounts, dropped them into a text document, and compared the lists. There are two followers that follow both animal accounts."

"Only two?" Charlie said.

"Don't get excited." Lamb showed him a picture of an old man with deep hollows in his cheeks, wearing steel-rimmed spectacles and standing by a beat-up Ford pickup truck. He was wearing gray coveralls. "This is one of the accounts."

"Okay," Charlie said. "Older male, farmer type. He fits. Where does he live?"

"New York State," Lamb said. "But I don't think this is our stalker."

"Why not?"

"Because it's a legitimate account." Lamb scrolled through photographs. Charlie saw the old man and a teenager working on the Ford and an old Chrysler. "He's not a farmer. He's a mechanic. He runs a shop that specializes in restorations. All the information we want about him is freely available here. There's his wife. There's the son. There's the front of the shop."

"You don't think the stalker would have a real account?"

"I think they'd have something like this," she said. She showed him another account. There were two pictures in the profile, one of a ginger cat sunning itself on the deck of an aboveground pool, one of the Golden Gate Bridge.

"Pretty sparse." Charlie finished the Clark Bar and rubbed his hands on his jeans. He felt the sugar rush tingling in his empty veins.

"It's a skeleton account," Lamb said. "The stalker probably set it up, never filled it out. Then he started using it to search for and source videos and images to sell his story to Ruby about being an animal-loving widower who could use a helping hand."

"Okay." Charlie shifted closer to her. "Okay. This is good."

"So I took the two images in the account and I reverse-searched them, tried to find out if they appear anywhere else on the internet," Lamb said. "Just like I did with Ruby's videos."

"And?"

"They don't. Which means they're probably real. The stalker took them himself. And there's more that tells me we're in the right place. Look who the account is following." Lamb tapped a number, and a list dropped down. She scrolled, hit an account, flashed a heavily filtered picture of a beautiful girl with chocolate ringlet curls on the screen. Charlie felt another energy bump in his body.

"Ruby Monacco."

"You're damn right."

"Nice work, Lamb."

"We need to know who owns this account," she said. "There'll be an IP address attached to whoever made it. We just have to hope it's a cell phone or a home computer and not an internet cafe or stolen Wi-Fi. It's a start. I'll text Surge, and he can have Binchley look up the address."

"That's going to be a problem," Surge said.

Lamb and Charlie looked up. The big man was standing over them, his sunglasses dangling off his chubby fingers. The slicked quiff he'd been wearing when Lamb saw him last was windswept.

"I just dumped him."

Lamb got to her feet. Charlie could see goose bumps had risen all over her lean forearms. "You . . . you killed him?"

"No, Lamby." Surge laughed. "I just drove him into the middle of the desert and left him for dead. I didn't actually *kill* him." He gave Charlie a quizzical frown. "I'm not an animal."

"We should have discussed that." Charlie raked his fingers over his skull. He had that bottomless feeling of feverish dreams, of realizing he had to catch a flight with only twenty minutes' notice and trying to pack his bags. Things forgotten, things lost, things left behind. "Saskia doesn't know Binchley was behind the Hertzberg-Davis thing. When she finds out it was him and that we let him go, she's going to flip."

"But I renegotiated with him." Surge shrugged. "And I'm a man of my word. I said I'd let him go, so I had to."

Lamb looked dejected.

"I made the game interesting, of course." Surge was looking down the hall at Bailey and his team. The comment was so offhand Charlie almost didn't hear it.

"You what?" Lamb asked.

"I evened the odds," Surge said. "I drove Binchley out into the middle of nowhere, gave him a bottle to catch his piss in, a ball cap to keep the sun off, and a compass to find his way. Then I stood there and called three police stations and let them know where he was. The chase is on! Cops and robbers was always my favorite game as a kid. You, too, probably. Right, Lamb?"

Surge nudged her in the ribs so hard she stumbled backward.

"We still needed Binchley," Charlie grumbled.

Lamb tapped her phone against her thigh. "I guess I'm going to have to try to look closer at these two pictures. Try to find a source. The Golden Gate Bridge isn't going to tell me much. Maybe the cat has a tag on its collar I could zoom in on." She lifted the phone.

"We don't have time for that now." Charlie turned her by the shoulder. Surge had walked off toward the officers blocking the hallway, a long and swift stride. "We just brought a *T. rex* to a cockfight, and we need to get ready to move."

Charlie and Lamb took up a vantage point by the vending machine, where they could hear the exchange.

"What the hell are *you* doing here?"

"I'm looking into the Delaney case," Surge told Bailey. "I heard you got a problem with people doing that."

"We do. You're denied access to this ward until—"

Surge's hands closed on Joe Bailey's shirt and jacket, taking two huge fistfuls of the fabric, the way an eagle's talons close on rabbit fur. The seams that joined the sleeves to the chest of Bailey's jacket popped open. Surge lifted and threw the man backward in one motion, sending him smashing into a large whiteboard hanging at the back of the hallway. Surge pivoted and rammed his elbow into the throat of the officer on his left, using the momentum to rake back a haymaker into the other officer's face. Charlie dragged Lamb through the fray as Bailey and one of the other officers leaped on Surge together, the trio crunching into the drywall as an alarm began sounding from the nurses' station.

CHAPTER 30

Charlie had visited secure wards plenty of times in his career. Here, the patients that hospitals needed to restrain were kept away from the public. The screamers and thrashers and criminals; junkies trying to fight air demons; howling dementia patients brought in from days wandering the streets, scabbed and stinking of urine. Occasionally, when multiple patients needed police supervision or protection at once, they ended up here. He'd responded to the aftermath of a prison riot once and found three members of the same stickup crew sporting puncture wounds, resting up in the same ward, planning their next caper from their neighboring beds.

The lights were dimmer here, and the distant alarm sparked by Surge's violence seemed muffled. Charlie and Lamb paused in a doorway. Ashlea Pratt was sitting in a bed by a window that was covered by a blind, holding an older woman's hand and wiping her nose on a well-used tissue.

"If the scans are all good, I don't know why I can't go home," she was saying. "I just want to go home and have a shower and go to bed."

The ward was clear of other patients. They passed two rooms full of empty gurneys, cleared whiteboards, pushed-back curtain dividers. In the fourth room, they found the curtains drawn around a single bed. Charlie tugged the curtain back, and the sound of the rings sliding on the metal rail jolted Jonie Delaney from her sleep.

"Oh, sorry." She sat up, shoving back her wilted, sleep-mussed curls. "Wh-what time is it? Do we have to go?"

"Jonie, I'm Charlie Hoskins. I'm a police officer," he said, taking a chair beside the bed. Lamb checked the door and pulled the curtain back around Jonie's little section of the big, lonely room. "This is my partner, Lynette Lamb. We're here to talk to you about Tilly."

"Is she okay?" Jonie asked.

Charlie glanced at Lamb.

"Tilly?" He was suddenly lost for words. "Uh, we don't know yet."

"No, I mean my mom." Jonie rubbed her eyes. Her movements were slightly stiff, like she was cold. All her limbs were pulled in toward her center. "Someone said she was in the hospital somewhere. In surgery. She got stabbed."

"I think she's still in surgery," Lamb said. "We can find out for you."

Jonie nodded vaguely. Charlie was about to speak when Lamb surprised him.

"I'm sorry this is happening to you, Jonie," she said. "All of it."

Jonie and Charlie looked over at the aspiring young police officer. The words had been so simple, so human and rudimentary, Charlie scolded himself for not thinking to say them first.

"I deserve it," Jonie said. "I killed Tilly. This is what you get for murdering someone."

Charlie felt his whole chest seize. He'd heard those kinds of words before, but never from someone who looked the way Jonie did now—so small and alone and frail.

His partner sat on the edge of the bed, and they both listened to Jonie's story. It was clear to Charlie that the young woman was still shaking off the effects of whatever sedative she had been given. She paused midsentence twice to stare at the ceiling, her lips parted and her eyes wandering slowly. When she was done, the empty room seemed to echo with the confession, like it had changed the very nature of the space around them. Widened and deepened it.

"That was what the dumpster thing was about," Charlie murmured to Lamb. He tried to slow his racing thoughts, the sudden desire to grip onto this and bring the whole day to an end, no matter how unbelievable the girl's claim was. Then reality hit him. The hard facts. He felt his feet on the floor suddenly, like he'd been shoved back down to earth.

This wasn't the answer.

He needed to find out why she was telling them it was.

"Jonie," he said. "Whatever happened to your sister that day, I don't believe it was your fault. I don't believe this story you're telling us right now is true."

"But it is true." Jonie's face crumpled. She hitched her sleeve down her wrist and wiped tears from her eyes. "I killed her. I remember doing it. I remember the sound of her head hitting the sink. Her hair was all wet. There was blood in it."

"But there were no dumpsters down at Santa Monica Beach that day," Lamb said. She put her hand on the lump beneath the thin blanket that was Jonie's restless foot. "You couldn't have gotten rid of Tilly's body the way that you described."

Jonie became still. She watched Lamb's face, her knees pulled tightly against her chest.

"There was a dumpster right near the parking lot."

"No, there wasn't," Charlie said.

Jonie looked at Charlie now, at the bruises on his jaw and the stitches in his scalp. If she had been more conscious, more clear-minded, Charlie supposed she might have questioned him about them. But for now, they were just passing visual curiosities as she tried to untangle her mind.

"Even if there were a dumpster," Lamb said, "you didn't dump your sister's body in it."

Charlie waited. Dents and spaniels.

"Think about it," Lamb continued. "A big dumpster like that, down on the waterfront? If the lid was open, it would be besieged by gulls all the time, looking for scraps. Leftover fries, ice cream cones, burgers, whatever. People bringing food down from the pier to eat on the beach. They'd hurl their leftovers into a dumpster standing open like that. You think the people searching for Tilly wouldn't have glanced into a big, open vessel sitting there at the edge of the parking lot a few yards from where she went missing?"

"The lid was shut," Jonie said. "Probably. And maybe . . . you know. Maybe somebody came and got the dumpster after I dumped her but before the police came."

"Okay, say the lid was shut." Lamb shrugged. "So, what—you carried Tilly's body out of the bathroom, laid her on the ground, lifted the lid, picked her up, put her in the dumpster, folded the lid back again? Without anybody seeing you?"

Jonie's chin wobbled. Charlie wanted to hold the girl.

"Ask Tanner," Jonie said.

"Who's Tanner?" Lamb frowned.

"My boyfriend. Tanner. He knows," Jonie said. "He knows I did it. He's better with the details than I am."

"Was he there that day?" Charlie asked. "Did he help you?"

"He was out in the water," Jonie said. "With the others. My friends. And when I raised the alarm that she was missing, and all the police came, he stuck around for a while to help with the search. It was only later that I told him the truth."

Lamb was frowning hard. She rubbed her brow like she was trying to scrub out the skepticism, but it didn't seem to work.

"How long after the day Tilly disappeared did you tell Tanner what you'd done?" she asked.

"Maybe a few weeks," Jonie said. "He's the only one I've ever confessed to before today. He was there for me after she went missing, when everyone was going crazy all around me. Tanner was calm, and he . . . he was supportive. He knew I'd done it even before I said I did."

Charlie looked at Lamb. He felt his mouth turn dry and his jaw lock tight.

"He knew I'd done it, and he helped me realize that and confess."

"He 'helped you' confess?" Charlie said.

"I'd blocked it out, in my mind." Jonie tapped her temple. "Like, my brain took the memory of what I had done and tucked it away somewhere. And Tanner, you know, he got it back. I was so scared that someone had abducted Tilly and they were . . . ah, like, they were doing horrible things to her somewhere." Jonie crumpled again. She hitched a series of sobs. "But Tanner just kept saying, you know, 'Maybe you did this' and 'Maybe you did that.' And then I remembered what I'd done. And it was kind of a relief that it was me, you know, and she wasn't . . . she wasn't . . ."

"Jonie"—Lamb was still holding that small foot shape under the blanket—"it is possible Tanner *suggested* to you that you had killed Tilly, when really you didn't?"

"No." Jonie dried her eyes. "Because once I'd told him, he promised me he would keep my secret. He covered things up for me." The girl wiped her nose on her sleeve. "He went through my clothes while I was out, and he found the bloody T-shirt. The one I'd been wearing when I killed her. He said he burned it."

Charlie nodded, took out his phone, tapped out a text message to Saskia Ferboden. For a moment or two, then, he couldn't move. Fury and disgust had paralyzed him, and he was afraid that if he forced himself up out of the chair that words would rattle loose and fly out of him. Some remote corner of his mind knew that revealing to Jonie Delaney right now that she hadn't killed her sister would be a cruelty, because it would take away the one ally she thought she had in the whole world. And it would open up all those dark possibilities she'd been so relieved to dismiss. So, instead, he simply sat there until the muscles in his shoulders and neck had loosened, and his knees had unfrozen, and his balance had been restored, and then he got up. He beckoned Lamb, and they thanked Jonie and went back out into the hall.

Ryan stood in the doorway to the hall outside lab 21, the gun hanging by his side, his eyes on the distant automatic glass door in the foyer. Bendigo watched him, thinking how strained the man looked, how a few hours of a situation like this could hollow a person's cheeks and sink their eyes and bring out their veins in a way that made them look like they were in a pressure chamber. In the days after Bendigo's wife, Cora, had left him, after the night he'd returned home from work to find her side of the closet empty and that fateful note propped on the kitchen bench, he'd looked like that. Bloodless. As the minutes passed, the duffel bag slung over Bendigo's back began to feel heavy. He could feel odd shapes inside it against his love handles and the curve of his butt. A corner. A wide, sharp edge.

"What's taking so long?" Bendigo asked.

Ryan didn't move. Didn't react to his words.

"Is he going out or not?"

"He's just standing there beside the doors," Ryan said. "I can see him in the reflection in front of the reception desk."

"He must be scared," Bendigo said.

"I would be," Ryan replied. "Last time a hostage went out, the snipers decided to light the place up."

Bendigo felt the hairs on the back of his neck stand on end. Outside, he could hear a female officer shouting.

"*Ibrahim Solea! We can see you! Please put your hands on your head! Walk through the doors slowly and carefully! Stop three paces outside the doors! Do it now!*"

Bendigo's knees felt weak. He leaned against the steel tabletop and looked at the burned and twisted fragments of destroyed DNA samples there. At the detritus of Ryan and Elsie's day taking command of his lab. Used water bottles. The plastic wrappers of consumed protein bars. He felt so full of hatred. He could taste bile at the back of his throat.

"He's moving." Ryan beckoned with one arm.

Bendigo gripped the duffel strap across his chest. "Come on. Get ready to go."

CHAPTER 31

Through the binoculars, the image of Ibrahim Solea wobbled and swayed. The muscular security guard was standing just inside the automatic glass doors, not close enough to set off the sensor and cause them to open but close enough that Saskia could see the expression on his face. He was open-mouthed, panting, his eyes wide and fixed on the handicapped parking spaces just beyond the curb outside the doors. Saskia couldn't tell if he was shifting gently from foot to foot, rocking, or if it was a trick of the binoculars in her hands. She put the lenses down and heard Curler sigh with frustration beside her.

"Six minutes," Curler said. He was checking his big silver watch. "Six minutes he's been standing there. He's scared stiff."

"Or he's psyching himself up, because this is some kind of trick," Saskia said. "We heard it loud and clear: Ryan knows we miked up the lab. Probably assumes we've got cameras in there, too. He might have slipped Ibrahim a note forcing him to do this. Whatever this is."

"Let's hope, if that's the case, the instruction was just to keep us busy while Ryan and Bendigo go up to the first floor," Curler said.

"Maybe. Maybe it's a suicide mission," Saskia said. "Ryan might have told Ibrahim he'd kill Bendigo if the boy didn't come out here shooting."

"Hell of a worst-case scenario," Curler said.

"It's all I can think of right now," Saskia said. "Worst cases."

"Why aren't they moving?" a voice said. Tanner Court was standing three feet away from Saskia, bent at the waist and watching a laptop feed of the interior of the lab. "Look. They're just standing by the lab door, waiting to go."

"Would you get your ass away from there?" Saskia said. "Jesus, kid, you're not a consultant on this. You're stuck here because you can't go with Jonie, and you can't go home because we might need you for something. Just sit."

"I've been sitting here for hours," he grumbled. "I'm losing my freakin' mind."

Saskia's phone bleeped. She watched the kid slink back to the fold-out chair and then picked it up. She had to read Charlie Hoskins's message three times before she could comprehend what it meant. Then she showed it to Curler and stood there holding the phone while he tried to take it in after several disbelieving reads.

They moved wordlessly to where the boy sat. Curler grabbed a handful of the back of Tanner's T-shirt and hauled him to his feet. The officers manning the tent watched, blank-faced, as Saskia and Curler marched the protesting boy over to the gap between the cruisers and the BearCat. Curler shoved him hard into the railing that ran the length of the oversize vehicle. The boy yowled.

"Explain this to me." Curler snatched the phone from Saskia's hand and showed the boy the message. Saskia was fighting the urge to take the kid away from Curler and throw him down onto the asphalt.

Animalistic desires driven by rage were ticking in her fingertips as the boy read, his face and neck steadily draining of color.

"Oh," he said. "Ohhh. Ohhhh."

"'Oh,' *what*?" Saskia hissed.

"It wasn't, uh . . ." Tanner gazed off at the checkpoint to the parking lot. "It wasn't exactly like that."

"It wasn't exactly like you convinced Jonie Delaney that she killed her little sister?" Curler flashed his teeth as he spat the words.

The boy tried to shift away from the big, lean man, but the only refuge was Saskia's presence, which wasn't any less threatening.

"Please explain to me what it was like, then."

"She just, uh, she just, she just, she just—" Tanner clawed at his neck, gripped two handfuls of his own T-shirt, his eyes fixed on the horizon, anywhere but the faces crowding in on him. "She kept talking about, like, uh . . . She kept asking over and over and over, like, 'What happened? What happened to her?' To Tilly. She was desperate to know. Sad and desperate and worried about all the kinds of things that might, you know, be happening. She had all these terrible ideas. And eventually I, um . . ."

"You *what*?" Saskia roared.

"I kind of just . . . gave her an answer."

"And what an answer it was!" Saskia said. "A very elaborate and detailed answer. An answer that conveniently left her indebted to you. Connected to you. Seeking a specific kind of comfort that only you could provide."

"No, I—"

"You told her you got rid of a bloody T-shirt you found in her closet?" Curler asked.

"It just—"

"Spit it out!"

"It just *grew*." Tanner palmed at tears running down his cheeks. "It started as, like, a little story. I just threw it out there: *Maybe you did it.* And then suddenly it was like, *Okay, you did it.* And then it just grew and grew and grew on its own." His eyes darted back and forth across the horizon, searching for an out. "She had questions about how she could have done it a-a-and how it would have worked, and so I just kept adding details. And then she was remembering the things that I had added. I'm sorry. I'm so, so sorry. I'll tell Jonie that it's not the truth. I'll go to the hospital and tell her now, if you let me."

"Honey, you're not going anywhere." Saskia grabbed the boy and yanked him off the side of the BearCat. She opened the door of the nearest cruiser and shoved him in. "You're gonna sit in there until I can figure out what criminal charges I'm going to lay against you. You think you're the only one who can get creative around here, boy? Guess again."

Saskia and Curler went back to the command tent. They stood in silence by the comms table, panting quietly with rage.

"Damn," Curler said eventually. "I've done some stupid, selfish, crazy shit to get a girl in my time. But that really takes the cake."

Saskia couldn't speak. She was tapping a message back to Hoss when the radio in front of her crackled with Delta Hodge's voice.

"We're losing him," Hodge said.

Saskia took up the binoculars. She focused them on the automatic doors just in time to see Ibrahim disappear back into the shadows.

Charlie tossed the car keys to Lamb as they headed across the lot. She was still focused on her phone but caught the keys in one hand without looking up.

"You drive," Charlie said. "I'm too angry."

"No, you drive." She tossed the keys back. "I'm busy. I might have something here."

They slipped into the car. Lamb leaned over and

showed Charlie the picture from the Instagram account she had been examining that was linked to Ruby Monacco. He looked again at the picture of the fat ginger cat lounging on the wooden deck, the slice of neon-blue water rimmed by white fiberglass pool edging.

"See that?" Lamb pointed.

Charlie leaned in and squinted. Lamb spread her fingers and zoomed in on the image. Behind the cat, on the side of a distant structure that might have been a garden shed, a small sign with blue lettering was hanging crookedly.

"Life's a garden . . . ," Charlie read.

"Dig it," Lamb said. "*Life's a Garden—Dig It.*"

"What does that even mean?"

"Nothing. It's cutesy novelty household shit like those *Live Laugh Love* signs white women hang in their living rooms." Lamb took back the phone and tapped. "But look. I found the seller. The sign is sold by Hobby Lobby."

"Oh. Good." Charlie rolled his eyes and started up the engine. "There's only one of those on every street corner in the country. Even I know about Hobby Lobby, and I've never hand-made anything in my life."

"It's something," Lamb said. "It's not just something, it's all we have right now. I'm gonna call the head office in Oklahoma City and see how many of these signs have ever been made and sold in the U.S."

"You think they're gonna tell you?" Charlie said. He pulled out of the parking lot and paused in the driveway to watch Surge being guided into a police cruiser. He turned left and drove into the street. "You think they're happy to just give away that kind of information?"

"You're not the only one who can act," Lamb said. "I'll feed them some bullshit about being a real cop. I've been making a convincing show of it all day."

She waited, selected an option, was put on hold.

Charlie drove, not because they had a destination, but because he needed to stay in motion. Because a dark, dreadful weight had settled in his belly, an unshakable certainty that they were not going to find Tilly Delaney. That she was going to remain lost, not only throughout the siege at Hertzberg-Davis that day but throughout all time. He knew in his belly and in his bones that the little girl with the big brown curls was going to appear on the front page of every newspaper in the world for the next few days, and then she'd go right back to where she'd been for the previous two years. In a database somewhere, on a handful of websites, and lodged in the memories of those who'd known her. Charlie recognized this sensation in his gut. The sickening inevitability attached to a hopeless case. Before, when he'd felt it, the hopelessness had been hard to dislodge. But as he looked over at Lamb, he felt it shift a little. Twist and wriggle. She was chewing her bottom lip and waiting on the phone and watching the sunset streets of Los Angeles pass her with restless eyes like she was going to spot the missing child any minute now, taking a walk with her captor in the falling evening.

He felt a tiny surge of something that wasn't dread but wasn't quite optimism. He thought for a while, then took out his phone and dialed. Olivia Zaouk answered after three rings.

"Hello?"

"Detective Charlie Hoskins. I have a few more questions for you."

"Oh, okay, sure. Sure. Whatever I can do to help."

"When you saw Tilly at the beach"—Charlie stopped at the lights, watched a couple with a stroller passing before his bumper—"what was she wearing?"

Charlie heard a sigh. "I think she was wearing the swimsuit. Like in the pictures in the paper."

"You saw images of Tilly in the newspaper?"

"Yeah. I think so. The next morning," Olivia said.

"At the hotel. Daniel and I were having breakfast. The searches were still going on, with the choppers and all that."

"Olivia." Charlie reminded himself to be gentle. Not to let the anger, the frustration, leak into his voice. "I'm trying to figure out exactly how sure you are about what you saw that day."

"Um . . . I mean, I'm sure."

"You talked to the other witness, Leanne Browning, at the beach on the day Tilly went missing," Charlie said. "Then you talked to her again this afternoon, as you arrived to see me and my partner, Lamb. My concern is that, both times, Ms. Browning might have given you details about what *she* saw, or you might have given her details about what *you* saw."

"Well, maybe. I guess," Olivia said. "What are you trying to say?"

"I'm trying to say that yes, you were at the beach that day. And maybe you even saw a girl. But I need to know exactly how sure you are that it was *Tilly Delaney* you saw, and that she was stomping off down toward the water."

"Well, shit, I don't know, sir. I'm as sure as I can be."

"What about the bag?" Charlie said, pressing the phone hard to his ear. "Are you sure about that?"

"Uh . . ."

"I've got your statement here in front of me. In it, you said that Tilly was carrying a beach bag."

"Oh. Yeah. Yeah, I did."

"What color was it?"

"Uh, I don't know if I remember the color exactly. I just know it was striped. Black and white or blue and white. A dark color with white."

"Okay." Charlie nodded. "Okay. Great. Thanks a lot."

He ended the call. Lamb was still on hold, watching him.

"Do me a favor," Charlie said to Lamb. "Close your eyes."

She did. He drove on.

"Imagine a beach bag," he said. "You know, the kind you carry sunblock and towels and stuff in. Maybe a paperback to read on the sand."

"Okay," Lamb said.

"What color is it?"

Lamb shrugged. "Blue and white stripes?"

She opened her eyes and looked at him. "What?"

"I just fed Olivia Zaouk a bunch of bullshit about her seeing Tilly Delaney carrying a beach bag the day she went missing," Charlie said. "She ate it up. Even told me the bag was stripy, just like you did. Because your classic beach bag is stripy."

"Right," Lamb said. "Tilly wasn't carrying the bag. Jonie was."

"And if Olivia saw Tilly stomping off toward the beach, like she said, that means Jonie would still have been in the bathroom. With the bag. Which was plain red, not stripy."

"So you're thinking, if you could insert that beach bag into Olivia's memory so easily, maybe Leanne Browning could do the same about seeing Tilly storming off toward the water."

Charlie nodded again.

"But how do you know it's Leanne who's influenced Olivia and not the other way around?"

"Because Olivia said Tilly was marching 'very determinedly' toward the water," Charlie said. "Who's more likely to use the phrase 'very determinedly'? Leanne is, what, midfifties? Olivia is twenty-three."

"I'll check the statement." Lamb took up her phone again, put the hold music of her call on speaker. Charlie waited and drove while his partner flipped through digital pages, zoomed and read and scanned through handwritten text.

"*The child turned and strode determinedly toward the water,*" Lamb read. "*She was visibly upset. I later recognized the child as being the one in the photographs police were circulating. I recalled seeing her distinct brown ringlet curls.*"

"Leanne Browning?" Charlie asked.

"Yeah." Lamb put the phone down. "So you think Leanne Browning was the one who actually saw Tilly come out of the bathroom and walk off, and Olivia Zaouk just thinks she did."

"I'm leaning that way," Charlie said.

"So where does that get us?"

"Nowhere exactly, but—"

Lamb flapped at him. Her call had connected.

"Good evening. My name is Detective Sergeant Lynette Lamb," she said, straightening in her chair.

Charlie scoffed. "There's no way you sound old enough to be a detect—"

Lamb elbowed him in the ribs.

"I'm calling because I'd like to speak to someone in management about a critical police matter."

Charlie grinned. Lamb saw it and turned away from him.

He walked on jelly legs, trying to make a beeline for them down the hall but instead coming at them in a wide curve, brushing against the wall. Ryan and Bendigo stood back and let Ibrahim come in the doorway, his throat hitching with what might have been swallowed sobs or nauseated gags.

"I. Can't. Do it." The security guard ignored Ryan completely, coming so close to Bendigo the scientist wondered if he was trying to get a hug, or to be caught if he fell. "I can't go out there. They're gonna shoot me. They're gonna shoot me."

"If you stay in here, *I'm* gonna shoot you." Ryan gripped the kid hard by his elbow and tried to drag him back toward the door. "Get the fuck out there!

I'm letting you go, for the love of god! You want me to change my mind?"

"Listen." Bendigo took Ibrahim by his shirtfront and looked at his glassy eyes. They stood there in silence, the two of them, Bendigo arresting the boy's attention for a soul-surging pep talk he couldn't imagine giving. Because, the fact was, he'd never encouraged anyone to do anything in his life. He wasn't a father; he'd never roused his son from the edge of a ball field into saving the day for a bunch of underdog Little Leaguers. He'd married Cora because she was a determined and hard-nosed woman who would have ignored or defied his encouragement to do anything even if he gave it, and he was the kind of boss who simply expected his lab scientists and their techs to do what he asked, under threat of reprimand or dismissal. Now he was tasked with talking a young man into facing a literal firing squad. But, somehow, for reasons beyond his understanding, the words started coming.

"Listen," he said again. "Ibrahim, you're going to stop thinking about the snipers and go out there. Ryan's going to cut your ties, and you're going to walk out those doors with your hands held high in the air, and the whole world's going to see you as the police come forward and guide you out safely. You're going to look like a fucking hero, okay? Because you got through this. Because you held on, and you kept your head, and you've got a good heart."

Ibrahim listened, nodding hard.

"That girlfriend who ran off with the personal trainer is going to have to take up residency at the local bar to drink away her sorrows at having dumped you," Bendigo said. He shook the kid by his shirt. "She's going to be the talk of her town. The village idiot. You're gonna be picking women off you like lint after this."

Ibrahim huffed a few short breaths and kept nodding.

"You can do this," Bendigo said, feeling cheesy and phony and racked with guilt, because he sure as shit knew *he* couldn't do what he was asking the boy to do. "You've got to say it: *I can do this.*"

"I can do this." Ibrahim shuddered.

"Cut his ties," Bendigo said. He turned the boy around to face Ryan. "Give him that, at least. Let him walk out there like a man."

Ryan tucked the gun into the front of his jeans and took up a knife that was sitting on the table beside them. He slipped the knife inside the loop of the middle cable tie, the one that connected the ties around both of Ibrahim's wrists, and bent the tie down around the blade. The tie gave a *snap* as Ryan cut upward through it.

Then, in a move so swift Bendigo could barely follow it with his eyes, Ibrahim lunged forward and snatched the pistol from out of Ryan's waistband.

CHAPTER 32

Charlie stopped the car in the parking lot of a Ralphs grocery store, the huge red lettering reflecting off the hood and now and then crisscrossed by evening shoppers wheeling carts of groceries toward their cars. Lamb had found a pen in the glove compartment and was sitting with one leg folded across her lap, the hem of her jeans pulled up, making notes on the pale, taut skin on the side of her calf. Charlie couldn't follow the progress of the calls, the numbers, the inferences in Lamb's questions. His thoughts were too tangled, and the new metal plate in his skull felt like it was rattling loose with the beat of his heart. Lamb hung up and completed a note on her messily scrawled calf, and Charlie sat back and waited for her report.

"Here's the bad news," Lamb said. "There have been four thousand, eight hundred, and seventeen of those *Life's a Garden—Dig It!* signs sold in the U.S. since Hobby Lobby started importing them from Malaysia in 2017."

Charlie put his head against the steering wheel.

"All's not lost." Lamb gave his arm a pat that had the briskness and roughness of a mother tired of her child's tantrums. "All's not lost."

"It is with this thread," Charlie said, sitting back in his seat. "You're working off a random photograph on a nameless online account that's only thinly connected to someone who isn't even Tilly Delaney. You're assuming too much with this, Lamb. You're assuming the photograph in the account was even taken in the U.S. If the company in Malaysia exports to the U.S., they probably export all over the world. Ruby's stalker could be in Australia, or England or . . . *Nigeria,* for all you know."

"Charlie—"

"And even if we ever find her stalker," Charlie went on, "we don't know that they went anywhere near Ruby on the day Tilly went missing. They might have stayed at home trying to scam some other lonely, famous sap with too much money on their hands."

"Charlie—"

"We need to go back to the beach." Charlie clawed his hands down his stubble, tried to draw on some untapped reserve of energy in his body. "Work the hotels. Find out if there was anyone staying in the area who's ever been convicted of—"

"Charlie, I found Ruby's stalker," Lamb said.

He looked at her.

"I asked the sales analyst at Hobby Lobby to cut the four thousand, eight hundred, and seventeen purchases of the garden sign down for me," Lamb explained. "I focused only on the signs that were bought online. That accounted for about half the signs. Then I asked her to cut down those numbers to purchases that were shipped to California. Yes, it was a flawed request. I assumed a lot. I assumed that whoever we're looking for, they didn't just walk into a Hobby Lobby and buy the sign in person. And I assumed that whoever we're looking for, they live in the same state as Ruby."

Charlie waited.

"For the first assumption, I took a chance," Lamb said. "I worked with what I had, not with what I wished I had. And for the second assumption, I wondered why the stalker chose Ruby. Of all the people in the world. Of all the rich people. Of all the rich actors. Of all the rich *child* actors. They chose Ruby Monacco. They constructed a very specific, very targeted scam. The animals. The father-figure type. They came up with a scam that she fell for completely, and they maintained that scam for months. *Months.* Being there for her when she was down. Listening to her when she needed an ear. Providing those heart-wrenching stories when she was ripe to be convinced to give out emergency cash."

Charlie put his head on the steering wheel again, his eyes closed, listening. Thinking.

"They knew the scam wouldn't be discovered by Ruby's handlers or her accountant or her parents," Lamb continued. "Because they kept the amounts they were asking for well under the limit of Ruby's monthly allowance. How did they know what her monthly allowance was?"

"They knew her," Charlie said.

"The parameters I asked for," Lamb said, "of purchases made online and purchases shipped to California, brought the numbers down to nine hundred and forty-four signs. I sent that list of names to Ruby to see if she recognized anybody."

"Lamb." Charlie shook his head. "I—"

"You can thank me later." She pointed to the road beyond the parking lot. "Turn right and head out to the highway."

On the laptop screen, Saskia watched Ibrahim Solea appear in the doorway of lab 21, his steps stilted and his eyes howling in the grainy image. She didn't look up when she felt Delta Hodge arrive at her side. The SWAT commander had her own tablet displaying the feed tucked under her arm.

"Motherfucker's backed out," she said. "I'm gonna keep the extraction team in place. You never know. A pep talk from the old man might do it."

"In the meantime, let's hook you up to the PA system," Saskia said, walking with her to the comms desk where Curler was standing, listening to his phone. "We can start talking Ibrahim through the extraction over the speakers. We'll tell him he's safe and that the shot from earlier was a deliberate tactic that's not going to happen again. We need to convince him to get out of there before Ryan doubles back on his decision."

"Jesus." Curler dropped his phone from his ear and stared at the screen. His thumb was hovering over the End Call option, and Saskia could see that it was shaking. "Oh, Jesus. Not now."

"What is it?"

Curler beckoned Hodge and Saskia closer. "I got a call from an officer I know down at the South Bureau. She said a guy just walked into Seventy-Seventh Street station with a handgun and tried to hold up the front of the building. Said he wanted his sister's cold case reopened."

"Oh my god." Saskia could barely form the words. "What—"

"They shot him," Curler said. "He's dead. But he got off two rounds. There's one officer dead and one on his way to the ER."

"The fucking radio host," Hodge said. "He played the interview with Ryan, and other stations must have picked it up. That host is a dead man. I'm gonna kill him myself."

"We can think about what charges to lay on him later," Curler said. "At the end of the day, this is all the Delaneys. This whole stunt was bound to inspire some other person on the edge, interview or not."

"We can't let this get out," Saskia breathed. She looked at Hodge. "If the officers in that building hear that a colleague has just been killed in a fucking copycat attack, they're going to go right off the rails. They'll storm the lab and kill Ryan and whoever else gets in their way, and there won't be a thing we can do about it."

"Yeah, sure, and I'm havin' a hard time disagreeing with that as a concept." Hodge's chin was twitching with rage, her mouth downturned. "Ryan Delaney has done enough damage here today. People are dying, ma'am. We need to take that fucker down right now."

"And we will," Saskia said. "Safely. We gotta think about the bomb."

"Fuck the bomb," Hodge snarled. "We'll hit him before he has time to scream, let alone grab any kind of detonator he's got on him."

"We can't contain this, the story about the officers from the Seventy-Seventh," Curler said. He weighed his phone in his hand. "If I've heard about it, other officers are going to hear about it any second now."

"Make sure your teams are all the way back," Saskia told Hodge. "I don't want anyone anywhere near the ground or first floors."

"He's got the gun!"

Saskia, Curler, and Hodge whirled around as the comms officer nearest them leaped back from the desk, her chair clattering to the asphalt. She was pointing at the screen.

"Ibrahim's got Ryan's gun!"

"Put the knife down," Ibrahim said. He had a double-handed grip on the gun, a finger on the trigger, and a palm under the butt of the weapon, the way Bendigo had seen cops point guns in TV shows. But the kid's eyes weren't right. They weren't cold and menacing, controlled, the way the posture suggested they should be. They were the eyes of a terrified child, watery and blazing white all around the dark pupils.

Ryan did exactly what Bendigo assumed he would, and yet the old man was so stunned by what was happening he could make no move to intervene. To play his part. To help his fellow hostage. He just stood there dumbly as Ryan put his hands up in a sign of surrender, backed around Ibrahim in an arc, and made for the steel table like he was going to place the knife on it. In a mere three steps, he'd backed into Bendigo and then slung his arm around the doctor's neck, the point of the knife now jutting into Bendigo's jugular.

"Don't be stupid," Ryan said. He yanked the strap of the duffel bag down at the front, so that the bag rode up and became sandwiched tight between Ryan's chest and Bendigo's back. "Don't be stupid, Ibrahim. You hit the bag and you'll blow the whole bottom half of the building out."

"Put the knife down," Ibrahim repeated.

"Don't do this," Bendigo begged the kid. "Just back out and fucking *leave*! This is your chance!"

"I'm not going without you!" Ibrahim roared.

Ibrahim took a step forward, a slow boxer's shuffle, his feet never leaving the floor. Ryan shifted his grip on the knife, and Bendigo felt the blade strum up the stubble of his throat like the comb of a music box. Ryan leaned backward, and Bendigo was forced to go with him, the two of them doing a slow waltz to the end of the steel bench.

"Listen, listen, listen," Bendigo said. "Both of you. You know they must be watching us! If they come through that door right now—"

"Shut up!" Ryan hissed in his ear.

"Ibrahim, you've gotta go!" Bendigo howled. "Just turn and go! I'll be okay!"

The boy winced. That was his mistake. In the quarter second between making the decision to shoot and shooting, while his finger pulled the trigger and the springs tightened and the lever depressed, he closed his eyes and screwed up his face and told Ryan with that simple, unconscious expression what was about to happen. Ryan yanked Bendigo to the ground. The round blasted out a window as Bendigo hit the floor behind the steel table, his head smacking against the linoleum, causing a buzz in his ears that drowned out the shouting and the thumping and the whiz of the zipper on the side of the duffel bag. Bendigo flipped and got to his hands and knees in time to see Ryan pulling the spare pistol from the side pocket of the bag.

"Ibrahim!" he cried.

He was too late. The name was only half-formed on his lips by the time Ryan had popped up from behind the table and fired twice into Ibrahim's chest.

CHAPTER 33

There was barbecue smoke on the wind, the sound of children laughing in the last blue glow of twilight. When Charlie opened the picket gate at the front of the property, the jangle of the latch set off a small white terrier, who came rushing toward the screen door. Charlie went up the steps but ignored the door and the dog, instead turning right, Lamb following at his heels. The porch opened into a large yard. The barbecue was hand-built, sandstone, surrounded by men with beers. A small knot of women had commandeered a table on the grass that was covered with plates, glasses, baskets of bread. Lamb felt a surge of excitement as she scanned the faces of the curious kids in the pool, who had made their way to the edge to watch the entrance of the interlopers.

"I'm looking for Shane McMasters," Charlie announced.

For a moment, nobody spoke. The meat on the grill sizzled. A spiderweb of exchanged curious and worrisome glances spread out around where Lamb and her partner stood. Then one of the kids in the pool, a boy with popped-out ears and two missing front teeth, called, "Dad?" and Lamb followed his eyes to Shane.

He was standing by the barbecue with a pair of tongs in his fist. The men around him took a step back. Lamb watched the man glance at the meat, like he was trying to decide whether whatever was about to happen would take long enough to burn the turkey patties. Over Shane's shoulder, Lamb spied the sign on the shed wall. *Life's a Garden—Dig It!*

"That's me." Shane raised the tongs. He was rippled and roped with veins, his T-shirt deliberately a size too small, hard work and clean eating on display. "Can I help you? Who are you?"

"We're here about Ruby." Charlie beckoned him with a low flick of his fingers, the kind of gesture a guy makes to a dog who won't come in from the rain. It made the men around Shane bristle. "Into the house. Let's go."

"Sorry, what's this about?" one of the men asked.

Lamb could hear the women shifting their chairs back, gathering behind the men. The air shimmered with tension, suburban paradise interrupted.

"We're kind of busy here. And this is private property."

"Shane," Lamb warned, "please come toward the house. It's about Ruby and your mutual friends, Jacob and Harrison."

Shane dropped the tongs. They landed soundlessly on the grass. The kids in the pool all turned in unison, two girls and a boy, watching Shane cross the lawn with his head down and his stride long.

The big man led them to the porch at the front. When they arrived there, Lamb realized a woman had joined them. She had the same popped-out ears and big, worried eyes as the boy in the pool. The white terrier was going crazy in a living room off the porch, a whirling, bouncing ball of furry terror.

"Jamie, go back to the kids, will you?" Shane told his wife.

"What's happened?" She focused on Lamb. "Is Ruby okay?"

"I said go back to the kids!" Shane snapped.

The aggression was obviously uncharacteristic. Shane's wife was so shocked by the outburst that she backed away sharply, bumped into Lamb, and trod on her boot. Lamb steadied the woman and turned her gently toward the yard. The big man was silhouetted against a gold porch light that was being dive-bombed by moths.

"Who are you guys?" he asked. "Are you police? Or are you with Ruby?"

"We're both," Lamb said.

Charlie had his phone out, reading off the white-lit screen.

"*You stinking, rotting whore,*" he read, his voice flat. "*I know where to find you. I know people to send after you who will enjoy making you their pretty little baby doll punk.*"

"Oh, Christ," Shane twisted away, covering his face with his big hands. "Don't read it, man. You don't have to read that stuff out loud. I know what it says."

"*Fuck you, mouthy, betraying little bitch.*"

"Dude. Dude, please."

"You're Ruby Monacco's life coach," Lamb said, watching the moth shadows dance over Shane's arms. "And you talk to her like that?"

"It was a role I was playing." Shane lifted his hands helplessly. Made a high, squirming noise inside his throat. "I didn't mean any of it, obviously."

"'Obviously'?" Charlie asked. He looked at Lamb. "Is it 'obvious' to you that none of that was real, Lamb? Because it wasn't obvious to Ruby. It wasn't obvious to me."

"Oh, maaan." Shane paced to the railing of the porch a few feet away, paced back. "*Maaan*. This is bad."

"Now there's the understatement of the century," Lamb said.

"I'm really, *really* sorry." Shane reached out, made to place a reassuring hand on Lamb's shoulder. She sidestepped it. "I know that doesn't mean anything to you guys, but I'm sorry. What kind of charge am I looking at for this sort of thing? Is it . . . is it stalking? Will I be charged with harassment?"

"Harassment?" Charlie laughed. "Try felony extortion, you towering piece of human garbage. That's slammer-worthy. And that's just where your problems begin. When these messages are read out in court and some of your fellow criminal scumbags hear them? You don't talk about a ten-year-old's body that way and expect word not to get out across the prison yard."

"It was just a *role,* though."

"I don't care what you call it," Charlie said.

"I can give the money back." Shane paced to the railing again, gripped it with both hands, paced back. "If I give the money back, then it's just . . . it's just words, right?"

"You and your lawyer can try to figure out how you're going to dig your way out of this grave," Lamb said. "Right now, we want to know where you were the day Tilly Delaney disappeared."

"Who?" Shane stopped pacing. He was standing at the railing, the night beyond dark, an abyss beckoning him. "That's . . . You mean the kid on the news? The little girl?"

"October 19 that year." Lamb jutted her chin at the phone she could see forming an outline against Shane's tight jeans. "Tell us where you were."

"Okay, no." Shane forced a couple of hard breaths, rubbing his sternum. "No. You've got this wrong. I'm not . . . I didn't say those things to Ruby because I'm a pedophile. I don't know any pedophiles. I said them because . . . It was about the money. It's not about little girls."

"I'm trying so hard right now, Shane," Charlie said. "I'm trying to find a reason not to believe you were at Santa Monica Beach, attempting to make good on the threats you'd issued toward your employer, Ruby Monacco, when Tilly Delaney disappeared. Ruby was at the same beach where Tilly went missing, at the same time. They look almost identical."

"No." Shane shook his head wildly. "No, no, no, no." .

"Your golden goose has stopped laying," Lamb reasoned. "You get angry. You try threats. They don't work. You know, because of the schedule that's shared between all of Ruby's staff, that she's at Santa Monica. You go to the hotel. Have a wander around. You go to the beach. You spot her."

"No, no, no, no."

"Tilly comes out of the bathroom," Charlie said, picking up Lamb's thread. "You're waiting for her, thinking she's Ruby. You grab her, realize too late that you've got the wrong kid. She squeals. You hit her to shut her up."

"Oh, Christ!" Shane's mouth was hanging open. He reached for his phone. "No, wait, guys. Wait a minute."

"Maybe you hired someone," Charlie pressed. "Because she knows you, right? Ball cap and dark glasses isn't going to cut it. So maybe you asked a friend to come with you. You say there's money in it. You wait for him somewhere, and he comes back with the wrong girl."

"Okay, what is going on here?" Jamie was back, marching up the porch toward them, a few other women hovering in the dark by the stairs down to the yard. "This is bullshit. This is my house. I need to know exactly what this is all about. We have guests over."

Shane ignored his wife and seized Lamb by her upper arms, blocking out the light from overhead as he bent over her. "Please, just listen to me. It was just a scam. I had nothing to do with a kid going missing, okay? Okay? I needed the money for the house, and Ruby was—"

"Hands off," Lamb warned.

His grip tightened. "Please let me show you—"

Lamb flipped her hands up, swung her forearms out and down, and was instantly free of his grip. His abdomen was hard as stone as she jabbed him in the gut, using the sudden distance between them to jam her boot into his testicles.

"I said hands off!" she growled. She heard Charlie's surprised laugh as she got down and put a knee in Shane's back, twisted his arm behind him.

The darkness beyond the porch was filled with faces now. Lamb looked out at the audience of startled families and felt a wave of hopeless sorrow cascade over her. Because she could feel it now, feel the electric signals pulsing through her brain, connecting instincts to thoughts to conclusions. It was the way Shane had reached for his phone. The swift, natural, unthinking way he'd grabbed at his pocket, as though the phone were a gun and he was facing down a wild hog. Discharge. Threat neutralized. Lamb knew that Shane didn't recognize the date Lamb had given him, but he knew he hadn't done anything like what they were accusing him of, whatever the date. He knew he was innocent, and proof of that innocence would surely exist somewhere, somehow, because that was how the world worked. Lamb warned the big man to stay exactly where he was, then got off him and leaned against the porch railing in the night and tried to continue breathing as the enormity of the dead end she and Charlie now found themselves in closed in on her.

"Oh god." Lamb felt the boards moving under her feet as her partner came to stand beside her. "We've been wasting our time. This was all a waste of time."

"Lamb," Charlie said.

She looked at him. The warmth of his palm on the back of her hand on the railing brought her slamming back to the moment unfolding around them. The porch. The yard. The house in the suburbs. Shane McMasters was lying on his belly, crying at his wife, who was crouching over him, shushing him, trying to follow his blubbering stream of explanations about Ruby and the money and the fake messages. The guests were leaving, hustling their children, making their excuses. Lamb followed her partner's gaze, and she saw that he was watching a little blond girl being pushed toward the street by her mother.

The child was wrapped in a damp towel. Her still-wet curls were slick and lank and hanging down around her ears, dripping on her shoulders.

"She was all wet," Charlie said. "Tilly. Jonie said they had just been rumbled by a wave, and they'd come out of the water and walked up the beach. So Tilly's hair would have been wet and heavy and hanging down."

"Not soft and curly." Lamb looked at him. "Like Leanne said."

Two pops. Two flashes, sharp and distant and white around the frames of those six covered windows, the ones the world was watching. A window blasted out, a blind torn. The shots signaled the beginning of the chaos. Saskia left her post and sprinted for the front of the Hertzberg-Davis building, arriving beside Hodge, whose team was following close behind. Saskia drew her pistol from her holster and backed against the wall by the glass automatic doors to the foyer of the building, Hodge's arm pressed against hers on one side and the shoulder of some nameless member of Hodge's team on the other. It disturbed her, briefly, how quickly she had abandoned her command position and fallen in with the ground team, but Saskia knew in her soul that she had more control over the men and women here while she was among them. Behind the comms table in the command tent, she had experienced information leaks, verbal abuse, open sabotage, the wanton endangerment of one of the hostages by rogue officers. It was time to stop watching helplessly from atop her high horse and get down among the hunting dogs if she were ever going to catch the fox alive.

Hodge swiped a card, and the automatic door slid open. Saskia watched her duck forward and then whip back, glancing up the hall toward the lab.

"Ryan Delaney! Gary Bendigo! Drop your weapons immediately and get on the ground!"

"Alpha team, we have a visual on the suspect," came a voice from the radio attached to the officer's shoulder beside Saskia. The group stiffened around her, silent, waiting. "He's in the northwest junction of the hallway, stationary, one civilian in custody. One civilian in lab 21, southeast corner of the building. Over."

Delta Hodge directed two SWAT officers to peel off from the end of the row. Besides the sweat glistening on the curve of her neck, Saskia could see the SWAT commander was stony and rigid, giving no further physical clue to the tension boiling inside. Saskia was dressed for the cameras, striped and buckled and pouring sweat beneath the unforgiving fabric. Yet she followed Hodge into the hall, crouch-jogged to the edge of the lab, and moved in. As the second into the room, she knew to step to her left and clear the corner by the door. Her old boot training kicked in as she swept the cold, sterile room with her pistol before crouching at Ibrahim's side.

It was the eyes that told her he was dead. His skin was warm, soft to the touch, still tight, but there was nothing behind those dark orbs fixed on the fluorescent tubes lining the ceiling. Hodge instructed two SWAT officers to commence CPR, and something about that low, uttered command made rage crackle like fireworks in Saskia's brain. Because Ibrahim was dead. They all knew it. A cold, clean, double tap to the chest had taken him, probably before Saskia and the others had even entered the reception area of Hertzberg-Davis. But protocol dictated now that Hodge's officers should try to render some kind of medical assistance, to pump his chest a few times, look for a pulse, turn him on his side, something. Saskia watched them do it, hating them for adhering to this single ridiculous edict when all day the officers around her had been ignoring her directives aimed at keeping the man alive.

"He's gone, you idiot." Saskia grabbed the nearest SWAT officer and shoved her. The woman tumbled slightly, righted herself with a knee on the linoleum, glanced at the chief with indignation behind the visor of her helmet.

"Comms," Hodge was saying. "Can you confirm that the suspect has a duffel bag with him? Over."

"Affirmative. Civilian has a bag. Over."

"Shit." Hodge glanced at Saskia from the doorway. "Bravo team, anyone from up there comes down to the first floor, I'm gonna put a bullet in their ass. This is your commander directing you to hold position. Confirm that, Bravo. Over."

They waited. There was no answer. Saskia lined up with Hodge at the door, the two remaining SWAT officers at her side.

"Weird," one of them said. He was a small, wiry guy with big gums. "They're not answering. The radios must be playing up."

"Maybe the body cams, too." The other smirked. "Who knows?"

"They'd better not be." Hodge whipped around, lined up the man with her blazing eyes. "This isn't Afghanistan, motherfucker. Somebody else in this crew steps out of line, they'll be trading in their badge for prison greens."

"We all want Ryan Delaney brought down for this," Saskia said. "But if this extraction turns into a free-for-all, a police officer's going to die tonight."

"You mean, *another* police officer's going to die tonight," Big Gums said. "We got one in the ice truck already and one circling the drain. Or did you think we wouldn't hear about that?"

Saskia had no words. She eased a breath, tried to shake off the question. Hodge moved into the hall, and the team followed. Ahead, they saw the stairwell to the first floor.

They rode in silence, Lamb on the edge of her seat, her phone bobbing in her hands as Charlie took corners at a worrying speed. She braced a palm against the dashboard as they careered through an intersection, wincing as horns too close to her window made her skull rattle and headlights swept over her face.

"The son," Charlie said. He swerved slightly to avoid an old man using a cane to walk across the road. Lamb had to squint through her light-affected vision to watch the man tumble over in shock, bystanders rushing to his aid. "How old was the son? Leanne Browning was midfifties."

"I'm searching now," Lamb said.

"He's got to be an adult. What's she doing accompanying her adult son to a doctor's appointment?" Charlie asked.

"I said I'm searching now."

"We should have asked that. We should have asked what kind of appointment it was. Should have checked if there even was a doctor or a shrink or whatever the hell in that strip of storefronts."

"Charlie," Lamb said. "Just drive."

He wasn't silent for long.

"She convinced Olivia of what she saw," Charlie said. "That day. At the beach. Leanne saw Olivia hanging around while the search was going on. She got to talking to her. Found out the young woman had been at the beach near the parking lot at the time Tilly went missing. So she planted the story. Olivia was young. Suggestible. Kind. Helpful. She made the perfect backup for Leanne's tale about seeing Tilly walking off angrily toward the water. Leanne planted the story that day, and then she reinforced it today when they arrived to meet us."

"Charlie."

"But she *didn't* see it," Charlie said. "Olivia didn't see Tilly walking away from the bathrooms with those big, soft, bouncy curls. Neither did Leanne. Leanne only saw them later. After they were dry. After she got the kid home."

"We might be wrong about this." Lamb heard the uncertainty in her own voice. "Maybe Leanne added the bit about the curls after she saw the news coverage of Tilly."

"She gave her statement the same day, before the news coverage came out."

"Maybe . . ." Lamb struggled. "Maybe . . ."

"Who's the son?"

Lamb tapped.

"Her son's name is Flinn Browning." Lamb flashed her partner an image; Charlie hardly looked at it. "He's twenty-eight. I've got birth records here but no social media."

The plastic on the steering wheel shuddered as Charlie wrung it. He put a hand out and steadied Lamb by the shoulder as he leaped the curb to avoid traffic at a set of lights.

"Oh." Lamb exhaled.

"What?"

"I just found him."

"Where is he?"

"He's in prison."

"What for?" Charlie asked.

Lamb couldn't form the words.

He looked over at her, and in the dark of the car, she could see real fear in his eyes. "What for, Lamb?"

CHAPTER 34

The stairs seemed impossibly steep. Bendigo crouched on the concrete landing, looking up them, sweat running from his eyebrows down his temples and into the corners of his eyes. The first set of stairs had seemed like a mountainous climb for both him and Ryan. Dread at the thought of their destination, and terror at what might occur along the way, had increased the gravity in the room a hundredfold. Bendigo gripped the strap across his chest and tried to haul it up over his head.

"Don't," Ryan panted.

"I can't do it," Bendigo pleaded, dropping the strap. The duffel bag slammed against his lower back, trying to drag him to the ground. "I can't."

"That's what Ibrahim said." Ryan poked Bendigo in the shoulder with the gun. "And look where he ended up. Get up those stairs, old man."

Voices were leaking into the stairwell, from above or below them, he couldn't tell.

"Bravo team, confirm you're holding! Over!"

"Bravo team, respond!"

"You go through the door first." Ryan shoved Bendigo up the last three steps so that he fell on his knees on the landing.

The double doors to the first-floor offices were

propped open by a tissue box, the swipe sensor flashing red and bleeping irritably on the wall. Bendigo glanced through the gap but only saw a dark row of desks, a distant glass-walled conference room.

"I'll be right behind you, so don't try to run."

Bendigo pushed open the door and crawled through, rising slowly, shakily to his knees. A long row of windows sprawled before him, showing a broad slice of star-speckled sky. Bendigo kneeled for a second, simply watching the lights out there, the gold loom from the press trucks on the hill and the chaotic spray of white specks signifying trillions of miles of gaping universe. As he got to his feet, the city came into view. The hill. The trucks. The people. He glanced around the dark room. Cluttered desks, cubicles, laptops, monitors. Signs of other humans everywhere: coffee mugs and framed photographs and little yellow sticky notes. Nothing moved.

"There's no one here," Bendigo said.

Ryan got to his feet beside him.

"Get the blinds," Ryan said. He closed the double doors, followed Bendigo toward the front wall of the building, his pistol pointed at him. "There. There. Pull the—"

The glass in front of Bendigo exploded. He heard two shots punch through the office behind him, blasting through a cubicle wall, puffing out insulation. Bendigo and Ryan hit the ground, hugging the carpet, their voices united in a terrified howl.

Delta Hodge shouldered her way through the door to the stairwell ahead of Saskia, flipped her helmet light on, and swept the wide concrete space. Saskia ducked instinctively as, above them, the sound of long-range shots puncturing the building seemed to shake the very air.

"Jesus," Saskia panted. "The snipers."

"Come on," Hodge beckoned. Saskia followed the

SWAT leader up the stairs, crouched in time with her as she pushed open one of the double doors.

"Alpha team entering the first-floor offices!" Hodge said into her radio. "Snipers, hold your *fucking* fire!"

A gaping office. The night breeze swirling through the blown-out windows, lifting papers, knocking items from desks. Saskia saw two SWAT officers appear in the hall to her left, guns up and heads low, gliding along on soundless steps toward the end of the room, where Bendigo and Ryan presumably had gone.

"Bravo!" Hodge hissed.

The SWAT officers across the room glanced up.

"I told you fuckers to hold back!"

The crew assembled in the center of the room.

"Are there any other officers on this floor?" Saskia demanded. "Or is it just you two?"

The SWAT members looked at each other.

Hodge shoved one toward the double doors. "You four, retreat to the ground floor and wait for my command. Do it now!"

Saskia and Hodge went on. When Saskia looked back, she saw the four SWAT officers gathered by the door to the stairwell—dark, motionless shadows, watching them, defiant.

When Charlie saw Leanne Browning standing on the steps at the front of her house, he knew deep in the core of his being that Tilly Delaney was dead. He parked the car in the driveway, bumper to bumper with the red station wagon that Surge had identified in the images of the Santa Monica Beach parking lot on the day that Tilly went missing. Charlie turned off the headlights, watched his partner exit the car, and then did the same. There was no explanation for why Leanne was standing there waiting for them. Probably, if he'd asked her, she would have told him she just had a sense that things were coming to an end. Charlie had heard that line once at a scene he'd responded to as a rookie from a guy who had shot his wife and then gone out to meet police in the driveway. He'd just gotten the idea that it was his time to go, to leave the free life and enter the fold of police custody.

Leanne Browning's empty eyes followed them from the driveway to the garden path. Then she seemed to lose control of her knees, and she crouched unsteadily and sat hard on her butt on the steps.

Charlie looked at Lamb. There were no tears, not yet. But he was going to make room for them, because if ever there was a time to let everything go, it was now. His own vision was shimmering as he sat down beside Leanne on the step. She peeled yellow dishwashing gloves off her hands and let them flop onto the path, soap suds flicking onto the lamplit grass. Lamb had gone to the immaculate hedges at the edge of the property to try to catch her breath.

"He was on parole," Leanne said. Her hands were shaking as she wiped her face, catching the skin beneath her eyes, pushing it harshly up into her temples. "He'd been so young when he . . . when he assaulted the girl at his school. So I . . . I believed the parole board when they said he'd been rehabilitated in prison. You know, your brain isn't properly formed until you're twenty-five. I thought Flinn had been cured. He was so happy and so optimistic about his future. Then he gets up one day and drives down to Santa Monica to go to his psychologist's appointment, and he comes home with a little girl in the trunk of the car."

Charlie listened to the crickets in the bushes beneath the window. He couldn't give the confession all of his attention. That would make it harder to escape from. Harder to forget. He had to keep half of his brain occupied with something else, try to absorb the horror and protect himself from it at the same time.

"I wasn't supposed to be home," Leanne said. "I'd told him I was going to the mall. Then at the last minute, I changed my mind."

"What did you do with her?" Charlie asked.

"I put her in the closet." Leanne swallowed hard. "I sent him away. Then I went straight down to the beach." The woman broke into sobs, let them fall out until she was wheezing. Had to suck in a big breath just to carry on. "I guess you know all this already. You know I went back there, and I pretended I'd seen her by the parking lot where he said he'd grabbed her."

Charlie was silent.

"That night, I cut up the swimsuit and took it down to the rocks. I was hoping it would give them some peace if they thought she had simply drowned."

Charlie nodded.

"It was all for nothing." Leanne shook her head, her eyes squeezed shut. "Flinn left here in a rage. He'd snatched the girl and brought her back here thinking he could do what he wanted while I was out, and instead, he didn't have time to do a single thing to her. He drove up to Santa Barbara and got drunk at a bar and hit a woman. Hit her so hard she couldn't walk properly afterward. They put him right back in prison that night."

"Leanne, where's Tilly?" Charlie asked.

The woman beside him put her head in her hands.

"Oh god, I can't do this," she sobbed. "I can't do this."

Lamb followed the little path down the side of the house, past a shed and a row of garbage cans into a neat garden. She didn't know if what was boiling in her chest, trying to force its way up and out of her, was sickness or sobs. She found a wrought iron rail beside a small set of steps, gripped it, bent her head, and breathed. To have the hope of finding Tilly Delaney alive torn from her was a physical thing. A stripping of her insides. She stumbled up the steps into a brightly lit kitchen, found a sink still filled with suds. She grabbed a clean glass from the drying rack and started filling it with water, the glass feeling like it was made of lead, her whole arm trembling with the effort of holding it.

The water gushed up and over the rim of the glass and down her fingers as her eyes wandered over to the rack of clean items. She gazed at the two dinner plates standing at the back of the rack. Her gaze then drifted to the curved section at the front of the rack that held the cutlery. She counted two forks, two knives. Lamb let the glass fall in the sink. She walked past the stove, where a pot was still sitting, the burner turned off, a few lumps of macaroni adhered to the bottom of the saucepan.

She walked into the hall, listening hard, Charlie and Leanne's muffled and burbling conversation on the porch reaching her from behind the distant door inlaid with stained-glass flowers. She heard nothing. Just the old house ticking as the ghost of the day's heat departed it. As she walked alongside the staircase, her breath a hard ball of pain lodged in her chest, she heard a whisper from low down, by her knees.

"We have to get to the castle," the voice said. "Come on. Let's go."

Lamb found the knob on the door in the dark and pulled it open. Soft gold light flooded out of the tiny space, the glow cast from a couple of dozen fairy lights strung around the closet under the stairs. Lamb crouched in the doorway in front of the girl, who was frozen in place, a plastic toy lion in one hand and a Barbie doll in the other. All around the child, thick, white foam padding had been stapled to the walls, the winter-wonderland-scape decorated here and there with pictures of mountains and forests of painted cardboard trees. There was a setup of toys on the floor before the girl, a congregation of farm animals and LEGO men. A stuffed Herbie the Millipede toy lay on its side in the corner of the small space, its fluffy legs limp and resting.

"Hi," the girl said.

Lamb slid onto her knees and tried to speak. "H-hi," she managed.

"Welcome to Narnia." The girl smiled, gesturing around at the lights and the foam snow. She pushed back her brown ringlet curls to reveal a cardboard crown secured with a rubber band. "I'm the queen here."

"What's . . ." Lamb shivered. "What's your name, Your Majesty?"

"Tilly," the girl said.

Lamb nodded. Then she burst into tears so loud and so hard the little girl curled in on herself, looking up at the woman, horror on her perfect little features. Lamb wiped at her tears, and as she did she felt small, warm hands encircle her wrists. When she opened her eyes, Tilly was almost nose to nose with her.

"What's the matter?" Tilly asked.

"Nothing, I'm okay," Lamb sobbed. "I'm just really, *really* happy to meet you."

They crawled on their hands and knees, around a wall and into the kitchen annex, Bendigo's breaths now so hard and loud he knew trying to listen for SWAT officers in the dark was a useless exercise. He'd looked back and glimpsed a knot of them standing in the shadows in the first office they'd entered. Now it seemed that every shape in the dimness was a man with a helmet with arms extended, a gun pointed down at him. Bendigo saw his own death in a thousand different manifestations, all of them grim and red and violent, another bullet punching through the side of the building, right through the bricks, hitting the bag on his back and blowing his body to pulp. Officers rushing up and cornering them in the kitchen, spraying them with bullets. Ryan turning and pressing the pistol to his head, deciding to cut the deadweight so he could make a last hopeless sprint for the storage cupboard.

"Where is it?" Ryan hissed. "How far?"

"Through there," Bendigo huffed. "In the next office. By the watercooler."

Ryan didn't kill him. He just sat there on the crumb-dusted floor, his eyes fixed on a laminated sign reminding people not to dump their used teaspoons in the sink. Bendigo traced the path in his mind. Around the corner of the kitchen annex. Past another big, long window looking out over the parking lot. Through a door. Past a vending machine, a row of filing cabinets, and a watercooler. Before Bendigo could trace the entire route in his mind, he was completing it, his hands sore and aching on the carpet as he passed beneath the window, the big closet rising before them, white and wide and scuff-marked and cast in long shadows from the gaping night.

Bendigo heard voices behind them. He thought they sounded distant, perhaps beyond the kitchen annex and back in the first office, but he couldn't be sure.

"*Ryan Delaney! Put down your weapons! Put your hands in the air!*"

Bendigo looked back, saw only Ryan, on his hands and knees, coming after him. They reached the door to the cupboard. Ryan looked up, seemed to try to judge the angle of the windows, the likelihood that he could be seen by snipers if he stood. But there was no assessing that. Bendigo knew it, and Ryan seemed to as well, because he rose to his feet and threw open the cupboard door.

"Where is it?" Ryan asked.

Bendigo shuffled back onto his knees. The duffel bag rested on the carpet behind him.

"It's all the way in," he said. "Top shelf, at the very back."

Ryan placed his gun on the middle shelf and reached up, shoved aside a wire basket of recycled paper, and reached into the dark.

Bendigo got to his feet, walked forward, and took the gun from the shelf where Ryan had placed it.

The hostage-taker seemed to sense what had happened. Or perhaps he froze because, somehow, in all the noise that must have been thundering in his ears—his heartbeat, his breath, the choppers on the wind, and the people shouting in the other rooms—he still heard the gun sliding on the wood and being lifted. Ryan let his hands slide down to the edge of the top shelf, and then turned to face Bendigo and the gun pointed at him.

"It's not there, is it?" Ryan said.

Bendigo shook his head. It was all he could do for a long moment while his throat tightened around tears.

"Where is it?" Ryan said quietly. He looked smaller, older somehow, without a weapon in his hand. "Do you know?"

Bendigo shook his head again.

"You never saw it?"

"I don't know," Bendigo confirmed. "I'm sorry. It got lost. Things just get lost sometimes. It's no one's fault."

Bendigo jolted as the door to the first office burst open behind them.

"*Ryan Delaney, put your hands in the air!*"

Ryan's body bucked three times as the bullets entered him.

Saskia was standing right beside Hodge when the SWAT commander fired the shots. She felt them pulse in her eardrum and in her chest, sonic booms that hit harder than they should have, perhaps because they were so unexpected. So hurtful. She watched, over the sight of her own pistol, as Ryan lifted his eyes to Hodge and took the three bullets in the torso. Two in the chest. One in the stomach. His hands had been by his sides, empty, so she saw the red holes bloom, the stains cast purple in the light from the windows, before the man even had time to fall.

Saskia dropped her weapon and ran to be with Tilly's father as he twisted once on the ground and then fell still. As she kneeled there, the old man, Bendigo, crawled forward and kneeled beside her.

"Boss lady, gettin' the job done," someone said.

Saskia heard Hodge huff a small, humble laugh. The sound of leather gloves giving high fives, back slaps, fist bumps. More fabric squeaking and groaning and straining as the room filled with officers. Saskia had a strangely clear thought, that the office sounded like a men's locker room after a football game. Or a nightclub being emptied after the music had died. Someone flicked the lights on. There were radioed reports of the suspect being down. Saskia couldn't look at it, couldn't take any of it in. She kneeled by Ryan Delaney as he lay dying and felt the sharpness of her phone vibrating in her pocket.

"Clear this place out," Hodge called. "Send in the bomb squad."

Saskia drew her phone out of her pocket, an unconscious gesture, wanting to strip off everything that associated her with the seconds before the shots had been fired. She felt the desire to rip off her uniform. Discard her gun, her belt, her radio, her boots. She put the phone on the carpet and looked at Ryan's eyes. They were watching Bendigo. The old man Saskia had observed for a day rattling around the confines of his cage like a terrified, abused dog was sitting against the wall, blank-faced, clutching a gun and the strap of the duffel bag.

Saskia didn't know what to say to Ryan, so she said words she'd uttered twice before when a victim of crime had lain dying in her arms.

"It's okay. It's all over now."

Ryan reached out his arm, gestured for the bag sitting beside Bendigo. Saskia felt fear ripple through her.

"It's not . . . ," Ryan managed. He coughed blood, gurgled. "It's not . . ."

Saskia went to Bendigo, unhooked the strap from around the numb scientist. She dragged the bag back to where Ryan lay, aware that SWAT officers were watching her with a mixture of curiosity and disdain.

She unzipped the bag. On the top of the pile of objects inside, Saskia found a plush toy giraffe. She took it out and gave it to Ryan, who held it against his chest. There were more items in the bag. A handful of books. A doll. A bear. A lush toy insect. A sweater. A clock shaped like a pig. The smell of a little girl's bedroom came out of the bag, mixed uncomfortably with the scent of spent gunfire and blood and sweat. Saskia heaped the toys and things around the dying man, and as she did so, her eyes drifted to her phone, which bleeped again. A name flashed on the screen. She unlocked the phone and looked at the image waiting there.

"Ryan," Saskia said. His eyes wandered to her. She held the phone in front of him, and Ryan Delaney looked at the photograph of his daughter wearing a painted cardboard crown.

"They found her," Ryan wheezed.

"They found her," Saskia said.

Ryan looked at the picture again and smiled a bloody smile.

"She's so big," he said.

He was sitting on the brick wall outside Leanne Browning's house when Lamb found him. She probably followed the cigarette smoke, he figured. The wannabe police officer took up residence beside him, and they watched the red and blue lights of the squad cars that had attended the scene bounce off the houses across the street for a while. It was a big turnout. Five squad cars for one suspect, an ambulance for the girl. As far as Charlie could tell, Tilly Delaney didn't need an ambulance or anything like it. The child had seemed confused at worst, annoyed at best, as she was escorted out of the house by officers, Charlie and Lamb shielding the kid's view of Leanne Browning sitting in the back of a squad car as she went by. Charlie hadn't said anything to the kid. He didn't want to add to the confusion.

From what Charlie could gather from a distraught, mumbling, and remorseful Leanne Browning, keeping Tilly Delaney after she rescued the child from whatever horrors Flinn Browning had been about to inflict on her had been a nondecision. Something Leanne simply did for a day, not feeling like it was safe to leave the house with the child and dump her somewhere on a street corner when the kid was all over the news. Then, that nondecision, that impulse to keep the kid rather than finding some way to get rid of her, had turned into a temporary arrangement. The fact was, Leanne liked the girl. She was agreeable. Sweet. Scared and vulnerable, and Leanne felt good comforting her, felt like a mother for the first time in years, maybe ever. Then the temporary arrangement morphed into something else as the child learned enough about her new carer and the house she lived in that Leanne feared setting her free only for some recalled detail to bring the police right to her door. The woman and the child fell into an unusual but unquestioned routine—Leanne schooling her during the day, letting her play in the private yard at night, teaching her to run to the closet and play silently whenever someone came to the door.

Charlie didn't know what kind of story Leanne Browning had cooked up for Tilly about why the child had come to live with her and why her existence had to be kept a secret. It was probably so elaborate it would take decades' worth of therapy to completely expunge. For that moment, Charlie was happy to simply watch the girl go by. Lamb hadn't stopped grinning since she'd burst out of the front door of Leanne's house, screaming to Charlie about the child in the closet. She was kicking her legs now like a kid, making the rubber of her boots bounce off the brickwork.

"All right," she said eventually, standing up with a decisive clap. "Let's go. We gotta go tell Jonie Delaney the news. Then we gotta go to Hertzberg-Davis. There's no time for sitting around, partner."

"You can go do all that stuff." Charlie waved his cigarette at her. "I'm tired. I'm going home."

"No problem, no problem." Lamb watched him get to his feet. "It's a good idea. You should get some rest. Tomorrow morning, you'll have a big meeting with Saskia Ferboden, and, damn, will you have a lot to say."

Charlie drew on his cigarette, said nothing. He saw her confidence falter.

"You'll have a lot to say," Lamb pressed, "about why I should be allowed back on the force."

"Lamb," Charlie said. "I'm going to tell you something. And I want you to listen very carefully, because what I'm about to say I am never, ever gonna say again."

Lamb watched his eyes.

"You're the best damn police officer I've met in a very long time," he said.

Lamb's mouth fell open.

"Your instincts are pure gold." He shrugged. "You're fast. You're clever. You're decisive. You know how to handle a suspect. You know how to handle a gun. And you know how to handle yourself. That nutshot on Shane McMasters today was like something out of a bare-knuckle cage fight. I saw a pair of ex-military special ops guys fighting in a bar once, and they were gentler with each other than you were with that guy. And you knew about Rojer. Without you, Angela Lu would be languishing inside that forgotten place under the construction site, or she'd be dead. You're a natural-born police officer, Lamb, and it's plain and clear for everyone to see. I can't count how many times today you've made me feel like a damn fool. And I would never have found Tilly Delaney without you. That's a fact. I lost hope, and I lost it too easily. You—you've got the kind of hope about things that's lodged deep inside you, so deep nothing's ever gonna reach in and extinguish it. That's a gift I wish I had."

Lamb's eyes were huge and sparkling with blue and red light.

"But I'm not telling Saskia Ferboden that," Charlie said. When her face fell, he shrugged again. "I'm not telling anyone that."

"Why not?" she asked.

He barely heard her voice above the blips of the police radios. "Because you're not ready to do this job."

All the wind went out of Lamb's lungs. He felt the hot huff of air against his cheeks. He stood there smoking, his face free of emotion, and watched the rage boil up and out of his partner's soul. Lamb was shaking when she raised a finger to his face. Her gaze was so hard and so fierce he struggled not to look away.

"Okay," she said. Her voice rose steadily from icy to snarling. "Okay. Good. Good. Good. You know what? That's fine. Because I'm going to tell her myself. I don't need you. I don't need you, Charlie. I don't need you, or anybody, to tell me that *I was born to do this job!*"

She beat a fist against her heart. Charlie heard the rap of knuckles against bone. Her voice made the officers standing nearby look over at them.

"*I know that I was born to do this job!*" she roared. Charlie watched as she turned on her heel and

stormed off. He waited until she was safely gone before he flicked the ash off his cigarette, watching the
little red sparks hit his boots and scatter in the night.

"*Now* you're ready," he chuckled to himself.

He extinguished the cigarette on the bricks, walked
back to the driveway at Leanne Browning's house,
and slipped into the car Surge had given them. Lamb
was nowhere to be seen. Not in the front yard. Not
in what he could see of the gold-lit hallway or the
front room. He backed out and turned around in the
street, tried to figure which way he'd need to drive to
get to Universal Studios. He was thinking of the bed
there, the thin pillows, the cold sheets. He could see
himself sleeping there, a still and stone island in a sea
of activity on the lot. He liked to sleep in the midst of
noise. There was such delicious rest ahead.

Then the impulse hit him. The one he'd been
having all day. The kind that made his heart flutter
a little in his chest. He weighed the options, figured
he could spare the time. He was tired, sure. But now
that he was in the grip of it again, of those thoughts
and wonderings about her, he knew a thing like that
could keep him awake through the heaviest fatigue.
He parked a few houses down from the Browning residence and took out his phone.

CHAPTER 35

LEE: Ranchos Palos Verdes Parks and Recreation, this is Ranger Lee.

HOSKINS: Hi. This is the ranger station covering East Beach, yeah?

LEE: It is. It is. You actually just caught me. I was about to start closing up. How can I help?

HOSKINS: My name is Charlie Hoskins. I'm a detective with the LAPD.

LEE: Oh.

HOSKINS: I'm . . . I'm actually trying to find someone related to an incident that occurred at East Beach four days ago. I'm wondering if you can help me.

LEE: Um.

HOSKINS: A woman rescued a guy down there. He was out in the water and she brought him in, and—

LEE: Sorry, sorry. I'm . . . I don't understand.

HOSKINS: Okay, so there was a rescue. Maybe you didn't hear about it. Down at—

LEE: No, I know about the rescue. But you already called here. You called here this morning, and we went through this . . . Are you still there? Hello?

HOSKINS: What do you mean?

LEE: I mean we spoke about this already, buddy.

HOSKINS: When?

LEE: This morning.

HOSKINS: No, we didn't.

LEE: Yes, we did. You called. You were looking for the woman from the beach rescue. We already had this conversation. This *exact* conversation. I even wrote your name down. Charlie Hoskins. Detective. LAPD.

HOSKINS: Oh god.

LEE: What? Hello? Hello? Are you there?

Charlie put the phone on the seat beside him, covered his mouth and nose with his hands. He was afraid to close his eyes, because he knew behind his eyelids lay graphic visuals of the dark imaginings already besieging him. The woman from the water. Dean Willis, head of the Death Machines. Charlie picked up his phone again, frantically opened it, and then froze, staring at the screen. Ranger Lee from Palos Verdes Parks and Rec had said that Charlie called there that morning. It was the natural place to begin, the most obvious source for information about the rescue at the beach. If Dean had begun that morning to try to track down the woman who had rescued Charlie, he was hours and hours ahead of Charlie's search. Charlie knew in his bones that Dean had her. That whoever she was, she was now a victim of the Death Machines, of Dean, the most vicious criminal Charlie had ever known.

Charlie put the phone down again. Picked it back up. Put it down. He twisted and looked back at the collection of blue and red lights assembled outside Leanne Browning's house.

Even if he described to the police on-site what was happening, how would they help him? Charlie had no idea who the woman who had rescued him was. How to find her. He turned the car on, the sound of the phone ringing on the seat beside him startling him so much that he swore hard and scrambled to pick it up.

Unknown number. Charlie eased a breath and accepted the call.

"You know," Dean said. "I got a newfound respect for what you do."

Charlie forced himself to unlock his back teeth. He could see Dean crouched before him on the boat, hacking strips of flesh from his chest with all the calm concentration of a kid drawing with crayons.

"You do?" Charlie managed.

"Yeah," Dean said. "Not being an undercover, I mean. I got no respect for that. I mean the way you track people down. Pick up a thread, follow it, find another, then another. Follow those. Hit a wall. Double back. It's taken me all day to find this girl. I had to get real creative. Think sideways, you know?"

"I know." Charlie sucked in a long, silent breath. "I know."

"It ain't easy. But I did it."

"Is she dead?"

"Not yet."

"Tell me where to go," Charlie said.

"Just hold your horses, Chuck," Dean said. "I got a couple of prospects heading your way. That's all I can spare for something like this at the moment. Can you believe that? I'm down to prospects and old-timers with nothing to lose. What you did sent a whole army underground. You must be proud of yourself."

He didn't answer. Now was the time for quiet, for calm. If he let the rage take him, he'd lose control. He watched as two shadows emerged from the darkness of the street behind him, outlines of thin bodies against the blue and red and gold lights. He put a hand on the steering wheel and kept the other on the phone, pressed to his ear. Prospective members of the gang were always trigger-happy. Ready to throw down, to prove themselves. The kid who slid into the passenger seat was barely eighteen. Charlie eyed him, listening to Dean's heavy breathing through the phone, trying not to imagine that noises in the background of the call might be the woman from the water fighting for her life.

The kid in the front seat was acne-scarred, gym-muscled under an expensive T-shirt. Charlie figured he was probably a dropout from some other gang, Armenian drug-runners or Russian human traffickers. Some of the new prospects were like that—not the grandsons or grandnephews of foundation members but fatherless idiots who were too dumb for the army but needed structure. He was twitchy, nervous, looking around. Charlie was more worried about the one who'd slipped into the back seat. His eyes were empty, almost distant, which was not how an amateur was supposed to react to escorting a man to his death.

"Give me the phone," the gym junkie said.

Charlie handed it over, put both hands on the wheel as the kid slipped a hand down the small of his back and took his gun. He watched the prospect in the back in the rearview mirror as the gym junkie reported in to Dean.

"We got him."

CHAPTER 36

Crowds of people. Crime-scene techs, cleanup crews, the odd reporter who had slipped through the cordon during the shoot-out and was now being rounded up by patrol officers. Saskia took the stairs back down to the ground floor, skirted around the cluster of people standing in the doorway to lab 21. She didn't look in. She didn't want to see Ibrahim Solea's limp feet lying there or her own footprints in his blood. When she was out in the night air, it was like an iron collar had been released from around her throat. She realized when she reached the command tent that she had a little blue stuffed bunny in her hand. The chief had no idea what to do with it, so she stood there staring at its limp figure in her fist.

Ronnie Curler came and took the toy from her and set it on a table nearby. Then he folded her in his arms and held her, and she focused on his hand rubbing up and down her back, counting the strokes, trying not to howl with anger.

"We should get a drink," he said.

She nodded, and the tiny flicker of something in her stomach at the idea of sitting across a table sharing a glass of wine with the man who was holding her told Saskia she wasn't dead inside. That there was life for her after this. That the most horrific day in her career was closing, would soon be sealed, would one day be tucked away in her memory. She would have smiled at that if she'd had the strength.

"I've got to make a call first," she said and took out her phone. She dialed Charlie Hoskins but found the line engaged.

"On second thought, I guess I don't," she said.

Curler took her hand and led her toward the checkpoint at the exit to the parking lot.

The kid in the front seat switched off Charlie's phone and threw it out the window after about five miles. He sat sideways, his gun pointed at Charlie's stomach, his back to the door. Watching. Smiling now and then. Pleased with himself. In the back, the icy one was watching the world go by, eyes flicking over the billboards lining the 210, reading every one. TRUCKING ACCIDENT? NOT YOUR FAULT? WIN COMPENSATION OR YOUR MONEY BACK! Charlie shifted up in his seat and gripped the wheel. He wondered if a billboard with Viola on it would come along, how he'd handle maybe seeing his sister for the very last time dusted with grimy city haze and smeared with neon lighting. No one spoke. He headed out past the low, stucco-covered houses at the foot of the San Gabriel Mountains and turned north at the big lights of the raceway.

"So you're gonna be a Death Machine," he said eventually to the kid in the front when he couldn't bear the quiet smiling anymore.

"Damn straight."

"I don't remember you. Either of you."

"You wouldn't. You and Dean and Franko and Mickey, you probably thought we all looked the same. Treat prospects like dirt, all of you."

"That's the whole point," Charlie said.

"I always thought there was something off about you." The kid squinted in the dark, the smile broadening. "I would have warned him. Dean. Told him he had a parasite on his belly. But I knew my place was to be seen and not heard."

Charlie nodded. "This your first real assignment?"

"Yeah." The kid grinned. "Things are a bit crazy at the moment. Dean needed someone he could rely on."

"He needed someone disposable," Charlie said. "He knows I'm going to kill you both as soon as we get where we're going. Saves him a job he would have had to do later anyway."

The kid laughed, looked at his partner to see if he'd heard. Took his eyes completely off Charlie for a full second. The iceman didn't react.

"You gonna kill us both, you reckon?" the kid asked.

"I am."

"And just how you gonna do that? You got no gun. No phone. Nobody knows you're out here. It's two on one. This guy back here?" He gestured to the iceman. "He's killed before."

"Shut up," the iceman said.

The gym junkie was wary, but pressed on anyway. "You heard of Krav Maga? I'm a level-four black belt."

Charlie said nothing.

"Level four," the kid repeated.

"That's not gonna help you," Charlie said.

The kid laughed at his friend in the back seat again. Charlie drove on. They reached a sprawling property rimmed by barbed wire. Dry, cracked earth and black hills, a little house in the distance. Charlie didn't recognize it, and that was bad, because small glimmers of hope had been flickering in his mind for the whole drive out there, about being assisted in what he was about to do. Maybe Saskia would try to call him. He wouldn't answer. She'd get worried, figure the gang had gotten ahold of him. She'd assemble a team, look back through the case file, and hit every known Death Machines location looking for him. The embers of hope, which were tiny to begin with, died as he drove up the long driveway. He was alone in this. There were lights on at the house. He parked in the moon shadow of a big blue aluminum garage and turned the engine off, put the car in park.

"There's one thing that could help you," Charlie said.

The kid adjusted his grip on the gun. "What's that?"

"Running," Charlie said.

The kid turned back to the iceman again to see if he'd heard. Charlie waited until his dark pupils had shifted over, until the smile had bunched the corners of his scarred face, until the kid was momentarily arrested by his humor, his joy, his excitement at this moment; this dangerous moment in what had already been a wonderfully dangerous and rebellious life. Then Charlie yanked the eight-ball gearshift out of its place and swung it back, ramming it into the kid's throat. The thin edge of the metal tube collapsed the flesh at his jugular. Charlie twisted and shoved his feet down for traction and leaned over hard, threw all his weight behind the stick in his hands, forcing the gearshift into the kid's neck right down to the ball.

Two guns went off. One, he knew about. The pistol in the kid's lap bucked and fired into the dashboard as his whole body curled inward with the force of the blow to the throat.

The second gunshot came from the iceman. Charlie hadn't known about that gun, hadn't been sure, carried only an inkling that the young man in the back seat was probably keeping a pistol on him as he drove. Because that was smart. That was something someone who had killed before would do. The shot went right through the seat, took him in the back as he was twisted sideways, lodged under the skin covering his ribs. A flesh wound. Charlie opened the door the gym kid had been leaning against and tumbled out into the dark with him. He rolled on the gravel, scooped up the pistol the kid had dropped, and waited for the iceman to come around the back of the car. He did, the taillights making his face a pink, waxy mask, the eyes black and hollow.

Charlie emptied the pistol from where he lay. The gun was slick with blood, his aim shaky from the shot to the back. The iceman took a bullet in the shoulder, and that was all, the rest of the blasts useless, swallowed by the night sky. The guy was on him then, lank hair hanging down in Charlie's face, hands around his throat. Charlie clawed at the iceman's face and shoulders and hair, the world growing red, the hard hands crushing tendons and pipes and veins in his throat and making his eyes bulge.

He forced himself to wait. In time, the guy adjusted his legs on the gravel, shifted up. It was a bad move. Charlie got a knee up under his stomach, shoved upward, kicked him off. It took almost all the physical strength he had left. Rolling over and snatching the iceman's pistol from the ground where he'd dropped it, turning, and shooting him in the skull drained him of the last drops, and he fell against the gravel and blacked out.

He was gone for only seconds. When he woke, the kid with the gearshift in his throat was finishing his last soft gurgle. Charlie clawed his way up the car, leaned against it, tried to feel around his back for the bullet wound there. The landscape of his right side below his shoulder blade was foreign, swollen, wet. A warm breeze was sweeping across the plains, making his shirt flap where it wasn't adhered to his skin with blood.

He walked to the house, stepped up onto the porch, put the pistol down on the railing where Dean would see it, and knocked on the door. Dean opened it for him. Charlie lifted his shirt to show there was no gun in his waistband, reached down with difficulty, and flapped the calves of his jeans on each side to demonstrate the same thing. The stocky, greasy-haired biker watched Charlie with a quiet kind of disappointment on his face, like a father greeting his son at the front door after the child had snuck out the bedroom window. *I'll deal with you in the morning.* There were four fingernail scratches down Dean's stubbled cheek, a red and angry nick above his milky left eye. Charlie ignored the old man. He walked into the house, followed the lights on in the bare rooms until he found one with a mattress on the floor and a chair blocking the doorway.

He saw her, and he remembered her arms around him, the hardness of her chest under the back of his head. She was still clothed and still alive, two things that filled him with a joy that was almost paralyzing. She watched him come in and let out a yelp of fear and relief and hurt, and he went to the bed and gathered her up. She had a broken hair clip hanging from a tendril of silky caramel hair, and her nose was clearly broken. Charlie didn't even know what her name was, but they kneeled there together and gripped each other's bodies while the man who would kill them both watched from the doorway.

"I'm sorry," he told her. He held her face and said stupid, meaningless words. "This is all my fault. I'm sorry. I'm sorry. I'm sorry."

"I was looking for you," she said. She pressed her forehead against his. Her tears were on his face. "When he called, he said he was you, and I believed him. I thought maybe you'd been calling around, too, and—"

"I was going to." Charlie gave a sad laugh. "I started. It's just . . . It's been a busy day."

"This is so cute," Dean said. "It's like I'm watching a scene from some faggy fucking romance film. In fact, you know what: it's inspiring me. I was just going to watch you slice her up, but now I think I want to see a different kind of show."

"Dean." Charlie got to his feet.

"Take her clothes off."

"This is what's happening," Charlie said. He put his bloody hands up. "You're going to let her walk out of here."

"Now, why the hell would I do that?" Dean cocked his head, actually curious.

"Because I can tell you what they have," Charlie said. "The police. I can tell you what I gave them. If you're smart now, Dean, you can use me to get it all down on paper. Every crime you admitted to while I was recording you. Every body you need to move. Every scene you need to clean. Every confession you're going to have to convince some low-life prospect or some jailhouse lifer to make for you." His mouth was running dry. Charlie reached down and held the woman's hand and squeezed it, and tried to bring some certainty into his voice. "You can get out in front of this."

Dean tapped his gun against his leg. The wind moaned through the back of the house, rattling shutters, making them bang against the thin cladding.

"Maybe." Dean shrugged a round shoulder. "Maybe. It's an interesting offer. You sure know how to squirm your way out of things, don't you, Chuck?"

"Stand up." Charlie tugged the woman's hand. She was too scared to move. "You're going."

"Whoa, whoa, whoa." Dean lifted the gun. "I said I'd think about it. I need plenty of time to think. I don't like to rush these things."

"You haven't got time," Charlie said. "People are going to be looking for me."

"You're a great bullshitter." Dean smiled, shook his head. "But you're not that good."

Charlie squeezed the woman's hand once more. She was sitting, crying into her other hand, knowing just as well as he did that talking his way out of this wasn't an option. That their only hope was to stall, and there was only one thing that was going to buy them time.

"Take her clothes off," Dean said.

"No," Charlie replied.

Dean raised the gun and shot him in the thigh. The pain didn't come immediately. He fell and twisted and lay on the mattress holding the limb, his mouth open on the fabric, her hands fluttering helplessly around his head. In time, he clamped his jaws shut and growled, and their sounds pushed back through the pain to him: Dean's laughter, the woman's screaming.

In all the chaos, he saw Lynette Lamb. She was standing in an open doorway twenty feet behind Dean, across what looked like a big, bare kitchen. Her stillness, the rigid blankness of her face, made Charlie think she was a hallucination brought on by the gunshot. But then he saw the big gold gun in her hand. He saw her eyes move, saw her thinking, calculating the distance between herself and where Dean Willis sat in the chair in the doorway of the little room, watching Charlie. All those dangerous yards of creaky floorboards. She couldn't shoot from where she was standing and not risk hitting either Charlie or the woman hunched over him.

Lamb disappeared, and Charlie forced himself to roll over and take the crying woman in his arms.

"It's okay." He pulled her tightly against him. "It's okay. I've got you."

"I can't do this!" she cried.

"We have to do this." Charlie gripped her head, her soft hair, pushed his lips against her ear. "We have to keep his attention on us. Understand?"

She pulled back and looked at him. Hope sparkled like electricity in her eyes. She understood. She put her hands on his face and kissed him, hard, and he heard Dean snicker from the doorway.

"She wants it." Dean laughed. "She actually wants it."

She let her head hang in his hands. He could feel her heart thundering under her skin.

"What's your name?" Charlie whispered in her ear.

"Mina," she said.

"Mina, we're gonna get out of here," Charlie promised her.

They took a booth at the first place they found. It was dimly lit, thrumming with people, ten screens hanging in a row over the bar showing everything from an ice hockey game to some kind of game show where contestants had to swing on ropes over water. Saskia sat stunned as Curler bought the wines. The world had been continuing on outside the siege. There was evidence of it all around the room. Tourists with their bags dumped at their feet. The regular Sunday night crowd slouched in booths. Bartenders checking boxes of beer bottles off a delivery list at the door to the parking lot. An old man sagged at the adjacent table, obviously having been there for hours, his splayed elbows surrounded by empty beer glasses. There was football on the screens. Saskia had experienced it before: the jarring sense that whatever trauma and violence she had experienced that day on the job was somehow separated from the outer world by an invisible shield. But, this time, it seemed doubly painful. No one she had dealt with that day had been an experienced or hardened criminal. The Delaneys and their hostages had been ordinary people. She looked around the bar and tried not to believe that something as bizarre as the Hertzberg-Davis siege could happen again, could reoccur right here, in fact, right now, with these ordinary people. Because to believe that would be to sign herself up for a life of terror.

She was safe. These people were safe. It was over for now.

Curler had drained half his glass of wine without speaking to her. He put a hand on her thigh and woke her from her reverie.

"We don't have long," he reminded her. "Quick breather, then it's back for the handover."

Saskia nodded, inhaled, tried to get some of that life-affirming air into her. But the wrongness of it all wouldn't shift. She took out her phone again and dialed Hoss. Now the phone was switched off.

"This doesn't feel right," she said.

"What?" Curler took his hand off her thigh.

"Hoss isn't answering," she said, taking his hand and putting it back where it was. She dialed again. "Last time that happened, the guy was playing shark bait."

Curler watched her eyes. She drank her wine, slowly, thoughtfully, playing with the promises the taste of it contained. Of a quick handover. A shower. A bed. Delicious darkness. Maybe Ronnie Curler sliding in between the sheets with her.

"That girl," she said instead, tapping the corner of the phone on the tabletop. "Lamb. Last time I saw him, he was with the rookie."

Charlie pulled Mina's shirt off. It was damp with sweat. She had bruises on her ribs and the taut, brown body of someone who felt at home in the waves. She peeled his shirt off, started crying anew as it left blood all over her hands and wrists and forearms.

"I'm okay," he told her.

"This is perfect," Dean said from the chair in the doorway. He was shaking his head, stroking his hand down his beard in thoughtful relief. "This is even better than it would have been on the boat."

Charlie didn't answer.

"Grab her tits," Dean said.

He did as he was told.

"Now take the bra off."

Mina nodded. "It's okay," she said.

"I had a backup plan," Dean said. He was shifting in his chair, probably feeling the crotch of his jeans grow tight. "Don't get me wrong. I had other ideas. I always have other ideas. My plan B was to go for that skinny little thing with the big mouth you've been hanging around with all day. Lamb. I saw her parents, the ones with the shoe store. Weren't they something?"

Charlie remained silent.

"You and Lamb in a room." Dean's voice was distant. "The parents. Some knives. Plenty of interesting options there. But this is better. This is perfect."

Charlie burned with silent rage, thinking about Lamb, trying to remember if the gravel of the driveway ran all the way up to the house. His hands were moving, stroking back Mina's hair, sliding down her waist, lifting her and guiding her back onto the mattress, but his mind was swirling with panic. Because their chances of being saved depended on far too much. They depended on twenty-one-year-old Lamb; exhausted from a day crammed with foreign horrors, with ridiculous hope and crushing disappointment and countless scrapes with death. Lamb, alone and matched against a man who'd not only been killing since before she was born but who killed as an oil painter strokes and plays with canvas. A man who made killing his life. They depended on Lamb remembering what Charlie wasn't even exactly sure *he* remembered telling her—that Dean Willis was blind in his left eye. Because if Lamb chose to open the back door of the house and sneak up on Dean from his right, she would be seen, and she would be shot. He was certain of it. Dean knew the two prospects at the front of the house were dead. He had to know that anything that made a sound or entered his peripheral vision in the next few minutes would be a threat. Lamb would be dead before she hit the ground.

She had to remember the story Charlie had told her, had to remember one tiny detail in a conversation in a day filled with details and conversations. She had to remember left, and not right. Lamb had to come through the front door. If she didn't, they would all die.

Mina was slipping his jeans off. There was blood all over the bed. Charlie chanced a look at Dean sitting in the doorway, and as he did, he saw the trembling nose of a gold pistol emerge painfully slowly from the right side of the doorway. Dean's left. The correct side. The gun barrel shivered as Lamb inched it toward Dean's head.

Then a phone rang.

Charlie watched as Dean jolted in the chair, leaned hard to his right, turned, and fired. Lamb's bullet took him in the temple, blew his brains all over the doorjamb, the wall inside the door, the polished floorboards. Charlie heard a thump as Lamb fell in the hall. The ground shook, and the windows all throughout the house quivered in their frames.

He forgot all about the two bullets lodged in his own body and got up and ran to her. Lamb was lying on her back in the hall, clutching her neck and writhing soundlessly, the heels of her boots slipping and squeaking in blood and brain matter. Charlie straddled her and forced her to peel her hands away from the wound. Her huge eyes found his, and her gasping mouth spewed out words.

"Oh god! Oh god!"

"You're okay, Lamb," he said. He tried to resist the urge to squeeze her. "Oh, Lamb. How the hell did you find me, you crazy kid?"

"I came back," she gasped. "I wanted to keep yelling at you. I saw you pull over. The guys. In the car. I saw them get in with . . . and I followed, and—" She gulped air, held her shoulder. "Oh god! I'm dead! I'm dead, Charlie!"

"You're not dead." He laughed with relief, closing his big palm over the wound and holding on tightly. The bullet had entered the hard muscle just above her collarbone. He felt a hand on his arm, turned, and found Mina pressing her T-shirt into his chest. He took it and held it down on Lamb's bullet wound. "You just took your first bullet on the job, that's all."

"My *first*?" Her panicked eyes locked onto his, her brow creasing with a frown. "But y-y-you're not supposed to take any!"

"Yeah," Charlie said. "And when was the last time you did anything you were supposed to?"

EPILOGUE

A week and a half after the Hertzberg-Davis siege, the *LA Times* was still running full coverage of the event itself, the aftermath, profiles, and check-ins with the players both major and minor. Charlie Hoskins sat on a bench in the sunshine that poured through the big windows of the ninth floor of the Civic Center, flipping through a copy of the paper he'd found sitting there and drinking a latte from a paper cup. The sunlight filtered through the thin pages, casting pointy shadows across the faces of the late Ryan Delaney and his victim, security guard and hostage Ibrahim Solea. There were stills of Ashlea Pratt appearing on NBC's *Early Today,* clutching her baby bump and wiping tears from her cheeks. Delta Hodge answering questions on the steps of Hertzberg-Davis, her helmet under her arm. Dr. Gary Bendigo had gone to ground, it seemed, and Saskia and Curler had filtered all their comments to the press through the LAPD's dry and warmthless media liaison officers. The *Times* and other newspapers were trying to pick apart the siege and declare someone at fault, but as the stories drained away to silence, Charlie wasn't seeing a strong contender for villain emerge outside those obvious seats occupied by Brad Alan Binchley, Ryan and Elsie Delaney, and Leanne and Flinn Browning.

Leanne's picture dominated page 2, the same one that had been floating around since the siege, of the broken-faced woman being led from a car in cuffs to a holding cell. There wasn't much sympathy for Leanne Browning. But what little there was painted Leanne as a kind of underdog, whose criminal actions paled in comparison to those of Elsie and Ryan. In keeping Tilly Delaney secret but safe for two years, Leanne had acted to protect her monstrous son. Again, Charlie didn't have the energy, or the heart, to place Leanne Browning somewhere in a hierarchy of bad people doing bad things. He flipped past her page quickly, avoiding her empty eyes.

On page 3, Brad Binchley's arrest at a gas station outside Rimrock was relegated to a side column between a story about an actor arrested for drunk driving and one about a drive-by shooting on a nail salon. Binchley was pictured in cuffs, pressed against a squad car, wind-whipped and cracked-lipped and angry-looking. Charlie wished the picture were bigger.

Among the regret-inducing images of the Hertzberg-Davis building and its blown-out windows, Charlie did notice one image that settled his stomach somewhat. It belonged to a new piece on page 4 that was focused more on the events since the siege than on the day itself. The picture was of Jonie Delaney holding open a car door, the arm of a little girl with curly brown hair extending from inside the vehicle to brace herself as she got out. The caption told Charlie that Jonie and Tilly were depicted arriving at Century Regional Detention Facility to visit with their mother while she recovered from surgery in the infirmary. While a columnist had filled half the page with a scathing rant about Elsie Delaney being allowed to see her children, Charlie found himself looking instead at the girl he'd last seen drugged and curled up on a hospital bed, alone in the dark.

In a mere week, Jonie Delaney seemed to have filled

out, aged, grown taller, her elbow resting on the top of the car door as she leaned confidently and caringly into the car to catch her baby sister should the kid stumble. She looked like a mother, Charlie thought. He didn't know how to begin forming an opinion on whether or not Elsie should be allowed to see the little girl for whom she'd given up her freedom, and the lives of others, to prove she still existed somewhere. He didn't know who was more at fault—the police who hadn't looked hard enough for Tilly, or the parents who had looked too hard. But something about the image of the child and her older sister getting out of the car in the parking lot at CRDF made him feel like the great storm of news around the siege was going to blow away and, with it, the heartache of the two girls in the picture. And that was all right with him.

Charlie heard voices rising in Saskia Ferboden's office, like goodbyes were being said. He quickly flipped through to the back of the newspaper to see if there were any mentions of him or the aftermath of Operation Hellfire, but there were none. As he'd hoped, the siege had completely obscured any and all notable incidents around Los Angeles from that week. There was also nothing about Surge or his part in the investigation into Tilly Delaney. The ex-police officer's assault charges against Bailey and his men had dissolved magically within a few hours of his arrest, and he'd been set free. That's the way it always happened with Surge. The only mystery was whether it was his past favors performed for the criminal world or police world that melted his legal complications. As usual, Charlie assumed he'd never find out.

There was nothing about Lamb. Charlie expected that her involvement in recovering Tilly, along with his, would be a tightly held secret for the LAPD. It wouldn't look good for anybody that it had taken the efforts of a recently fired twenty-one-year-old police rookie and a deeply problematic victim of a botched undercover job to find the missing kid. Better that the public believed simply that it was a "crack investigative team" who had brought Tilly home. Which was true, Charlie thought.

When Lynette Lamb opened Saskia's door and stepped out into the hall, Charlie was struck with the same impression he'd had when he looked at Jonie Delaney in the photo in the paper: that he was looking at a person who had arrived sometime recently on the edge of their adulthood. Lamb did a double take when she saw him sitting there, her body already turned toward the elevators. She adjusted the sling around her neck and came to him, and he handed her the second coffee he'd bought, which had been sitting on the bench by the paper. She looked briefly at the boots on his feet. Wide-bridge, classic-cut Waybournes in what she guessed was a size twelve and a half.

"How'd you know I was here?" Lamb took the coffee numbly. "You didn't—"

"No, I didn't." Charlie lifted his crutch from where it leaned against the wall. "I told you I wasn't going to plead your case to Saskia, and I meant it."

"Oh, good," Lamb sighed. "Because if I'd just given that whole speech in there without needing to, I'd have kicked somebody."

"I was keeping an eye on your hospital admission," Charlie said. "I knew you'd stay in for the full amount of time they told you to. So I know you were released three hours ago. I figured you'd go home, shower, change, and come straight here."

"You were right." Lamb smiled. "Good instincts."

"What did she say?"

"She said I'm back in." A smile was dancing about the corners of Lamb's mouth, but she was managing to keep it contained. "Turns out you can get reinstated, even if you're dumped on your first day on the job. All you have to do is solve a cold case, almost get murdered by a biker and crushed by a palm tree, then kill a guy, and they let you right back in."

"So you'll go back to Van Nuys?" he asked.

"I don't know," she said. "I was too scared to ask. But I've got a month off, no matter what happens." She adjusted her sling again. "Can't do anything for four weeks. Doctor's orders."

"Great," Charlie said. "That's exactly how long I've got on the bench, too."

She stopped beside him, made curious by his strange tone, and he took the file he'd been carrying under his arm and handed it to her. It was a thin file. Light. Filled with unanswered questions, just as the Tilly Delaney one had been. Charlie watched Lamb flip through it, and then she lifted her eyes to his, and the two officers stood in the hall and grinned at each other.

"Imagine how much we could do together," Charlie said. "With more than one day to do it."

ACKNOWLEDGMENTS

As an author, I'm not only a product of my lived experience, but also of the time, effort, and care that was devoted to my training in the craft by good teachers. So as always, I'd like to thank the people who honed my writerly ways at the University of the Sunshine Coast, the University of Queensland, and the University of Notre Dame.

I also have a brilliant (and always growing) team of publishers, editors, and agents across the globe. Beverley Cousins and her crew at Penguin Random House Australia take care of me at home, and Kristin Sevick and her team at Tor/Forge look after me in the US. I'm so grateful to be with Thomas Wörtche and Suhrkamp Verlag in Germany and so many others around the world for both my solo and collaborative works. My hardworking, long-suffering, and always supportive agents are Gaby Naher in Australia, Lisa Gallagher in New York, and Steve Fisher in Los Angeles.

This book is dedicated to the *Troppo* team. While writing it, I got to experience the almost unreal process of having a book adapted into a blockbuster tv series with skilled writers, an awesome cast and crew, and a relentless production effort. Business turmoil, funding sagas, a global pandemic, and a host of other challenges stepped in the way of this fierce group of people, but they adapted and overcame because they believed in the project. Thank you to every single person who worked on *Troppo*.

When it comes to research for this particular novel, I'd like to thank Lauren Gadson, an emergency room superhero, who has provided medical advice to me on demand for books for years. The notorious and wonderful former homicide detective Gary Jubelin provided context on undercover operations and hostage crises for me. Homicide detective Adam Richardson of Santa Barbara took me on a tour of the Hertzberg-Davis Forensic Science Center and has been ever ready to answer my questions for a long time. Gaby Naher gets another mention here, not for her work as an agent, but for answering questions based on her experience as a sea witch. Thank you to her family of other ocean dwellers for naming Mina and for their encouragement.

Thank you to the friends I have made in the Australian crime writing community, who listened and helped me through, particularly in those tough lockdown times. Tim Ayliffe, Loraine Peck, Andy Muir, and Anna Downes, in particular. My friend and mentor James Patterson was also an absolute rock during this time.

And to Tim, Violet, and Noggy. My beautiful family. In the end, it all comes down to you. Thanks for loving me and letting me love you back. Famwich!

Read on for a preview of

DEVIL'S KITCHEN

CANDICE FOX

Available in summer 2024 from Tor Publishing Group

A Forge Book

ANDY

"We know you're a cop," Matt said.

Andrea had been waiting for those words. All the way out to the forest, as they pulled off the highway and onto the thin dirt road. The unsteady headlights between Matt's and Engo's shoulders cast the trees in a strangely festive gold. The killing fields. In a way, Andy had been waiting for the words a lot longer than that. Every morning and every night for almost three months. The potential for them clinging to the lining of her stomach like an acid.

We know.

Now she was kneeling on the bare boards of a run-down portable building in the woods, the sound of boats on the Hudson nearby competing with the moan of skin-peeling wind. The corrugated-iron roof rattled above all their heads. The property—a massive, abandoned slab of woods that probably belonged to some absent billionaire who'd had ideas of building a house here once—was dead silent beyond the little shack. Andy knew she was in a black spot on the river's otherwise glittering edges, so close to safety, yet so far away. Ben was breathing hard beside Andy, sweating into his firefighting bunker uniform. The reflective yellow stripes on his arms were trying to suck up any and all available light. There wasn't much. Matt, Engo, and Jakey were faceless silhouettes crowding her and Ben in. Strange what a person will long for at the end. A sliver of light. To breathe the sour air unfettered, as Ben did. They'd taped her mouth.

Matt put his gun to Ben's forehead, nudged it hard so that his head snapped back.

"You brought a *fucking cop* into the crew."

"She's not a cop! I swear to God, man!"

"I *raised* you," Matt growled. "I found you in a hole and I dug you out and this is how you want to play me?"

"Matt, Matt, listen to me—"

"Benji, Benji, Benji." Engo stepped forward, put his three-fingered hand on Ben's shoulder. "We *know*. Okay? It's over. You got a choice now, brother. You admit what you've done, and maybe we can talk about what happens next."

"*She's not a cop!*"

I'm not a fucking cop! Andy growled through the tape. Because it's what she would say. Andrea "Andy" Nearland, her mask. She wouldn't go down quiet. She would fight to the end.

Engo came over to her and tried to start in with the same faux pleasantries and soothings and bargains, and she flopped hard on her hip, swung her legs around, and kicked out at his shins. He went down on his ass, and she let off a string of obscenities behind the tape. Andy had always hated Engo. Andy the mask. And the real Her, too. Jake got between them. Little Jakey, who had until now been hovering in the corner of the dilapidated portable and gnawing on the end of an unlit cigarette, muttering worrisome nothings to himself.

"Get her back on her knees."

Jakey came over and helped her up. His hand was clammy on her neck.

Don't fucking touch me!

"Benji," Big Matt said. "There's an out here. I'm *giving you* an out. You gotta take it."

"I don't—"

"Tell us that you turned on us. That's all you have to do, man."

"She's not a cop!"

"Just tell us!"

"Matt, please!"

"Tell us, or I'm gonna have to do this thing. I don't want to do it. But I will."

Andy looked at Ben. Met his frantic gaze. She saw it in his eyes, the scene playing out. Andy taking the bullet in the brain. Her body rag-dolling on the floor. Ben next. All the vigor going out of him, like his plug had been yanked from the socket. Matt, Engo, and Jakey strapping firefighting helmets onto their dead bodies and lighting the place up around them. Driving back to the station car parked at Peanut Leap. They'd make the anonymous call to 911. Then respond to Dispatch when the job came over the radio.

Hey, Dispatch, we're up here anyway. Engine 99 crew. We took the station car for a cruise, and we have basic gear on us. We'll head out there while the local guys get organized.

It would look like an accident. The crew had taken the station car out for a spin, parked to watch the lights on the river and sink beers, and picked up a run-of-the-mill spot-fire call. They'd rolled up to the property, spotted the portable that had probably served as a construction-site office once, starting to smoke out. Ben and Andy had taken the spare gear from the back of the car and rushed in ahead of Matt and the rest of the crew, no idea that the blazing building was full of gas bottles and jerry cans that some local cuckoo had been hoarding.

Kaboom.

A tragedy.

Oh, there'd be an inquiry, of course. Wrists would be slapped—about the rec run with the station car, the beers, the half-cocked entry. There would be whispers, too. Especially after what happened to Titus.

But then everybody would cry and forget about it.

Matt and his crew did that: they made people forget.

Andy watched Ben weigh his loyalties. His crew, against the cop he'd brought in to destroy them.

"I don't want to do this, Ben," Matt said. The huge man's voice was strained. He shifted his grip on the gun. "Just tell us the truth."

The wind howled around the shack and the boats clanged on the river and Little Jakey started to cry.

THREE MONTHS EARLIER

BEN

Fire is loud. It calls to people. Probably had been doing that since the dawn of time, Ben guessed. When it was old enough, when it had evolved through its hissing and creeping and licking phase and was a good-size beast learning to roar—that's when they came. Stood. Watched. Felt the heat on their cheeks and felt alive and part of something, or some hippie shit like that.

By the time Ben's boots landed on the wet sidewalk of West Thirty-Seventh Street there were huddles of people in darkened doorways across the street and gawkers hanging out of apartment windows above them. The pinprick white lights of phone cameras. He hardly noticed, was hauling and dumping gear onto the concrete, his mind tangled up with the next eighteen steps. Engo, who had a cigar clamped between his jaws and was drenched in sweat, started stretching the line.

"This is a mistake," Ben told Matt as the chief jumped down from the engine. The flashing lights were making Matt's angry red neck stubble a sickly purple.

"It'll be fine."

"A fucking fabric store?" Ben ripped open the hatch on the side of the engine and started grabbing tools fast and efficiently. A looter in a floodlands Target. "It's a tinderbox."

"The building is right on our path. It was the best way in."

Clouds of singed nylon were pouring out of the building above them. "It'll go up. And Engo and Jakey won't be able to—"

"Stop bitching, Benji."

Ben stopped bitching, because you didn't bitch too long at Matt. By now, two windows on the third floor of the fabric store had blown out and the crowd in the street had doubled. The windows were glowing up there, not just the ones that were blown. Ben had been doing this ten years, longer. The window glow told him the fire was big enough that it was probably into the foundations.

He tanked up, slapped on his helmet, shouldered a gear bag, and went in. Engo was in front, of course, his chin up, the hose hanging over his arm like a great limp dick. A guy walking into a fancy museum. Engo made a show of marching into fires like that, like it was all routine. Like nothing was a big deal. *What happened? Granny left the iron on?* Ben had seen the guy step over bodies as if they were kinks in a rug. His tank was unhooked because smoke worried him the way water worried fish.

Ben dropped his hose, split from Jakey and Engo, and went down the stairs while they went up toward the fire. Things passed before him, curiosities his mind would pick over later as he tried to sleep. Walls of buttons in a thousand shapes and colors. Giant golden scissors. Cutting tools and rulers. There were stacks of leather lying folded on shelves, colors he hadn't imagined possible. He was glad they'd decided to set the spark device that ignited the fire on the third floor. It was all fur and feathers on the basement level—this part of the store was going to vaporize when it caught.

Ben dropped his bag and helmet. The bag was so heavy with tools it shook the floor, made a jar of pins jump off the nearby cutting counter. He took a knife from his belt, slit a square in the carpet, raked it back, and exposed the boards. Lifting up six floorboards with a Halligan tool took fifteen seconds. He dropped his gear bag down onto the bare earth below the building and slipped in after it, landing right on top of the concrete manhole. He didn't have a pit lid lifter but the Halligan did the job, slid nicely into the iron handle of the forty-pound manhole cover. He adjusted his mask, worked his jaw to make sure it was sealed tight before he popped open the cover and stepped down into the blackness.

Something about being surrounded by toxic gas makes a guy breathe harder. He'd thought about that for the first time as he hauled bodies for overworked paramedics in COVID times, then while putting out car fires while the NYPD doused the streets in pepper spray during the George Floyd days. It had occurred to him again now in the dark, working his way along the disused, hand-bricked tunnel beneath West Thirty-Seventh Street, as he thought of the hydrogen sulfide swirling in the air around him, built up from decades of moss and sewage and whateverthehell percolating in the old, sealed subway access. It made him suck on the oxygen like a hungry baby at the tit.

He didn't use the flashlight down here. Engo had tried to argue that H_2S wasn't that flammable, and an LED didn't spark like that anyway, but Ben wasn't going to turn that corner of New York into Pompeii because he didn't like the dark. He had about eleven minutes to get where he was going, do the job, and get back again. The blindness would make the timing tight. The radio crackling in his ear canal with the voices of the crew behind him made him twitchy.

"Engo, you on site?"

"Yeah, boss. We got a nice little campfire here."

"Ben?"

"Checking for a secondary ignition site," Ben lied. His voice felt trapped behind the mask.

"We better black out the whole block," Matt said. *"We don't know who shares a distributor."*

Ben fast-walked, imagining Matt on the street, ordering the backup crews, who were probably already arriving from Ladder 98, to shut down the power to the whole Garment District. The guys from 97 and 98 would probably think that was over the top, that blacking out the singular block would do. But Matt needed to make sure that not only the fabric store was powered off, but also the jewelry store on West Thirty-Fifth, where Ben was heading.

Left, right, left, he reminded himself. Just like the marching call. He turned the last corner, walked for three minutes, his gloved fingers trailing the wall, all sorts of landscapes passing under his boots, most of them wet and squelching. He found the steppers he was looking for—rusty iron rungs concreted into the wall—dropped his gear bag, and went up. His arms were shaking as he lifted the second manhole cover. Nerves.

It had been a year or more since they'd done a high-end job like this, something that required blueprints to be memorized and on-site scouting in the lead-up. A dry spell ended. Ben didn't like these kinds of jobs; scores they *needed*. Don't rob when you're broke. That was a mantra he'd always believed in. Desperation makes guys stupid, dissolves trust. Because at the end of the day, did Ben really know for sure that Matt had gotten the best fence for this take? Someone who could move what they stole tonight without making ripples? Or had Matt settled, because the crew chief had three ex-wives with their hands out and a bun in the oven with baby mama number four? And did Ben really know for sure that Jakey had double-checked on all the construction sites in the Garment District for late-night workers who might be in the tunnels? Did Jakey know the local police response times? Or was the kid into the horses again? Was he hocking old PlayStation games to fend off loan sharks?

Ben realized, as he hauled his gear up through the manhole and into the two-foot-tall crawl space beneath an apartment building on Thirty-Fifth, that he didn't trust his own crew on a job anymore.

And that was bad.

But there were worse kinds of mistrust.

There was the one that had made him write the letter to the detective.

Ben lifted the manhole cover back into place, raked his oxygen mask off, and lay panting on the compacted dirt floor. The crawl space was as black as the tunnel, but years of working in roof cavities and basements and tunnels and collapsed buildings had given Ben the ability to maneuver in the dark like a night creature. He found the flashlight on his belt, clicked it on, and got his bearings. Wide, raw-cut floor beams stretched into the nothingness just inches above where he lay. They'd probably been built when they still called this place the Devil's Arcade, and it was an army of prostitutes and bootleggers, and not fancy types shopping for diamonds, stamping over them. Ben started crawling west, found a gap in the brick foundations that separated one building from another, and kept on. A hundred yards from the manhole, three buildings over, the subsurface power-distribution board belonging to the jewelry store was just where he expected it to be, bolted to a brick strut.

He pulled wire cutters and a charge tester and the bug from a vest strapped under his turnout coat, started working the board to insert the bug. Sweat ran into his eyes. His mind kept trying to wander away from what his fingers were doing and drift two blocks over to the fabric store, to twenty-three-year-old Jakey, shoulder-to-shoulder with an eight-fingered, potbellied psychopath who wanted to die in a blaze of glory. The two of them battling a decidedly glorious blaze. The men trying to let the magnificent thing eat through enough cotton and satin and jersey and whatever else to give Ben the time he needed to do what he had to do; but not so long it would become a monster and turn and eat them, too.

Ben finished installing the bug in the jewelry store's security system and was shifting around to crawl back to his gear bag and tank and the manhole three buildings away when he heard a woman's voice.

"Hello?"

Ben froze. Instinct made him flatten on the dirt like a threatened lizard. His toes were curled in his boots. His eyes bulged and his lungs expelled all the air that was in them. He heard the floorboards somewhere to the right of where he lay creak with footsteps.

The radio in his ear crackled.

"Engo and Jakey, you got it in hand?"

"Yep. Yep. We got it."

"It don't look like it from here."

"I said we got it."

"Ben, give me an ETA. They need you up there."

Ben didn't breathe. Whoever was in the jewelry store above him walked across the boards right over his head. He heard a muffled snap, and then, even through the layers of carpet on the boards above him, he saw the glow of a light.

"Fuuuuuuck," he mouthed.

"Hello?"

"Ben, give me a sitrep," Matt insisted.

He didn't speak. Slowly, achingly, he lifted his hand from the dirt and reached for the radio on his shoulder. He clicked the transmit button twice, the code for trouble.

There was a long pause. Ben counted his breaths. The counting made him think of time. Seconds ticking off. With a recognition so filled with dread it sent a bolt of pain through his spine, he remembered the PASS alarm on his belt and reached down and shook the safety device so it wouldn't sound a pealing alarm at his immobility. Sweat was dripping off his eyelashes.

"Two for hold, three for abort," Matt finally said. Ben could hear the tightness in his chief's voice. He clicked the radio twice.

Another three minutes. Ben counted them. The woman in the jewelry store moved some stuff around, opened and closed a cabinet.

"Ladder 98 crew are comin' up to join you, Engo," Matt said. Ben could hear the quiet fury in his voice now.

"Tell those pricks we got it!"

"I'm telling you to haul ass!" Matt said. *"They're comin'!"*

Ben swore under his breath. It probably sounded to anyone monitoring the radios that Matt had been talking to Engo, encouraging him to get the fire under control before another crew came in and claimed the knockdown of the fire. But Ben heard the real message. Matt was telling him to haul ass out from under the jewelry store and back to the fire before the guys from 98 geared up and entered the site, climbed to the second floor, and asked where the hell Engine 99's third guy was.

Or worse, they came looking for him. In the basement, maybe, where he'd opened up the hole in the floor to access the tunnel.

The light clicked off above him. Ben guessed whoever was in the store had decided the sound she heard wasn't a person. He counted off ten breaths, then slithered for his life back to the manhole, tanked up, and popped the cover and dropped his gear into the shaft.

He was sprinting so hard down the home stretch his fingers almost missed the steppers on the wall under the fabric store. He grabbed on and yanked himself to a stop, almost slipped in the toxic sludge. Ben climbed to the top of the ladder, shouldered open the manhole, got out, and threw it back into place, then heaved himself up through the hole he'd cut in the floor. His body was screaming at him to just lie there, take a minute. Three-quarters of his oxygen tank was gone just from his own panicked breathing. The air in the mask tasted rubbery and thick. Soon it would start shuddering on his face, a sign he was about to max out. He rolled over instead, got up, and dragged a heap of furs to the edge of the hole. He lit them with a cigarette lighter and bolted up the stairs.

He arrived in the foyer as the Ladder 98 guys were marching up the stairs to the second floor. Ben came up behind them. He couldn't think what else to do. A guy he didn't recognize whirled around on him.

"Da fuck?"

"We got a secondary ignition site in the basement," Ben said. The Ladder 98 guys looked at each other for a moment, probably trying to decipher how the hell a secondary fire could start on the basement level of the building when the main fire was on the third floor. And what the hell Ben was doing down there looking for a secondary site before his own crew had taken hold of the primary site. But they shook it off. They probably guessed Engo was behind the split in manpower, and they'd all seen stranger things happen with ignition sites. Fires creeping through walls and popping up in two apartments on opposite sides of the same building. Fires reigniting two weeks after they were put out. Fire had no rules. It was the only magic left in the world.

"Go to your crew," the 98 guy said. "We'll take the basement."

Ben watched them go. He could see flames licking up the walls of the basement stairwell. Just as he'd predicted, the basement was already just a room full of ash and memories.

It was 4 a.m. and they were in the squad room before anybody could talk about it. Matt's crew had a room of their own, mainly because nobody from the other crews could stand the idea of Matt coming in and sitting down to watch the TV and them having to sit there with him like there was a full-size lion lounging on the end of the couch. Ben and the guys, they all stank. Ash and sweat and monoammonium phosphate. Engo was in his armchair nursing his paunch, a wet basketball under his T-shirt. Matt was throwing shit around in the kitchenette. Jakey stood by the door, wincing like he was expecting to be the next thing picked up and hurled against the wall.

"Who *the fuck* was she?" Matt bellowed.

"How do I know?" Ben shrugged. "Hard to make her out through the floorboards."

"It was *your* job to watch the ins and outs." Matt turned and stabbed a sausage-size finger at Engo. "You said nobody would be there."

"So somebody pulled an all-nighter," Engo said. "What do you want from me? I watched the store for two months. Nobody ever stayed past nine."

"*Did* you watch the store?" Ben piled on. "Or did you sit in your car eating burgers and jerking off?"

"This guy." Engo shook his head sadly at Ben.

"'Member that time you landed that nineteen-year-old on Snapchat? You let those security guards creep up on us at the Atrium."

Engo sat grinning at him.

"What if we'd put you on watch duty at the fabric store instead of the jewelry store? Huh?" Ben asked. "What if someone pulled an all-nighter there, and you didn't notice them? We could have had a civilian on the second floor when the fire started. Or in the basement, when I was cutting through the goddamn floor."

"You're really mad, huh?"

Ben held his head.

"Would it help you feel better if you took a swing at me, babycakes?" Engo tapped his stubbled chin. "Because you're welcome to try."

"Jesus Christ."

"Yeah. That's what I thought."

"We can't go on with this job." Ben's hair was still plastered to his skull with sweat. He thought about giving up and going home to bed. He made one last appeal to Matt. "The 98s saw that I was split off from my crew. They'll know something was up. They're going to wonder why I went looking for a second site when the primary site was getting so out of control."

"It was never out of control," Engo said.

"If I hadn't got back when I did, you and Jakey would be sandwich meat between the third and fourth floors of that place right now."

"You're delusional."

"It was into the foundations!"

"No, it wasn't."

"Maybe we should think about it," Jakey piped up, already glowing red in the neck and cheeks like a parakeet. "Because there was, uh . . . You know. There was the radio call, too. 'Hold or abort.' That'll be on the record. That's not good."

"We're not pulling the pin on this job," Matt finally said. "We're too deep."

"We've been deeper before and walked away," Ben reasoned.

No one spoke.

"The woman. What if she figures the noises under the carpet were rats?" Ben asked. "Maybe she sends a pest guy down there."

Matt was white-knuckling the kitchen sink, staring out the window at the training yard. "Some dumbass rat guy's not going to know anybody else was down there messing with the electrics. He'll be looking for rats, not bugs."

"'Rats, not bugs,'" Engo laughed. "That's funny."

"What if she *doesn't* figure it's rats," Ben said. "We hit the jewelry store in three weeks, and she remembers the noises she heard under the floor. Reads about the fabric-store fire in the papers. Sees it was the same night she heard the noises."

"So we wait a month," Matt said.

"We can't go ahead," Ben insisted. "A job this size has got to be perfec—"

"*I said we're doing it!*" Matt grabbed a mug off the counter, gripped its rim and handle and sides like a baseball. Like a grenade. "You got a hearing problem I don't know about, Benji?"

He didn't answer. No one did.

In the end, Ben just shrugged, because he was tired and he didn't need a coffee mug to the temple right then.

And what did he care, anyway? They were all going to jail, whether it was a month from now or sooner.

He was staring into his plate of eggs at Jimmy's when she came in. Ben's hands were still shaking. Had been all morning. But he couldn't figure out if it was last night's near-miss under the jewelry store or The Silence, as he'd come to think of it. The great big Nothing-At-All that had happened since he'd left a handwritten letter on the windshield of a car belonging to a homicide detective from the South Bronx.

Eighteen days. Not a phone call. Not an email. Not a sound.

He poked his eggs with his fork and listened without really listening to the people bustling in and out of the diner, their moaning about the heat. A Ferris wheel of possibilities was turning in his head, each carriage a different explanation for why nothing had happened since the letter. Maybe the guy had figured it was a prank. Maybe the wind had swept the envelope off his car. Maybe his girlfriend and her kid going missing had fucked Ben's brain up so bad that he'd imagined the whole damn thing—choosing the detective, writing the letter, putting it on his car. He'd been so jacked, walking there and placing the envelope under the windshield wiper, that he barely remembered doing it.

Maybe it was much worse than any of those things.

Maybe Engo or Jakey or Matt had followed him the day he left the letter. Maybe they'd taken it off the windshield. Read it.

Maybe they *knew*.

His fork was doing Morse code on the edge of his plate. One of Jimmy's guys banged a fry basket into the hot oil and the fork leapt clean out of Ben's hand. He had to stop thinking about it. He looked at Jimmy's terrible clumsy handwriting on the greasy whiteboards above the fry station and picked off items and tried to think about them instead. About salad. About burgers. About soup.

Ben stared at his eggs.

The woman had to say his name a couple of times before he heard her.

"Benjamin Haig?"

He looked over. The woman was sitting on the stool next to his, her hand on the countertop near a steaming coffee. He had no idea how long she'd been sitting there, got the feeling that it might have been a while. Her bobbed blond hair was slicked behind her ears, and she was watching him through navy-blue reading glasses. His rattled brain took down some things about her. She was beautiful. She was expensively dressed. She was a stranger. That was all he got.

When the woman knew she had his attention, she unfolded the newspaper on the counter in front of her and set about scanning the headlines.

"I'm here about the letter," she said.